M000031804

THINGS THEY BURIED

THINGS THEY BURIED

a Thung Toh jig

AMANDA K. KING &
MICHAEL R. SWANSON

Copyright ©2019 Amanda K. King and Michael R. Swanson

All rights reserved. No part of this book may be reproduced in any form or by any electronic or mechanical means, including information storage and retrieval systems, without permission in writing from the publisher, except by reviewers, who may quote brief passages in a review.

ISBN 978-1-7335783-0-1 (paperback edition)
Library of Congress Control Number: 2019930804

All characters and events in this book are fictitious. Any similarity to real persons, living or dead, is coincidental and is not intended by the authors.

Edited by Stonehenge Editorial
Design by Amanda K. King
Cover painting, *Cenotaph*, by Michael B. Fee
All photographs by Michael R. Swanson unless otherwise credited

Printed and bound in the United States of America
First printing February 19, 2019

Published by Ismae Books
740 N Shortridge Rd. #199182
Indianapolis, IN 46219-9998

ismae.com

To Jeffrey Lincoln Swanson,
whose enthusiasm lit the fuse.

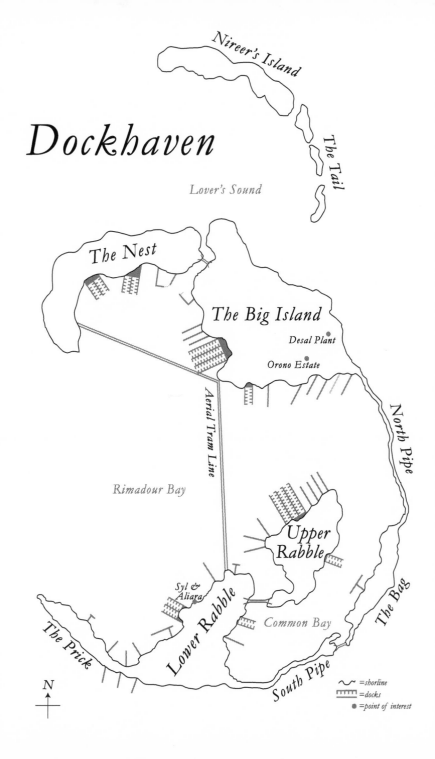

The Calendar

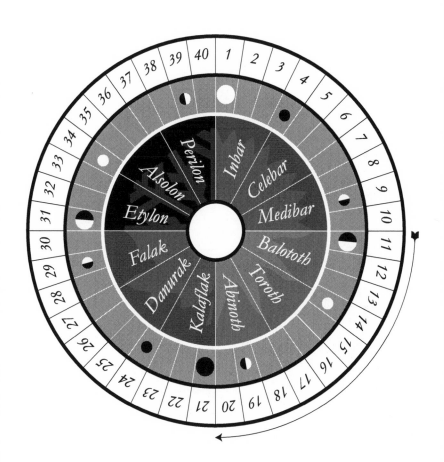

PROLOGUE: **MALOOSE**

Mother was lost.

It seemed only moments ago Maloose had been tugging at the collar of his temple suit and wishing Mother would finish her dreary haggling when a curious sound drifted to him on the autumn air. He'd left off watching a young baluut chase a frisky seabird through the aftermid sky and closed his eyes, the creature's ovular shadow still visible against the sunbaked brightness behind his lids. When the muddled noise resolved into the pings, pongs, and hoots of a music box, his heart leapt. Something delightful was coming to relieve his boredom!

Maloose had stepped away from the spice-seller's booth then, away from Mother to scan the mixed crowd. A grinder emerged from amongst the shoppers, one hand winding the silver crank of the music box strapped to his chest, fingers of the other dancing over its pearly buttons. A crowd of laughing, clapping children trailed him like a school of minnows as he wound his way through the vendor-lined market path.

"O, the cat did dance for sailor's pants and was given nothin' but a skirt," the ruddy-faced karju man sang.

The grinder and his song were gloss, but Maloose was captivated by the white kitty leading the ragged parade. It wore a red cap and matching skirt that whirled gaily above its fluffy tail while it danced and capered. It was the funniest thing Maloose had ever seen, and he had been there when old man Mushta's donkey ran right off a dock and swam all the way to the Prick.

Unable to resist the show, he'd drifted toward the group, clapping and smiling with the others.

When the grinder's song ended, the children chattered among themselves as they dispersed, and Maloose was left alone. He looked around. Nothing was as it should be. He'd intended to stop following at the first cross street, but he'd gone too far. The smile dropped from his face. Something in his core tightened and tears welled.

He hurried back down the narrow way, desperate to find the booth where he'd left her—or any of the booths they'd visited that day. Far ahead, he spotted a grey figure wearing a blue dress that looked like Mother's temple-best, the one she'd worn today. Maloose followed, turning corner after corner, calling to her until his target was lost in the blur of the mixed-species crowd. Still he hurried on, searching this way and that, chest so tight his breath came in short gasps. He tried to catch someone's eye, even tugged at a few shirtsleeves, but no one looked down. No one cared about a lost little chivori boy. Tears filled his long eyes and dribbled down his cheeks. It was hard to think.

Aftermid was fast fading into evening. Shopkeepers with strange faces flicked open the shutters on their glowing lumia signs and scowled at the boy lurking near their shops. Nothing here was right, nothing looked familiar.

He looked around in search of anything safe and spied a zoet parlor with a pop-eyed rabbit on its sign. Smiling people ambled in and out. Maloose started in to ask for help, but the door swung open, almost knocking him over. A hulking karju man with zoet horns and skin the color of strong tea stepped out with a growl. Maloose jumped from the man's path and ran down a nearby lane until it ended, the market and its crowds replaced by tall, unfamiliar buildings. Beyond, he heard surf breaking against the cliff-side. He wasn't even sure he was still on the Big Island.

In the doorway of a shabby building, Maloose drew his knees close, buried his head in his arms, and wept.

It was cold when he woke. Blinking sleep from his eyes, Maloose turned his gaze down the sparsely occupied street. Handlers moved carts and crates to and from the buildings around him, their faces harsh and frightening beneath the streetlamps. He hoped Mother would be among them, ready to deliver one of her lectures on his foolishness. He'd take it with a smile and hug her tightly until she talked herself hoarse.

But she wasn't there. There was no lecture. There were no hugs. He'd lost her.

He sniffled, dragged the back of his hand across the fresh flow of tears running down his cheeks and whispered a prayer to the Duin that someone would arrive and rescue him.

In the dark space between two buildings, something stirred. A misty figure drifted out of the shadows. Maloose rubbed his eyes. It appeared almost to float toward him, but that couldn't be right. It glided closer, coalescing into a round old karju man in a checkered robe, his nearly bald head glinting in the streetlights almost as brightly as the array of gem-studded rings clogging his fingers. The old man's puffy pink face crinkled in a smile. He raised a hand, beckoning Maloose toward an alley that led to the enormous collection of conjoined towers Mother called the "desal plant."

Maloose stood but didn't move. He'd wished for a savior, and here was one. Things didn't work that way. Or so Mother always said. He took a hesitant step forward, bit his lip.

The man waggled plump fingers at Maloose, encouraging him to follow.

A distant street vendor shouted promises of the juiciest sausage in town, and for a beat, Maloose looked away from the stranger toward the handlers packing their carts. The tightness of panic returned to his throat. His eyes snapped back to the old man. The workers didn't care, but this old gaffer did. Why?

Maloose nibbled at a fingernail.

The stranger might know where Mother was.

Yes, that was it. She must have sent someone to find him.

The man's smile widened, soft chins wrinkling beneath his jaw. The tension inside Maloose unwound like a clock spring. He took a small step forward, then another. The man bent and patted his thighs as if summoning a pet, then turned and wandered back into the darkness. Maloose glanced back down the street once more before hurrying after his new friend.

The alley curved along the plant wall to a narrow trail, overgrown with weeds and spotted with puddles of birdlime both dried and fresh. It wound down the cliff-side, so well camouflaged by time and nature that Maloose would have missed it altogether if not for the old man. In the dim light of the moons, he calculated his steps, leaping over gaps where rock and soil had crumbled into the sea, worrying he might encounter one too wide for him to dodge or, worse yet, the path would give way under the old man's bulk. His rescuer moved gracefully forward, though, oblivious to the boy's anxiety.

The grandfatherly figure stopped at a weather-worn door set into the cliff face, ajar just enough for a slight body to pass. He grinned and gestured Maloose inside.

Maloose paused, again nibbling his fingernail. This was an odd place for Mother to be. He glanced behind him. It was a long, dangerous way back for a little boy alone, but at least it was known, not strange and scary. As he bit his lip, mind flashing between the two pitiful options, Maloose became aware of a smell, one familiar and happy.

He sniffed deeply. Spices, sweetness, and comfort curled around him. Cookies. His mother's cookies were baking inside! She was in there, waiting, wondering where her little boy was. This was what the old gaffer was trying to tell him. He looked up into the round, smiling face. The stranger tapped his snoot and nodded. The fear in Maloose's chest withered.

He scrabbled forward and squeezed through the gap into a dim corridor. Weak moonlight eked through the cracks in the door, revealing two other children, a boy and a girl roughly the same age as he. Their eyes were blank, jaws slack. They looked a little ill.

This wasn't right. Maloose took a step back, ready to bolt when, as one, the children raised their arms and waved a greeting. Like a cool burst of wind, comfort washed over him. They too had been lost. The old man had helped them, just as he helped Maloose, and now they were here to make him feel welcome. He just hoped Mother had made enough cookies for all three of them.

Maloose hurried further in, barely aware of the soft swish from the darkness above. Before he reached his new playmates, something warm and firm and terrible slammed into his skull.

PART ONE
UNDERGROUND

ALIARA

Aliara slow-blinked the pain away. With every few swings of his dangling legs, the tippled man across the table kicked her just below the kneecap. She shifted position, yet no matter how she sat, the errant foot always found her. He didn't notice, but continued regaling her with his nonsense, brew-foam flying across the table at her with each sibilant. She decided to allow him one more kick and two more cups-full before leaving him behind the Barnacle for the gulls and alley cats, gurgling on his own blood.

"—so Hink said we wouldn't do it," he said, words slick and slurry from the liquor Aliara's coin had bought, "but Luula, she goes, 'that a challenge?' an' I says 'ho-ho, sounds like one,' but Brunk, he didn' like that—"

When she had slid into the seat opposite him, offering a full cup and sympathetic ear, he'd introduced himself as Frabo. Given or surname, Aliara didn't know, didn't care. He was a scrawny, cocoa-skinned minikin, one of the unnaturally small karju, and his diminutive frame enjoyed a surprising capacity for drink. One equaled, it seemed, only by his capacity for rambling drivel.

He was seated alone when she arrived that evening, bawling about the horrors he'd witnessed the previous night while patrons and employees went on with their business around him, unconcerned with his trauma. It was a tirade familiar at the Bitter Barnacle and other bars of its ilk, and one most patrons had learned to ignore. But Frabo was loud and insistent.

Despite her best efforts to ignore him, Aliara had picked up the thread of the story. It was clearly embellished by drink and retelling, but when Frabo had begun yelping about the desalinization plant, her interest was piqued. She completed her business, slipped into place at his table, and made her offer. That was long before she'd realized just how tedious the minikin's tale would be.

"We needed tools, ya' catch? So Brunk he goes to ol' Purdy's pocky lil' shop—you know the one over on Pier Road? Right, well, he goes with Hink an' they grab this thing." He laid a finger across his snoot, the extra olfactory organ unique to his species, snorted deeply, and swallowed.

Aliara's stomach revolted. The little flap of flesh across the bridge of the karju nose was nauseating enough when used only to bolster the species' sense of smell. She did not enjoy seeing it employed so vigorously.

Waiting for something worth hearing, Aliara let her gaze drift across the room. It seemed as though every ship in the harbor had disgorged its crew on the wharf that led to the Bitter Barnacle's door. A crowd of boisterous sailors, reveling in their brief time ashore before returning to the sea, drank and laughed and shared exaggerated tales. The karju among them, broad and tall and all brownish-pink skin, curled over the little bar tables, almost dwarfing their sinuous, grey-faced chivori comrades. The biggest karju among them whooped with laughter and slapped his table, sending the coins and glasses on its surface skittering.

At the bar, a puka woman threw her dice at her opponent, her hairless head flushing a darker shade of olive with drink and annoyance. Her partner ducked, and the dice bounced off the shoulder of a mountainous rhochrot sitting behind him. The rhochrot rose, snatched both protesting pukas from their seats and scuttled across the room, all four feet moving nimbly between tables and patrons, and threw them out the door.

Over Frabo's shoulder, a pack of inebriates threw silver Callas, tarnished coppers, and strips of sinewy meat at a sun-leathered karju woman, who gyrated in the swirling glow of the red glass lumia pillars flanking the stage. She waggled her unfettered breasts to the melody engine's loping beat, pausing occasionally to gather coins and nibble food. One of the onlookers dared to reach out and stroke the dancer's zoet-grown tail, an expensive addition that likely netted her extra tips for its outlandishness. She whirled and rubbed one of the greasy chunks of meat in the audacious chivori's long, grey face.

"—an' an'…listen to this: It goes tink! And Luula, she laughs." Frabo licked the rim of his empty cup, stubby fingers of his free hand tapping against the table in rhythm with the music.

His foot again slammed into her knee. Aliara winced and shifted, trying once more to adjust out of his range, her mind rolling over an image of shaking him until the right answers fell out.

"Now, now, this is important." Frabo reached across the table and patted Aliara's hand, his eyes wide, face earnest as though this part of the story was vital. "Like I said earlier, it's 'cause Brunk loves a good 'venture. Came back with a bottle'a khuit—strong stuff, left trails, ya' catch? Not that we needed it." He snorted out a chuckle, then his face turned down and he sighed. "Gonna miss Brunk…" The melancholy faded as quickly as it had come. "We downed that thing in oh…well, we drank it fast."

Aliara poked at the discolored globs of tonight's special in the tin bowl before her, small pools of grease congealed on the shiny surface. Dockhaven didn't see much meat. Given the island-city's location and size, seafood dominated the markets and restaurants. What livestock the Haven saw mostly passed through unbutchered, changing ships or waiting while the crew enjoyed leave. The Barnacle's cook, however, considered red meat a specialty of the house. He frequented the stockyards, paying a pittance for the sick and dying among the herds.

She dropped her fork, pushed the plate away, and held up a hand as grey as the meat in her dinner. "Stop."

Frabo looked at her, expression curious, then tilted his head back to drain the already-empty glass. He grunted in annoyance, slammed it on the tabletop, and ran his tongue over his bottom lip in time to catch a tendril of ale-stained drool.

"How 'bout another?" he asked, leaning across the table toward her.

"Fine." She glared at him through narrowed eyes. "Then you *will* arrive at a point."

"I'm gettin' there." He nodded, wobbling in his seat. "Gotta tell the whole story, or it don' make sense."

"No, you don't," she said.

He grumbled.

"You were half-seas over. You were behind the abandoned part of the desal plant. Start there."

"It's that Orono," he blurted.

This time it was Aliara who bent closer. "What's 'that Orono?'"

Frabo leaned away reflexively. "The thing …the thing that got 'em. Hink 'n Brunk 'n Luula."

She twirled a hand for him to continue. Frabo raised his glass in a silent reminder of his needs, and Aliara signaled for another drink.

"Haunts the Haven, ya' catch?" Frabo said quietly, as though someone might be listening. "The mayor an' all, they say he died down there, but…" He shook his head, clicked his tongue.

"I know the story," she said.

She knew far more than the tale spread by locals. Aliara and Syl had been owned by and subjected to Kluuta Orono for nearly two decades. When he disappeared in the incident at the desalinization plant years ago, the Dockhaven chinwaggers transformed him from eccentric inventor to folktale bugaboo. She and Syl knew the reason for Orono's disappearance, just not its result. That was what she sought, why she had sat here for what seemed like hours listening to this tepid little moron.

"Continue," Aliara said.

"We was playin' round with the junk back behind the plant—you know what a mess'a feck that is—an' Brunk, he starts diggin' in this pile. Said he saw somethin' sparkly, but it was dark, ya' catch? He was full'a plop."

The fresh ale arrived. Frabo took a long drink, his eyes fixed on the empty space over Aliara's shoulder.

"He just wanted salvage, so he's pullin' out bricks'n tiles an' tossin' them behind. Almost hit Luula once." Frabo chuckled. "Did hit Hink a couple'a times. Pretty soon, Brunk, he calls back, 'found a hole!' an' we all hurry over. Now we can't *not* go in, right? So Hink digs 'round an' finds a length'a rope. We hook it up, drop it in, and down we go."

"Where is this hole?"

He didn't seem to hear. "Was dark inside. Really dark. Neat stuff lying 'round, mostly dross, but Brunk pocketed a couple-few bits. Luula, she started actin' like she worked there, and we all had a good laugh… Slippery. Fell down lots. Kinda' happened slow."

He shrugged, took another drink, eyes still distant and glassy. "Suddenly Hink says 'what in the depths? It's gettin' light already.' An' we look round, and it's like dawn's comin', but not dawn, right, 'cause it's blue." He caught his breath and squeezed his eyes shut. "Luula never saw it comin'."

Aliara waited as he gulped the ale.

"It was big," he said softly. Frabo's eyes blinked open, and he flailed his stubby brown arms to indicate something grandiose, splashing brew-foam on his balding head. His voice rose, catching attention all around. "So big! An' glowy, all blue-like. But not watery-like like lumia, but blue-blue. I ran. Ran so hard. I…I…I left 'em all behind." Tears dripped down his cheeks.

"Wait," Aliara said. "What was big and gl—"

The stuttered scrape of a chair against the battered wooden

floor intruded.

"Give me that." The darkly tanned hand of a reveler from the table at Aliara's elbow groped at the lip of her bowl.

Without shifting her eyes from Frabo, she snatched up the fork from her dish and drove its tines into the offending hand.

The man yowled and leapt up, looming over Aliara, the sheer breadth of his karju frame casting a shadow across their entire table. The pong of sweat and dead fish washed over her. She couldn't imagine how his sensitive nose could stand such a reek.

"You twitching quim," he growled as he yanked the fork out.

Aliara's gaze slid up to the man's florid face. He was only a bit taller than her, almost twice as broad, and far more tippled than he realized. She could rid herself of him in a heartbeat, but a death in the Barnacle on such a busy night would only cause her aggravation.

She uncoiled the fingers of her right hand, exposing the blackish nut of the bane gland embedded in the valley of her palm. She allowed the fine, bony needle at its core to emerge, poised to deliver its toxin.

The man's eyes lost their heat as they shifted from her face to the hand. "My, uh, my mistake," he said. He tossed the fork back to her, wiped the bloody back of his hand on his pants and returned to the next table with his friends.

Aliara coaxed the needle back into place and laid her hand palm-down on Frabo's forearm. "Where?" she asked.

He winced, bleary eyes never leaving her hand. "Where, uh… where what?"

"The hole in the wall. The one you entered."

"Oh…" He licked his lips and gently withdrew his arm from her grasp. "Don't 'member just right. 'Round the back. Nothin' but a crack 'bout my size. Hard to see if you're not lookin' right." He lifted the glass to his lips, only to realize it was again empty.

"What part of the wall?"

"Where a couple'a towers meet. We just kinda fell into it…" He yawned elaborately. "Just went in...fell..." He trailed off, dropped his head to his chest and feigned a snore.

Aliara threw a Calla on the table to cover the drinks, drew the hood over her short black hair, and left the Barnacle.

She slipped through the streets, anonymous among the masses in the marina's grimy spring mist. Traders, sailors, dockworkers, and street people blended with the ubiquitous thieves in a jumble of commerce and chaos. Aliara drifted between the bodies, their stench dissipating with each gust of sea air. She turned down a rough, cobbled alley hidden between towering heaps of tenements and businesses too vulgar or too shoddy to populate the northern islets.

A couple dozen strides down the backstreet, she was jerked from her thoughts by a loud "*psst*" from the shadows. She froze, crowd breaking around her, and cocked her head toward the sound.

"Hey Rift, over here."

Her eyes easily penetrating the gloom, she spotted the squat, shadowy body of Schmalch crouched behind the Order of Omatha. He rose, only so tall that his head reached her waist. When he smiled, his skin, the drab green of a not-quite-ripe olive, crinkled around the enormous brown orbs of eyes set so far apart they were almost on either side of his thoroughly hairless head.

Aliara was doomed, it seemed, to spend her evening with an array of irritating personalities. She stared down at his bald pate. "What?"

Schmalch looked up and gave her a dirty-toothed smile. He wiped a sleeve under the bony nose that sprouted from his forehead before running down his face like some wicked beak. He pulled open his grubby coat to reveal two sad daggers and an ornately engraved scattershot mag-pistol. Its ebony stock was inlaid with mother of pearl, the under-barrel opoli chamber shrouded in silver filigree. It was a curiously posh item for such a pathetic thief to have acquired.

"Picked 'em today. Got a buyer for the stickers, but not the swish pistol. Still got opoli in it. I came to you first, Rift." He nodded enthusiastically, hand extended, palm up.

Aliara raised an eyebrow. She didn't use pistols, but Syl enjoyed a good firearm. She offered her own hand.

Still nodding, Schmalch drew the weapon and passed it to her. "Right, yeah, you'll want a look."

She wiped his dirty fingerprints from the curved handgrip. It was lovely. Expensive. On a whim, she flicked the power switch with her thumb, and the magnet inside hummed to life, tickling her palm. She pointed the flared muzzle at Schmalch's head.

He recoiled. "No, no, no, no!"

Her black-painted lips curved in a smile. "Tested?"

He gulped and shook his head as enthusiastically as he'd nodded. "Not yet. Didn't want the noise. City Corps don't much like me."

"Loaded?"

"I—I don't know," he whined.

She coughed a small laugh, held her position.

"C'mon, Rift," he whimpered.

She pulled a Calla from her cloak pocket and studied the moody face of the coin's namesake on both sides before lowering the pistol. Schmalch relaxed. Aliara fished out two more coins and tossed all three at his feet.

"But it's worth more—lots more," Schmalch said. "I brought it to you first, Rift. To you."

He wasn't wrong. The pistol was worth many times what she gave him. Why Schmalch continued doing business with her and Syl, Aliara would never know. This was not an unusual exchange.

Two more Callas tinkled to the ground. Schmalch snatched them up, alternately muttering giddy gratitude and whining complaints. She threw a final Calla over her shoulder and resumed her trek home through the turbid city.

Unlike most islands across Ismae, space on the atoll known as Dockhaven was at such a premium that the urban sprawl here spread vertically, not horizontally. Buildings nestled into the sides of bridges, towered as high as sanity allowed, and burrowed underground until sea pressure forced a stop. Entire islets were consumed by single, massive structures. Even dockside, the hulks of abandoned freighters became apartment blocks for residents more plentiful than former crews.

Thanks to the perceived status of her mate, Duke Sylandair Imythedralin, they'd long ago obtained comparatively spacious accommodations in all this congestion. Though his duchy, Isay, sat on the low-caste rural island of O'atlor in the Dominion of Chiva'vastezz, neither she nor Syl shared that detail, instead trading on the locals' fanciful concept of a Vazztain duke. His clout was such that they could have chosen a more exclusive building on Dockhaven's Big Island, but both preferred to live in the seedier and more colorful Lower Rabble.

Aliara skimmed up the basalt stairs, their protective railing long since lost to wind and weather. The building, overlooking busy Rimadour Bay, had once been only three levels. Over the years, stories had risen atop stories, some in line, some askew, until its modern incarnation gave the impression of mismatched, awkwardly stacked packages.

Eight flights up, the steps ended at a weather-pocked patio. Aliara turned the key and slipped into their penthouse.

Sunk into the cushions of a wood-framed chair before a dying fire, looking as though he were posing just for her, Syl paged through a large book. He looked up and smiled.

"Pet," he said in that honeyed voice she knew so well, "done befuddling the City Corp so soon?"

She slipped out of her cloak and boots. "I met someone with an interesting story."

He placed the book on the smoking stand beside him, took a draw off his uurost pipe and patted his lap. "Sit and tell me about it."

Aliara drifted across the room, feet sinking into the plush Norian rug Syl had won in a card game months earlier. She stroked the long, black tail of his hair, flecks of silver starting to reveal themselves, and bent to breathe him in, a scent as familiar as her own. They'd been together as long as she could remember, both owned by that whinging monster.

She laid the pistol atop his book. He picked it up and stroked the silver tracery with nimble, pale-grey fingers, examined the barrel, tested the grip.

"Beautiful," he said. "Where did you get it?"

"Schmalch."

"Pocky little douse must be growing better at his craft." Syl smirked. "Or he found the corpse of an affluent suicide to pick before the Corps arrived. It's wonderful, Pet. It will complement the topcoat I purchased last quartern."

Aliara settled onto his lap, threw her legs across the chair's arm, and kissed him.

Syl ran a hand down her thigh. "And this interesting story you heard?"

"Most was tippled rambling. Something dangerous in abandoned section of the desal plant."

"Really? That *is* interesting." His forehead creased. "This is the first we have heard anything more than 'my poor baby disappeared' in quite some time. Who was your chatty friend? Were there any details?"

Her shoulders bobbed. "Some minikin named Frabo."

Syl pulled a face, nose wrinkling in disgust. "Why the karju don't drown their kind at birth, I'll never understand."

Aliara grunted. "Whatever it was, he called it 'big' and 'glowy.'"

Syl's brows went up. "Curious." The brows lowered. "Is that even a word?"

"His group uncovered an access behind the plant. He claims he's the only survivor."

Syl caressed her breast absently as he considered her words, ending with a gentle push encouraging her off his lap. Aliara curled into the cushions of the matching chair. He rose, smoothed the blackberry jacket across his shoulders, closed the last few buttons he'd undone for comfort while seated and began a slow pace before the fire, boot heels clicking against the slate.

"He claimed it was Orono," Aliara said.

Syl paused, brows shooting even higher before resuming his stride. "What in the depths put that in his head? Simply because he's the local haint? Or something more…tangible?"

She shrugged.

Though they'd been present for part of Orono's last great experiment, neither were certain of the fate of their former captor after the explosion, the one that had permanently closed a large portion of the plant. The city had presumed Orono dead in the blast, even erected a statue of him near the entrance, but she and Syl remained unconvinced. Whether out of fear or respect, city officials left that wing in its ruined state. Rather than rebuild, they rerouted broken pipelines and hoped the rest would need no maintenance or demolition; an astonishing decision, given the value of both land and plumbing in Dockhaven.

In the few years since they returned to the Haven, Syl and she had heard stories of children vanishing from the city streets in that neighborhood, their bodies never found. While such things were far from unheard-of in the city, the concentration of disappearances around the desal plant was notable. If it was the work of their old owner, his experiment with The Book had succeeded. If that were the case, they had good reason to return.

"We should have a look." Syl stopped pacing and tapped his upper lip. "We left him deeper in when we ran, not in the plant proper. The concussion and its accompanying flames reached the plant, so I am curious, did he move with them?" he asked, not expecting an answer. "It is an ill sign that only one of the runt's group returned. Did he say how many went down with him? Were they armed?"

"Three others, all half-seas on khuit. He didn't mention weapons."

"This glowing entity?" he said with a smirk.

"They could have come upon a vagrant with a crank torch."

"True. Was he the only minikin among them?"

"Didn't say."

Syl took the poker from its rack and used it to turn one of the logs. He stood back and watched the fire for a few seconds.

"We may have the advantage here. We are both properly formed, unlike your friend, and we know how to handle weapons. Nevertheless, should we hire an escort? I do not relish the idea of involving others, but I like the thought of dying even less." He walked to one of the windowed walls flanking the fireplace.

"Abog Union mercs?" she asked, tone dubious.

In the glass, Syl's reflection made a face. "They're as common as gulls, and about as loyal." He ran a finger down the silver loops that lined the length of his ear, all the way to his lower lug, tucked where long lobe met jaw. "This will be an exploration, nothing more."

"More feet, more noise," Aliara said.

"And we do not want that."

"A single person to reconnoiter?"

"Yes, someone compliant, with sharp eyes and poor judgement." He turned to face her, lovely mouth spread in a wicked grin. "You said you saw Schmalch. Would he be up for such a trip?"

"Most likely." The Duin knew they'd persuaded the puka to do far worse. "For silver."

"Yes. He'd cut off his own finger and eat it if enough Callas were at stake. I suggest we keep our true purpose confidential. The instant that idiot puka learns that we seek proof of Orono's continued existence, no force in all the isles will compel him to join us. No, I shall explain to him that we are pursuing something mysterious. Imply value, financial gain. Allow his mind to conjure possibilities." Syl bent over Aliara, hands on the arms of her chair, his nose to hers.

"We are agreed?"

"Yes."

He smiled in that way she knew so well, ran his hand across her cheek and down, working the long line of buckles that held her catsuit closed. She arched to meet him as he wound his hands inside, fire-warmed fingers dancing over the scars that covered her like armor. He let his lips run the long line of her lobe.

"But that…" Syl murmured, "…is for tomorrow."

ALIARA

2085 MEDIBAR 18

The sky didn't yet hint at dawn when Aliara slipped out of bed, leaving Syl coiled in the inky sheets. She showered and strapped herself into tight amber pants and a loose black shirt, ran a hand through still-wet hair, raising it like nails in a board. She drew a black line around her wide-set eyes and tapped black tint on her lips, working around the old scars that split both upper and lower.

She padded quietly down the stairs, donned her cloak, and ducked into the kitchen to snatch one of the muffins left by their domestic, Sviroosa. Aliara stepped outside, frightening a group of stray cats busily gobbling kitchen scraps. She gave them a few moments lead before following into the haze of the morning.

She spied Schmalch slumped in a pool of vomit outside the Barnacle, its shuttered lumia sign and windows denying any early morning customers. His head lolled to one side, brown saucer eyes half-closed, something unpleasant dripping from his prow of a nose. She wondered idly if he stewed in his own vomit, or if it belonged to some passer-by.

She kicked him lightly, careful to avoid fouling her bespoke leather boots, cobbled without soles for a silent tread. After a second, more enthusiastic kick, Schmalch twitched and released a resounding belch. Aliara kicked harder. He blinked dazedly, wiped his nose with an already-streaked sleeve and looked around.

She squatted, careful to drape her cloak away from the vomit. "Get up."

"Rift?" He scooted away from her, only to find himself already pressed against a wall. "Nothing wrong with that pistol, right? It was gloss when I found it. Really. I already spent the Callas."

She waved it off and rose. "Up."

He stood. She grabbed his collar and dragged him, muttering protests, to the nearby water's edge and pushed him in. He squawked loud enough to send a cluster of gulls into the sky, spluttered and flailed, and finally paddled back to the ladder. On solid ground, he shook like a wet animal. He still stank, but his clothing was a bit less vile.

"Why'd you do that?" he whined. "I could'a found a bucket or somethin'. Garl'll even let me wash up in the Barnacle sinks if I help out."

She gave him flat eyes.

He looked at his feet, voice lowered to a mutter. "Didn't need to throw me in the drink. Plenty of other ways to get clean 'round here."

"Follow." Aliara turned and started home.

"Sure, Rift, sure." Squishing with each step, he scurried to keep pace with her gentle stride.

Syl sat at the dining table, drinking caba and staring out the window. Beneath the fin of his nose, a finger tapped pensively against narrow lips. He looked like a painting, blue dressing gown bright against the dark-stained chair, dark hair spilling over his shoulders.

When Aliara cleared her throat, he turned those potent slate-blue eyes to her. She pushed her hood back with one hand, shoved Schmalch forward with the other. He tripped on the rug, fussed with his hands, and glanced around, looking at anything but Syl.

"Schmalch." Syl stood, his smile somewhere between gracious and unnerving. "Welcome. Come, sit. Enjoy a spot of caba with me. Have you eaten yet?"

Despite any misgivings, Schmalch shuffled to the indicated chair, unwilling to refuse food or liquor. They both sat, Syl waiting while the puka clambered up, and arranged himself in the chair.

"It seems I owe you my gratitude for this beautiful pistol." Syl drew the weapon from the pocket of his robe and laid it on the table, muzzle toward his guest.

Schmalch sat very, very still.

"I've not yet had an opportunity to fire it. She swears you claim the power cell still works." Syl tapped a manicured fingernail against the barrel. "Shall we load it and find out?"

Sviroosa skittered out from the kitchen in a blur of sage-green skin and brown cotton, hurriedly set plates of lox, eggs, and warm bread on the table, and vanished back through the swinging door.

Schmalch's eyes followed her. When she disappeared, they circled from the food to the pistol and finally up to Syl. "Uh, sure, um, if you'd like to, Duke."

"Duke…?"

"Duke Imi—Imith—" Schmalch produced some unintelligible series of sounds.

Syl scowled. "Repeat. Im-ith…"

"Im…ith…"

"uh-drah-lin."

"uuuh…drah…lin." Schmalch nodded and bit his lower lip, eyes drifting to the food.

"Again, all together."

"Imythedralin," he repeated slowly.

"Good man." Syl pocketed the pistol and scooped eggs onto his plate. "We shall leave a test firing for another time. Eat."

Schmalch pounced on the food, his jacket sleeves dripping

seawater on the table.

Aliara slid into the chair opposite Schmalch. She picked up a slice of bread and chewed, her black eyes following the conversation.

"Before she so fortuitously bumped into you last night, my darling girl enjoyed drinks with someone else interesting," Syl said.

Schmalch shoveled food as his eyes swiveled from Syl to the plate and back.

When it was clear his only response would be sloppy chewing sounds, Syl sipped his caba and continued. "This person discovered something awe-inspiring beneath the abandoned region of the desalinization plant. You're familiar? Yes. You see, we are considering taking a look ourselves, but what he found…" Syl paused, breathed deeply, and waved a hand in the air. "Well, it may be too much for the two of us to handle alone. We would need another pair of hands."

Schmalch slowed his voracious eating at this. "What'd he find?" Bits of egg spewed from his mouth. Syl brushed them from the table with his napkin before continuing.

"He wasn't specific," Syl said, leaning forward conspiratorially, "but he did mention something about a glow."

Aliara watched Schmalch's brain work behind his enormous eyes. There was only one glowing object he could conceive of that would be worth Syl's and her time—opoli.

"Yes, I see you understand." Syl leaned back. "Naturally, you were the first person we thought of to provide that extra assistance. Who better than our good friend Schmalch? We intend to gather some supplies and set out in two dusk's time. I realize it is a lot to ask, but would you consider joining us?"

Schmalch nodded vigorously and dangled another slice of lox into his mouth. Remnants of his meal spangled his damp tunic.

"Excellent. We would pay for your services as scout and assistant up front…say, fifteen Callas? You would, of course, receive an equal portion of anything we brought back." Syl sipped his caba, allowing the words to form their own picture in the little scug's brain.

Schmalch's chewing slowed, his eyes distant, dancing with imaginings.

"Tonight, while Aliara and I make preparations, you will locate a breech in the plant's wall." Syl refilled his guest's glass. "The man she spoke with indicated the fissure was on the Promenade side of the building, relatively obscured from view in the junction of two towers. He and his companions found it quite by accident during a drunken excursion. Can we depend on you for this, Schmalch?"

Clearly pleased with his luck, Schmalch swallowed his food with a gulp. "Sure, sure, I can do that, Duke Im-Im-Imythedralin. You know I can find things real good." The little puka beamed, thoroughly unaware of what he'd gotten into.

SCHMALCH

Schmalch could do this. He was an excellent thief. More or less. Finding a hole in a wall was no problem. The thought of scouting ahead in some towers crumbling off the side of a big, old building, though, that was a little scary. But he could do it for a big pay-off.

Squatted near a dreary workshop whose doors had closed for the day, he studied the ruined towers of the desal plant. From where he stood, the plant's bulk stretched out for blocks along High Road, almost disappearing in the growing dusk were it not for a few lit windows. Schmalch didn't like looking directly at the building; it was so big that trying to take it all in made his stomach turn on itself.

For the most part, he avoided the thing, easy since it sat on the Big Island, and he rarely left the Rabbles. He'd heard bits and pieces about what had happened to close down this section. It may have been long before he was born, but rumors got around. Some kid from the Spriggans told him the guy who built the plant went on a rampage, killing everyone and everything in his path. Another story, from Garl at the Barnacle, claimed the same guy had killed little kids trying to make himself immortal by drinking their blood. A third story said he'd set off some explosive that left this part of the place too dangerous to reopen. Schmalch couldn't remember where he'd heard that one.

He didn't know which of the stories was true, so he believed them all. Whatever the truth, it scared the pants off everyone, including the local government types. It was crazy for them to leave so much space idle. Schmalch grew giddy just imagining how much the unused land might be worth. More than even the Duke and Rift had, he bet. Standing in the growing darkness, watching the plant's shift-change, he passed time considering what he'd do with that many Callas. Most of his dreams involved impressing friends and enemies, but there was a corner of his mind that thought warm thoughts about the Duke's housemaid. He needed to learn her name. Maybe he could charm her with his wealth once he had his share of the boodle from this venture.

Almost in chorus, the shutters on the streetlights and various lumia signs opened with a whoosh, the city shifting like a moored boat under their dull rolling glow.

He'd had to wait for dark. True, it would have been far simpler to look during the day, but Schmalch knew he'd be rousted if spotted—or worse, followed by someone wanting to horn in on his job. Now that night was officially here, however, he stared into the darkness behind the plant and reconsidered the wisdom of his plan.

He glanced back at the squat little farspeech office that sat a ways down High Road and sighed. Maybe if he'd managed to pass the farspeaker test they gave all the puka kids—the one he'd taken at the orphanage half his life ago—he wouldn't be here. He'd be rich from listening to all those messages that came in from all over the isles. Instead, he was alone in the dark, assigned to investigate the scariest spot in all of Dockhaven. He couldn't hear the farspeakers in his head. He was just another ordinary puka, doing someone else's work.

Schmalch scuttled across High Road and down Salt Street along the dark side of the plant, its cobalt-domed clay towers looming alongside him. The hum of the ever-present crowds dimmed with the streetlights' glow. With both moons in sliver tonight, he headed into thick blackness, an endless potential array of terrors waiting within.

Having spent his whole life in a city full of noise, this stillness was alien. He loved sneaking around and eavesdropping, but the uncertainty here flustered him. Being well-informed of his surroundings was integral to survival on the streets of Dockhaven. The more familiar the environs, the safer Schmalch was. Places didn't get much less familiar than this. Schmalch tugged at his ears and picked up his pace.

He rounded the damaged end of the plant and allowed his eyes to adjust to the gloom behind it, heart hammering in his chest. He couldn't see much detail, but what he could see sure did look abandoned, like a place you came to die, not to get a drink of water.

The whole yard back here had once been quite swish, according to some of the older tipplers who lurked around the Bitter Barnacle. Way back when the desal plant was all new and shiny, people came from all over the islands just to see the one-of-a kind place. The city built this spot behind the plant, called it "the Promenade." Visitors had picnics in the lawn and strolled along the boardwalk and looked out at Lover's Sound. It was all very romantic, he'd been told. Now it was all very terrifying.

He eased into the area, the smell around him fusty and dank. Dark patches of moss dotted the brownish clay, and the wood of the cliffside boardwalk seemed squishy and worn away by storms and neglect. Blue roofing tiles peppered the unkempt yard alongside an array of abandoned dross, dropped by skivers or left over from that initial incident. Schmalch swallowed his creeping fear and worked his way across the exterior of each domed tower, moving from the security of faint moonlight into the shadows.

Too deep in to escape, he jumped when a low, scraping creak shot through the silence like the roar of a blunderbuss. Panic flooded his mind. He dropped to the ground and scooted across the yard onto the rotting wood of the boardwalk, eyes searching the night, until his back slammed into a chunk of punky railing. He drew his knees close as he scanned the area, dinner-plate eyes struggling to absorb every drop of light.

Minutes passed. No footfalls, no creaks. On hands and knees, he crept back toward the building, prepared to dart away should the need arise. Every few steps, he paused to listen for the mystery sound, his stubby hands anxiously plucking at the spongy decking and dirt.

Halfway back, his palm slipped on something round, twisting his wrist. Schmalch bit his lip to silence a yelp of pain. He patted the rotten wood around him in search of the wounding item, hand finally brushing something cool and smooth. It rolled away. He groped the ground until his fingers closed over it. Holding it up to what light he could find, Schmalch saw it was spherical, about size of his fist, with a rounded nub on each end. The thing shone with a metallic glint. Silver, maybe. It might be a watch, though not any kind he'd seen before. A toy, maybe. Or even jewelry. Didn't matter—it looked expensive, and that meant payoff. Schmalch pocketed it.

One treasure usually led to another. Fear exchanged for greed, Schmalch pawed across the ground, undeterred by the abundant puddles of gull lime. He groped and discarded a broken cup, a soggy, bug-laden cushion, the bottom half of a broom and something that felt like it may have once belonged to a pistol. None of it was worth keeping. He kept at it, sure that if he stopped, he'd miss that one gloss bit of swag only arm's-length away.

When his knuckles rapped something bulky and rough, he sat back with a groan, sucking his scraped fingers. He grabbed the wounding item with his free hand, and explored its shape—boxy but rounded, hammered metal, a circular furrow, a latch, a handle. A lantern. Worthless. He shrugged and was about to toss it aside but paused. If the lumia was still alive in there…

Schmalch pulled the fist from his mouth and fumbled with the lantern, flipping open the bull's-eye with a pale, metallic scrape. Watery aqua light rolled out. He giggled. The sound bounced back at him from the building's high walls. He snapped the lantern shut and crouched against something that felt like a coil of sailing line. HIs eyes searched the area for movement, ears strained to detect sound. Satisfied no one had heard, he again opened the lantern, happy to have more than moonlight to aid his search.

He hadn't realized he'd crawled so close to the building during his hunt for boodle. Only a cart's length in front of him was the thing he'd been sent to find. A crack about his own height gaped from the shadowy crotch of two cylindrical towers, a recently disturbed mound of rubble at its mouth. Dangling into its depths was the limp end of the heap of rope he'd hidden behind. About a hog's width at the base, the crack tapered jaggedly to a point at the top, black and foreboding. The lantern's weak glow didn't touch the darkness within.

Schmalch sat back on his heels, staring, doubt seeping in. With the sleeve of his jacket, he wiped away the mist beading at the tip of his nose and sniffed. Something nasty was in the air, something that smelled like the time the Barnacle's heat eater had died, and all Garl's meat had gone bad. His skin crawled like it was trying to escape. Schmalch hopped up and ran, stumbling over the coiled line, yet managing to keep his feet.

If this was where the Duke and Rift planned to take him tomorrow, he was going to spend every coin they'd fronted him living it up tonight.

SYLANDAIR

Syl stood in the ramshackle shop of the Lower Rabble's finest metalwright, examining his well-manicured fingernails. At the counter, a soldier in the crimson and khaki of the Norian marines was several minutes into his attempt to complete a purchase with the stone-deaf vendor.

"What?" Mardo shouted at his customer.

"You remember my order from last month?" the soldier shouted, gesturing frantically in an attempt to draw an air picture of this mysterious order. "The wallarmbrust."

Mardo frowned, rosy brow crinkling. "What? Reimburse you? You haven't bought anything yet."

The soldier sighed.

Bored, Syl edged past the frustrated man, withdrew a slip of paper from his pocket and passed it to Mardo.

"Right, Duke," Mardo said, grinning wide enough to expose a silvered tooth adjacent to a missing one. He disappeared into his storeroom, leaving the soldier unaided.

As a genuine Vazztain duke, Syl enjoyed a favored position among Dockhaven's merchants. In the imperial court of the Dominion of Chiva'vastezz, the Duchy of Isay was considered rather pitiful, known only for its blalal berries and amphibious livestock. Syl had earned the title and its land, but the whole thing was something of a joke, and one he preferred to rule in absentia. To the Haveners, however, Syl was a duke, and one who held such a title was better served than some random soldier.

"Forgot your purchase order?" Syl asked the exasperated soldier while he waited.

The man nodded.

"Perhaps write down your request for Mardo to read in lieu of making such a din next time?"

The man's face brightened as though the idea had never occurred to him.

Mardo clomped out of his storeroom with a rattling wooden box, smile still in place.

"Quite'a challenge," Mardo said. "What's your plan for 'em, Duke?"

"An experiment," Syl said, voice raised. He slid the box under one arm.

Mardo opened his mouth, undoubtedly to ask "what?" but Syl stopped him with a palm. He laid his silver on the counter, donned his sunshades, and left Mardo and the soldier with a nod.

He strolled along the steep shore toward home, glancing at the harbor littered with floating tenements, once sturdy barges and freighters now abandoned, punky and infested with squatting poor. A karju woman lolling from the upper window of a bright-yellow three-story affair called greetings to Syl. He waved at her with a small flip of his hand. Had he ever known the woman, her name had long since escaped him.

He veered away from the coastline, past a string of shops, most still rolled up for the night. Simple shutters blocked the higher levels, bars added on the ground floor. The only activity, a seamstress on the third story hanging out her fashions for the day's display. Syl paused to examine them, deemed them garish and sub-par, and continued on toward the neighborhood's finest produce market. The young shop-caller, stationed as always below a painted mural of a buxom lady eating carrots, urged Syl to stop in for vegetables delivered fresh from the docks that morning. Certain Sviroosa would see to such things, Syl strode past with only a pleasant nod in the boy's direction.

As he passed through a cloud of greasy steam billowing from an early-morning diner, a canker-ravaged woman fell into step with him. One glance gave her profession as cut-rate trull.

"How 'bout a quick suck, chivori?" she asked. She twirled a lock of greasy red-brown hair around a dirty finger. "Only two coppers for a pretty one like you."

"You would likely have better luck with the night-shifters heading home from the fisheries." Syl kept walking.

"Sometimes a girl wants something sweeter than a fish gutter." She hopped in front of him, blocking his path. "Slip down the alley with me, I'll let you box the compass." With one hand, the trull lifted her skirt to reveal something so unkempt and grubby that even the night-shifters would have run. With the other, she fumbled for his crotch.

Syl knew this routine, had run it himself with Aliara years ago. Sidestepping, he swung around to catch her partner's hand halfway into his coat pocket.

"Watch where you place that." Syl wrenched the errant hand, felt the bones inside grind. "Or be better at your craft."

The man yelped and tried to jerk away. Syl held tight. The man pulled a dull sailor's knife, brandishing it awkwardly in his off-hand. Ducking under the lurching weapon, Syl twisted the arm behind the man's back. His shoulder popped neatly out of joint. The thief fell to his knees and bawled, knife forgotten.

"You windless fid!" Ragged nails bared like claws, the trull charged.

Syl put a foot on her partner's back and shoved, rolling him into her path. She tripped, momentum carrying her across the rough cobbles of the street. Syl left both of them in a heap, moaning and bickering.

Lurking seagulls and stray cats scattered as he scaled the steps toward home, where Aliara waited, her whip-thin form hunched over the dining table. Precisely arranged before her were a length of rope, two crank torches, a fresh canvas rucksack, her leather work pack, and other assorted tools of her trade.

"Before you store all that away," Syl said, "you'll want to consider these as well."

He unlatched the box, revealing a fist-sized canvas bag, a mallet, and a collection of steel pitons, the type used as climbing anchors. Near the head of each piton was a narrow band of resin filled with glowing lumia algae.

"Return guideposts." Syl said. "I've no intention of being lost in that monstrosity again."

"And that?" Aliara nodded at the bag

"A bit of shot." He spilled several large-gauge steel balls into his palm. "You didn't think I would leave on this little escapade without my new pistol, did you, Pet?"

SYLANDAIR

Syl stood before the desal plant in dusk's waning light, staring at its clay walls, but seeing something else entirely.

"You see here the finest zoetic science has to offer," Orono said on the day he guided young Syl through the enormous water-purification plant. Only days earlier, he'd purchased Syl, purportedly as a houseboy. Reality had been quite different. "This city...no, all the civilized world would be lost without my work."

The memory rolled through Syl's mind, unwanted, insistent. He could still see the old karju through his eight-year-old eyes: hunched back, wispy white patches of hair, fleshy bulk draped in a colorful, flowing robe. He was as ancient as he seemed, though young Syl couldn't have known. The old man still drew breath only by the grace of heavy anti-agathic dosing. Without the drugs, he would have been dead years before Syl's life even began.

Orono leaned heavily on his cane, his wheezing breath as loud and real in Syl's mind as it had been at that moment. The old man gestured at the plant's complex network of harnessed lusca, zoet creatures whose genome he had designed. Their squishy, semi-transparent bodies sucked seawater from hoses, gushed freshwater into the troughs below and thick salt paste into the dangling collection-bags.

"Before I developed these zoet wonders," Orono said, "the masses relied on solar stills. Always a shortage. My tinkering with genomes put water in their mugs." He wagged his finger at Syl. "You be proud your master created this. Always remember that you belong to a great man."

Caught up in the reminiscence, Syl abruptly spat in the direction of the statue erected to Orono. "Great man," he muttered with a scowl.

Aliara's sloe-colored, almond eyes slid his way, but she said nothing. She had her own memories of the monster's greatness.

Shaking off the unpleasantness, Syl tugged at the bottom of his vest and plucked rogue bits of lint from his clothing. He'd foregone his standard finery in favor of more practical blue trousers, ivory sweater, and black leather vest, pistol holster tucked beneath. Aliara had gifted him his own pair of soft-soled boots for the occasion. Though he preferred a solid click with each stride, he found a hushed tread preferable for this undertaking.

Picked clean of all vestiges of disarray, he adjusted the rucksack slung across his back and tapped his foot mutely against the brick of the street.

"Where is that little puddle?" he muttered.

Around them, the shift change brought fresh plant workers in while exhausted ones shuffled home in the growing dusk. Shopkeepers and their patrons concluded business while tipplers emerged as unfailingly as the stars overhead, and couples held hands and smiled obliviously at the darkening sky. Pedicabs rang bells at pedestrians who ignored them, and shop-callers changed their song from housewares and pantry items to liquor and entertainment. Weaving among them all, the obligatory pickpockets executed their craft.

Schmalch was not among their ranks.

Aliara ignored the dwindling crowd, seemingly unbothered by the delay. She stretched and looked out to sea, the catsuit she wore clinging to every gesture. A blackened-steel stiletto hung at each of her hips, their holsters strapped to her thighs, ubiquitous black boots tight to her knees, familiar leather bundle on her back, tools particular to her craft tucked within.

"Look, Duke, look!" The clipped, nasal voice preceded Schmalch, who appeared as though conjured by Syl's impatience. Still wearing the same revolting clothes, a rusty old lantern held before him like a talisman, he wound his way through the press of bodies toward the quiet space where Syl and Aliara waited. He skidded to a stop and swung open the bull's-eye. "Still glows. Even fed it."

"Good," Syl glanced at the lantern. "You did as requested?"

"Yeah, 'course. Got this, too." He held up a new pack, dotted with bright, youthful patches. "Nicked—I mean, bought it from a kid down in the Rabble. Real good one." He opened it to display color sticks and a pair of school books mixed with his assortment of other looted possessions. "Holds a lot—think I got a good—"

"Show us," Aliara said, cutting him off.

"What, Rift?"

Syl sighed. "The entry, Schmalch. The one you were dispatched to locate."

"Uh, yeah, sure." Schmalch's lip twitched as he glanced uncertainly toward the back of the plant.

"Now," she said.

Pace decreasing with each step, Schmalch led them down the boardwalk toward the rear of the building. When he stopped, he chewed on a dirty fingernail for a moment before pointing at a dark opening nestled where two towers met. It was the height of an average puka, tapered at the top. A length of fresh rope dangled into the darkness beyond, its end coiled and anchored with a heavy block. Even standing several feet away, Syl caught the odor of musty desertion, something foul beneath it.

Aliara crouched and stuck her head into the breach, pressed her ear against the wall. Satisfied with what she heard, she slipped inside. Syl heard a gritty hiss and a soft thump. He crossed to where she'd just been and placed his own ear against the cool clay. He felt the familiar thrumming in his lower lug, the resonant tickle of vibration in his jaw. He heard only the expected from the still-operational areas of the plant—churning of the distant lusca, thudding of boots, conversation of plant employees, rush of water in the pipes. He peered inside. The floor was sharply canted. Two smooth lines led from the opening to where Aliara leaned against a cracked wall, peering into the room's upended doorway. A scatter of other streaks and footprints, remnants of the minikin and his friends, surrounded her path. The charnel odor was heavier here.

"It's safe," she said quietly. "Corpse in the hall."

He chuckled. Only Aliara would relate safety to the presence of a dead body.

Not as nimble as his mate, Syl wound the rope around his forearm and eased himself down into the room, dropping with a quiet *whoof* beside her.

He'd irrationally expected to enter through a hallway or foyer, but this was hardly a formal entrance. It was just a random hole in the wall opening onto a long-abandoned office, its state a clear illustration of damage dealt to this section of the building. Tables, chairs, and miscellaneous office detritus had tumbled across the floor, accumulating on the far side. Walls fell away into nothing, and the ceiling gave a fine view into the many stories above. How far their group could travel before the floors fell away altogether remained an open question.

Schmalch followed, riding the slanted floor like a playground slide, landing with a thud and a whine. He got to his feet, both hands holding his prodigious nostrils protectively closed.

Aliara dropped through the one-time doorway into the dark hall. Syl crouched and watched her. He had no intention of jumping in indiscriminately and landing on a putrefied carcass.

She took the crank torch from her pack, wound it, and sprayed the pale-yellow light down the windowless corridor of sea clay. On its floor, tiled in a bright-blue echo of the obnoxious roofing, slumped the decaying body of a youngish karju man. His gut was bloated, his skin yellowed and rodent-pocked, the top half of his skull smashed to bits. What remained of his face was a tight rictus Syl interpreted as fear.

Aliara hopped over the drooping corpse, arranged herself with one foot on the wall, one on the skewed floor, and bounded down the corridor, light bobbing like a buoy on a rough sea.

Syl lowered the rumpled puka into the canted hallway and followed. Schmalch spied the body, reversed direction, and tried to climb back out. Too short to reach the exit, he managed only a few hops before Syl put a hand on his shoulder.

"Step over him." Syl jerked his chin toward Aliara. "Now go. Follow her."

Schmalch took one step forward and gagged, cheeks puffing out comically. He shook his head. "Isn't there another way in?"

"I believe you were the individual in charge of locating the entry. If you found nothing else…" Syl shrugged and held out his hand, palm up. "Climb over him or return my Callas."

Schmalch whined, head drooping heavily against his chest. With a sigh, he shuffled toward the unfortunate explorer and climbed gently over his recumbent body. Safely on the other side, the puka awkwardly loped away, grousing under his breath.

Syl took a piton and the mallet from his pack and drove the glowing marker into the wall before joining the procession.

ALIARA

Aliara shone her crank-torch around the old processing room, a space so vast her light didn't reach the far side. What was visible seemed surprisingly undamaged; the floor level, the equipment still in place. Rows of cracked hoses hung limply from pipes in the ceiling alongside decaying harnesses, once occupied by the working lusca. They now held only wispy bits of the zoets' desiccated corpses, pale and fluttery like the fragile ash of burned paper. The distant ping of aging metal told Aliara some of the rigs still dribbled seawater into the collection troughs below.

With a light shove, Syl urged a reluctant Schmalch into the big room. "Go," he said. "Earn your Callas."

Schmalch fished the aging lantern from his pack, took one last imploring look over his shoulder and, upon seeing no sympathy, slowly trudged into the room.

Syl placed another piton, leaned against the wall and slid down with a weary sigh. "This will likely take a while," he said. "At least the fantasy of imminent treasure will keep him moving."

Aliara dropped her pack and joined him. Syl slid an arm around her and together they watched Schmalch's bald head and bobbing light move through the room, intermittently disappearing behind collection troughs. His pace was far from hare-footed, and he showed no discernable pattern. With such a haphazard effort, he was certain to miss something. Or maybe Frabo's mystery creature would dart out and eat him.

Aliara chuckled at the thought. Syl gave her a sidelong glance. She shook her head.

"Fine then," he said with a smirk, "keep your secrets."

He kissed her cheek and traced a finger over the crescent-moon scar that spanned the left side of her head. She leaned into him and closed her eyes. A low rattle and creak from somewhere in the room disturbed the moment.

Aliara opened her eyes, waiting for Schmalch's light to move. After several moments it was still in place. "He's been still too long."

"Who?"

She elbowed Syl. He chuckled.

"Schmalch, are you alive?" Syl called into the room.

The words bounced back in layers.

"Looting, most likely," Syl said. "We can review the contents of his pack when this is over. Provided we care enough to do so."

"Maybe."

Aliara pulled out of Syl's grasp, rose, and headed toward the stationary light, his soft tread in rhythm behind her. Deep in the room, she found Schmalch's lantern alone on the floor. Halfway down the row of troughs, its owner squatted by a heap of old bones, humming softly as he dug through the pockets of long-dead plant employees.

"Find something interesting?" Syl asked.

The puka lurched forward with a squeak, banging his head on the rusty trough. It thrummed and wobbled in protest. He grabbed his skull and flopped back in a puff of dust.

"Just some goodies, Duke. We can look at them together later." He scrambled to his feet. "I knew you'd want me to pick up anything I found. Like we talked about, right?"

"Yes, the purest of intentions," Syl said.

That rattle and creak came again, louder, longer.

"Quiet," Aliara said.

Syl fell silent. Schmalch did not.

"I didn't want you to be mad at me for not picking it up, Duke. You'd be really angry if I let something expensive go, right? We can look at everything now if you want." He reached into a pocket and held out a handful of worthless dross. "See? You want anything?"

He took one step toward them and vanished as a sharp crack reverberated through the room. A long, low ringing, like the strike of an enormous gong, droned beneath the echo.

As the sound subsided, Schmalch's voice, distant and small, said, "Help?"

Aliara edged toward the new hole, testing the floor, listening for more warning sounds. She pointed her torch into the jagged opening, its light barely effective in the cloud of stale dust kicked up by the collapse.

Schmalch and scattered bits of floor lay atop the gently arcing cap of a huge metal drum she recognized as a freshwater cistern. It was old and coated in corrosion, untouched for decades. Narrow pipes ran from the collection troughs through the floor into the tank. Larger lines extended from both sides, passing water from cistern to cistern down the main.

Syl squatted beside her. "Still alive down there?"

"Sure, Duke, can you get me out?" Schmalch asked.

Syl stretched out flat on his belly, hand extended. Schmalch hopped a few times, but never came close.

"I'll get the rope." Aliara passed her crank-torch to Syl and started back toward the dim glow of the piton.

She'd only just hefted the gear onto her back when another clattering racket banged through the room.

Aliara's heart skipped. She sprinted toward where she'd left them. Schmalch had been lucky to land on the cistern when he fell. Had he missed it, he would have fallen much farther, likely broken something if not killed himself.

She found Syl lying on the cistern at the base of a long ramp formed from broken floor. His torch was clutched in white-knuckled fingers, his hair powdered by dust. He shifted onto his elbows and coughed.

"Did you find the rope?" he asked.

She crouched and dug into the pack.

"Pet…" Syl said.

"What?"

Syl pointed to the base of the new collapse. The tip of the ramp had punched through the tank's rusty surface. Fragments of rust flaked away from the tear, plinking into the hissing water below.

Schmalch stirred and groaned. The metal popped and buckled with each movement.

"Hold still," Syl hissed at him. He sat up slowly, long eyes wide on Aliara. "The rope, Pet. Quickly."

Aliara dumped the pack, snatched the coil of rope and flung one end toward him. Syl lurched forward, but the rope sizzled through his fingers. The metal beneath him screeched, split further. He scrambled to his feet, stumbling back, bits of corroded steel crumbling in his wake.

Aliara tried to retrieve the rope for another toss. She felt slow, clumsy. She wouldn't get it to him in time. She dropped it, raced to the solid side of the opening and flopped onto her belly, arm outstretched.

Syl reached for her, glanced back, saw the cascade of metal rushing toward him and jumped. His fingertips brushed hers. He dropped back onto the cistern with a clang. The metal wailed, shattered, and Syl splashed into the water. Aliara made one final lunge for his groping hand as he slid away into the rush of the trunk line below.

She rolled away when the floor beneath her creaked warning. She grabbed the torch from Syl's pack, wound it, and flicked it on, looking down into the ruined cistern. The water flowed east-to-west. Syl travelled with it.

Shouldering their gear, Aliara flew out the first westerly exit she found.

The fate of Schmalch never crossed her mind.

SYLANDAIR

Syl spat and cursed, mouth full of water and rusty flakes, banging against the pipe as the water carried him along, head-first. He groped the metal above him in search of purchase, but his fingers only banged painfully against unidentified protrusions. He spread his limbs against the smooth walls to try and create drag, but the pressure was too strong. He was borne along like any other piece of debris. Pushing aside panic, he let himself bob, stealing gasps from the thin pocket of air above. His waterlogged brain struggled to recall Orono's lectures on the Haven's plumbing network.

"Four lines leave the plant," the old man had said. "Two serve the business district and Temple Row here on the Big Island. Another curls northwest toward the Nest. The final dips south to feed the dullards of the Upper and Lower Rabble."

Syl was certain he could survive two, maybe three of those routes. If he'd fallen into the Rabble line, though, this would be a long, dangerous, and most-likely lethal trip. Impulse urged him to continue his struggle, but instinct told him to save his energy and focus only on keeping his head above water. He closed his eyes and searched his mind for any other useful morsel of information.

A few feet behind Syl, however, Schmalch enjoyed no such instinct. He writhed and wailed, raking his nails against the metal, sucking in mouthful after mouthful of water until his terrified gyrations quieted, becoming sleepy shadows of earlier efforts.

Just as Syl had resigned himself to a long and excruciating trip through the city's pipes, his back and skull slammed into something hard and immobile. The water still moved, gushing over him, shooting up his nose, and filling his eyes. He had no idea how or why they'd stopped, but this was different, and at the moment, different was welcome. He probed the blockage with pruned fingers. It was a crude metal grate that halted the passage of anything larger than a grape. He felt chunks of rust, remnants of his fall, caught in its weft just as he was.

If there was a screen to catch debris here, there had to be some way to clear it. As he reached up to inspect the area above, the unconscious weight of Schmalch slammed into his chest. Syl retched water, spots dancing before his eyes. He rolled the little, limp body to one side and cast about the top of the pipe. His fingers found the edge of a gasketed hatch, possibly large enough for his body to fit through. He fumbled around its edge but found no latch. Obviously. People weren't intended to be inside the line; it opened from the outside. He banged on the hatch, determined not to die trapped inside plumbing. He tried to shout but received only another mouthful of water for his effort.

As though waiting for his arrival, the door swung upward. Syl was jerked from the water and tossed on a hard dirt floor, Schmalch deposited beside him with a splat. He caught a brief glimpse of brilliant green through his wet, loose hair before something struck the back of his head, and the world swam into darkness.

ALIARA

Aliara hardly saw the rooms she ran through. Here and there, she paused, ear to the ground, checking the pipe's bearing. Twice, she backtracked from dead ends, fear whispering in the back of her mind. When she reached a third dead end, fear did more than whisper.

Only in the drug-induced dark nothingness of Orono's delirium experiments had she previously felt this alone. She still tasted the bitter tang of the drug, heard the echoes of Orono's long-gone admonitions about The Book. The old emptiness within teased as she searched the room, tossing broken furniture and equipment, clawing at the cracked walls. She flung aside an overturned bench, revealing a constricted hole where a portion of wall and floor had given way. The panic withdrew.

Aliara shone the light into the small opening. A short, rough tunnel sloped abruptly into darkness. A breeze, light as a sleeper's breath and bitter with the tang of tainted soil, escaped, hinting at another exit beyond. She slipped in and slid down the mounded rubble left over from the collapse. Rolling to her feet, lantern held high, Aliara found herself at the dead end of a tunnel whose crude construction left no doubt she'd left the plant proper.

She half-shuttered the lantern, drew one stiletto, and crept forward. The tunnel looked to have been dug with picks or some other sharp implement. Its height and width varied irrationally, course veering left and right with baffling illogic. Here and there, sections had collapsed, only to be shored up with shabby salvage boards.

She paused at an alcove nestled in an abrupt turn. Whoever had dug this tunnel was disorganized, unskilled. They might still be in residence. If they approached everything with the same haphazard effort, she could likely avoid or end them.

Assumptions were for fools, though; craftier inhabitants may have moved in.

SYLANDAIR

As his senses returned, Syl was overcome by a musky reek that brought to mind a reptile house he'd visited years ago. The smell had offended his nose then, and his appreciation of it had not improved over time. Nearby, a deep voice spoke in a sibilant language foreign to his ears. It trailed off into a raspy laugh, joined by others.

Lying on his side in a muddy puddle, Syl cautiously opened one eye. Across a small, dirty room, three draas, ostensibly he and Schmalch's rescuers, were crouched on their haunches in a semi-circle, their abdomens unnaturally distended by a recent meal. They looked like a troop of hideous, bickering pregnant women.

Even from his squat, one loomed over the others. His body was jade green, his flat, rounded snout a rusty-red. He sat with his long tapering tail strung out behind, thick claws tapping wearily against the hard-packed dirt as he watched the conversation bounce between the others. Syl mentally dubbed him Red.

The other two squabbled enthusiastically, most likely over the dispensation of their find. Though both were more heavily scaled than Red, the rows of spikes running down their backs more pronounced, they sat with tails curled guardedly beneath them. The more enthusiastic speaker had grey-green scales and a body built for crude strength. His tail twitched nervously as he spoke, his comments punctuated by the occasional sinister hiss and menacing glance in their prisoners' direction. His opponent, all gold-edged green scales, spent more time barking protests than actually commenting. Twitchy and Goldie.

Though he was far from thrilled by the discovery, Syl was hardly surprised to encounter such a pod in this little space hidden beneath Dockhaven. Once the dominant species of Ismae, the draas now almost universally cringed in the neglected corners of the world, far from polite society. During one of Orono's long-ago vacations, Syl had the displeasure of meeting a lone draas kept by a traveling circus. He found the thing crass, smelly, and erratic—and more than a little terrifying.

As determined as he'd been not to die in an underground pipe, Syl was further resolved to be no one's dinner. They had some time, thanks to the draas' obviously recent meal, but soon the trio's minds would turn back to food.

Syl closed his eye and assessed his position. His pistol may or may not have been lost in the pipe. He felt the holster beneath his vest, but without moving, he couldn't be sure if the gun was inside. Still, it may not function after the recent dousing, and even if it did, he had no ammunition. That was in his pack, which he'd dropped by the door to the lusca chamber.

It was possible Schmalch carried the short kris he used to mug the old and infirm in the streets above, but there was no way Syl could be sure. That was even assuming the puka was alive. At the very least, Syl knew he was unconscious. Had Schmalch been alert, Syl would have heard whimpering or weeping or worse.

With an empty pistol and a puka whose best use at this moment was as an appetizer, guile was Syl's only sure defense. Failing that, he'd find a way—life hadn't always been silver and duchies. When he'd escaped captivity with a barely younger Aliara in tow, they'd had nothing more than one another. Over the past three decades, he'd shaken off the stigma of poverty and larceny, but some skills could not be forgotten. Facing this brood was little different from being backed into a corner by a rape gang while armed with nothing more than a sharp stick. He'd escaped then, he would now.

He reopened his eye a slit.

Twitchy and Goldie continued yammering and gesticulating, their dialog heating up. Red's beady, black eyes followed with a bored expression. He huffed, the naris atop his snout ejecting a misty puff. The conversation stopped. Red spoke a few solemn words to the pair, who bobbed their heads in return—though neither appeared satisfied. Red spoke a few more words, tapped his thick, sloping skull, and turned to lock with Syl's surprised eye.

"I know you wake, chivori," Red said in Plainspeak, his speech slow and deliberate, obstinate tongue struggling to form the phonemes.

The others swiveled toward their captives, mouths slack with disbelief.

Syl sat up and smiled the smile he used when striking bargains with reluctant parties.

Goldie returned the smile before realizing he was alone in the gesture. His rows of jagged, yellow teeth did little to encourage Syl.

"I was hesitant to express my gratitude," Syl said. "Apologies."

"Gra-ti-tude?" Red repeated slowly.

"For retrieving me from that vile pipe. How may I repay you?"

Red huffed again, though no cloud appeared. He poked a clawed thumb toward his companions. "They say eat you."

Syl rose to his feet.

As one, the group followed suit.

Syl raised his arms in supplication, sodden sweater dripping on the floor.

Red nodded, and the trio relaxed.

"Not much here to eat, I fear." Syl turned full circle. "Perhaps I can arrange for a nice, plump karju or two to float down your pipe?"

"What of him?" Red grunted, jerked his chin toward the soggy, wheezing figure of Schmalch.

Syl kept his eyes on his enemies. He would hate to lose such a malleable lackey, but not so much as to lay down his own life. Some effort, however, was advisable.

He sighed. "That one is the reason I was in the water," Syl said. He hesitated, looking at Schmalch, tapping his lips in a pantomime of mental debate. "I can't say I have had opportunity to sample puka meat. Though from the smell, I suspect he's quite gamey."

Red yawned.

Goldie exclaimed something, concluding with an obligatory hiss. Though Red growled angrily at his brood, one side of his lip rose in what Syl considered unsettling amusement. Another huff produced a mist, and Twitchy stomped toward their captives with a length of sailing cord.

Syl took a step backward. "There's no need for that. I assure you we will both be on our very best behavior. The little one's not even conscious."

Red said something to Twitchy, who produced a strangely giddy laugh.

Recognizing his efforts were futile, Syl bowed and held his arms behind his back, fists clenched, bicep obscuring the bulge of the pistol holster. Twitchy wound the rope around his wrists and jerked it tight enough to threaten blood flow. Syl braced for a frisking, but the burly draas was so eager to poke through Schmalch's purloined backpack that he gave no thought to concealed weapons. He sank to the ground and watched the nest-mates finger and taste Schmalch's precious trinkets.

ALIARA

Rounding yet another bend in the tunnel, Aliara heard voices, gruff and guttural. No words were clear, but gradually she differentiated two speakers. Others might be present, but silent.

If she'd come upon a pack of pukas, Aliara would have mowed through them without a pause, but these voices were deep. Only broad, thick chest cavities rumbled that way. A fight with large, potentially armed opponents was risky.

She shut the lantern and eased forward, seeing only by the ambient light ahead. She spotted no side corridors bypassing the obstacle. She had to go through. If she retraced her steps now, she would waste even more time than she had getting here. Given the rate of flow in the water line, Syl would have needed only a few heartbeats to cover the same distance. She refused to consider how far away he may already be.

As the voices grew louder, the area grew brighter. She made out details in the walls, dull stones, broken shells, and most unsettlingly, excavation marks that looked more like furrows dug by powerful claws than simple shovel scrapes. She stopped where a cap-light's yellow glow blazed around a corner. When her eyes adjusted, she stole a quick peek. Ahead was an opening, possibly the entry to another tunnel. She held for several heartbeats and glanced again around the corner. No, not a tunnel, a room of some sort. Shapes shifted inside.

She crept closer. Beyond the shadows of movement within, she made out a pipe running along the far wall, knotted debris spread about, and a damp lump on the floor. The two voices were more distinct.

"But I want to eat it!" one moaned. "Grey ones are delicious."

"You had grey one last time," the other voice said.

"I'll give you a thigh *and* the green one."

The second voice spat a curse.

"The whole leg." The first voice grew louder, more agitated. "That's more than fair. You can't expect me to split—"

"Quiet!" A third voice joined in.

Aliara flattened herself against the wall.

The voice changed to Plainspeak. "I know you wake, chivori."

"You've caught me."

Syl. A thrill danced in Aliara's chest.

"I was hesitant to express my gratitude. Apologies."

"Gra-ti-tude?" the strange voice said.

"For retrieving me from that vile pipe. How may I repay you?"

Aliara slunk closer to the entrance, the whole room in view. The damp lump on the floor was Syl. He sat up, his expression the one he used for difficult negotiation. His usual natty appearance was absent. His hair was matted and loosed from its lash, sweater damp and heavy, vest tight and shrunken, and every bit of him was speckled with mud. But it was the face she knew.

She pulled her gaze from him to examine the group. Three draas of varying size and color stood opposite him. Schmalch lay immobile between them, possibly dead. One of the draas was tall but slender. One was broad as a rain drum. The last was middling but wore a well-armored hide. They all showed the gut bulge of having recently fed.

"They say eat you," the tall one said.

A pause as Syl stood, still smiling. "Not much here to eat, I fear."

He was safe for the moment. She would trust him to remain so a bit longer.

Silently, she shifted away from the door and hurried back down the tunnel, past a sharp bend to where the den's light barely reached. She piled their gear in a corner. It was too awkward, too noisy for what she had planned.

A blitz would do little good against three overlarge males, each with three-fingered claws for hands and armor for hide, all packed into a small space. Even given her skills, she could dispatch one, maybe two before they overtook her. No, this had to be done her way—subtly, quietly. A surprise.

Since the moment she was delivered to Orono, she'd been adept at hiding from her master for hours or days, often concealed only feet from him as he ranted about the "disobedient girl." Though she still bore the scars of the punishments, the temporary freedom had been worth the pain. And it had taught her to move like a cat in the fog—a skill that benefitted her profession as an adult.

She would need that skill now. She had encountered draas on only two prior jigs. Each time she found them surprisingly challenging. Their claws cut deep, their teeth tore and ripped. With a whip of their barbed tail, they could flay flesh, break bones, or knock enemies to the floor. Worse yet, since she had no gun, dispatching the draas with gold-tinted saucer scales would require a precise attack at close range. To her advantage, however, the species was stupid and short-sighted. Though there were few places to hide in this shabby tunnel, she could use its meandering course to her advantage. All she had to do was lure them out one by one.

She emptied Syl's pack and went to work.

SYLANDAIR

Syl willed Schmalch to remain unconscious. The puka had no gift for coping calmly with stress. They had at least a day before the draas' hunger returned. He was confident Aliara would arrive and dispatch their captors before either he or Schmalch hung from the roasting spit. If the puka woke and panicked before then, however, no amount of guile could save them.

Reclining against the pipe he'd so recently emerged from, Syl cast his eyes over his surroundings. The room, cramped for three such ample creatures, was hollowed from the island's basalt, and framed with steel. Flickering capacitance lamps dangled from the ceiling, a long cable connecting them to a hand crank mounted on the wall. Given this technology, it was hardly likely that these ham-fisted draas were the original architects. Syl could imagine the pod stumbling on the old maintenance room, delighted to find free water, shelter, and light. The only visible entryway was an irregular hole in the wall, handiwork easily attributed to the draas.

Beside the entrance was an unsavory mound of matted clumps of hair and chalky bones, mostly rodent-size, though enough larger ones were mixed in to unsettle Syl. This pile lay next to a haphazard collection of objects that likely passed for treasures—seashells and shiny rocks, mateless shoes, lengths of rope, rusty and broken weapons, and more useless dreck. That junk spilled into the pod's communal nest, undoubtedly the source of the room's funk. Housed in an alcove in the wall opposite Syl, it was matted with dried plants, old shredded cloth, and more cherished pieces of the junk-treasure. Beside it, three large rocks were arranged around an inverted Billidoc Coalition shipping crate to form a makeshift table and chairs.

It was far from an impressive lair.

Red napped in the nest while Goldie and Twitchy manned the table, most likely assigned to guard Syl and Schmalch. They played a game with old bits of metal, hissing and swiping at one another after each turn in what Syl supposed was a playful manner. A fan of such diversions, he passed the time studying the mechanic, which combined stack-balancing with counter-attacks against an opponent's success. He'd almost fully grasped it when a distant metallic clang echoed from the tunnel.

Syl smiled.

Twitchy and Goldie's heads jerked to attention. They looked at each other, then at their sleeping leader. Another clang. They scowled at Syl, who merely shrugged. A third clang.

Another argument ensued. Twitchy gestured to the exit and grunted something. Goldie replied in a petulant tone. The quarrel's tempo increased until another clang reverberated through the cramped space.

Goldie grabbed a muck-caked crank torch from their treasure pile and smacked Twitchy in the head with it before strolling out of the room, muttering some final insult. Twitchy rubbed his thick skull and flopped back on his rock, flicking claws at the metal game pieces.

Syl began slowly working his hands free of their bonds.

ALIARA

Perched high on the tunnel wall, body still, breath slow and quiet, Aliara waited like a hungry spider. She clung to a ladder formed from Syl's pitons, stripped of their lumia chambers. Her torch lay on the floor below, a curious and irresistible lure. She ignored the rocks pressing into her spine, the jittery muscles in her arms, attentive only on the sounds around her.

The rustle of incautious shuffling approached from the direction of the den, the tread heavy and slow. The thick-scaled one strolled into sight, grumbling in a tone of one bemoaning his lot in life. His step faltered as he spied the light. He cocked his head to the side, scratched his chin with a lethal claw and gave the device a light kick. The torch spun, flashing dizzily like nightclub lights. He squatted, leaned forward.

Aliara dropped onto his back.

Off balance, the draas tipped to one side, barking with fury. His torch went flying, its scattered light further confusing the scene. Aliara slipped her right arm around his neck like a harness, stiletto in her left probing the base of his skull for an opening between his overlapping scales. He righted himself, rose to his knees, and pawed frantically at the intruder on his back, claws tearing her clothes, scoring her skin. She ignored the discomfort and clung on, stiletto scraping uselessly against his scales, refusing to find purchase. She bit back a cry when he clawed at her forearm. Blood burst from the wounds, soaked her sleeve.

The draas wobbled to his feet and slammed Aliara against the tunnel wall, bulk knocking both the breath from her body and the weapon from her hand. Coughing and sucking air, she dragged her left arm around his throat, linking it tightly with the blood-slicked right. She braced her knees against his back and jerked. Something inside him grated and popped.

He released a gagging groan and pitched forward, scales of his neck opening invitingly as he stumbled around the narrow corridor. Aliara drew her other stiletto before he could recover and drove it between two of his gold-tipped plates, up into his brain. He crumpled to the dirt.

She rolled away onto her feet. Blue-black blood trickled down her arm, dribbling off her fingertips onto the dirt. She ripped the sleeve from her suit and tied it around the deep gashes. Both stilettos holstered, she switched off the cap-lights and climbed back up the ladder of pitons. The attack had been brief but noisy. It wouldn't be long before the next draas appeared.

SYLANDAIR

At the yelp from the tunnel beyond, Twitchy shot up and scowled at Syl, who shrugged with feigned bewilderment. The yelp became a frenzied scuffle, a gurgle, then silence.

Twitchy's eyes shifted from the doorway to Syl and back, finally lighting on his sleeping leader, coiled comfortably in their nest. He crouched and shook Red, who sat up, his inner lids blinking drowsily. Twitchy spoke. Red snarled. Predictably, the discussion became heated.

Syl quietly slipped free of the sailing cord.

With a sharp bark, Red released a cloud from his naris and Twitchy fell silent.

The sound woke Schmalch, whose reaction upon grasping his situation was blind panic. Still bound at the wrists, he squeaked and scooted into the nearest corner, dinner-plate eyes scanning frantically for escape.

Neither draas seemed to notice. Red rifled through the pod's treasure horde while his subordinate scowled at his back. When it became obvious the leader would not change his instruction, Twitchy spat quietly and stormed into the tunnel.

Syl slid across the muddy floor to the cowering Schmalch and lifted the puka's pant leg to find the kris strapped in place. Drawing the small dagger, he slit Schmalch's bindings, then pressed the knife into the puka's hand. Syl jerked his head toward Red, still busy scouring the nest.

In most circumstances, Schmalch groveled and scraped in order to excise himself from difficult situations. When those efforts proved futile, when he was pushed into a corner with no alternative, the Schmalch of everyday Dockhaven transformed into a maniac, behaving irrationally, even throwing himself deeper into danger. Years ago at Saxelyt's Gatehouse, an inebriated rhochrot had mistaken Schmalch for a puka who'd pinched some coin, or so Schmalch claimed. Dangling from the rhochrot's massive fist as bar patrons cheered for his blood, Schmalch abandoned whining and pleading. He drove his tiny dagger into his attacker's hand, swung onto the brute's shoulder, and took bites until little was left to call an ear. The rhochrot's friends had tossed Schmalch out a window into the sea, but as always, he'd found his way back to shore.

It was then that Syl had settled on recruiting Schmalch into his service.

Red rose from his squat by the nest, brandishing the broken and corroded stub of a longsword.

Quite literally backed into the den's corner, the maniacal Schmalch returned. He leapt, surprising Syl by digging his motley teeth into the fine scales behind Red's knee. The draas roared, rust-red frills flaring from his cheeks. For an almost comical moment, he spun in circles, swiping in vain at the puka latched to his leg. When Red connected, Schmalch flew across the room, a gory string of tendon trailing from his mouth, his eyes wild, almost feral.

Red dropped to one knee, his blood mingling with the dirt and pipe-water. He dragged himself awkwardly forward, the broken tip of the sword aimed at Syl.

"I should have—" Red's threats cut off with a yelp as Schmalch drove his kris between the scales at the base of his spine. He dropped his weapon, groping at his back for the invading blade.

Syl dove for the abandoned stub of longsword. With a quick stab upward, he jammed it through Red's long, flat snout. The draas' eyes went wide. He tried to yowl, only managed a groan. Using the blade like a handle, Syl heaved the creature forward, cracking his skull against the pipe. Red's body went limp. Syl released the pommel, and Red's corpse slumped into the dirt.

As Schmalch stabbed the corpse a few more times, Syl turned to the tunnel entrance. Aliara's soft tread sped toward him, the powerful thudding of a huge creature behind her. Drawing his still-damp pistol from the shoulder holster, Syl filled its barrel with Goldie and Twitchy's game pieces. He flicked the switch that brought the weapon to life, felt the thrum and hitch as its mag-field grabbed the metal hunks. There was no time to test; he had to assume it would work.

Syl stood wide and aimed into the darkness of the tunnel. The slim shape of Aliara took form in the gloom. She burst into the room, dove out of the line of fire.

Slavering and roaring, Twitchy pounded in behind her. He skidded to a stop, the thrill of chase replaced by bewilderment at the sight before him: Syl unbound and armed, Schmalch awake and bloody-faced, Red nothing more than a gory, lifeless heap.

Syl pulled the trigger.

High-velocity fragments peppered Twitchy, ripping through his tough hide like stones breaking the water's surface, shredding his face and upper torso. One pierced an eye while two others tore burgundy gashes in his throat. Still more buried themselves in his muzzle and forehead or shattered teeth. A cluster spangled his chest.

The big draas stood in place for a moment, expression perplexed, staring through Syl with his remaining eye. His shoulders twitched once. Blood dribbled from his mouth. He raised an arm, whether for help or to attack, Syl couldn't tell, then dropped to his knees and pitched forward on his snout with a crunch.

For a moment, everyone remained still. When nothing stirred, Syl lowered his weapon and grinned at Schmalch.

"It seems you were correct," he said. "It functioned well."

SCHMALCH

While Rift and the Duke enjoyed a passionate reunion, Schmalch explored. He'd already retrieved the Duke's discarded and water-withered vest, as baggy on him as it had been snug on the chivori. He was quite certain there were treasures to be found here. Certainly in all of this, the draas had managed to collect something useful. Probably not the opoli the Duke and Rift were after, but Schmalch wasn't so picky.

He skipped over the bone pile and headed straight for the boodle horde. Most of it was junk, even by Schmalch's standards, but he found some sea glass and a broken copper bracelet he might be able to pawn above ground.

Certain he had retrieved everything of value, he moved on to the stinky nest. As he burrowed in, past gnawed-on bones and fragments of things that had once been useful, he spied the glint of silver. He dug faster. At the bottom of the heap lay a scratched, but intact belt buckle, puny strip of leather still clinging to its oval frame. Silver, he was sure. Down here under a bunch of sleeping draas, doing nobody any good. Schmalch picked it up, but it snapped out of his fingers. He tried again. The stitched leather pulled taut, stuck on something beneath the nest. He traced the strap to the floor, found it was attached to a steel loop, the loop attached to a door. He dug in, matted leaves and moldy fabric flying as he cleared it.

"Schmalch!" the Duke snapped. "What in the depths are you

doing?"

"Apologies, Duke," Schmalch said, "but com'ere. You're gonna want to see this."

The Duke left off washing up at the pipe hatch and crossed to the nest, picking bits of debris from his wet sweater. Rift floated up behind them.

"You found a pearl?" he asked.

"A door, Duke, I found a door." Schmalch struck the surface with a metallic clang. "Some sort of trapdoor. Weird. Why would they sleep on that?" He looked at the door, scratched at a random itch. "What do you think's down there?"

The Duke looked at Rift. She nodded as though he'd asked her a question.

"Open it," the Duke said.

Schmalch yanked until the old hinges gave way with a jarring creak. A mildewy stink floated out. He peered in and saw only darkness.

The Duke stretched out on his belly and lowered the lantern into the opening. The walls were smooth, reinforced with metal banding. A steel ladder ran down one side.

"Too deep to see much." The Duke sat up, brushed bits of the nest from his clothes and looked at Schmalch. "Time for you to scout."

Schmalch winced. He'd hoped his valiant performance with the tall draas had earned him a reprieve from the recon job. After all, Rift was better at this sort of thing than him, sneakier and slick. He licked his lips, scratched his nose, tried to dawdle until the Duke changed his mind and sent her instead.

"Now," the Duke said.

Schmalch sighed. His shoulders sunk. "Yeah…right."

He plopped down at the lip of the hole and anchored his feet on the ladder, lantern gripped tight in one hand. With a last, pleading look at the pair of indifferent faces, he climbed into the chilly blackness.

It was quiet. Really quiet. Weirdly so. He wanted to make noise just to hear something, but that might announce his presence to whatever lurked below, waiting to tear him to pieces. More draas could be down here. Or worse. He tried not to picture what "worse" might be.

He lost count of the number of rungs he'd climbed down by the time a soft breeze wafted up his pant legs. He stopped, sniffed. The sea, he smelled the sea. Not the sea smell he was used to in the streets and boardwalks of Dockhaven. This held only the salty-clean smell of water tinged with fishy pong, the scents of rubbish and sweat absent.

Fear forgotten, he scurried down the last few rungs and dropped with a soft thump onto solid ground. The sea air called him. He could almost smell the moonlight on the water's surface. In the lantern's glow, he saw the walls of a tunnel, crisply cut and braced, around him. At its near end loomed a dark opening. Something seemed to shift beyond. He edged forward, clinging tight to the wall. The scene outside the doorway came into focus and he rushed forward. There was the sea, the moons, and stars! He stepped out onto a shallow ledge high above the pounding surf.

A gritty scuttling from the left sent a surge of panic through him. Schmalch shuffled back into the tunnel, fumbling for his kris as he retreated. The sound grew closer, louder. He'd disturbed something. Now it was coming to get him, punish him for his intrusion.

He shuttered the lantern and crouched against the tunnel wall. A squirming shadow rose in the moonlight. Schmalch held his breath, caught between running and fighting. A brief parade of fuzzy grey bodies each no bigger than his foot, scurried through the doorway. They skittered past into the darkness, as frightened of Schmalch as he'd been of them. Nothing but a bunch of rats. He giggled, the laughter only slightly nervous.

"Schmalch?" the Duke called. Then more firmly, "Schmalch,

come back here. Now."

"Right, right, Duke," Schmalch called as he jogged back down the passage. "I got excited. Fresh air down here. I started walking before I knew I was doing it."

"Fine. What did you find?"

"Another tunnel. Opens onto the sea down this way." He pointed first one way, then the other. "And some rats."

"The other direction?"

"Gimme a few beats and I'll check."

The Duke grumbled a response.

Schmalch travelled a ways in the unexplored direction, finding only a boring old tunnel. He returned to report.

"Pretty nice that way. Long," he said, round face tilted up toward the Duke's silhouette. "I don't see anything special."

The Duke turned his head and spoke to Rift, who materialized in the glowing square from the room above. She slipped onto the ladder. When both had dropped into the tunnel with Schmalch, the Duke ran a finger over one of the ceiling supports and studied it in the lantern's glow. He showed it to Rift, who said nothing, though her eyes narrowed in a way that historically did not mean good things.

"You have been out there?" the Duke asked with a nod toward the sea exit.

"Yep, that's where the rats came from," Schmalch said.

"Anything besides vermin?"

Schmalch shrugged. "The sea?"

SYLANDAIR

The view was spectacular. When they'd entered the ominous crack in the plant's wall, the night had been new. Now the slip of the white moon of Dormah hung high in the black dome, its veiled face shimmering on the water as the waves blew sea spray against Syl's damp clothing. The lonely arc of the green moon, B'hintal Dadeyah, peeped over the horizon, chasing its sister in a sky salted with stars. Opoli's shattered corpse was a glittering ghost arcing between the two.

Syl sat, feet dangling over the edge, and listened to the rhythmic din of surf against the rocks below. Aliara lowered herself close behind him, legs and arms wrapped around his body, head resting against his back. He did not need to ask to know she too wondered what they would do if they actually found what they sought. If Orono was still here to be found, they were close. The tunnel beneath the draas nest was the same they'd escaped through almost three decades past, fire and death nipping at their heels.

Back then they'd watched, passive and terrified, as Orono sacrificed child after child to his amalgam of science and mysticism. Only by the luck of age had the pair escaped the dagger's edge. When Orono had slain more than half, Syl saw the old man's exhaustion, his distraction, and seized Aliara's hand. He still could feel her clammy palm tight against his as they ran from the concrete chamber into the tunnel they traversed tonight.

The blast came while they were still underground, still finding their way. Whether real or imagined, both felt the heat of the explosion pursuing them. They scrambled up the nearest access ladder, bursting from the floor among startled plant employees, barely clearing the room before the blue flames blew through the hatch behind them. Bewildered workers screamed and died, some burned, some were crushed by falling wreckage. The mayhem was so great that no guard, no supervisor hassled the two ragged youths racing through the facility.

Syl and Aliara cleared door after door, pandemonium swelling in their wake, until they saw the blue of midday sky peeking through a haze of soot. The blast had jettisoned soil into the air, cracked streets, and blown fragments of equipment and employees into the sky. Crowds too foolish to stay away swarmed the building, ignorant of the two chivori youths rushing through their ranks, away from Orono and into independence.

Under the moons, they shared this memory.

With a purgative breath, Syl released the images. His eyes panned around their perch, lighting on an almost invisible path sloping off to the left—narrow, but passable.

"Scout?" he asked.

From his position relaxing in the dirt, Schmalch groaned. Syl wasn't sure why the puka kept complaining. It made no difference. Perhaps it made him feel better.

Schmalch rose, not bothering to brush the clinging dirt from his clothes. "Scout what?"

Syl pointed to the ledge. "Do us a favor and inspect that path. Find out if it leads back up to the streets…or to anything useful."

"Sure, Duke. How far you want me to go before coming back?"

"Until you find something or the path runs out."

SCHMALCH

When Schmalch returned, Rift sat straddling the Duke, who lay sweaterless in the cool dirt. They were both so stretched-looking and bony, almost like they never ate, but then all chivori looked that way to him. Half-dressed, her bubs bared to the night sky, she raked her short nails across his chest. Schmalch wondered absently if these two had any other hobbies. He cleared his throat and stayed out of their reach.

Rift looked at him, and the Duke rose to his elbows, their eyes glinting in the moonlight like an alley cat's. Schmalch always found the effect unnerving.

"Welcome back. What did you find?" said the Duke.

"Looks like a big cave. I didn't go far in 'cause I didn't want to be pinched and thought I heard somebody coming, but…" he paused thoughtfully, "…it, uh, seems to belong to someone pretty rich."

"Oh? What makes you draw that conclusion?"

"Lotsa' rich stuff in there. Boxes, kegs, expensive looking dosh sitting around." He held out an artfully engraved silver ring inset with a smooth moonstone the size of a blalal berry. "Like this and bigger."

The Duke took the ring. Swiveling between his fingers, the metal glinted, the pearly stone glowed with its namesake's light. "Very nice. Excellent quality." He placed it on Rift's index finger. "More like that in there, you say?"

"Not exactly like it, but swish like that, yeah." Schmalch frowned at the loss of his filched bauble. He'd had big plans for that ring.

"Aside from this path, how would one reach this cavern of riches?"

"Some complicated thing that looks like it can go up and down from the cave to a dock below. A big lift, you catch?" Schmalch didn't know how to work the device, but he'd seen many like it clinging to Dockhaven's bayside cliffs and overlarge buildings. They always had an operator on duty. "Kinda hidden in a…a whatsit…a nooch?"

"A niche. How far off is the cave?"

Schmalch shrugged. "How long was I gone? Half that."

The Duke smiled grimly. "I do appreciate your precision."

"It's around a bend." He pointed. "Ledge follows the wall. Easy trip."

The Duke sat up, forehead against Rift's chest. "Sadly you'll need to dress, Pet. I see a little foray in your future."

Swinging off of the Duke, she stood and snapped back into her ripped suit.

"Dump the bags," she said.

The two chivori emptied their gear. Schmalch unstrapped his pilfered pack and hugged it close.

"Why are we doing that, Rift?" he asked.

Face puckered with irritation, she took the bag and dumped all his precious belongings into the dirt. She made as if to sling his pack over her shoulder with the others, but hesitated. She squatted. Her hand dipped into the jumble of his stuff and returned with the little metal sphere. She held it between them, brows raised in question.

"I found it last night," Schmalch said, "when I was behind the plant looking for the door, er, crack or…you know, the place we came in."

She studied him with a doubtful expression before handing the bauble to the Duke, who chuckled as he hefted it. "*This* was lying abandoned on the boardwalk behind the desalinization plant?"

"Yeah. I wasn't sure what it was. A Mucha toy, maybe? Or a watch? Is it a watch? I thought I could get some nice coin for it. I was gonna try to open it last night, but I got busy at the Barnacle…" He let his words trail off as the Duke's chuckle bloomed into full laughter.

"You—and everyone else at the Barnacle—are quite lucky you forgot about it." The Duke tossed the shiny ball to Rift, who slipped it into her tool bag. "That is a grenade."

ALIARA

Aliara skimmed the ledge, empty packs strapped on her back. She edged around the thick pipes that ran down the cliffside, connecting the plant above to the sea, and hopped over the occasional half-rotted timber jutting from the cliff wall, remnants of what must have once been a platform linking the maintenance tunnel and cave.

The puka's trail was so ridiculously easy to spot, he may as well have dribbled paint. He'd even stopped at one point to piss against the wall. She scowled at the stain and kicked dirt over it, wondering why he hadn't simply turned around and aimed into the sea. When the cave's owners returned, they didn't need to know anyone had paid them a visit.

Peering into the dimly lit space, Aliara agreed with Schmalch's assessment—the cave was, in fact, full of "rich stuff." Crates, kegs, and ceramic vessels lined the walls—some bearing the tariff marks of their nation of origin or shipper's name, others blank. The jumble rose to the ceiling and stretched back so far she couldn't see the rear wall. This wasn't someone's home or bolt hole, it was large-scale storage of what she assumed were ill-gotten goods. And no one seemed to be on guard.

She stepped back, scanned the area around her. The dock below was dark and empty. The screw that drove its big lift was old and rusty, but bits of clean metal still glinted in the moonlight, evidence of its continued use.

It was an ideal site. This portion of the Big Island faced the open sea. Few captains anchored outside of Rimadour Bay, which lay safely in the atoll's embrace. Those that did had their reasons for not mentioning the doings of others.

She held at the entry, listening for movement, searching for signs of inhabitants. Catching nothing, she stole inside and drifted between the haphazard stacks and rows. Here and there, she lifted this or pocketed that, careful to leave no obvious signs of trespass. Sealed crates were out. Prominent items as well. Things underneath and unseen, however, were fair game. If no one noticed missing boodle, no one came looking for a thief.

"When at all possible, your targets should not realize they have been robbed," Orono had instructed her during the first of their burgling trips.

Vacations, he called them. Perhaps to him they were. To Aliara they were little more than uncomfortable and compulsory expeditions to old temples and museums scattered across the islands, where Orono made rubbings of messages and images etched into ancient walls or artworks, copied text from dusty books, or chatted interminably. Once he found what he wanted, he spent the rest of each vacation giving orders and diddling Syl.

Not until their visit to the city of Monicene on Elnor, was she given a role in the vacations. That time, Orono needed an artifact, one owned by a family with no urge to sell it. Suddenly, Aliara was a tool to be employed, something only slightly more than luggage.

"You are so proud of finding your way unseen into places you are not allowed," he told her, fat finger jabbed in her face. "That talent will make you a marvelous thief in my service. My research of The Book has revealed many answers, but I require the keys. You will assist me in separating them from their current homes. Start with this." He'd handed her a map and a sketch, opened the door to their suite and waved her outside.

Aliara only stared, unsure why he trusted her to return.

"Ah yes." He patted her narrow face. "You *will* come back to me, and you *will* have the bowl I need. Or Sylandair will reap the consequences of your disobedience. Nushgha has been aching to dole out some punishment." He nodded at Syl, who sat on their balcony, reading in the day's failing light, Orono's one-eyed thug in a chair beside him.

And she understood.

Alone in the unfamiliar city, armed only with instructions and a threat, Aliara was overcome by the strangeness of it all. She'd never been allowed to socialize with Orono's visitors. Her whole world was Syl, Orono, and the four servants. She didn't know how to act around so many people, how to deal with so much freedom and open space. Strange faces assaulted her, their smiles like menacing snarls. She bit back panic and tears as she stole through the city.

After hours of bumbling around, dodging the endless sea of accusing eyes, she found the walled estate. Slipping into the extravagant home was no challenge. She slunk in and out without disturbing so much as a mote of dust.

It was one of the few things Orono had been right about—Aliara *was* a marvelous thief.

Since that lonely day, she'd expanded and refined those skills tremendously.

One pack already stuffed with salable items or ones she intended to keep, she crept deep into the cliff cave, pausing at an open crate marked "*Ossquere*" that vomited clothing of all kinds. Glancing at the condition of her catsuit, Aliara selected new garments for them all, shuffled the clothes so nothing would be missed, and continued on.

At the cave's rear, the boodle gave way to a collection of bunks stacked against the back wall, a stove and long table in front. It was the first evidence of life she'd seen. She crouched behind a barrel labeled "*Mondala Vineyards of Imtnor*" and listened. Muffled grunts and moans of sex came from the living space. She peered around the barrel and saw the rhythmic shifting of blankets atop one of the bunks. The guards, it seemed, were more concerned with their own pleasure than the security of their storehouse.

She worked her way around the periphery, careful not to disturb the lovers. On the back wall hung a huge flag. In green and black on a yellow field loomed the blocky image of a yawl pierced by a scimitar. The symbol of the Yenderot, raiders who robbed travelers, merchants, and Billidoc alike, harrying the seas and skies, vying for dominance with the Bankal and Suul clans. Caught stealing from any of them, punishment would be swift and severe.

Aliara sped back through the loot. She was almost outside when the gleam of dark metal caught her eye. Atop an open crate of rather pedestrian weapons rested a dagger, its oil-rubbed bronze hilt and sheath adorned with relief designs. Though she'd never seen one before, she recognized the pattern from a block print of ancient weapons she'd given Syl years ago. It was a Voshar dagger, a relic from lands lost long ago beneath the seas. She drew the curved steel blade, its surface gleaming like oil on rippling water. Voshar weapons were coveted for their rarity as well as their reputed ability to hold the finest edge without dulling.

She wanted it. It would be missed. Weighing the risk and finding herself indifferent, Aliara slipped it into her pack and hurried back.

Syl wasted no time, flinging his wrecked sweater and pants over the cliff's edge before donning the new black trousers and shirt the same slate blue of his eyes. She traded the dark blue catsuit for simple black pants and a ginger linen tank. Schmalch replaced his timeworn clothing with tan cotton trousers—short-pants on any chivori—and a red tunic beneath the now-favored vest rescued from Syl. Over it all, he resumed his bedraggled burlap jacket.

As Schmalch reloaded their packs, Aliara placed the Voshar dagger in Syl's palm. He drew the blade and slashed abstractedly at the air for a moment before slipping it into the back of his pants.

"Exquisite, Pet." He kissed her cheek and whispered, "We should put distance between us and that cave."

SYLANDAIR

They left the ledge and backtracked, heading deeper into the tunnel, past the ladder leading to the draas nest. As they walked, Syl made every effort to avoid thinking of the last time he'd been here. They were here now only to confirm what the city assumed, what neither of them believed. He tried to occupy his mind by watching Schmalch scamper ahead of them, his lantern casting eerie shadows on the walls. The effort proved fruitless.

It didn't help that the only notable break in the tunnel's unrelenting sameness was the collapsed passage leading to Orono's ritual chamber. Schmalch scaled the mound of dirt and rocks spilling from the entryway and pronounced it thoroughly blocked. Syl stepped over the room's deformed metal door, now lying across the tunnel, without a word.

Schmalch scampered past him and Aliara into the dim corridor ahead. In moments, the puka's happy voice bounced back at them.

"Duke! Rift!"

The lantern's glow rushed toward them, accompanied by the flap of Schmalch's footsteps. He stopped in front of them, panting and grinning.

"Another door's down there! This one's still shut, not blown across the hall. C'mon. C'mon!"

He hurried away, shouting encouragements. They found him bouncing with excitement beside a gasketed door, wheel handle set in its face. Aliara laid her ear against the cold steel surface. Syl joined. At first he heard nothing, then slowly he picked up a dim, rhythmic pulse.

"Music?" Syl asked.

She nodded.

He opened the door onto a tight, narrow room lined with shelves of tools, plumbing paraphernalia, and cleaning supplies. The music was a faint undertone. Syl puled the shutter cord of the lumia lamp dangling from the ceiling. Only a dim, last gasp of light eked out. He cranked his torch and stepped inside.

The glorified closet continued to one side for some distance, its length lined with more crowded shelves. At the far end stood a steel tool case so tall it reached the ceiling. Syl shoved past Schmalch, now busy pawing at the plumbing equipment in search of something worth stealing, and opened the hulking cabinet. He expected an array of rather banal plumbing equipment. Instead, he found another gasketed door, this one painted with wild swirling patterns of green, gold and red, its wheel handle striped like a child's candy.

Something familiar tickled Syl's memory. Before it could take shape, Schmalch squeezed between Syl and Aliara.

"Ooo, pretty," he said. "What's it doing here?"

"An excellent question," Syl said.

Aliara listened at the door. "Definitely music."

Syl pressed his ear to the riotous pattern. Within he heard the same rhythm, distant at the first door, now distinct, its cadence lively. He could make out other instruments, strings and brass, as though a full ensemble were entertaining a crowd within. Curiosity overtook caution and Syl spun the wheel, tugged the door. It hissed open with a sickly-sweet odor, a puff of dust, and a cacophony of discordant instruments. A dust-shrouded scarlet curtain waved gently in the doorway, blocking any view inside. Syl pulled back the hem. Even his chivori eyes, adept in the dimness, found only blackness. He aimed his torch into the room. An old saloon of some sort, deep enough that he could only barely make out its rear wall.

"Schmalch," Syl smiled, "enter."

Schmalch pointed to Aliara. "Can't she go this time? She'd be in and out before anything knew she was there."

"Save your flattery." Syl crouched down and smoothed the lapels of the puka's ratty old coat. "Take a look inside as you were paid to do. If something starts to eat you, be sure to shriek so we know it is not safe."

SCHMALCH

Schmalch stared at the timeworn fabric hanging limply before him. It was weird that there was a crazy painted door and some fancy red curtain in a plumbing maintenance cubby. Anything could be lurking on the other side of that tattered old thing. It could take his head off. He gulped. He should have stayed on the surface. He knew all about the dangers up there. As usual, he'd let these two talk him into something he'd never do on his own. Though they did pay well—and they never hurt him, which was more than he could say for most others. If he wanted that to continue, he needed to screw up his courage and scout ahead.

"Now." The Duke's voice was icy.

Schmalch leaned forward into the curtain, but his feet wouldn't move. He tried to will his body through. It refused. He groaned with effort, still rooted in place.

Rift resolved his conflict with a soft boot to the back. He flopped through with a whoosh of fabric and a fresh cloud of dust. He rolled away, coughing violently before he remembered stealth was the better option. Frozen in a tight ball on the floor, eyes squeezed shut, he waited for something to leap out of the dark and devour him. Thanks to the noisy music, he'd never hear it coming.

As time passed and nothing pounced, Schmalch slowly opened one eye, then the other.

He flicked open the lantern. The room was gloomy, long and

narrow, though wider than the closet and tunnel. A hulking real-wood bar ran down the center of the room, all swish with a shiny metal tube along the base. This was way swankier than anything at the Barnacle.

Schmalch got to his feet. Behind the bar's far end, he could see a hump-shape. He raised the lantern, stared hard, but was unable to distinguish details from this distance.

"We're waiting," the Duke called from beyond the curtain. "Is it safe?"

He crept toward the bar. One step. Two. Three. Shutters flicked open on the room's many lamps, filling the room with the feeble glow of sickly lumia.

Schmalch leapt backward, startled. In the improved light, the hump-thing looked like a person, though not a very healthy one. Its back was to him, thick dust coating its hair and shoulders, its once-elegant crimson jacket a wreck of moth-holes and rips. It vibrated as though chilly.

Schmalch chanced another step forward. The figure lurched, arms jerking out to its sides. One dangled unnaturally from a drooping shoulder.

"Um…vrasaj?" Schmalch whispered in greeting.

The figure made no reply, it simply shivered. Schmalch dared one more step.

The thing's head spun toward him like some crazy underground owl. The face was fixed in what it thought was a smile, eyes wide, artificial lips pulled back to bare painted-on teeth. Once, when he'd been stuck in a drainpipe during a storm, Schmalch had met a man with that same expression. He didn't like it then and he certainly didn't like it now.

With a yelp, Schmalch scurried backward, tripping over his own feet. He flopped onto his bum and crab-walked through the curtain until he was safely pressed against the Duke's shins.

SYLANDAIR

"So?" Arms crossed, Syl eyed the fetal figure of Schmalch at his feet.

"It looked at me," the puka whimpered.

"What in the depths do you think that means?" Syl asked Aliara.

"He wasn't eaten," she said and slipped inside.

Syl followed, the sensation of familiarity again niggling at the back of his mind.

The room was dim, its lumia nearly dead. Behind the far end of the ornate bar, highlighted by the glow of Schmalch's lantern, stood a figure shuddering with accumulated energy. Though its damaged torso was turned away, its shadowed face, a rictus of mechanical design, followed Aliara, who stood there examining it with cocked head. She slunk toward the bar on silent feet.

At her approach, the mechanical body whirled around to align with the head, loose arm flapping out in a disjointed arc. It zipped down the length of the bar toward her with a hum, audible even over the blaring music. Her hands went to the stilettos at her hips, her shoulders hunched forward, knees bent and ready to spring. When the automaton reached her, its functional arm gestured gleefully, jaw wagging in silent greeting. She released her weapons, climbed onto a stool, and bent over the bar to investigate.

Unable to resist the tempting sight of her upturned ass, Syl gave her a playful pat.

"It has no legs," she said.

Syl leaned past her. The barman's head and torso were supported by a thick metal pole set in a channel that ran the length of the bar.

"The Mucha, no doubt," Syl said. "Who else would want something so unsettling to serve drinks?"

"Agreed." Aliara settled onto the stool, eyes crawling over the rest of the room.

Trained in the Colleges of Ukur-Tilen, the Mucha were the world's best-known collection of intellectuals. As dinner companions, Syl found them obnoxious, what with their braggadocio, absurd titles, and ridiculous and competitive fashions. When not in their presence, he appreciated them for their brilliant inventions and finely-honed skills. They were peculiar at best, dangerous at worst, and bizarre regardless.

"Is it safe?" Schmalch asked.

"Yes," Syl said. He raised his voice over the music. "Yes. Nothing to fear."

Schmalch tiptoed in, looked around, and cowered behind Syl's legs. "What *is* this place?"

Syl shrugged. It was obvious no one had patronized the establishment for quite some time. The entire room was smothered in a layer of dust that dampened the dark red walls, the gold-glass lumia tubes, and the vibrant array of bottles. The elegance beneath remained. At one time, the establishment had been quite swank.

Syl pushed away from the bar and straightened the seam of his new, stylish trousers. "Let's see what else we have here."

The automaton followed as he strode down the aisle, Schmalch at his heels. It was a fairly standard saloon—café tables, comfortable chairs in red and gold crushed velvet, etched glassware. Other than its existence, he found nothing particularly odd about the place. When he rounded the end of the bar, however, Syl found himself facing another ragged red curtain. This little area was only the beginning of the mystery.

He sniffed. The foul odor was richer here, the music more bombastic. He glanced over at Aliara and jerked his chin toward the curtain. She slid from the stool and hurried across the check-patterned floor to where he waited. The barman whirred down to meet then follow her, pleading mutely for her to deliver an order so he could do his job. Aliara paid him no heed, leaving him to peddle his stale liquor to an empty saloon.

Syl pushed the heavy curtain aside. The putrid odor rushed in. He clamped a hand over his nose, searching vainly in his pocket for the handkerchief that had gone over the cliff with his old, ruined pants. Schmalch retched onto the floor. Aliara coughed, buried her nose in the crook of her elbow and slipped past the curtain.

Syl took the lantern from Schmalch and opened the bullseye, flooding the wide space with its aqua glow. Directly in front of them, café tables and barrel chairs lay in a tumult around an ornate steel cage that ran floor to ceiling, a collapsed elevator car listing like a drunk from its maw.

He tensed, every muscle in his body so taut he felt they might snap if he so much as moved. Realization hit him like a kick to the stomach. He knew where he was. Long-buried dread threatened to overwhelm him. He took control before it had a chance, softening his expression, relaxing the rigid muscles, shoving the anxiety into that pit in his mind where it always lurked.

He stepped into the room, lantern held high. The lofty ceilings were swathed in garish frescos and twisted chandeliers. Below, the downward-sloping house floor was lined with chairs upholstered in crimson velvet that matched the saloon's decor. Some were bolted in place, others in shards. Most lay scattered pell-mell throughout the auditorium.

In front of it all was a vast, ornate stage. Set into its back wall was the source of the obnoxious music: a massive orchestrion. Flanked by tattered black drapes, the thoroughly out-of-tune contraption still pumped giddily away. An enormous bank of organ pipes led the ensemble. To one side hung a huge bellows, wheezing air into fanciful brass piping to power a throng of blatting horns. Tiers of drums and cymbals, complete with mostly functional striking apparatuses, clogged the opposite side. In front of it all was a troupe of automatons, drooping and motionless despite the gleeful, if unfortunate, tune.

"Certainly needs some adjustment, doesn't it?" Syl shouted.

As if in reply, the piece reached its crescendo and ended. The beastly thing sat silent for a few breaths before launching into a lilting woodwind approximation of birdsong. It was no less dissonant but offered some relief from the grating din.

Aliara left him and threaded her way through the chairs. As she neared the stage, the automatons jerked to life. As one, they raised their heads and commenced their pre-assigned patterns of movement, whirring and clicking, arms waving, jaws flapping, their spastic dance a stark contrast to the silvery tune. One of the dancers raced toward her, its body flailing like a convulsive circus bear on the loose. She watched it, again braced for attack. Its support pole slammed against the end of the track with a metallic snap, momentum driving it from the stage into the house. Aliara pivoted, sidestepping its charge. The machine careened across the floor. Syl tracked its path with the lantern. As it came to rest against a row of chairs, his eyes rose. His breath caught.

Tiny bodies in assorted stages of decay filled the still-standing chairs like some ghoulish audience waiting to be amused by the antics of the mechanical performers. Rot eroded their soft tissues in a slow, predictable pattern. Some were near-skeletal while others appeared fresher, perhaps only a month or two past death. All were arranged like engaged viewers, hands crossed in their laps or crumbling bodies reclined against arm-rests.

"Bah!" Schmalch yelled. He hopped closer to Syl and Aliara, eyes wide.

Syl pasted on his best wry smirk. "Well, we've found the missing children."

He followed Aliara to one of the fresher corpses, a little chivori girl in a blue dress and black buckle shoes. With the tips of her long, grey fingers, Aliara gingerly leaned the girl's head forward. Her little ear slid off, plopping onto the dirty theater floor. Aliara hopped away and took a long, slow breath before resuming her examination.

The back of the child's head was smashed crown to neck. Skull fragments and an overlong, object like a needle formed from bone were embedded in the putrefied soft tissue within. Aliara's hand hovered over the bone needle for a moment, then she shook her head and returned the girl to a comfortable position. She looked at Syl for a long moment, eyes grim, before picking her way between rows, inspecting other tiny bodies. Each one displayed similar trauma.

Syl dismissed his roiling stomach and panned the lantern across the gruesome scene while she worked. Schmalch, fear exchanged for avarice, busied himself by digging through the corpses' pockets. Nothing else stirred. As he passed the light over the collapsed lift cage, Syl stopped. Behind it, the dappled amber paint was broken by a dark archway, another curtain hanging within. He knew what lay beyond.

"It appears there's more to investigate, Pet."

Syl headed up the aisle, Aliara alongside. He drew back the short curtain, its hem ragged as though torn off in a fit of pique. A short corridor, dotted with a few closed doors, ran perpendicular to the entryway.

"You go this way, I go that?" he asked.

SYLANDAIR

Syl loved the theater, which was admittedly odd, given his initial theater-going experience. It had been during his first outing with Orono, purportedly a treat for a child on his best behavior. Later Syl understood that the aging inventor had brought him along not to share the experience with his young charge, but rather to flaunt his new acquisition to friends.

It offended Syl somehow that he'd never realized that this theater—the same place that prowled his memories—had lurked beneath his feet all those years. He'd recognized it, realized where he was the instant he saw the ornamented lift cage listing uselessly from its wrought-iron shaft. It was the same vehicle that took him to this underground playhouse, into the beginning of his torment.

Syl waited until Aliara ducked into a room on her end of the hallway, set his shoulders, and stalked into the first room he came to. A tall mirror jutted from a grimy dressing table, matching stool overturned nearby. Empty racks, now bare of costumes, stood stoically against the wall, a fainting couch and full-length mirrors at the fore.

Syl stepped to the vanity and examined the selection of desiccated creams, evaporated potions, and grooming tools made brittle by time. He had been taken to a room like this that night. It may even have been this one. He couldn't be certain.

They'd attended *Quill of Grandeur*, a play in which the Duin,

Nys, visits a young skald, inspiring her to pen poetry to enthrall her country, only to withdraw it again when her works failed to please him. A fairly pat, cliché plot to him now, but at that time, the story was a revelation. Syl was catered to that night, plied with candies and the tooth-numbingly sweet liquor, quincitaba. He believed this was his wonderful new life, that for some inexplicable reason this codger wanted nothing more than a son to dote upon. He felt like the luckiest boy in all the islands.

Naturally, the pampering was a ruse.

The play had dazzled Syl's tippled mind. He followed his new master happily to a lonely dressing room.

"You are a lucky boy to have been bought by me, no?" Orono asked.

Syl nodded, still nursing a sour lolly given to him by another friendly older man called Herrenny. His legs swung happily, dangling over the settee's edge, Orono beside him, hand on Syl's knee.

"Lucky boys must earn their rewards, you know," the old man said. "Do you know how to repay me for the joys of tonight?"

The words made little sense to young Syl, but this was an adult—and one who'd given him this happy night—so he smiled in response. "How?"

If only he could take back that question. Though he knew it would not matter.

"Let me show you…"

In the withered dressing room deep underground, Syl shattered bottles, tubs and mirrors against the walls until no more remained to break. He wanted to scream and curse, but that would bring Aliara and Schmalch. He calmed his ragged breathing, tugged at the cuffs of his new shirt and returned to the hallway.

The other rooms were similar. He passed them with only cursory glances inside. The last was a curtained doorway opposite the others. It opened onto a long passage above which a faded sign declared "*To Stage*." Following it would put him too far from Aliara. They could investigate it together later if need be, though he suspected they'd find nothing but cobwebs and putrid air.

Hands still clenched, Syl returned to the doorway where they'd separated, and reclined, eyes closed, against its frame, forcing the reminiscence from his mind.

Two months after that visit to the theater, Aliara had arrived, another import from Chiva'vastezz for the old buzzard to violate.

ALIARA

Unlike her mate, Aliara despised gathering spaces like this theater. They were universally loud, crowded, and suffocating. Syl had long ago accepted her revulsion, and no longer pestered her to attend with him. Plenty of others were delighted to appear on the arm of the Duke of Isay at bustling social events—and to entertain him afterward.

Many times she'd come home to find him occupied with some random escort. Like any chivori, she'd enjoyed her share of diversions as well. She simply didn't *need* the variety, the sense of control in her encounters as he did. She recalled one occasion on which she'd avoided a reception for the visiting Norian Queen Marastrava. Aliara had returned home to find Syl with his escort, a well-sculpted karju, with his face buried in Syl's lap. When she slid into the opposite seat, brows raised, Syl smiled and drew on the uurost in his pipe.

"He joined me tonight at the mayor's reception for the Queen," Syl said by way of explanation. With a cocky waggle of his eyebrows, he gestured at the man busy at his lap. "Met the illustrious split-tail herself. Asked how he could repay me for such an honor."

The icon on the first door in the little hallway announced that Aliara had successfully located the ladies washroom. Its walls were red and cloying. A circular couch sat at the center. Sinks hung from one wall, a row of small closed stalls behind them. Powders, balms, and perfumes littered the counters. A dried-up lip tint lolled in the sink. The communal use of such items baffled her. It was repulsive.

She poked her head into each of the wood-paneled latrines, greeted only by the lingering pong of the long-dead dibucs that served each stool. Whatever happened here, those affected had been as concerned with these zoets as the plant employees had been with the lusca dangling helpless in their harnesses. Both groups of creatures had been left to starve and die.

As she finished with the final stall, a brief motion caught the edge of her vision. She turned, hands on the blades at her hips, but found nothing, no one.

She revisited all the empty stalls, but again, when she turned to leave, something fluttered just out of sight, like a wisp of smoke gusting past her. She whirled around but found herself alone. Swearing under her breath, she hurried to the hallway.

The men's washroom was next, a gold mirror of the ladies'. The dehydrated unguents and colognes spread over the counter were different, and she found some curiously abandoned undergarments in one of the stalls, but no flickers of movement taunted her here.

At the end of the hall, the remaining door stood in contrast to every other element of this place. In lieu of welcoming and comforting patrons, this door did everything it could to discourage them. Its cold, steel surface sported large red letters declaring "*No Entry*" in Plainspeak. Three locks supported that directive.

It attracted Aliara like a parched sailor to a saloon.

She squatted, unshouldered her pack, and withdrew a sleeve of tools, each molded into a shape appropriate to a specific use. The first two locks required almost no thought; a quick tick of pins and the bolts retracted with satisfying clicks. This third, however, was a Mucha favorite, the magnetic lock.

She'd once been hired by a very angry Mucha master to eliminate a rival who'd stolen his schema for a modified baluut genome. Aliara found the thief busy in a workshop filled with plans for mechanical and zoetic creations, documents filched from dozens if not hundreds of victimized inventors. Among them was the plan for the lodestone cloud, a device that confused magnetic locking mechanisms. When her elimination contract was complete, she snatched the cloud's plans along with several others that seemed intriguing. Mardo had fabricated the device for her in exchange for some of the doubly stolen plans. It had become an essential tool in her kit.

Placing the cloud's cone-shaped mouth beside the lock, she twisted the small connected box one-quarter turn. The cloud hummed. When the sound waned, she turned it back. The hum rose to a whine, the cloud warming in her hands. Then snick, the lock popped free, the door opened, and the aroma of disuse wafted out.

The room was an archive of liquor, packed tight with row upon row of shelved bottles. She eased past the racks, finding more around a corner. Toward the rear, the shelves became crates, then a cramped office. Two cabinets flanked a desk of sculpted resin. At a desk slumped the remains of a well-dressed woman, pen clasped in her withered hand, ledger open before her. Time had dried and split her skin. Once well-coifed hair dangled in wisps from her scalp. Her long red sleeves could not hide the faded markings of the Seers on her puckered skin.

Aliara chuckled quietly. All this Mucha nonsense ultimately had been controlled by a Seer.

She turned her attention to the more interesting feature of the little office—the huge safe looming behind the desk. Hands stroking the black cast surface like a desperate lover, she squatted and studied the unfamiliar lock. Its seamless circular casing, which protruded from the door, was set with ring of small studs cast from white metal, an egg-shaped knob of the same material at its center.

She tried the obvious—pull the handle, open the door. As her fingertips brushed its surface, however, the knob crackled with a discharge of sparks. Aliara sprang back, shaking her hand and producing a string of Vazztain invectives. Thanks to her years as Orono's lab pet, she was no stranger to the sting of shock. She rubbed the wounded fingers against the rough weave of her shirt, forcing the tingle away. With her other hand, she tentatively stroked one of the white studs. No reaction. Only the knob had bite.

With soft puffs of breath, she cleared the dust from the lock. A few dark swirls in the familiar shape of fingerprints clung to three of the white studs. She placed her own finger over the first print and pressed until the stud clicked into place. When nothing happened, she depressed the other two. She drew long breath and quickly tapped the knob. It sparked again, sending white-blue lightning up her arm. She tipped back onto the floor and swore some more.

As it had in the ladies' lav, something danced just outside Aliara's vision.

"*Pretty*," a strange voice said.

Aliara jumped to her feet. Someone had been close. The voice was quiet, but nearby, almost on top of her. Yet looking around, she was alone. She walked a few steps down one row of shelves, saw nothing, and tried the others, even walked around the corner to the exit. No one was in there with her. Perhaps a trick of the ventilation? She scanned the ceiling in search of potential sources.

From the auditorium, the orchestrion hooted. That had to be what she'd heard, a distorted combination of notes. She shook her head once and returned to the safe.

She tried the buttons a few more times before she found the right sequence, but not before her hand had gone numb from the repeated shocks. When she finally was able to touch the egg-shaped handle safely, she pulled it out from the door until it would go no further. A camshaft jutted from its back, three cams notched into its length. She rotated the knob until the egg's tip pointed to the first stud then pushed it back toward the door. With a snap, the camshaft stopped. The stud popped up. She repeated the turn-and-press maneuver with the second and third studs. The safe creaked open.

Aliara stared into the long-sealed vault for a moment, unsure she could trust her eyes. Then she rose. She needed to find Syl.

SCHMALCH

Having plundered the last of the tiny cadavers, Schmalch was ready to share his windfall. Instead of the appreciative ooos and ahhs of his comrades, though, he found himself surrounded only by the hooting music and the chilling stares of the dead.

"Duke?"

No answer.

"Duke Im-Imythedralin?"

Still nothing.

"Rift?"

They'd left him alone. He'd been good. He'd been helpful. Why would they do that?

Last he'd seen the two chivori, they were poking around the stage. Schmalch scampered over and with a hop, pulled himself up to where the automatons still hummed menacingly in their weird little dances. Springing from one's path, Schmalch scurried toward the rear corner, the only visible exit. When he opened the door and stepped in, no shutters clicked open, no automated lights winked on. The Duke had his lantern, leaving Schmalch to face this utter blackness, more unsettling than the auditorium full of dead kids.

He squatted and dug through his pack, hoping he'd thought to pick up that nasty old crank torch from the draas lair. He pulled out the previous owner's writing board—now smeared with draas gore—a clump of knotted rope fragments, the silver belt buckle, sea glass, and all his other assorted possessions, but found no torch.

A low whine built in his throat. He looked from the well-lit, prancing mechanical men to the darkness backstage. The Duke had to have gone this way. He'd want Schmalch to follow. With a sigh, the puka fished the head of a doll lifted from a dead audience member from his pocket and jammed it beneath the door.

He took another step inside and forgot his fear. Twinkling in the pale stage light was a wall packed with machines and control panels.

Schmalch had never been able to resist the lure of un-pressed buttons, a compulsion that had resulted in more than one bitter scolding from the temple staff when he was a child. Faced with so many options, he scurried in, poking at buttons, yanking random levers then stealing peeks at his effect on the automatons. As he reached for a particularly big and shiny lever, Schmalch tripped and fell on something that sounded like twigs snapping beneath him.

He scrambled up in search of an attacker but found only the shadowy form of a newly crushed corpse on the floor. This one was no child. She lay on her face, writing board near her hand, brittle grey hair cascading over her pink-clad shoulders as though she'd collapsed mid-step. He poked her with the toe of his boot and dried-up bits crumbled off, like an old moth's cocoon he'd found years before. In the dimness of the shifting light from the stage, her jutting shoulder blades and hip bones looked like strange creatures struggling to escape a bag. The discovery sucked the joy out of his antics.

He squatted and made a half-hearted attempt to rifle the body before creeping deeper into the room, unease building with each step away from the light. He hopped back when something soft brushed his outstretched fingers. He snatched a wistful glance back at the lighted wedge of the stage door then reached out cautiously, the softness again at his fingertips. Another curtain. He relaxed, released his breath.

"Duke?" He pulled the fabric back a sliver. "Rift?"

Only the cheery music replied. Mustering courage, Schmalch

dashed past the curtain, into darkness, slamming almost instantly into a wall. Something in his nose made a terrible grinding sound. He tasted blood. Dazed, he groped around the area in a frantic attempt to orient himself—the curtain was behind him, wall to the left, another wall ahead, empty space to the right. He scurried off to his right. Even the melody's meandering whistles seemed dulled by the suffocating lightlessness.

After a few terrified moments, he stopped. Something smelled like cookies, ones like he'd smelled outside that fancy pastry shop in Pukatown. Sniffing, he pawed the air around him. If someone was baking, a kitchen must be around here. Maybe it was a way out. As he moved deeper into the delicious smell, tummy rumbling, the air changed, grew colder. The soft scents of mildew and death hid behind that of baking. His hand brushed the wall and, like the sea breeze earlier, a cold draught blew up his pant legs. This one did not refresh. He froze, hunger forgotten, and listened.

Somewhere, something was moving. He heard a faint dragging sound like an artist's dry brush against canvas.

Schmalch ran.

A hazy light blossomed ahead, grew into a doorway. He sprinted, straining to reach it. With a triumphant cry, he rushed toward the light into yet another hall. Nearby, the Duke reclined against a wall, examining his ragged fingernails.

"Duke!" Schmalch locked his arms around the man's waist.

"You're bleeding on me," the Duke said. He used both hands and a knee to pry Schmalch off him. "What did you do to your nose?"

"I didn't know where you went," he said. "There's dead people all over."

"Clearly. There are what, fifty-odd dead children out there? You were ransacking them. Remember?"

"Yes, but…" his protest died as Rift materialized from the darkness.

"Follow me," she said.

SYLANDAIR

The three of them stood at the open door of the decades-sealed safe, mesmerized by the items within.

Schmalch snatched a resin box filled with Callas from a low shelf and clutched it to his chest.

Syl eyed him curiously. "Yours?"

"We'll share it, Duke," he said, "but we can't leave it there. What if the door suddenly shut and we couldn't get to it? It'd just be locked in there again, doing nobody no good."

Syl held Schmalch's eyes for a long moment before returning to the safe. Aside from the coffer the puka had claimed, the safe contained a stack of overlarge accounting books, two bags he assumed contained more Callas, a brick of uurost, a set of pill molds, and two shelves of delicate, cork-stoppered glass vials. The shimmery dust inside the vials shifted hue from purple to green in the undulating glow of the room's lumia lamps. "*Portent*," was scrawled on their labels in an ornamented hand, though Syl could hardly fail to recognize the Seers' exclusive drug. He and Aliara had spent enough time under its influence, after all.

Syl slid her a knowing glance. Her lovely black eyes were fixed on the tiny bottles.

"Find three clean, dry heavy-glass bottles," he told Schmalch, who scooted away.

"We're taking it?" Aliara asked.

Syl nodded. The drug wasn't just something to be sold for coin, it was power. The Seers of Dream and Waking rarely released any of the hallucinogen to outsiders. When they did, it was only a pressed tablet or two. Nothing like this. The Seers guarded its formula closely, and the Dominion of Chiva'vastezz considered it a cultural treasure. Syl wasn't sure how he would use it, but having it might later be an advantage.

"He bought it here," Aliara murmured.

The thought hadn't yet occurred to Syl, but she was right. This pile of bones in the red dress was likely the source of the tablets Orono had fed them during his delirium experiments.

Syl cupped Aliara's troubled face in his hands, kissed her. "It will never again pass your dear lips."

"Got 'em," Schmalch interrupted.

"Shall we see what he's found?" Syl's mouth brushed Aliara's forehead as he spoke.

Schmalch beamed at them, bottles hugged to his chest.

"Excellent," Syl said. "Now fill those with the powder from the vials. Carefully. Stopper them firmly." He stared at Schmalch for a long, emphatic moment. "Do *not* spill a drop. Do *not* inhale it. Do *not* rub your eyes or nose or mouth. If it touches your hands, rinse them. You will not like what happens otherwise. When you are finished, deliver them to me. Understood?"

Schmalch's forehead crinkled with concern, but he nodded and set to work.

"What else did you find?" Syl asked Aliara.

"A couple of public toilets."

"Lovely."

"Gaudy."

"I found nothing but dressing rooms. Gaudy as well."

"What's next?" she asked.

"After we clear this out? There was a hall labeled *To Stage* on my end. We may take a look together if you are interested."

Aliara opened her pack, dropped in a substantial bag of Callas and the uurost. She offered the other bag of coins to Syl.

"Wise," he said. "We'll divide the bottles between packs when Schmalch is done."

"These?" she held out the ledgers.

Syl's brows drew together. He weighed the clout of possessing evidence of this place against the awkward size and extra weight. He hefted his pack. The silver Callas inside were cumbersome enough as it was.

"Let me see them," he said.

She handed him the stack and disappeared into the shelves of liquor.

Bound in black leather, each ledger bore the name "*Club Perpetual*" surrounded by the same colorful design seen on the entry door. Each appeared to track different income streams. The first was the standard accounting of any nightclub: liquor, foodstuffs, admission, salaries, equipment, and so on. The second clarified the presence of uurost and Portent. This establishment had seen more income from these drugs than from door fees or even liquor. Quincitaba had cost guests an outrageous one Calla per glass. The hallucinogenic Portent ran fifty-two Callas for a single pressed pill. It would have been easy for those sales to overtake the normal day-to-day income.

The staggering sums calculated in the third ledger mystified Syl until he recognized a monthly pattern. Every forty days, the same entries appeared—same name, same amount. Sylandair Imythedralin was quite familiar with the rhythm of blackmail. He wondered what sorts of things went on among the intelligentsia at Club Perpetual to result in such a hefty extortion-based income.

The final ledger, like the blackmail record, listed only names, dates and amounts. Here, instead of a single name, each entry listed pairs.

2031 Kalaflak 4 ...... Woren Polt / Samir ...... 14,100 C

2031 Kalaflak 8 ...... Zygar Alag / Ran'rika ...... 21,080 C
2031 Kalaflak 19...... Nasheng Naareth / Leerka ...... 8,900 C

They went on like that, a baffling code with only the faintest commonalities. The structure clicked into place, though, when Syl spied a familiar pair of names and dates.

2048 Alsolon 1 ...... Kluuta Orono / Aliara ...... 16,170 C

Syl flipped the pages back two months prior.

2048 Danurak 32 ...... Kluuta Orono / Sylandair ...... 38,900 C

At least he'd sold well.

He couldn't be sure what the listings meant, but given the dates and mention of their names, he assumed it to be the record of their sale. Though neither he nor Aliara had memory of an identity or life before sale to Orono, the connection here was too strong to be coincidence.

Syl snapped the book shut and wedged it into his pack. For later.

He closed his eyes and pushed his rage down. This was not the time to share with Aliara.

"Are you done yet, Schmalch?" he asked, voice harsher than intended.

"Just about, Duke. Only a few more little bottles to go. Where do you want the big ones?"

Eyes still closed, he held out a hand. "One to each of us. Wrap them in the clothes for padding. Do *not* lose any." His eyes flicked open to glare at Schmalch, who withered in fear.

"Never, never," he attempted a smile as he laid one of the bottles in Syl's hand. "What next? Want me to load up on hooch? We going somewhere else? Back up top?"

"Out of here."

With drugs to touch the Duin and Callas to ease their lives loaded in their packs, Aliara and Schmalch wound their way out of the room. Syl hesitated, staring at the desiccated husk of the Seer. With a growl, he shoved her corpse from its chair, crushed her skull with his heel, and followed his companions, leaving the witch alone in her mausoleum.

"Follow." Syl tossed the lantern to Schmalch and marched out of the room. He led them down the short hall to the doorway marked *"To Stage"* and drew back the curtain. "It is time for you to scout."

Schmalch's brown eyes pleaded.

"You made it once without being eaten."

"Right, Duke, right." Schmalch gulped and ducked inside.

Schmalch panned the lantern's light over the gold-flocked walls and gritty floor. Beneath the puka's panicked footprints from his earlier passage were phantom prints from even smaller feet, coated in varying levels of dust. Schmalch scurried forward, stopping midway down the corridor. He shone the light along the east wall and backed away.

"Duke? Uh…hey Duke?" he called, his voice distant over the domineering music, now some discordant piano dirge.

"What?"

"I really think you're gonna wanna see this."

With a shrug from Aliara, the pair entered. Schmalch crouched by the wall, squinting at it, his head bobbing curiously like some courting parrot. The grime on the floor around him was smeared and streaked with a surfeit of footprints. As Syl and Aliara approached, he pointed at a ragged hole torn into the plaster, large enough for a young child or a grown puka to walk through comfortably.

"Smell that?" Schmalch asked.

The faint odor of baking hung in the air. The scent was off-beam, masking something else, something rotten.

"Smelled stronger earlier," Schmalch said. He poked his lantern into the opening. "Where d'ya think that goes?"

SYLANDAIR

The crawl was proving tedious, mucky, and more than a little chilly. Syl's breath puffed out in faint misty clouds as he lugged the coin-laden pack through the passage. This was not how he'd expected to spend his evening when they entered the plant only hours before. His nails were broken and filthy, his whole body ached, and now another pair of fine trousers had been sacrificed to this Duin-forsaken place. The Callas, he reminded himself, would more than compensate for the damage, but the principle remained.

He glanced back at Aliara, who crawled behind him. Her expression was bland and unbothered by the discomfort, but then she faced far less pleasant circumstances regularly as part of her work. She gave Syl a slight lift of the corner of her mouth—her version of a smile.

"Looks like a really long stretch," Schmalch called. He and the lantern had disappeared around a corner ahead. "Dark, too. I can't see the end."

Syl grunted.

"I'll keep looki—" Schmalch yelped, metal clanked, and a pair of hurried feet slapped their way back.

Syl picked up his pace, reaching the corner just as Schmalch skittered into sight, grimace on his face. Down the new stretch of tunnel stood a karju boy, quiet and unmoving. Schmalch's lantern lay at his feet, casting eerie shadows on the drooping, vacant face. His skin had the quality of moldering burlap and his muddy hair, once the color of flame, hung limply over his face. He didn't move or look up. He didn't seem to be aware of Syl, Schmalch, or even the lantern.

Syl pushed the puka aside and crept cautiously forward. He passed a hand in front of the boy's dull face, but received no reaction. He sat back on his heels and examined the back of the boy's skull, careful not to touch.

"He has the same damage as the others," he whispered to Aliara. Syl retrieved the lantern and returned it to Schmalch. "Walk around him. Do not touch him."

Body flat against the dirt wall, Schmalch eked past. Though Syl was prepared for the boy to leap into action and sink fingers or teeth deep in the green flesh of the puka's throat, nothing happened. He simply stood there.

When he'd passed successfully, Schmalch jumped out of the boy's reach and hopped from one foot to the other, anxious for Syl and Aliara to join him. It was unlikely he would blunder ahead again.

Soon enough, another boy, this one chivori, blocked the passage.

"Is he the same?" Syl asked.

Schmalch shrugged. "Looks like it."

"Walk up there and find out, you douse."

Schmalch crept forward, lantern wielded like a shield. He wiggled fingers in front of the dull face. Nothing. He tried to inspect the skull but was too short for a good view. He shrugged at Syl.

"Move on," Syl said.

Schmalch screwed up his mouth and darted past. Safely on the other side, he waved both hands. "Psst…hey, Duke?"

Still helping Aliara move their packs past the obstructing child, Syl sighed. "What now?"

"There's a little girl over here. Looks the same."

"Keep moving."

"You sure they're not gonna reach out and get me?"

"No, not at all."

They passed two more inert children before a dim, wintry light materialized ahead. Schmalch's enthusiasm for the point position dwindled as the light grew. Tired and desperate to stand again, Syl shoved past him and held at the exit, examining the scene within. The room, colder yet than the tunnel, reeked like spoiled meat and unkempt animal cages.

Dozens of motionless children stood clustered in small groups throughout the space, one knot close enough to touch.

"Look at all of 'em," Schmalch murmured.

Aliara clamped her hand over his mouth.

Syl knew this room all too well. Its walls of smooth concrete, long ago constructed by Orono's workmen, were soot-covered and splotched with mold. Cobwebs and dust, as motionless as the children, clung to every surface. At the room's center, ringed by a litter of bones and shackles, sat a glassy, puka-sized heap reminiscent of the melted remnants of an immense candle. It glowed a wan blue from within; not the comforting aqua of lumia, but something more intense and flat. The object was new, but Syl knew the source of the bones and restraints. A long-forgotten pang of guilt nipped at his gut.

Orono had referred to the Portent sessions as experiments, though only to rationalize the procedure as legitimate in his own mind. They were the only experiments Syl had been subjected to. The rest were Aliara's alone to bear.

"The girl is most likely too stupid to accomplish this by herself," Orono had said as he shoved the chalky Portent tablet into Syl's mouth. "You shall be fine. This won't leave a mark on you."

Like Aliara, Syl's experience with the drug was largely that of a vast nothingness, though if the Seers were to be believed, they both had touched the minds of the Duin each time Orono fed them Portent. Syl had to believe this was true, had to believe he had touched the divine, otherwise he alone was responsible for all those little bones. Aliara may have helped him entice the children from the street, but the idea had sprung from his lips.

Only once during the months of experiments had his young mind conjured something miraculous. As he slipped under the drug's influence, a woman came to him, a creature with the beauty of an otherworldly, outlandish Aliara and an air of calm wisdom unlike any he'd known. She had enfolded him in two pairs of arms, cradled him against skin the brilliant blue of sapphire. Her touch revealed paths and patterns he'd never known existed.

"My poor boy." Her lips brushed his forehead. "This man, he has studied my book, yes?"

Syl nodded, unable to speak.

"He will want children," she whispered close to his ear.

Syl's body became mist, and she breathed him in.

"Two score, less three," she sang sadly, releasing him from her lungs.

"He will coerce you, compel you to ensnare them." Her long fingers, keen with extra joints, stroked his face, solid once more. "He need only a spark, but he will consume them. In his self-induced madness he will deviate from true intent. He has eaten of the First's gift, one tainted by unscrupulous hands. The sublime path will elude him."

Expression melancholy, she cupped his chin and raised it for a kiss. "You will know when to free yourself."

She took Syl up in her palms like water from a brook and cast him back to rain down on the world, where Orono waited like a fat osprey anticipating his next meal.

Syl gasped back into reality.

"Did you find her this time?" Orono asked, beady eyes bright. He leaned forward on his cane, dry tongue creeping over his lips. He smacked Syl's shoulder with the cane. "Sylandair! Tell me, what did you learn? What did you hear?"

"Thirty-seven...thirty-seven," Syl muttered.

"What? Thirty-seven what?" He prodded Syl with the cane. "Tell me."

Syl blinked at the puffy face. "Spark…children," he said before toppling from the chair onto the cold marble floor.

He'd long regretted speaking before taking a moment to calculate.

Syl slid out of the tunnel into this place of nightmare, Aliara tight behind him. He had revisited this room in his dreams more often than he admitted even to her. Here was where they'd witnessed Orono's final, terrible experiment—or part of it.

He crept between the catatonic children, picked his way reverently through the ring of tiny skeletons, and squatted in front of the strange object, frozen eddies of copper pooled at its base. It *was* glass. He understood. He recognized it all.

Into an enormous copper vessel Orono had placed the keys, those items Aliara had stolen on the many trips to the many islands across the world. The final had been a luminous blue ball of unrefined and unshielded opoli—the source, Syl had no doubt, of the devastating explosion that followed. This melted mound of glass was the result.

Syl reached out to touch the object, but his hand faltered a hair's breadth from its surface. It was warm, though the air around it was frigid, as if it drew the warmth from the room. Beneath Syl's fingers, a distant pulse thrummed within the great glass thing. He hovered in place, unwilling or unable to touch it.

Schmalch, who'd wandered deeper into the room, broke the silence with a tumult of words. "Hey Duke, there's another hole in the wall over here. A door, I guess. But it's caved in. You think it's the other end of the one we saw earlier? It looks like a real door made by real workmen."

"Quiet," Aliara hissed.

"Sure, Rift, sure."

Syl rose and faced Aliara, who stood outside the ring of bones, unwilling to come closer. He picked his way back, almost reaching her when something deeper in the room scuffled and ripped.

SCHMALCH

Oblivious to the activity around him, Schmalch poked merrily around the strange room. He wasn't sure why such a place would be under Dockhaven, or even what purpose such a room could possibly serve, but after finding a big fancy theater down here, he was surprised by nothing.

He drifted between the silent, motionless kids in search of anything interesting. Exposure to them had made their weirdly still posture less creepy. They seemed harmless now. Some of them looked really sick, others a bit healthier, but they all looked wrong, off-beam somehow.

As he slipped into a cluster deep within the room, the glint of silver caught his eye. Around the neck of a particularly wretched-looking girl hung a swish, fist-sized locket. It must have taken the silver of ten Callas to make it, and here it was underground, unappreciated, and unloved. Schmalch puffed warm breath into his chilled hands, slipped up behind her, and unfastened the clasp, his fingertips brushing the nape of her neck. The fine chain slipped free and the locket clinked to the ground at her feet. Humming a favorite song he'd heard last night at the Barnacle, Schmalch edged around the girl, squatted, and retrieved the locket, dropping it into his vest pocket with a happy pat.

He stood, prepared to seek out more boodle, and found himself facing not a dull, unresponsive child, but a leering nightmare. The girl's eyes were open, milky and dry, her lips pulled back from long-rotted teeth. She sniffed at him.

For a moment, Schmalch could do nothing. His body refused to move. Then she hissed. The smell of death and rot rolled over him. He gagged and staggered backward. At his motion, she lashed out, snatching a fistful of his old coat. The oft-repaired seam at his shoulder gave as he jerked away, sleeve ripping off in her hand. The sleeve tumbled to the ground. The girl lurched forward, fingers clutching at empty air.

Schmalch backpedaled faster. He bumped another body, lost his balance, and fell to one knee. The girl's fingers closed around his bare wrist, nails digging deep, drawing blood. Trembling, Schmalch drew the kris from its ankle holster and waved it at her, his knuckles pale as honeydew around its hilt.

"Back," he said in his angriest voice. "Get back. I don't wanna hurt you, little girl."

She drew back her free hand and raked his chest with ragged nails. Only the Duke's still-damp leather vest saved him from injury.

Behind him, the body he'd bumped into began to move.

Schmalch squealed. He hacked at the girl's wrist, bits of bone and flesh and drops of thick, tacky blood spattering his face and arm and chest. She didn't seem to care, slashing again and again as he chopped away. She didn't seem to notice when her hand came free and plopped to the ground with a splat. He scrambled to his feet and started toward the exit, dodging the other moving children.

"Duke! The kids are—" The words died in Schmalch's throat as a hand dug into his shoulder. Schmalch ripped from the grip. All around him, the kids had come to life. They lurched and sniffed, swiping at the air in his general direction. A little girl in overalls grabbed his ears and tried to rip them from his head. He pushed against her, feeling some important part of her body give way. She let go and he ran, shoving bodies from his path, determined to reach the exit and remain above ground for the rest of his days. He bit and stabbed and kicked until he was slick with the kids' weirdly thick blood. None of them seemed to care. They just kept coming.

He leapt into the tunnel opening, only to be yanked back. Someone had a hold of his pack. He pulled forward, they tugged back, and with a gut-churning rip, the pack gave way. Clothing, jewelry, liquor, everything Schmalch had collected over the long night, crashed to the floor. Color sticks marred with draas' bite marks sprayed into the crowd. Callas poured from the shattered resin box in a heart-breaking cascade. The unwrapped Portent bottle rolled across the floor, bumping into the worn work boots of a chivori boy, his cheeks reduced to festering slashes.

Schmalch wanted to escape, but more than that, he wanted to be rich. He sprang from the tunnel and stuffed handfuls of silver coins into his pockets. The children scratched him, squeezed him. He slashed the kris at them with one hand while the other collected the boodle that was rightfully his.

"Schmalch! Leave it!" came the Duke's voice. "Move, you drab little son of a trull!"

Schmalch stood up. The two chivori were struggling through the sea of children. Rift was a hurricane of knives, slashing out at everything around her. The Duke raised his pistol and fired into the crowd. A few kids fell, but mostly they just took the hit and kept coming.

Schmalch jumped into the tunnel and ran.

SYLANDAIR

Syl had never harmed children before, but given this situation, he fired a cloud of shot into their little bodies without hesitation. A handful of the monstrosities dropped. Aliara left his side and advanced into the gap, her stilettos piercing and goring their way through the diminutive terrors between them and the exit.

A child clawed the back of Syl's leg. No time to fumble for a reload, he pulled his blade with his off hand and spun on the assailant. The Voshar dagger, as finely honed as any of Mardo's work, sliced deep into the karju girl's neck, syrupy red-brown blood oozing down her checkered dress. She lunged toward him, collapsing in the process.

They were being surrounded. The children that had once been scattered around the room were now moving toward them.

Aliara was keeping the closest off as she tried to drive toward the tunnel mouth. A particularly large karju boy charged. She raised her arms crossed at the wrist and slashed across his throat. His head slid neatly off his shoulders. Aliara kicked his body into the group, bowling several over, giving them an opening.

Syl sheathed his dagger, grabbed the pouch on his belt, and dumped another load of shot into his pistol.

"Come!" he shouted, tugging at Aliara's pack.

She stepped back. Syl pulled the trigger, downing the few children that remained between them and the mouth of the tunnel.

Aliara sprinted toward it, hurdling the struggling casualties. She ducked inside and rolled. Just before Syl did the same, he caught a glimpse of blue light wriggling across the ceiling. There was no time to consider its implications.

ALIARA

She'd crawled six strides down the tunnel when Aliara heard a *whoof* and a thud. Behind her Syl, prone on his belly, was being dragged back toward the ritual room. She dove for his outstretched hand and tugged, but whatever had him pulled her along as well.

"Something has my ankle!" he shouted.

She pulled herself over his sliding body and grabbed the binding around his leg.

It was warm, like holding an eel.

Aliara slashed at it with her stiletto, severing the thing in two strikes.

Something back in the ritual room keened. Aliara rolled off Syl and glanced at the horror she held. It was thin and reedy, covered in something akin to flesh, but too white and waxy and slick. The severed end dripped blood as red as any karju's. At the other hung an approximately round mass of pale flesh, wicked ossein spike jutting from its end.

It twitched.

Aliara released an involuntary "ewch!" and dropped the oozing thing.

"The grenade," Syl said as he lifted himself onto his knees "Do you still have it?"

From Schmalch's direction came the sounds of a brief scuffle and a nasal yelp. Whatever was happening there would be her next concern.

Aliara unslung her pack and withdrew the little metal sphere some foolish stranger had abandoned behind the plant. The thing looked harmless; little wonder Schmalch thought it a toy. It was as simple as a toy, but she'd seen the results when the two chemicals contained within met. It was far from amusing.

Her eyes flicked up to Syl.

"We do not want to see what that belongs to." He nodded at the fleshy remnant she'd dropped.

A strange shape crossed the tunnel mouth, blue light and a collection of limbs that reminded her of a bug. It was big, far larger than any of the children or the entryway.

"We don't want to see *him*," Syl added, voice low and harsh.

Aliara nodded. The fastest way to get out of a tunnel this cramped—outside of being as short as Schmalch—was to scramble on hands and toes. Syl was too tall for the maneuver, crawling was the best he would be able to do.

"Go," she said. "Get a lead."

He frowned but nodded, kissed her, and crawled away.

When she turned back, a bloodied boy, more ambitious than the others, had almost reached her position. She met him halfway and drove a blade into his forehead. He collapsed in a heap, impeding passage through tunnel. A little girl with a missing pigtail shuffled in after him. She swiped at Aliara, momentum pitching her forward, over her friend's body. Aliara drove an elbow into the girl's neck, snapping it.

The sound of Syl's shuffling crawl was fading. She glanced back; he'd almost disappeared into the darkness.

A dry sound like old paper or dead leaves echoed from the ritual chamber. Aliara turned back, catching a blur of blue light and thin, knobby legs. It moved not from side to side across the tunnel mouth; this time, it scaled the wall.

Her breath quickened. She recognized the fear that bubbled up inside. It was a sensation she hadn't known in years.

Where had this creature been hiding? Aliara had a sense that it was enormous—bigger than an adult karju, maybe even as big as a rhochrot. And it glowed. Difficult to hide.

She squinted into the chamber. A few children stumbled toward the tunnel, while others resumed their catatonia. The lump of glass still squatted at the room's core, the ring of bones around it.

Aliara frowned.

She looked at the grenade then at Syl, the back of his now-dingy trousers still faintly visible. She'd give him twenty more heartbeats.

Before even half of those had passed, a lump of flesh about the size of Aliara's head descended into view at the tunnel mouth. Lightly twitching, it dangled from a narrow whip of a tail, the stub of a sharpened horn projecting from its tip. It was like the one that had grabbed Syl, but smaller. What had been waxy white flesh on the first was pinker and almost raw on this one.

She looked back. The one she'd severed still lay there, more grey than white.

After slowly circling the entryway, the smaller doppelganger darted inside and cast about like a blind man in search of something he'd dropped. It paused to grope the bodies of the dead children. It dragged the girl's corpse back into the chamber, flinging it across the floor as carelessly as a child discards the pickings from its nose. It removed the boy as well before continuing its spastic search.

Aliara stowed the grenade, drew a stiletto and crept toward the twitching tail, eyes following the sharpened tip as it flopped about. Squatted barely within arm's reach, she watched its exploration, calculated its path. When the tail whipped from wall to wall, she grabbed and slashed. Something in the chamber beyond screamed, the same keening she'd heard before. The remainder of the tail zipped out of sight.

Aliara retrieved the grenade and turned its timer knob as far as it would go. From the chamber, something hissed. The tail reappeared, something tiny and round expanding from its tip like a sickly balloon. Aliara clicked the activation knob and hurled the metal ball into the ritual room.

On all fours, she rushed down the tunnel. A few times she nearly slipped in what could only be the bodies of those dispatched by Schmalch during his rush to escape. Her foot caught in one of the corpses, costing her precious time.

The delay left her too close when the device blew. The tunnel went bright with white light for a heartbeat, followed almost instantly by a deep, roaring rumble like the dead giving voice to their anger. It consumed all other sound. The rattling and thumps of concrete and dirt pummeling the walls and floor filled the void when the blast faded.

Her upper lugs rang. Her lower lugs ached. She gritted her teeth against the pain.

Like canvas pulled over a window, the ambient blue light behind her winked out.

She drove harder, ass colliding with low-hanging chunks of the tunnel's roof.

"Pet!" Syl called. His voice was close.

The concussion wave caught up, pelting her with pebbles and dirt that lined her nostrils and dried her tongue. It bowled Aliara forward, bouncing her against the wall. She held her breath, squeezed her eyes shut. She couldn't see, but she knew it was Syl's arms that dragged her around the corner, out of the dust cloud. He wiped off her face and patted her down for injuries.

Aliara coughed and spat. She heard the tunnel collapse in her lower lug first. Even over the ringing remnant of the concussion, she caught the muted growl and heavy whump of falling soil.

"Move!" Syl bellowed.

ALIARA

Aliara woke to find herself alone in the enormous bed in their suite at the Ritora Doublet. She rolled onto her back and stretched.

The bedroom door creaked open. Syl reclined against the jamb, mug in hand.

"I thought I heard you stir," he sipped his tea, admiring her. "What a lovely sight this is."

She smiled and patted the bed.

"No, I think I'll enjoy the view for a moment longer." He grinned, a rare sight of late.

Syl's mood had been unpredictable since the events underground. Since they'd left the desal plant, he studiously avoided the subject of what they'd seen. She'd been unsure of how he'd react to the knowledge of Orono's continued existence, though this avoidance didn't surprise her; he'd behaved so in the past. It had been quarterns—almost a month—but she'd played along, steeling herself for what she knew would come next.

"Are we alone?" she asked.

"Yes, the wallflower left an hour or so ago. A bit shamefaced about last night's merriment, but quite satisfied."

"Hm." She propped herself up against a wall of pillows and appreciated the figure he cut. One side of his dressing gown hung as though heavy, pulling the garment open. She pointed. "What do you have there?"

"I think you know." He waggled his eyebrows.

"Yes, I'm quite familiar." She gave him a playful glare. "I meant in your pocket."

He withdrew a glossy wooden box ringed in black ribbon.

"This?" He tossed it onto the bed. "A little present."

She crawled across the duvet and opened the box. Inside, settled in a bed of silk lay a small bone-handled knife, its silver-plated blade a wicked hook. A leather holster, the perfect size for a bicep or ankle, was tucked beneath. Aliara sat back on her heels and drew the little blade.

"The package's arrival this morning woke our guest...what was his name?" He waved his hand dismissively. "No matter. I had Schmalch commission it from Mardo for me. An addendum to your arsenal."

"So I see."

Syl watched her slash the air, clearly enjoying her pleasure. It almost hurt to break the pleasant moment.

"Any other word from the Haven?" she asked.

Syl's face fell. He sighed and walked to the window. His reflection in the glass glowered at the snow-dusted black slopes of Mount Arra, its awesome beauty utterly lost on him.

"A chit from Schmalch accompanied the package. He says the news callers drone on about a rash of disappearances on the Big Island, concentrated largely near the plant. All children." He sipped his tea and watched the snow in silence for several moments. "We accomplished nothing."

"Not nothing. We know."

He shrugged, back still to her.

She returned the claw knife to its box and lay back in the still-warm bed. "Are we going back?"

"Not quite yet. I don't know what we could do if we did." He gave her a forced smile. "Schmalch sends fond regards. He is likely the wealthiest itinerant on the boardwalk."

"Until he blows it."

"Indeed."

Syl slid into bed with her, head resting on her breasts, lips pressed to the fading scratches on her arm as she ran fingers through his hair. She'd nearly drifted off again when he spoke.

"How would you feel," he asked, "about moving our little holiday to the duchy?"

PART TWO

HOME AGAIN

ALIARA

The aftermid light glinted off a hammered-copper urn sitting atop a cypress stump. Locals milled around it, wagging their chins about the man whose ashes were tucked within. The truth of his death didn't matter to them. The observance of their ritual did.

Aliara loitered in the umbrella of a willow on the periphery of the commons, passing another few hours by distracting herself from her restlessness, observing the banal dramas of rural life. A procession of grey faces drifted past her, each more bland than the last. She missed the wide array of life in Dockhaven, the uncertainty of who or what would cross her path next. Here, they were all proper citizens of Chiva'vastezz, thralls to the caste system they had been born into, alternately obsequious and conniving as convention dictated.

The dead man was rurabuthu, the caste of free workers, and a tenant farmer. She'd picked up the deceased's name—then promptly forgotten it—and that he had died in some unfortunate accident. Purported causes she'd caught in the circulating gossip ranged from drowning in his blalal berry bog to being partially digested by a dibuc. None of them made him sound particularly competent.

Behind the dark circles of her sunshades, Aliara watched two weathered bags settle onto the bench just outside her blind. Listening to the lilt of their native Vazztain, she yearned for the fractious polyglot of Plainspeak spoken back home.

"Lovely ceremony. I wasn't sure what they'd do, given his condition," said the one wearing a stained and once-fashionable jacket.

"Oh?" the other asked, brushing a marsh fly from the sleeve of her screaming-yellow overcoat.

"He fell into the berry masher." Her wrinkled mouth curled into a smirk, revealing worn and ragged teeth. "They won't be selling *that* batch of jam."

"No, no," the other answered, head wagging. "Halad told Muuraan, who heard from Belya that his son dropped a full crate on him in their barn. All set to go to town, they were. His wife'll still be able to sell *those* berries."

"Well…if Muuraan said it, then he knows—second cousin on his mother's side." The first shook her head to demonstrate her grief by proxy. "Too bad. Though I suppose the whole fracas frees up the widow. Maybe she'll get the family out of indenture."

They both cackled discreetly behind raised hands before settling back into their funerary facades. Aliara leaned from her cover and sniffed the curls poking from beneath the scarf of the one closest to her. Cooking grease, stale flatulence, and a vague hint of decay. Even the corpse couldn't have been so perfumed with rot.

"The boy will never be the same," the first said, oblivious to the intrusion. "We should go pay our respects."

"True, true." The second clicked her tongue and shook her head with affected sadness.

The first perked up and pointed across the plaza. "Muuraan's here!"

They scuttled away to sift their fellow mourners for fresh rumors.

Nearby, Aliara heard the solid thwack of a fist to flesh. Across the row, in the shadows cast by stilted houses, two little boys were beating on a third. She considered wandering over to put a stop to it, but found drawing attention to herself unappealing. Besides, why should she deny the beaten boy this lesson?

She drew her hood further over her bleak face and slipped from her blind, careful to avoid notice. If any of them recognized her, they would pounce. The assailant would reveal their name, bow and flatter, then commence with a thinly veiled lists of grievances. They all wanted something. And for the time, their duke wanted nothing to do with them.

Aliara paused at the entry to the manor house, taking a final look at the rites silhouetted against the setting sun. Syl would have risen by now. She touched the moonstone ring reflexively, rotating it around her index finger. She'd stay here as long as he needed, but she hoped he'd end this wallowing soon.

SYLANDAIR

Syl blinked against the offending gold glow of the waning sun reflecting off the plaster ceiling. Only the cypress beams broke the monotony of light. Each flicker of his eyes felt like sand lined his sticky lids.

He turned his head to where Aliara should have been, but she was gone, probably hours ago. More and more frequent of late. He couldn't blame her. On his other side, an anonymous woman drooled on his imported pillowslip. Also increasingly frequent. They came and went with shameful regularity, brief distractions whose names he forgot as quickly as he learned them.

His eyes returned to the beams overhead. Outside, the locals played some grinding dirge on their menagerie of homemade instruments. Somewhere in his mind, Syl remembered one of them had died. Yes, that was the reason for all the pomp. According to the footman, two days ago a pair of primped children had arrived at the door, requesting their duke's presence via song. He hadn't so much as deigned to respond.

He rolled away from his guest, turning his face into a pillow stained with his own drool and stinking of stale uurost and liquor. Knees curled to his chest, he scanned the room that had cost him so much to furnish, each piece bespoke or an antique, each arranged just-so after months of planning. Those had been the days; when being a duke was the pinnacle of his life, the goal he'd finally reached.

Now garbage and laundry lay heaped alongside those few things still important to him.

A half-drunk bottle of caba atop his dresser caught his eye. Syl swung his legs off the bed and waited as a wave of dizzy nausea rolled over him. After a bit, the episode passed. Using the carved swan's-neck bedpost, he swung into a standing position, retrieved the caba, and flopped back into bed.

"Good morning, my duke," the woman said. Her hand slid across the dark sheets toward Syl's thigh. "What do you have planned for us today?"

He brushed the hand away before it touched skin. "Leave."

In his peripheral vision, he saw her mouth open as if to protest. "Now."

"Take your eye," she cursed under her breath as she dug through the mounded clothes scattered across the floor.

"Faster, or I'll see you out myself."

She pulled on her dress and gathered the rest in a bundle. The door slammed behind her.

Syl lay there for a moment, nursing the warm, flat liquor, listening to the mournful tunes outside change from one to another and yet another, never changing key. He rolled over, looking out the tinted picture window over the upturned corner of the manor-house roof. The late aftermid sun had almost disappeared behind the city's outwall. Though it was too bright to go out now in search of Aliara and a new diversion, it soon would be dark enough.

Ideas for the evening's entertainment rolled over in his mind, the same theme, but he'd vary specifics. It had been a joy to joggle the locals, to demonstrate to them exactly who their duke was and what he was capable of.

As a plan took form, his eyes idly roamed over the room's contents, settling on the Voshar dagger atop his bureau. Memory dragged him back to the night he acquired it, conjuring the onslaught of defiled children, the pull of what could only have been a tail against his ankles. Syl closed his eyes, the images circled through his mind like unrelenting water down a drain.

He threw the bottle to the floor, glass shards scattering. What little caba remained sprayed the nearby clothing. Syl stood and examined his nakedness in the tall mirror. Some four months in this backwater had punished him. The flat, smoky skin beneath his eyes crinkled and edged toward black. The shining mane, always smooth and clean, hung in limp hunks around his face. Ill-groomed hair, more silver than black in some spots, hung over his lip. Its matching beard, restricted largely to his chin, was speckled with remnants of what he hoped was food. Ribs poked at his dehydrated skin. Even his ornamentation was missing.

"Enough," he told his reflection.

A polite knock, then a quiet, nasal voice inquired, "Duke? Is everything well?"

"Enter."

A dingy green puka turned out in a scrupulously clean dress and apron entered and bowed, broom and dustpan in hand. "Can I get anything for you, sir?"

"Clean this," he pointed to the shattered bottle, then swept his arm over the rest of the room. "All of this."

She scurried forward, picking at the bottle shards with great enthusiasm. He watched unflinchingly, well aware of how eager she was to leave his presence.

When she finished with the glass, he added, "Draw a bath, Quinch, and pack our things; Aliara's and mine."

"Sir?"

"We're leaving," he said. "I'm done with this."

SCHMALCH

Every copper gone. The coins had rushed through his hot little fingers so fast. The Duke had warned him about being too generous, but he couldn't help himself. Excess equaled respect, and nothing bought both like two pocketfuls of Callas.

Schmalch leaned over and vomited a bile-soured splash of beer and gristle into the gutter. The stray ginger cat curled up beside him hissed and scuttled away. Even the Vazztain duds Rift gave him were grubby and ruined—the red shirt, the tan pants, the Duke's swish leather vest, all tattered and stained. He rolled onto his back and hoped he'd pass out before he vomited again. That would make things quick and easy.

No word from Rift or the Duke for quarterns. They'd left him to waste away on the streets with the memories of what lurked beneath his feet...beneath everyone's feet. The only answer to his knock at their penthouse had been Sviroosa, the pair's domestic. Schmalch liked her, her bitter-brown eyes, her smooth sage skin, and the way her skirts swished around as she moved. On one occasion, when he still thought the chivori might come back and visit him, he'd offered her candies and a bottle of quincitaba he'd purchased from Garl. But Sviroosa merely held her nose and shooed him off the stoop.

Garl had suggested a bath and a thorough scrubbing of clothes. Schmalch had grudgingly complied before returning to the penthouse, this time with a smoked scorillion wrapped in seaweed—actually purchased, not pinched—from a gloss Dockhaven restaurant, Drift. As tall as Schmalch himself, the big fish had cost him twelve Callas, and he was nearly bursting with pride over the intended gift.

She'd not even opened the door that day. He'd knocked over and over. He even heard the flick of the peephole cover more than once, but no answer came. He left the treat by the door for Sviroosa or the neighborhood cats, whomever got to it first.

After that, he'd lurked around at the Bitter Barnacle or in its gutter until his coin had run out. He'd returned to pickpocketing two quarterns ago, but the thin stream of filched coin couldn't keep pace with his new lifestyle. He was deep in debt to Garl, among others. And each time he tried to care, Schmalch pictured those torn-up kids with their flat eyes and smashed skulls. He felt their little groping hands all over him. It didn't matter what he owed or did. Those things were under them all.

For a time, he'd even returned to the Temple of Spriggan, tried to salve his mind by helping others like him. He had intended to play with them and teach them sleight of hand, but during each visit, his mind twisted their happy smiles into dull stares, their playful hands into tearing claws. His panicked screams scared the little ones. In the end, the temple elders led him away with gratitude for his gift of time, but requested that maybe he could give of himself in other ways.

Behind him, the Bitter Barnacle's front door creaked open.

"Still here?" Garl's voice drifted out.

Schmalch rolled over and sat up. "Sure am. You open?"

Garl nodded and waved. "Am now. Got some dishes need done if you wanna keep drinkin' here. Couple'a toilets took some punishment last night, too."

Schmalch sighed.

"'Course, you can just pay up and come on in and drink. Or lay out here and keep bakin' in the sun and salt, all I care."

Schmalch dragged himself to his feet and started indoors. "I'm on it, Garl. I'm on it."

ALIARA

Aliara slipped through the front door of Isay's manor house, left her cloak with the wan, stooping footman perpetually lurking there, and headed for the dining room. She stopped short at the threshold.

For the first time in quarterns, Syl had arrived for the meal before her. He sat at the head of the table, hunched over, brow furrowed, eyes swinging from side to side as though waiting for a painfully late collection of dinner guests while his fingernails rapped a staccato against the tabletop. His freshly washed hair was slicked back from his drawn face and cinched at the nape of his neck. His mustache and beard, grown wild over his months of negligence, were trimmed into a respectable shape that hardened his features into something more rugged than pretty. He'd even dressed for the meal, complete with newly pressed shirt and coat.

Aliara wasn't sure if this was a good or a bad sign. Their time at the Ritora Doublet had been enjoyable, sometimes delightful. The months since had been difficult. At first he'd attended to his duties as Duke, entertaining, holding court, and the like. Within a few quarterns, though, he'd devolved, repeating the same tedious behavior day after day.

Today's change of routine could mean he was surfacing from his misery or he may simply be entering a new phase. She hoped for the former.

"What's for dinner?" she asked, striding into the room as though nothing had changed.

Syl picked up a fork and ran a tine under his fingernails. "We're leaving."

"Good."

He grunted.

"Back to the Doublet?"

"No. Leaving Chiva'vastezz altogether. We're going home."

"When?"

"Tonight if possible. Quinch still has to pack our trunks, and I've sent Crel to the farspeakers office to order our transportation. We'll be taking a ferry over to Gal, then a carriage into Vinex," he said, meeting her eyes for the first time. The dark bags beneath them had faded. Action became him. "From there, we find whatever means we can to reach the Haven."

"Home?" She raised a brow. "You have plans?"

"I'll be claiming my inheritance…the house, the coin, all of it."

Aliara dropped into her seat, lips parted in surprise.

Quinch skittered out from the kitchen, dropped two bowls filled with some sort of blackened fish salad on the table, and returned to her domain. Aliara picked up a fork and poked at the meal, eyes still focused across the table. Syl didn't bother feigning interest in the food. He held her gaze, sipped his tea.

All of Dockhaven had been shocked to learn that the tubby old pervert had willed everything he owned to his young ward, Sylandair, upon his death. Syl had never claimed a copper of it. He'd simply never wanted it before. The mansion, adjacent to Orono's precious waterworks, had sat empty for more than two decades since its owner was declared dead after the explosion.

The place could rot for all Aliara cared.

"Why?" she asked, struggling to absorb the drastic change.

"We both know that what we found beneath the city—beneath *his* estate…"

She nodded.

"Have you considered what that thing that grabbed my ankle might have been?"

She had. She'd examined every possibility, but no matter how she reasoned or compensated for coincidence, she came to the same, inescapable conclusion. "Orono."

"My thoughts as well. Given what you saw of his...his tail, it appears he can remake himself at will. He has gained some semblance of the immortality he sought." Syl's eyes narrowed. One side of his mouth pinched. "Though the side effects do seem extreme, beyond what one might expect from anti-agathics and exposure to unrefined opoli."

Aliara raised a brow.

"I believe I mentioned dispatching agents to investigate our options."

"No."

"Ah, well, apologies. I did soon after we arrived in Isay. They have yet to locate a viable entry. Our friends the Yenderot appear to have noticed our brief intrusion. My agents tell me that guards— ones more active than those you saw—are stationed along the cliffside path. That entry is no longer accessible without a direct assault. I would prefer to avoid such conspicuous actions. To operate so brazenly, they most certainly have allies within the City Corps... or perhaps even our Mayor."

Aliara nodded, unsurprised by the suggestion. Mayor Carsuure was not known for her integrity of her office.

Syl straightened, each movement, each word restoring the man she knew. "If we are to end him, we must understand this...thing he has become." His voice was clear and smooth. "All of his secrets were in that house. I can think of no better place to start."

"And the coin?" She stabbed some food and chewed.

"I shall pay a visit to Idra," Syl said, referring to Dockhaven's marginally effective mayor. His voice shifted ominously. "Her office has held the bequest all these years. I believe I can encourage her to expedite proceedings. She owes me a kindness or two, thanks to some favors. Among other things."

Aliara smiled, swallowed.

"When we have finished with all this, I am quite certain we can find something wildly scurrilous and wasteful to do with what remains of the chunky old diddler's hoard."

She dropped her fork into the bowl with a light *ting*. A familiar warm desire was building in her belly, one that had become merely perfunctory these past several months.

"We will gather Schmalch again, naturally." Syl waved a hand. "I am certain the little douse has wasted his whole nut by now."

"Naturally." Aliara pushed her chair back from the table.

"He will clean away the decades of debris and assist in sorting the home's contents. The place already was a confusion of flotsam. I cannot imagine the intervening years have improved that. The Duin know what things we might find stored in jars there."

She rose and slunk down the length of the table toward him, watching his eyes watch her, dusty blue stones set into features as beatific as they were baleful.

When she reached his seat, Syl stood and swept Quinch's carefully crafted luncheon to the floor. He rocked her back onto the table and slipped down her body. He buried his face in her, and those stagnant months of boredom became memory.

SYLANDAIR

2085 DANURAK 9

It took two quarterns and a fair number of Callas to travel from Syl's duchy on O'atlor back home to Dockhaven. Their arrival at the penthouse startled Sviroosa and a suitor, curled up together on the solarium's settee. When Syl came upon the happy scene, the little domestic squeaked, flushed from her scalp to the tip of her nose, and shooed the smitten man out with her apron as she would vermin from her kitchen. She took to her duties instantly, mortification written on every feature. As embarrassing as the situation was for Sviroosa, it was equally amusing Syl, a welcome distraction given the unpleasant tasks ahead.

While Sviroosa saw to the unpacking and Aliara ran her errand, Syl headed north, to the Nest and the mayoral offices. Upon his arrival, Idra claimed—through her assistant—that she was too busy to see anyone without an appointment. After a few moments to consider the balance of their relationship, however, wisdom prevailed. The assistant pronounced the Mayor free "for only a few moments" and ushered Syl into Idra's office with its panoramic view of Rimadour Park and the sea beyond.

The room was as opulent as its occupant. A deep rug of simple, rectilinear reds and oranges blanketed the floor, towering shelves filled with antiques and rare books lined the walls, and an aquarium burbled in the far corner. At the center of it all sat a large desk inlaid with woods from across the islands. The chivori woman seated behind it glared at him. Her pale cloud of hair was pulled back in a severe bun, bespoke pink blouse buttoned to her neck, hands folded tight atop the desk. She looked like a blister about to pop.

"Well?" she asked. "What is it that you need speak with me at such short notice, Imythedralin?"

"Mayor Carsuure…Idra. So good to see you." Syl removed his wide-brimmed black hat, using it to add flourish to a polite bow. He draped it and his rain-spattered topcoat over one of the more expensive chairs. "A lovely day for a visit, wouldn't you say?"

Idra glanced out the enormous window at the light, but persistent rain. "To you perhaps."

He crossed to the wall of glass behind her. "A stunning view as always. It remains a wonder to me that you keep the grounds in such a natural state of beauty. You could make quite a pile of Callas if the land were parceled off."

Idra's reflection in the window stared sourly at him. "All part of Rimadour's codicil, Imythedralin. I'm fairly certain you're aware."

"Ah yes. Yes." He knew the stipulations well but enjoyed the goad. "Too bad. I know how the council love their Callas. Though I must say that personally, I approve of the green space."

"What do you want, Imythedralin? I'm busy."

Syl turned from the window quickly enough to catch Idra's annoyed frown snap to polite interest.

"Very well. I will dispense with pleasantries," Syl said. "My needs are simple. I wish to take possession of the grounds and monies left to me by my benefactor, Master Kluuta Orono."

Uncontrolled amazement swept over her face. "You said you didn't want it."

"What I told our previous mayor—your late wife, I believe— was that I was leaving it in trust with the city." He shrugged and held his hands out as though helpless. "That arrangement no longer serves."

Idra stumbled over her words as she shoved back from her desk. "I…we…the city has found other uses for…for much of it."

"I see. I suppose you'll simply have to recover it then, won't you?"

She blinked several times then, as though a switch had ben flicked, the open shock on her face shifted to flirtation. She rose and slunk toward him, hips swaying with a roll to make the sea jealous. "Is that really necessary, Sylandair?" She took his hands in hers. "We've been such close friends for so long. I'm certain you can understand my position."

"Friends" was hardly the term, but he'd seen this act many times before, usually aimed at others from whom she needed something.

"Of course I understand." It was a simple position to understand: She'd spent his money. "My needs, however, are urgent. I am eager to acquire that magnificent property."

"Yes! Yes! The property, you want the property!" She brightened. "I can provide the deed easily. Two days' time, maybe less. You would have to rid it of the squatters on your own, however. Officially, it would be difficult for me to justify the use of the City Corps for such petty affairs."

Syl smiled at the idea of the city's wastrels urinating on Orono's rugs, then wrinkled his nose in disgust as he considered the smell.

"Yes, I hear there's been quite a crowd squatting there," Idra said. "They've polluted the place, I'm sure, but it shouldn't take long to shoo them off."

"And my accounts?"

"The coin…the coin *is* an issue. We have it…tied up…in a number of infrastructure projects currently." She sighed, held his hands tight against her chest and smiled, obviously pleased with her quick thinking.

Syl scanned the elegant room. He wondered how much of this extravagance had been purchased with his inheritance.

"You could wait a few months on the coin, couldn't you?" Idra batted long lashes at him. "For me, Sylandair?" She released the taut bun, hair spilling across her narrow shoulders and kissed his fingertips before cupping his palm over her breast.

Idra's dignity was secondary to her greed. This routine had worked on more of her constituency than seemed reasonable. It had been entertaining enough in the past for Syl to provide her a bit of leeway in their dealings, but today, this was not an acceptable trade. He bent toward her upturned face until his thin nose brushed her button one. Idra closed her eyes.

"Then you'll simply have to untie it," Syl whispered. He retrieved his hand from her bosom and stepped away. "I shall expect all funds in full by the start of Danurak's second quartern."

"That's only two days! How can you expect me to get that much together in so short a time?" Before he could answer, her panic reverted to forced seduction. She worked the lashes again as she made a show of unbuttoning her blouse. "Perhaps we could reach some sort of interim arrangement?"

"Idra, while I am familiar with your talents—and they are prodigal—none are worth the quantity of Callas left to me in that will."

"You can't believe that's realistic, Imythedralin! Two days!" She stamped her dainty foot and produced a petulant sound somewhere between a growl and a wail. "You can't expect me to gather that sum so quickly. It's—"

"I can and do expect you to assemble the amount so quickly, because it was never yours to touch, Idra." Syl slipped into his topcoat, retrieved his hat. "It should be sitting in a vault, gathering dust...and interest."

She opened her mouth to protest, but he raised a finger.

"You have such a lovely financial resource across the Bay." He nodded at the window, where the massive Bank of Dockhaven loomed on the Big Island. "I suggest you tap it. Unless you would like your constituents to learn so very much more about what their mayor has been up to."

"Ugh!" she said, the sound of protest used by many a child.

Syl paused at the door. "We *are* old friends, I suppose." He tapped a finger against his lower lip in an exaggerated show of deliberation. "I shall be generous. Take three days, Idra, and I'll gift you that First Epoch enameled ewer you showed such interest in."

Her mouth flapped like a landed fish.

With a bow and a blown kiss, Syl left the office.

ALIARA

As was the norm, Aliara was sent to retrieve Schmalch. In extreme circumstances, Syl would frequent areas haunted by their lackey, but given any alternative, he avoided the more squalid sections of both Rabbles. They had a tacit agreement: Syl didn't force Aliara to attend the public functions she so reviled, and she executed their business in the less palatable regions of the city whenever possible.

Now she hovered between two dingy buildings in shadows cast by the creeping dawn, sullen drizzle forming drops that rolled from her hood and dripped onto her nose. Soon enough, Schmalch emerged from the Bitter Barnacle carrying two buckets brimming with filth. He scurried away from the tavern, quickly returning with the same buckets now filled with clean water. She doubted he had bothered to rinse between loads. He swept dirt and litter out the tavern door, gathered garbage, and patched a mysterious hole in the building's exterior. A mangy dog dining on a pool of vomit beneath the front window growled and ran away when the puka doused it with one of the buckets of water. When he mounted a rickety stool and began smearing the rain-dampened grime uniformly over the windows, Aliara slipped from her hiding spot.

"Unlikely work for a wealthy man."

Schmalch wobbled on his perch, dropped the cleaning rag, and groped for the blade at his ankle.

"Unless you bought the place," she added.

He squinted, struggling to see her in the dawn light. When she pushed back her hood, his face exploded in a smile.

"Rift? Rift!" Schmalch threw himself at her, latching on with a painful hug.

"Let go."

"You left me," he said, sobbing into her shirt.

"You had money and friends. Let go."

"I spent it all," he hitched out.

"Of course you did."

She wrenched her hand between them and peeled him off. He blinked away tears and snorted something working its way from his nose.

"But you left me."

Aliara cocked her head as she regarded him. "Now we're back."

His eyes swiveled up to her face. "Really? You are? The Duke, too?"

She nodded. "Wash before you visit. We have work."

He wiped his beak on a filthy sleeve, leaving a dirty streak above his mouth. "Sure, sure, but I gotta finish up for Garl." He looked at his feet, cheeks darkening. "Owe him some money."

Aliara took him in. His new clothes were ruined, possibly even grubbier than the last set. His eyes were sunken, skin sallow, fingers raw from Garl's scut work. She'd seen Schmalch in desperate straits, but his present state was beyond anything previous.

She glanced up at the Barnacle, Garl's liquor-bloated face staring out the window. Schmalch was useless to Syl and her as long as he was here, especially working off a debt while simultaneously drinking his way into further arrears.

"Bathe," she said. "I'll deal with Garl."

"Really? You'll…you'll pay him?"

"Yes. A salary advance."

Schmalch gave her another hug, kicked over the window-washing stool, and hurried inside, stripping as he ran.

SCHMALCH

2085 DANURAK 12

Schmalch sat on the aging steel bench of the aerial tram carriage, staring at the little box in his palm. The Duke had sent him to deliver the box and its contents to the mayor's office all the way up in the Nest. Schmalch had learned long ago not to ask questions when it came to the Duke and Rift, but a message for *the mayor*?

He waited until his carriage companions shuffled off at the Big Island stop before sliding the lid open. The chit inside, about as big as a thumb, hopped and skittered about the little container. Schmalch pinched the zoet creature between his fingers, stroked its lumpy pink back, and stared into the black stone of its eye.

"Idra dear," the Duke's creamy voice said in Schmalch's head, *"I invite you to pay a visit to my penthouse this evening. You do remember where it is, I assume."* He chuckled in kind of a scary way. *"Yes, I know you do. I expect to receive you at sunset. We shall enjoy a drink or two and continue the discussion we began three days prior."* He paused so long Schmalch started to think the message had ended. *"For both our benefits, I hope you have procured the items we discussed. I look forward to a lovely evening in your company. Until then, Sylandair."*

The words all sounded pleasant, but even Schmalch recognized the threat hidden within. He stuffed the wriggling chit back into its tin, closed it, and stepped out of the carriage into the yawning green space of Rimadour Park. Beyond the park's trees and smattering of government-type buildings, rich people's mansions and exclusive businesses clogged the Nest. Everything was so clean and well-groomed. Seeing it make him itch. Or maybe that was just the swank clothes the Duke had insisted he wear for his errand.

He hurried across the green to City Hall, where the guard smelled poverty on him like an animal scenting fear, letting him pass only when Schmalch presented the chit tin and announced, "Duke Imythedralin has a message for the Mayor." She tried to take the tin herself, but Schmalch's instructions had been quite specific: He was to deliver the message personally. He protested. The guard refused—nastily—but he wasn't about to disappoint the Duke. He wouldn't leave until he'd delivered his message.

Without bothering to hide her annoyance and disgust, the guard ushered him into the big, official office like a fine guest. The cushness was so overwhelming, he lost his breath. Rich stuff was everywhere. The place almost smelled like Callas. The pluck he'd enjoyed with the guard disappeared. Schmalch dropped the chit tin into the angry Mayor's hand, bowed as directed, and backed out of the office.

He shook all the way back to the Lower Rabble.

When the Duke and Rift woke up from their mids, the Duke stationed Schmalch in the penthouse foyer with instructions about what to do when the Mayor arrived. He stood there, staring at the door, waiting for the bell to ring for what seemed like hours. Rift waited with him, but she got to relax, her body draped over the seat of the nearby hall tree. Something about her just sitting there, staring, not saying a word, made Schmalch sweat, which made his clothes just that much more itchy. He tried not to scratch, but he couldn't help himself. Each time Sviroosa pattered through the foyer, though, Schmalch straightened his spine and ignored the insistent prickling of the fancy clothes until she returned to her kitchen. He hoped she noticed how professional and clean he was.

When the doorbell finally bonged, Rift disappeared from her perch so quickly Schmalch thought he must have imagined her being there at all. He sucked in air and opened the broad wooden door with a bow and a sweep of his hand.

"The Duke will greet you in the parlor," he said, each word just as he'd been instructed.

The mayor—looking much less mayor-y, but just as angry—tossed a hefty dun-colored wrap at him and marched into the parlor without so much as a second look. Schmalch tossed the wrap in the general direction of the now-vacant hall tree before hurrying up the spiral stairs to the library, where the Duke waited.

"She's here," Schmalch whispered.

The Duke looked up from his reading.

"She looks…" Schmalch searched for the word he'd heard the Duke used so many times, but couldn't locate it and defaulted to his own lingo. "She looks pretty swish."

"Of course she does. I have something to finish across the hall before joining her. Tell her I am unavoidably occupied, but will be with her as soon as possible. Give her my deepest apologies."

Schmalch circled back down the steps, repeating the command to himself, "Occupied…join her…deep apologies." He was so distracted as he crossed into the parlor, he almost smacked headlong into the Mayor.

"Where is Imythedralin?" she demanded.

"The Duke…Duke Imythedralin has something to finish. I mean, he's unav—unav—…he's busy. Then he'll, uh, he'll join you."

With a huff, she marched over to one of the picture windows flanking the fireplace.

"He sends his deepest, uh, apologies," Schmalch told her back.

"Bring me a drink while I wait, puka."

Having received no instructions on what to do about drinks, Schmalch scooted off to the kitchen. He dodged the swinging door and tried to stand in a spot where he wouldn't be in Sviroosa's way. She was on her stool by the stove, stirring something that spattered and hissed. He waited until she returned the lid to the pot before speaking.

"Hey, er…Sviroosa?" he said.

Her pretty mouth turned down in a frown. "What do you want?"

"The important lady in there, the Mayor, she wants a drink."

"What kind?"

Schmalch shrugged.

Sviroosa sighed as though this were the stupidest thing she'd ever heard. "Then go back and ask."

Schmalch found the Mayor situated in the seat he'd come to know as the Duke's favorite. She was still frowning.

"What kind of, uh, drink would you like?" he asked.

She dragged her eyes from the painting over the fireplace to Schmalch.

"Quincitaba. And it best be the finest Imythedralin stocks."

Schmalch returned to the kitchen.

"Quincitaba," he told Sviroosa, who rolled her eyes.

"Duke Imythedralin doesn't keep that. Ask if she wants something else."

Again he passed through the swinging door, which seemed bent on whacking him, and found the Mayor now staring into the dead fireplace.

"The Duke doesn't keep quincitaba," Schmalch said. "What… what else?"

Her grey hand flicked out so quickly, Schmalch didn't even notice her move, only felt the slap, the sting of his cheek. He hopped out of arm's reach, unwelcome tears swelling in his eyes.

"If you are the kind of servant Imythedralin keeps around, it's a wonder he's a duke of anything," the Mayor said. "Bring me a caba. Good vintage. Next time, if your master doesn't stock something, be sure to tell his guest first."

Schmalch wiped his eyes and returned to the kitchen, face burning with both injury and embarrassment.

"She wasn't too happy about that," he told Sviroosa. "She wants caba now."

For a moment, what might have been pity flashed in the lovely housemaid's eyes, but when Schmalch sucked at the snot threatening to drip from his nose, the glint vanished. She poured a glass of caba and passed it to him with loads warnings not to spill any on the rugs or—the Duin forbid—on the guest.

He managed to carry the glass without dribbling more than a drop. Or two. The rugs were deep and busy with patterns. No one would notice. He sat it on the side table and left before the Mayor could strike again. As he hurried from the room, movement to one side of the door startled him. He paused, squinting. Rift lurked in the shadows between the gaming cabinet and a tall plant. She winked.

Schmalch wasn't sure what the two chivori had in mind for the evening, but it couldn't be good. He backtracked to the kitchen at a run. Sviroosa might be hostile toward him, but the worst he could expect from her was a conk on the head with a wooden spoon. Whatever was about to happen in the parlor was going to be a whole lot worse than that.

IDRA

"Idra dear. So good of you to pay me the courtesy of a visit." Imythedralin entered the room with snap of boot heels and a sly smile.

Idra rose from her seat and gave him a burning grimace. He'd kept her waiting for ages. She would have preferred that things went pleasantly, but Imythedralin's little manipulations had made that impossible.

He took her shoulders and brushed ear against ear, a surprisingly familiar greeting given the circumstance. When he leaned back, she slapped him in his smart mouth, immediately regretting the loss of control.

"My apologies for the delay, Mayor." Imythedralin stretched his face where she'd struck him. "I had unavoidable business to see to."

He tossed a stack of papers on the little table by her glass of caba, her third since arriving. She glanced at them, face firmly composed. They were all too familiar. He'd required one signed each time he procured another piece for her collection. It was an ill sign that he'd felt the need to bring the entire sheaf this evening.

Imythedralin stood back and ran thumb and forefinger down the silky hair of his chin, the newest of his affectations. "Do tell me you have all that I requested."

"Sylandair," Idra began, using her most mournful tone, "I've done the best I could."

"If it is your best, then I am certain I will be satisfied."

She wrapped a thread of hair around her fingertip and looked up at the ceiling in her best imitation of someone about to cry. She'd handled far smarter characters than Imythedralin in her rise to office. Idra bit her lower lip and glanced at her reflection in the window. The shimmering mist of a dress clung to her every curve. Were it necessary—and she doubted it would be—she'd have no trouble this evening. He'd caught her off guard when he visited the office. Tonight she was prepared, and had more than one lever to apply.

"As promised, the transfer of the deed to the house and grounds was a simple formality…though many of the council did not appreciate being convened at such an odd time." She eyed him, hoping to see the slightest sign of discomfort.

Imythedralin skimmed the document nonchalantly, tossed it onto the table with the others and returned to her. "Very well. You have my gratitude. And tomorrow, when I visit the bank?"

"The council and I have signed off on the release of the accounts to you, but you may find the funds insufficient for whatever it is you have planned for them." The words burbled out. She knew she was rambling, all her rehearsal ruined by caba and anxiety. "You must understand that the trust has been invested by the city into a number of projects over the years, and we have always—always—replenished what was diverted and often to your benefit, so the value overall is substantially greater. But it will be some months yet before we see yields on the latest projects."

His face disclosed no emotion, it barely even showed interest.

She let her lips quiver. "I—I've done everything I could, Sylandair. I've sold things and wheedled and bargained. I even tried some maneuvers that could get me removed from office, but…" Her breath caught. A lone tear ran down her cheek, mussing her artful cosmetics. "I simply can't get the money together now. Or… or anytime soon."

"Oh?"

Idra wiped away the ersatz tear. "Much of it is deposited in Locnor Bay as a security toward picket ships for the city; you know how badly we need them. The losses to raiders in the last few seasons have been astronomical! The Billidoc Coalition and the shippers' guild have pledged funds to be released upon completion of the fleet, and at that time the city should be able to reimburse your accounts. The keels have already been laid, I can't ask for return of our deposits from the builders. Imagine the political tangle that would create!"

Imythedralin watched her, his expression as sympathetic as the one she reserved for the city's gutter babies.

"You wouldn't...just maybe, consider donating your inheritance to the city, would you?" The pre-occupation Norian bracelet slid up her forearm as she swept open hands around the room. Imythedralin didn't need to know that she'd purchased the silver piece with a bit of the coin he'd left festering away in his purportedly unwanted inheritance fund. "You are a Vazztain Duke slumming at the center of the Middle Sea, I find it hard to believe you are short on capital. Perhaps a seat on the council? Wouldn't you like a say in what happens here?"

"You have overestimated my civic spirit, Idra. Perhaps if I believed you concerning the disposition of my funds, I would join your council and allow these projects to come to fruition." He scoffed. "We both know not a single copper went toward this fabled fleet of yours."

Idra's tears dried up, her pout hardened. "Fine. If you're not willing to be magnanimous..." She took a sheet of paper from her case and handed it to him. "I'm certain you've heard of Mister Flark."

Imythedralin took the page and read.

"He's quite convinced this building is unstable." She made a show of looking at the ceiling and walls, all of which appeared to be in excellent condition. "The way builders have stacked level upon level over the years. It's not safe. He's petitioned my office to have it demolished, with a taller, more stable one to be erected in its place."

Imythedralin looked up from Flark's petition, one brow raised. She had him.

"Flark even has two Mucha master engineers willing to present his case before the city council. He's built so many new buildings on the Upper Rabble already." She shrugged. "The council will no doubt appreciate his acumen in these matters and approve his appeal. I've used my influence to delay it because of our dear friendship, Sylandair, but I don't know how much longer I can continue to stall."

"Yes, Flark is a persistent little slumlord. Unpleasant, even for a puka. I cannot say I have enjoyed being his tenant," Imythedralin said. "You should proceed with his claim. Do not forestall progress on my account."

Idra stammered, unable to form a coherent word. He and his scruffy mate were notorious in the Haven for this pretentious cuddy, far too fancy for either of the Rabbles. She'd been sure he'd do anything to save his home.

"While I enjoy living here, I would hate for it to come down around my ears. If it is truly that unstable, the city should raze it. When you deliver the bequest in full, my darling girl and I will easily procure finer accommodations. Rumor reached me only last quartern of an available estate on the Nest. Quite close to your own." He handed the page back to Idra. "May I refill your caba?"

Left with no other cards, Idra snatched a handful of Imythedralin's shirt before he could leave to fetch the liquor bottle. At least with him, persuasion wouldn't be as unpleasant as it often was with others of her constituents. "I've been terrible, Sylandair," she said, putting on her best penitent expression. "The coin is beyond reach. I've tried everything I could think of to make up the balance. How can I convince you to forgive the debt for just a little while?"

One corner of his mouth quirked.

"I could…" She released him and slipped the knot at the back of her neck and the gown slid to the floor, revealing her calculated nudity. "…try to make it up to you in the meantime."

Imythedralin's arm circled her waist, the other darted behind his back before slipping between their bodies. She felt not the warmth of his hand, but the chill of metal part her thighs. A piece of jewelry, perhaps, or an exotic toy. Both intriguing.

He bent, closing the gap in their heights, and whispered, "I do not think you understand the strength of my resolve in this issue."

The metal bit so slightly into Idra's thigh. A drop of blood tickled down the curve of her leg, resting behind her knee. Insides dancing with fear and an unexpected excitement, she tried fruitlessly to wriggle out of Imythedralin's grasp.

Behind him, the shadows around a tall plant coalesced into a familiar woman; lithe, with dead eyes and a feral grin. Long, thin blades hung at her hips. She ran a hand over Imythedralin's shoulders and assumed a position beside the chair where Idra had been waiting.

The fickle excitement inside Idra chilled to uncertainty.

"I am a generous man," Imythedralin said. His face was grim and angry, not the usual mocking half-smile Idra knew. "I have permitted you additional time to procure funds that were mine by right. While your amateurish stratagems and hackneyed displays have been amusing in our previous dealings, I will no longer play this game with you."

"What do you—?"

Imythedralin shifted the blade ever so slightly. The sting at her thigh went raw. Idra shut her mouth and nodded. He watched her eyes, his hard, pale gaze daring her to speak again. In a moment the blade slid away, sending more rivulets down her leg.

"Now…" In a single, quick motion Imythedralin laced his long fingers in Idra's well-coiffed hair and bent her over the back of the chair she'd so recently vacated. He crouched beside her, one hand pinning her in place, the other resting casually on the chair's arm, as relaxed as though her were at a cocktail party. Lips grazing the back of her ear, he spat out words like a man with lye on his tongue. "You *will* return my coin."

She tried to nod, but he held her face tight against the cushion. Her toes barely touched the floor, the chair's wooden frame biting into her midsection. Her face flushed with blood and heat. It was hard to draw breath.

She gulped air and shouted, "Yes! I'll return it!"

"You will see that I have every copper by the fourteenth?"

"Yes!"

"Say it all."

"Your inheritance. Every coin promised in the Orono will. By the fourteenth."

"And the interest owed?"

"Yes, every bit!" She cried, choking on tears.

"Excellent." His fingers unwound from her hair. He straightened, tucked the blade into the sheath at his back, and covered it with his waistcoat.

Idra slid back onto her feet, unpleasantly breathless and a little queasy. Her fear had vanished with the blade, replaced by annoyance at being bested and anxiety at the prospect of gathering so much coin so quickly. Her mind raced with ways to obtain the Callas—liquidating her collection, emptying her accounts, selling favors to people far more terrifying than Imythedralin.

He crouched to pick up her dress and, Idra imagined, to ogle her nakedness.

"As for what you offer tonight…" His chill, blue eyes shifted to his mate. "Pet?"

The woman cocked her head like some curious bird and studied Idra. When her dispassionate gaze swiveled back to him, she shook her head once.

Imythedralin handed the blood-spotted dress to Idra. "We have no interest."

She yanked the dress from his hand and slid it over her head. Yes, she'd find all sorts of ways to pay him back.

ALIARA

Aliara threaded her way through the Lower Rabble, past the fishing piers and up the main road of the Prick. She passed a sad-faced girl with black finger-sized bruises on her forearms, tossed her a Calla without pausing. As she neared the westernmost tip, Aliara slipped down an alley then into a division between buildings too narrow to be properly called an alley, garbage cans and awnings concealing it from notice by any random passers-by.

The passage, darkened by the buildings lining it, took a sharp left and went on for blocks. She heard the scratch of rats' claws as they scurried from her path, smelled the reek of fetid water pooled in the bottom of garbage cans. A raggedy tabby cat growled and darted away, something dead flopping in its jaws.

Again the path turned sharply left, descending into a spiral of aging coquina stairs, chunks of the coral used as substrate poking through the treads like bulging scar tissue. Aliara stepped nimbly, familiar with their uneven surface.

More than two stories below sea level, the stairs ended on a damp, age-worn room. Threads of the burgeoning dawn seeped down the coiled staircase, but she needed no illumination to find her way through this small space. She swung beneath the staircase. Fingertips brushing the underside of each stair, she pushed a loose brick on the eleventh step from the floor. A low door behind her slid open with a gravely sizzle. She rolled into the cramped space beyond quickly, before the door ground shut again. Inside, a red lumia bulb dangled from the ceiling, contents pulsing and swirling. The effect left most candidates mildly seasick.

Facing the low door was a full-sized steel one, stained with rust and pockmarked with brutality. Aliara ran a hand along the outer edge, feeling the rivets that fused the layers of metal. She pressed them in correct sequence. Gears worked within, and an aperture opened to reveal an unnumbered dial, hand-crank, and keyhole.

Ear to the door, she slowly turned the dial, searching for the oft-changed combination. When the drive pins found their wheel flies, she withdrew a braided iron key from the lining at the collar of her cloak, turned it in the keyhole and spun the crank five times. The door swung open and her eyes swept the room's sparse contents and residents.

The damp smell was diminished here, replaced by stale sweat and old paper. Almost directly in front of the door, a small man sat at a careworn wooden table littered with loose papers, some of which spilled out of an enormous binder at his elbow. At his other elbow sat a jar of chits, crawling over one another in search of an escape. His lips moved as his fingers, the color of a tea stain, tripped through the splayed papers.

The man finished rifling, apparently having found the one he sought, and fished a chit from the jar. Glancing up, he smiled and dropped the wriggling creature. It bounced off the jar's edge and scurried across the table.

"Rift! I have a contract you're perfect for." He lifted his spectacles from glittering gold eyes, resting them on his fuzzy white hair. "If you want it, of course."

"Luugrar," Aliara said. She snatched the escaped chit from the table and returned it to its owner.

"Little douse," Luugrar said.

He held the creature up to the paper he'd selected and stroked its lumpy pink back. It attempted another getaway before noticing the document. Its frantic movements ceased while its black eye absorbed the information it was meant to carry. In a heartbeat, the little zoet resumed its struggle. Luugrar held up a finger to Aliara and turned to the smattering of huddled figures at the tables deeper in the room.

"Dreg! Contract's ready," he shouted, far louder than necessary for such a small space.

Several heads lifted, but only one of the waiting mercenaries stood. Aliara had worked with him before, found him unpleasant but competent. Thin and young, he was subtly shorter than her and dressed entirely in well-worn yet stylish clothes whose color blended almost seamlessly into his grey skin. His hair, pulled back into a stubby tail, was an unnatural mass of swirling, shifting colors. A matching nib of it grew beneath his lower lip. He'd undoubtedly paid a jig's-worth of Callas for the zoet alteration. She'd never understood why someone in their profession would do such a conspicuous thing.

His grey eyes met her black ones, and they stared a moment before raising their chins in greeting.

Dreg shoved the chit into a tiny canvas bag, muttered something to no one in particular, and slipped through the metal door.

"Now," Luugrar said, "you want that jig, Rift?"

She shook her head. "Hiring."

His bushy white eyebrows shot up. "You want to issue a contract, or just do some recruiting from this lot?" He tipped his head toward the room's other occupants.

Aliara scanned the small group, both listless and alert. They were spirits haunting the Thung Toh contract house waiting for purpose. She'd sat similar watches many times.

Neither she nor Syl had even considered hiring from the Abog Union's ranks. Union types were unreliable, and often lied about their skills. Aliara knew who to trust among the Thung Toh, who would do the job properly. Although Syl was endlessly amused by what he called their "trite, ultra-secret underground organization," he took her colleagues as seriously as she did. Filling the position well would come at a cost, but since Idra had delivered as promised, coin was little issue. After examining his account's balance, even Syl had struggled to envision something debaucherous enough to waste the entire amount.

Aliara recognized all the Toh sitting watch. She'd worked with them all, respected most, but one caught her eye: a swarthy man sitting alone in the far corner, back against the wall, fingers wrapped around an uncorked bottle he'd not lifted once since she entered. All karju were tall and broad in comparison to her species, but he was well beyond the average, his muscular bulk almost overwhelming the little table he leaned on. His restless hazel eyes, set deep and wide in his scarred, sallow face, crawled over the room in a slow, implacable pattern. Tracks of long-healed claw marks slashed across the bicep of his right arm were emphasized by tattoos telling the story of how he'd received the wounds. Tendrils of ink the color of chivori blood ran from the arm wounds to similar scars on his right cheek then up to puncture wounds dotting both temples. She'd worked with him often enough to know the scars extended to his chest. Aliara didn't understand the Estoans' snow-tiger trial, but she admired his—or anyone's—ability to endure it.

Victuur Haus was memorable by those details alone, but the ropey mass of scar tissue and steel that masqueraded as his left arm made him flatly unforgettable, even earning him the moniker "Fist" among the Toh. Though it was unpleasant to look at, the exposed metal bones and crude flesh functioned as well as any organic limb, sometimes better. A team member on a long-ago jig had complained about working with Haus, calling him "the gimp," claiming the deformity made the big man ineffective. With his crudely restored arm, Haus had grabbed the man by the throat and ensured that working together would never again be an issue.

Leaving Luugrar with his question unanswered, Aliara lighted on a rickety chair across from Haus. His roaming eyes slipped to her and lingered a moment before returning to their assessment of the room. He released the bottle and ran his hand through disheveled dark-brown hair.

"Rift," he said, voice deep, his speech deliberate.

"Haus."

They sat for a moment in silence, regarding one another.

She broke it by gesturing in the Toh's hand cant. "*I have work for you.*"

"Oh?" he asked aloud.

"Interested?"

"Could be."

"You still using a crew?"

"How many you need?"

"Three or four, you as binnacle."

He nodded.

Again, they sat quietly.

He took a long pull off the bottle. "What's the work?"

"Squatter eviction. Safeguarding the proprietor."

"Have a plan?"

"Barely. You'll want to detail it."

"Good. Where?"

"The Big Island, Temple Row."

He rubbed the pointed tip of his left ear. There was no longer a point on the right one to rub. "Tricky. What's the property like?"

"Walled grounds, large main house, handful of outbuildings, scattering of trees."

"Gates in the wall?"

"Main and two smaller."

Eye distant with thought, Haus' hand shifted, ran over the scar riven in his cheek. "How many squatters?"

"Unknown," Aliara said.

"When?"

"This evening," she paused, added, "if possible."

"How many besides my crew?"

"Me, the owner, an assistant."

"Calm and reliable?"

She doubted either word applied to Schmalch. "Perhaps you should meet them." She watched for any shift in his expression. "If you're interested."

"Fee?"

"Generous. Settle specifics with the employer."

He stood. "I'll meet them."

SYLANDAIR

Syl sat alone at the long birch dining table, watching the sun poke through the haze over Dockhaven and contemplating the unpleasant return to his childhood home. He slouched against the armrest, frowning, absentmindedly fiddling with the tasseled rope cinching his blue dressing gown. His foot tapped against the polished wood beneath him.

Aliara had left long before sunrise to see to some hiring. He felt her absence, missed the intimacy of their morning meal together, but his annoyance with this interminable waiting trumped any warm feelings he might have. She should have returned an hour ago.

The front door's creak roused him. Assuming a more customary stance, he flattened his spine against the chair's rigid back and wrapped a hand around his mug of tea. Aliara made almost no sound as she glided down the hall, but whomever she'd brought with her produced heavier steps, despite the obvious efforts to mute them.

The karju who entered dwarfed Aliara—not in that prodigious way of the rhochrot, rather he had a simple, dense form born from exercise and use. Despite brutishness, scars, and the mangled mess of metal and flesh his visitor had for an arm, Syl saw intelligence in the man's eyes as they roved the room, taking in all details.

"Welcome," Syl told the man. "Have a seat. Sviroosa has been holding breakfast."

The visitor nodded, pulled out a chair, and examined its design with some interest before he sat. Syl clapped, and Sviroosa emerged from the kitchen with a clattering cartload of plates, mugs, and carafes. She arranged them on the table and scurried away.

"Victuur Haus." Aliara nodded at the newcomer then gestured to Syl. "Duke Sylandair Imythedralin."

The men clasped wrists in greeting.

Haus' cheekbones jutted as though he was starving, but the corded muscles of his neck and arms said otherwise. His nose had been adjusted more than once, running a sloppy path down his rugged face. And his many decorated scars were more grisly even than the ones speckling Aliara.

"Help yourself," Syl said. "Sviroosa is a marvelous cook."

Haus obliged, somehow filling his plate without actually looking at the food. He sniffed approvingly. Across the broad bridge of his nose, his snoot twitched in response. Syl tried not to stare. It was a feature of the species he'd never quite become accustomed to.

"Do you prefer Victuur or Haus?" he asked.

"I'm Fist at the Toh," he said between bites. "Outside, most call me Haus. You call me whatever you like."

"Haus it is," Syl said. "Aliara has given you the particulars?"

"An outline."

"Do you require more?"

"I'd like to hear it from you."

"As you wish." Syl took a sip of tea, savored the liquor he'd laced it with, and nodded. "I own a property on Temple Row. According to our mayor, it is infested with squatters. Aliara saw as much from the wall last night. How long they have lived there is unknown. I was bequeathed the property some twenty years ago, so they may have their own little village with a school and militia for all I know."

Haus' brow creased, and he glanced at Aliara. "Didn't go in?"

She shook her head.

"How many buildings on the property?"

Syl answered for her. "The main house and four outbuildings. I asked that she not enter the grounds until we had obtained proper support. Neither of us has set foot past the gate since my benefactor's death."

"Lotta potential for trouble."

"Yes." He took a long sip of tea before continuing. "Understandably, these people have taken advantage of my inattention. It is, however, time they were evicted. I am unconcerned with the methods you wish to employ, but they must be out by the dawn of the sixteenth. Every last one of them. Two days should be more than enough time for them to pack up their chattel and go."

Shoveling corn cakes into his mouth, Haus turned his stare to Aliara. She gazed back, eyes hooded and mild as always.

He swallowed. "You said there was an assistant."

Aliara nodded and rose, returning with a sleepy and disgruntled Schmalch. Haus stopped eating long enough to assess the puka.

"Do you panic?" he asked.

Schmalch blinked twice, brow furrowed. "Huh? No…uh, not usually," he said tentatively.

Syl resisted the temptation to laugh at the half-truth.

"You run when there's trouble?" Haus asked.

Schmalch shrugged.

"You stay out of the way when there's trouble?"

Schmalch nodded vigorously.

Haus turned back to Syl. "He do as he's told?"

"More or less."

"Right." Haus resumed eating.

Syl flicked fingers at Schmalch, who hurried from the room.

"Rift mentioned you had a rough plan," Haus said.

"The thought was to rouse them all, announce our intent, and hope they leave peacefully. Naturally, I would prefer we not be forced to kill anyone, but…" Syl waved his hand to indicate the alternative.

Haus dropped the fork onto the cleaned plate, pushed it away and, crossed his arms, eyes fixed on Syl's. "Do it after dark, after the streets wind down. More will be there, settling in for the night. You'll get increased results, fewer gawkers."

Syl held the intense eyes. "Go on."

"Spike the small gates shut. Force them out the main, ensure no one slips back in. Put a lookout on top of the house with a mag-rifle. Rest of the crew in the front. Make a big ruckus, get them all into the courtyard, and say what you have to say. They give you any back talk, we put the fear into them."

Syl pressed his fingertips together, properly matched, and tipped them to his thin lips. "If I asked you to kill one of the squatters?"

Haus nodded.

"Your team as well? Without question. No compunction, no moralizing?"

"If I take the jig and you pay, we'll do what's required."

"How many are on your team?"

"Four, including me."

"How quickly could you be ready?"

His eyes grew distant for a beat. "Four, maybe five hours. We need to reconnoiter, check for surprises."

"How much silver will this cost me?"

"Five bars each. Up front. Another five in the wake."

"Done."

"And we're going to need the right rifle, that's another ten. I know a guy who's trying to off-load one cheap."

Syl hesitated a moment, eyes narrowing. "And is that all?"

Haus nodded.

"Then we have a contract."

They skimmed palms and relaxed into their seats.

Syl fished a corner of toast from his plate and chewed thoughtfully, still watching his guest. "We may require your services again later," he said. "Would you be amenable to us housing you at the Belvedor Inn for a quartern?"

"Ten days seems reasonable." Haus cupped a hand over the

back of his neck. "You cover costs plus a ten-bar retainer. Squatters come back, we oust them at no charge. Different work, we negotiate cost. Agreed?"

"Agreed," Syl said. It wasn't even a nick in Orono's bequest.

SYLANDAIR

Syl stood in the courtyard of the Orono estate, studying the once-opulent main house. The waxing white face of Dormah cast an eerie light over the deteriorating building. Beneath his dark trench, a chill crept across his skin. He stymied a shudder before it could begin.

Despite its decay, the house stood proud. The colorful, twisted tip of its spire stabbed the night, looking like a fool's cap on the head of an elder sovereign. Scattered bricks and boards in the yard showed the truth of the battle with the years. Though the sandy brown masonry had deepened pleasantly over time, the brilliant mosaic trimming had faded into an indistinct morass. Once the riot of patterns drenched in reds and corals and bright yellows had delighted a young Sylandair. Today he found it merely a gaudy corpse.

For all its lifelessness, the dark eyes of the mansion windows still mocked Syl for his inevitable return. He turned away and took in the courtyards, the decrepit outbuildings, and long-neglected gardens and paths. Languid music drifted over the dividing wall from the neighboring Mucha Hall, invoking memories of days spent as a prisoner amongst this luxury.

Shaking his head, Syl turned his attention to the others. Aliara and Haus conferred only a few strides away. A bear of a man, larger even than Haus, shuffled restlessly at the mouth of the open gates, spiked knuckle-dusters on his meaty hands. An athletic, freckled woman leaned casually nearby. A crossbow dangled at her side, a patient smile rested on her lips. Syl vaguely recalled being introduced to them as Uuron and Rej, respectively. Highlighted by the crescent moon, he made out the shifting shape of the final crew member scaling the main house. Her name had already escaped him.

Schmalch squatted beside him, one of Sviroosa's copper cookpots and matching ladle in one hand. The already-filthy fingers of his free hand traced patterns in the footpath's dusty soil as he scrutinized the decaying building.

"This where you and Rift grew up, right, Duke?"

Syl nodded.

"Pretty nice. Lots better than the orphanage."

Syl aimed a disconcerting smile at him. "Then you should enjoy staying here during its autopsy."

"Really?"

"A presence is required." Syl tugged at the bottom of his vest, straightening the wide indigo and black stripes, then drew a watch from its pocket and made a show of checking the time. "Aliara and I most definitely will not be spending the night in this…this eyesore."

Schmalch's olive-green brow creased. "Doesn't look so bad to me."

Syl shrugged almost imperceptibly. He'd allowed Schmalch to remain in the guest room of the penthouse the past few days. Despite her silence, Syl knew the puka's presence was driving Sviroosa mad, and she was far too good a servant to test the limits of her patience.

"Hey, Duke." Haus strode up to Syl, small, thick cudgel in one hand. "The moons are up as much as they will be tonight," he said, and pointed to the candy-tipped tower. "Nyyata's in place. You ready?"

"Yes."

Haus raised a cupped fist to his mouth and produced an appalling sound meant to imitate the call of a nightjar. He repeated the noise twice more. From the heights of the minaret, flares sparked and tumbled to the ground, bringing the courtyard to life.

"When you're ready, Duke," Haus said.

Syl looked down at Schmalch. "Proceed, maestro."

With an energetic smile, Schmalch raised the pan and ladle and began a one-man riot of sound that had Syl covering his ears and itinerants pouring from the outbuildings. When a crowd of twenty or thirty had gathered, Syl gestured to Aliara, who snatched the makeshift instrument from Schmalch, leaving only the hum of confused voices.

Syl smoothed the lapels of his charcoal trench coat. He was ready to perform. "I do appreciate your prompt response," he said, voice raised above the crowd. "And I apologize for the late hour."

"What do you want, you fop?" came a call from the crowd.

"An excellent question. I want you to vacate my property."

The crowd's murmur grew louder.

"Quiet!" Haus roared. He took a step forward.

The crowd quieted.

"This has long been my property, but until recently I have had no interest in it. You have been allowed to live here due only to my indifference. Today I am taking possession." Syl glared at the crowd, anticipating a reaction.

"What proof do you have of your claim to this place?" asked a deep, resonant voice, one accustomed to oration.

The squatters parted, and a sallow karju strode from their midst, tattered tails of his piebald overcoat swaying behind him.

Syl withdrew a chit tin from his vest pocket and extended it to the man. "An attestation from our mayor."

"Tell him of our mission, Rector," called a crackled voice from the assemblage.

The Rector raised his hand to silence his congregation. He popped open the tin and locked an eye with the chit inside. After viewing the message, he turned and examined Syl as if confirming something for himself. "He does not lie. The rule of law makes this property his."

A woman's voice called, "What do we do, Rector?"

"We must convince him of the evil that calls this place its home." The man raised his arms to the onlookers, panicked chit still wriggling between his fingers. "We must educate him on our place here. He will understand the obligation we all have to keep the malevolence at bay."

Haus seized the chit and shoved the man back into the crowd.

"There will be no convincing, no educating, no understanding," Syl said. "You will leave these grounds and you will not return. I am not without generosity, so I will give you until the sunrise after next to remove your belongings, such as they are, and find new living quarters."

"Rector, cast him out," called one voice.

"Who will defend against it?" wailed another.

Soon most of them were clucking similar entreaties.

Having recovered himself, their leader stepped out of the throng. "You will not oust us, sir," he boomed "We are all that withstands the evil of this place. Without us, it would run rampant across the Haven, slaughtering all who stood in its path."

He continued droning in a similar vein. Syl motioned to Rej. She shifted into position at his side, crossbow pointed toward the sky.

The Rector, having worked himself into an impressive lather, spread his arms and threw back his head. "We are the chosen protectors of this defiled ground, placed here with the knowledge and the devices to ensnare the fiendish wickedness that dwells within! We are the adherents, the lone vessels who possess the will and the resolve to hold the malevolence at bay!"

"Enough!" Syl bellowed, head lowered, eyes raised.

"You cannot put this city at risk, sir. Whosoever enters the forsaken place shall not leave. Without us—"

Syl stalked forward, crowding the Rector until he was close enough to bite the man's lip. "I knew the evil that dwelt here." He spat out the words. "I lived by its sufferance, served its whims, looked into its eyes daily. You will leave here and you will do so quickly, or you will need to find a way to keep *my* evil at bay."

He spun on his heel and returned to his position alongside Rej. "Now," he said, voice calmer, "you will vacate, and you will do so within two dawns, or you will be removed. By whatever means necessary."

"We will not!" the Rector shouted. Other voices joined him, cheering him on. "We cannot allow that to happen. There are fewer of you, sir, than of us. We will stay, regardless of what the law says. Our spirit is needed to hold this evil…" He prattled on, louder and louder.

With two fingers, Syl adjusted Rej's crossbow into firing position.

"…and I tell you, sir, none of us will have on our heads the terror that will infiltrate this great city, sending its streets dark with the blood of all—"

"Now," Syl breathed.

Rej's finger twitched. The bolt drove smoothly through the Rector's forehead.

As blood burbled from his nose and mouth, he managed, "—fight you, sir…evil…" and crumpled to the ground.

A handful of screams came from the group before it scattered. Some dashed for the buildings they called home, others for the spiked-shut gates. The wisest among them circled around Syl and the others to escape through the front gate.

"Have them all out by sunrise on the sixteenth," Syl told Haus before stepping into the streets of Dockhaven, Aliara at his side.

NYYATA

Nyyata Untere stood at the base of the polychrome nightmare of a house. It dominated everything around it; her diminutive grey figure virtually disappeared in its presence. She and the swish new Bildvald 700 mag-rifle Fist had picked up were to serve as spotter and, if necessary, sniper for this jig. Simple enough work—a much easier pile of Callas than the last contract she finished. That crazy douse had damn near taken Nyyata's hand off with a cleaver when he'd spotted her reflection in a window. Picking off the scum of Dockhaven from a distance seemed like a vacation after that.

Fist and she had decided she'd perch on the colorful tower's widow's walk. The horrible thing seemed designed specifically for her purpose. From there, she could keep eyes on the irregularly shaped property.

With a few simple hops, she nimbly scaled the projecting solarium. A quick toss of the grappling hook and she climbed to the main roof, hustling down the ridgeline. She easily scaled the band of narrow windows circling the tower, but struggled with the concave channels of the tower's screw-like roof, finally flopping inelegantly into the gallery. Bits of shattered glass speckled the floor, jagged teeth of it poking from the space where windows had once been.

Weapon assembled and round chambered, Nyyata scanned the property through the rifle's multi-lens scope. Lights burned in some outbuildings, revealing the stirring shadows of unwary residents.

Uuron and Rej stood at the gate chatting, Fist and Rift close by. Their employer stood studying the house as though perplexed by its very existence, a grubby puka at his feet.

At Fist's sign—a half-assed bird call—Nyyata sparked her flinter, lit the flares, and tossed them into the courtyard like a minor meteor storm. The puka made a racket, and curious people emerged. While their employer gave his speech, she alternately watched the main gate and swept the grounds. The tower creaked and moaned around her, protesting in the wind. Below, a troublemaker had emerged. She caught only a few words on the wind. Their employer seemed to be handling it, but the drama rolled on too long. Swift endings were good endings.

She smiled when the conflict ended abruptly. The troublemaker lay in a growing pool of blood. The crowd scattered like panicked hens, surging this way and that in search of exit. Finger hovering alongside the trigger, she watched for outliers who might confront instead of flee. When things calmed, she lay the heavy rifle at her feet and shook out her arms. The creak of the settling tower seemed louder now that the shrieking had concluded. She stopped. That couldn't be right. The thing was so old, it should have settled long ago. She looked down its smooth sides for any sign the structure might give way. Though its decorative façade had been abused, the frame looked solid. The tower creaked again. Something hidden in the walls must be failing. She wanted out of this place before it tumbled down, taking her along for the ride.

She squatted and broke down the rifle. As she reached for her bag to stow it, motion caught her eye. She put a hand on the knife at her belt. A strange shape was emerging from a shadow on the floor of the gallery. She squinted at it, confused. The indirect light from the moons and flares had to be playing tricks with her eyes.

She groped in the bag, but all the flares were gone. She crouched and half-crawled toward the movement, flicking the flinter to life. Something like fingers crept their way from beneath a slowly opening trapdoor in the gallery floor. They were wrong, like a child's drawing. These weren't the elegant digits of a chivori, the fat fingers of rhochrot, not even the stubs of a puka. They were pale as Dormah, each with an extra knuckle. The fingers became a hand, as pale and elongated as its digits. A shadow drifted off the low moon, and its white light caught eyes glinting beneath the trapdoor. Something hissed.

Nyyata stumbled back, startled. Chiding herself, she drew her blade, surged forward, and with a quick stab, pinned the fumbling hand to the floor. The hiss turned to a screech and the door slammed open.

SYLANDAIR

2085 DANURAK 16

A haggard and disheveled Haus greeted Syl and Aliara at the gates of the now-empty grounds.

"Every last one gone." He swept an arm over the empty estate. "Place is all yours."

"Any problems?" Syl asked.

"Not really. Couple who went on about this being their home or more babble about evil. All gone now."

The approaching rhythmic creak of metal interrupted their exchange. From the direction of the carriage house, a thin, brittle-looking old man rounded the main building, cheerless scowl emphasizing the furrows of his face. He struggled to pump the pedals of an equally frail tri-wheel. Behind him trailed a wagon topped with an uneven tarp.

Haus flicked a Calla at the man as he wheeled past. From behind his dark lenses, Syl watched the old razee disappear into the morning traffic of the Row.

"Like I said, all gone now." Haus jerked his head toward the shed. "Only living thing left is a clowder living in the shed. Stinks like cat piss. We left them be."

"Schmalch will see to that," Syl said. "Do you anticipate any will return?"

"Doubtful after what's happened."

"Very well. Your crew will be at the Belvedor as agreed?"

"Our sniper seems uninterested. Did her job and left after the hubbub." He paused, cracking his neck casually as he spoke, then added with a scowl, "Owes me a rifle. Rej and Uuron are already settled at the inn."

"Should you be needed, we or one of our pukas will call there."

With a nod, Haus stalked away.

Syl contemplated the obscene playhouse on his way up the drive. In the autumnal dawn, its dilapidation was even more apparent. Flakes of the multi-colored metal leaf from the minaret's twisted dome littered the roof, giving the thing a leprous appearance. Substantial portions of fanciful hardwood detail—so expensive to import to this island-city—had rotted away. Tiles had cracked, split, and fallen like ill-cared-for dentition. To Syl's surprise, however, nearly all the windows were intact, even the lower levels' art glass lacked only a dozen or so panels. And the walls, though in disrepair, remained strong and straight. If he'd actually wanted the thing, it would take only a modest amount to restore.

Restoration, however, was far from his mind. Demolition was more in line after he and Aliara had wrung every secret from within its walls. Perhaps he'd have a breeding stable built. The aroma would certainly chap the Mucha congregating in the estate of one of their long-dead luminaries next door.

He chuckled. Aliara eyed him. "Nothing," he said.

From the breast pocket of his dobby blazer, Syl drew a long silver chain, two ornamented keys dangling at its end. He watched the pair revolve slowly in the morning light and considered the past they represented, the future they could resolve. A heaviness far beyond the weight of two keys settled in his chest, supplanting the emptiness of the past months.

A familiar shuffling from behind broke his trance.

"Duke, Duke! Wait up," Schmalch called. Beads of sweat dripped from his brow down the copious bridge of his sweeping nose. He puffed a little and leaned forward, hands on his knees. "Sviroosa sent me ahead. She hired a crew of four for the cleaning. They're coming with her. A couple of 'em even agreed to spend the night here to get more done." He straightened, thumbed his chest. "I'll be in charge of them, of course."

"I see. May we enter now?" Syl asked.

"Sure, sure."

Two locks, two clicks, and the door swung open. The smell of dust, heated and chilled by decades of passing seasons wafted forth. In the circular foyer the oak hall tree was slightly askew and the brass umbrella stand lolled on its side, though the stuffed caracata in repose remained fixed in its familiar position, feline eyes perpetually in search of prey.

Syl stepped inside, Schmalch at his heels.

At the entry to the parlor, the puka whispered, "By the dead hand of Leb," before dashing out the house, down the porch, and into the drive.

The décor Syl remembered was still there, but not in any sort of recognizable arrangement. The furniture had been knocked over and scattered haphazardly, books appeared to have flown from the shelves of their own volition, and Orono's precious mementos and other feck were scattered and shattered all over the floor. The fading of years had done no favor to the garish orange walls, though now the paint was spattered with wild spray patterns, some a rusty hue, others inky. Much of the room's other contents had been similarly spattered. Most unsettling was the collection of bones beside the overturned sofa that looked disturbingly like they once formed an arm.

"I can only guess that this has something to do with the evil the rector ranted about last night," Syl said.

Aliara nodded and stepped into the mess, examining familiar objects and dried blood spatter with equal interest.

"Duke!" yelled Schmalch, still several strides away from the porch.

Syl leaned out of the threshold. "Yes?"

"Sviroosa can't see that."

"She's an adult."

"Yeah, but that's too much. That's a—that's a lotta blood and all. She hasn't seen the stuff you and me've seen."

"Someone needs to clean it."

Schmalch shuffled, watching as the worn toe of his boot scored the dusty soil. He sighed and lifted his head, shoulders back. "I'll do it."

Syl removed his sunshades and raised an eyebrow. "You? I have been told of the deficiency of your cleaning."

"Me and two of the others—the ones who said they'd stay the night—we'll get rid of the...the gory stuff." He pointed to some of the outbuildings. "Put Sviroosa and the others on the rest of these. She can come in and do it up right when the nastiness is gone." He drew a few more circles in the dirt with his boot. "I, um, I don't know if they'll want to spend the night here, though, when they see all this."

"Very well," Syl said. He pointed a finger at Schmalch. "But *you* will be staying the night. I leave it to you to convince your charges to do the same."

Schmalch emitted a long, low keening sound, his shoulders wilting.

"Unless, of course, we're all torn to ribbons before night falls," Syl added.

The whine grew louder.

Syl closed his eyes, drew in air. "Very well. Catch our friend Haus, tell him to come back here and sweep the premises for anything with a taste for puka."

The irritating lament ceased, and Schmalch perked up.

"His fee will come out of your salary."

Again, Schmalch drooped.

"The choice is yours," Syl said.

The puka looked over his shoulder in the direction Haus had gone, then back at the house. "How much?"

"Two-hundred Callas, give or take. That again for each of his companions, should he need them."

Schmalch scrunched his face in thought. He earned three Callas a day for this work, and he'd only just worked off the advance Aliara had used to pay off his debts to Garl. Syl saw the moment Schmalch understood he could never pay off such a debt.

He peeked one huge, brown eye at the dreadful house, sizing it up. "Two extra Callas for every night I stay?" he proposed.

Syl stared at him, for a long moment. "Very well." He stepped aside, arm raised in a gesture of invitation. "Now get inside."

ALIARA

While Syl and Schmalch negotiated, Aliara explored. The chaos and bloodshed evident in the parlor extended through practically every room of the first floor. Thanks to the shattered picture window, the dining room was especially unruly. One end of the massive table was in pristine condition, chairs in place, wood intact. The other end was warped and rotting, coated in years of litterfall from the surrounding gardens and evidence of visits by stray cats, gulls, and just about every other form of local wildlife.

She passed through the swinging door into the kitchen, zigzagging through fallen pans and cutlery, shattered plates and glasses. It was a mess she didn't even care to examine. She tried the locked door at the room's rear, which lead to the cuddy of Orono's irrationally loyal steward, Flibuul, a rare ray of kindness in her youth. A quick pick of the lock showed her the quarters had remained unscathed by whatever else had happened in the main house. Flibuul's rigid orderliness was in place, though cobwebs and sun-fading had had their way with his precious few belongings.

Aliara roamed through the line of narrow rooms divided only by sliding doors. In the bedroom she found the ancient puka's mummified corpse laid out politely on the well-made bed. She wondered if he'd lived out the rest of his life in the tiny railroad apartment waiting for them all to return or if he'd simply given up and died when no one did. After a moment, she left him in peace, re-bolting the door behind her. When time permitted, she'd send him back to the sea.

She deliberately bypassed the music room and climbed the stairs to the second floor. The first door she passed, her old bedroom, was also locked. She left it that way. The floor's only other rooms— the library and four guest quarters maintained for visitors whose interests mirrored Orono's—were in varying states of shambles similar to what she'd seen on the first floor.

In one of the guest rooms, she paused to study the missing window. Glass littered the flagstone patio beneath. It had shattered outward. Aliara didn't care for the implication.

A low whisper nearby startled her.

"Sylandair?" she asked but received no answer.

She eyed the room's false wall. Orono had not intended for her or Syl to know about this clandestine space where he observed his unaware guests. Intrepid explorer that she was, however, young Aliara had stumbled into its concealed entrance early in her tenure here. She'd spent many days cloistered inside, hiding from him. She'd also witnessed things both colorful and horrifying while there.

Someone was in there now, watching her, whispering.

She rushed to the stairwell landing that separated second and third floors, rotated the left antler of the mounted rugaelk's head and stepped back. A full-length mirror mounted alongside the hunting trophy slid back and to one side, revealing the narrow, unfinished room within. Aliara stepped in and waited for her eyes to adjust to the darkness. She saw no one, only two pinpricks of light oozing from holes in the walls. She worked her way through the claustrophobic space until she reached the twin openings and peeked into the room. Still empty.

No one waited in the stairwell or the other rooms. She must have imagined the whisper. Or perhaps she'd only heard the muffled sounds of Syl and Schmalch chatting below. With a shrug, she climbed to the third floor. Orono's chamber also was locked, a state she had no interest in changing. Across the hall, the study door stood open. It, too, had been battered and bloodied, and it smelled stale edging toward fetid.

The room at the end of the hall she knew would be locked. It always had been. She ran nimble fingers over the silver knob and keyhole. This was the first lock she'd learned to pick. Aliara smiled, laid a cheek against the old wood of the door before she snicked it open and entered.

The room endured exactly as she remembered. Everything was precisely placed: Dressers equidistant from one another, bed perfectly made, washstand tidily arranged, bottles and brushes in strict lines across the vanity. She settled into the fainting couch alongside the vanity. It coughed a puff of dust in reply. She'd reclined on that couch, watching him brush and primp many times over.

She could almost smell Syl in here still.

Tucked into a corner near the pocket doors that opened onto Orono's room was the oversized green velvet chair. She rose, stroked the aging fabric. This was where they'd first had one another. The doors could have slid open at any moment to expose them to their owner, a risk that made the experience all the more intense and exciting.

That was where Syl found her, curled up, head draped over the chair's tall arm, smiling wickedly.

"Traipsing through the past?" he asked.

She patted the cushion beside her. "Care to join me?"

He smirked, though his eyes showed no happiness. "A lovely thought, but I'd just as leave do what must be done and go home."

She shrugged.

"Quite the odor built up across the hall," he said. "Enough that I only ducked in for a moment. I avoided the room's lavatory altogether. I shall put Sviroosa on purchase of new dibucs for the sanitary system when she arrives." He looked out the window above his old vanity. "I believe I'll stroll the grounds, maybe the library next. Care to join me?"

She shook her head. "Music room for me."

"Ah," he muttered distractedly. "Re-opening old wounds, are you?"

"Someone has to open that door."

He broke his stare, looked down at her. "Then you are the best for the job, Pet, among us or any other company."

A long pause hung between them. She watched the eyes of the boy who'd once lived here scan across his old room before they grew hard again.

Syl jerked his head toward the open door. "Quite the horror show out there."

"Only the unlocked rooms."

"Have you visited all the locked ones?"

"Only two."

"This and?"

"Flibuul's quarters."

"Ah." Syl leaned down and kissed her forehead. "I'll check in when I'm bored with the library." He started to leave, but stopped, hand on the doorknob. "Would you relock this when you leave?"

SYLANDAIR

The grounds were overgrown and wretched. The once-beautiful gardens were trampled and largely dead. A last-gasp blossom crinkled on the rosebushes that lined the high estate walls. The scrupulously cobbled paths were broken and speckled through with moss and weeds. Shrubs once pruned into fanciful shapes now surrounded the house like brown skeletons. The squatters may have lived here, but they did little to make the place a home. Evidence of their unwelcome presence was written all over the estate. Crushed hay and dirty blankets littered the building that once had served as carriage house and stables. In the shed behind it, the Rector's people had kept a number of rusty barrels, those used as cooktops in one room, those used as toilets in the other. Syl did not envy Sviroosa the job ahead of her.

Past those buildings, he stopped at one of the surviving fruit trees, plucked an orange, and slid down its trunk to sit, settling in to contemplate the servant's cottage. Three karju men had lived there. Before his arrival, Syl had never met anyone of any species beyond his own. At least not that he remembered. The men had seemed enormous and frightening to young Sylandair. Like most karju, their bones were thicker and broader than the familiar, elegant chivori frame. In adulthood, the disparity in height between the species was minimal, but still karju bodies simply consumed more space. Today, Syl was unperturbed by the contrast. As a child, he'd been dazed by their size.

With time and proximity, he'd outgrown of his fear of two of them. Reye, a one-time street performer, maintained the grounds. He was kind enough to spend companionable time with Syl here and there, even teaching him some sleight of hand as well as volumes about gambling. Iruund was Orono's driver and groom. He was more reserved than Reye, but never hateful to either of the children. Syl had spent many happy, quiet aftermids with Iruund and the horses.

The third man, Nushgha, was a big, burly slab of an idiot who served as the guardian of the grounds. Nushgha was the reason Syl had remained trapped here long past the age when he'd become sexually unappealing to the master of the house.

"If ever you leave my custody or these grounds without permission," Orono had told his fresh wards, "Nushgha will hunt you down and snap your brittle little necks like the twigs they are."

The hulking man towered behind his master as Orono delivered the threat. "Nah, too easy," Nushgha interrupted, leering with his one good eye, lips curled in a snarl. "I won't make it fast. I'll cut off your pretty fingers and toes and feed them to you. Then I'll cut off your hands and turn them into lobe rings for your fancy chivori ears. Before I cut out your eyes, I'll make you watch as I slit open your belly and pull out your—"

"That is enough Nushgha." Orono waved him off. "I believe they understand the dire consequences of departing my company."

Thereafter, Nushgha delighted in Syl and Aliara's fear. He repeated his threats regularly, startled and frightened them whenever possible, and generally did all he could to maintain the children's terror of him. When they were disobedient, Nushgha doled out the punishment. When they were well-behaved, he only cuffed them now and again for fun. His satisfaction with this pursuit was unmistakable.

Once, at age eleven, Syl found the courage to refuse Orono's request for a communal shower. The old diddler huffed and puffed his way across the hall to the study balcony and shouted to Nushgha, who bounded up the stairs with a smile. He dragged Syl into the courtyard and beat him mercilessly. Two broken arms, several cracked ribs, and a fractured jaw were the punishment for the brazen rebuff. While the surgeon worked on him, Syl had pleaded with his eyes, but the man merely bandaged and medicated the boy before Nushgha chucked him into the carriage and took him home. No one, it seemed, questioned the activities of the brilliant Kluuta Orono.

When he dropped Syl in bed, the big man had leaned in close, the bitter tang of his breath in Syl's nostrils. "Next time you say 'no' to your master, it'll be your little girlfriend who takes the beating." Nushgha patted Syl on the head and left him with that thought.

Even after they'd won their freedom, the fear of Nushgha persisted. He became their singular obsession, the bugaboo around every corner waiting to grab them. Their first decision as free people was to rid themselves of him.

They found and followed him, learned his rhythms, and watched for weakness. Opportunity came at last when The Sword and Sheath arrived in town. The pleasure barge rarely anchored in Dockhaven's Rimadour Bay. When it did, anyone with coin in their pocket flocked to it, debauching until their Callas ran out. Nushgha was no exception.

They scrambled for two sleepless days to pilfer enough Callas to buy their way on board. They bypassed the gaming tables and erotic diversions without a glance as they searched the barge for Nushgha, finally locating him in an upper-deck cabin, joggling a buck-toothed blonde. He had her bent over the balcony railing, a liquor bottle in one hand, the other slapping the woman's generous rump as he pumped away. Syl and Aliara lighted on the edge of the room's unused bed to wait for Nushgha to complete his performance.

When he'd finished, Nushgha reached around his partner and squeezed her breast with an accompanying "moooo."

"Let's hit the bed for a bit, big tits," he said.

The woman giggled. Nushgha started inside, but hesitated,

liquor-blurred eyes straining to focus on his guests. Recognition didn't take long.

"What are you two puddles doing here?" he slurred.

"We came to pay you a visit," Syl said.

"Oh you have, have you?" he asked with a wobbling lunge toward them. He'd hoped for a flinch, but neither moved. He smiled. "What'cha got planned? You two gonna gang up on me?"

Syl raised one shoulder and dropped it.

"'T'zat why Master O never came home? You two do sumthin' to him?"

They watched the naked man impassively.

"Just gonna sit there and gawk at me?" He scratched his pimpled ass. "Me and the girl are gonna need that bed."

"We can share it, sweet thing," the woman chimed in.

"Wait. Share it? Oh-ho-ho. I get it now. You want some, too?" Nushgha laughed and stroked his dwindling member, near-empty bottle still dangling from his other hand.

Aliara smiled. She stood and walked over to him, unbuttoning her jacket as she went.

"Yeah, I knew it. We got unfinished business, don't we, little girl?" He wrapped his tanned paw around her pretty grey neck. "Let's see what I can do with this scrawny thing first." His eye shifted to Syl. "Then it's your turn, boy."

Nushgha pitched his head back to drain the final drops of the khuit into his mouth. From her sleeve, Aliara drew a push dagger. She made one quick slice. Nushgha dropped both the bottle and Aliara.

"What did you do, you quim?" he asked.

She handed Syl Nushgha's severed fid.

"Now," Syl said, drawing his own blade, "I believe…"

Nushgha leapt forward, swinging his brick of a fist at Syl, who ducked and drove his dagger into the man's shoulder. Booze-numbed, Nushgha came back for another attempt, blood spattering the cabin floor with each step. As he dove toward Syl, Aliara leapt onto his back and thrust the tip of her weapon into Nushgha's spine. He folded like a rag doll, lone gold eye rolling in his head.

The trull, still hovering near the railing, let out a small squeak. Syl held a finger to his lips and tossed the rest of the Callas he'd stolen in her direction.

Nushgha spat blood as he bellowed incoherently.

Syl stood straddling the prostrate figure, slowly drawing his blade from the meat. "As I was saying, I believe there was talk of feeding someone something. A few years past, perhaps, but a memorable conversation nonetheless."

"That was—that was just a threat," Nushgha said, fear in both voice and expression. "He wanted you to stay put. I was never gon—"

Syl shoved the amputated organ into Nushgha's mouth and ran a bloodied finger down the dent in the man's scraggly chin.

"Now where to begin?" Eyebrows raised, Syl looked at Aliara settled on the bed.

"Dealer's choice," she said.

Syl had ensured that Nushgha watched it all before he removed that shiny eye and tossed the bits that remained into the bay.

The orange now eaten, peel politely piled at his side, Syl stretched and yawned. He'd visited The Sword and Sheath more than once since that day, fully enjoying all the entertainment offered there. On each visit, he rented a very special cabana. Rising, he brushed loose grass from his trousers and returned to the main house.

ALIARA

Aliara stood in the music room, taking in the instruments that littered the floor, hung from the walls, and lined the shelves. It was a space only Syl, the household's lone musician, used with any regularity. She would have liked to learn, to join him, but that privilege wasn't for her. She was only allowed to pass through the room, hands slapped if she dared to touch anything. She'd spent hours as a child lying in her bedroom directly above, listening to him practice piano, clavichord, anything with keys, until she was able to hum each tune with him as he played. Once Orono was gone, he had quit music. A little piece of her mourned its passing.

Her eyes settled on the never-played chellarin, now flopped onto its face. When standing the bulky instrument covered the first of the secreted doors, its seams hidden by the patchwork of wooden tiles covering the walls. Each tile was cut at a different depth, so while some fit flush to the wall, others protruded into the room. The sculptural effect, while striking and effective in its purpose, must have been a nightmare for Flibuul to keep free of dust.

Behind this door lay another room and another door that would take her to Orono's basement lab. Though she knew the route well, she had never sussed out its secrets. Whenever Orono called her to the lab for one of his many experiments, he was sure to open both doors before she arrived. When she'd snuck in to uncover the secrets, the chellarin had proven too great an obstacle. Either she was too small to lift it or, when she'd grown sufficiently, it had been impossible to move noiselessly. No matter how delicately she handled the thing, its resonant thrum alerted the entire household to her activities.

As if to remind her of its purpose, the chellarin's remaining strings complained atonally when she shifted it into the corner. She discarded the urge to give the thing a good kick and ran fingers around the hidden door's seam, but found no triggers or switches. She moved out, probing the surrounding tiles. One near the top corner wiggled suspiciously and she pressed it. The door swung open with a soft wheeze.

The room beyond was swathed not with wooden tiles like the music room, but with large, rolled-steel panels bound in riveted bands. Even the floors and ceiling were paneled. It was like stepping into a long-closed restaurant's cooler. The air inside was stale and cold. She slipped in, the soft stroke of her steps rustling faintly against the metal. A steel door took up most of the wall to her left, combination dial flanked by two keyholes set at hip height into its face.

She crouched and studied the setup. The keyholes were curious, not straight up and down like the usual, but broad, almost squarish, yet rounded on two sides. She closed her eyes, picturing the shape of the shaft to fit the opening. Her lids flicked open and she smiled. She needed Syl's silver chain of keys.

Poking her head out of the room, Aliara called, "Keys?"

A distant voice replied.

She stepped into the empty hallway, catching a flicker of movement near the stairs. She turned. Nothing. Syl was playing with her. Peculiar, given their location, but perhaps he'd changed his mind about the green chair. She scaled the stairs, found his bedroom door still locked. She let herself in. No Syl lounged in the chair, sprawled on the bed, or even lolled in the oversized tub. Unaware she was doing so, Aliara stuck out her lower lip and pouted.

Movement flickered at the edge of her vision. A whisper tickled her ear, louder now. She could almost make out words. She turned, expecting to find him behind her, smiling that rapacious smile of his, but found nothing. She frowned. The prize at the end of this game best be worth her effort.

After finding the third floor empty, she travelled down. She'd only just stepped on the second floor when the whisper returned, this time coming from her old room. So that was his game. She jimmied the lock and scanned the room. Everything seemed the same—things slightly chaotic but in place, bed mostly made, closet door firmly closed—yet it felt different, like a dusty phantom of the hole she'd once called home. Her things had always been second-hand, old and worn, but now they looked almost brittle. Her few books' spines were broken or absent, dolls had no hair or worse, cosmetics were merely stubs plucked from the trash. Her eyes fell on the bed, where faded black speckles stained the sheets. Reminders of the many surgeries. It had been a pathetic life.

She peeked into the lav and found it vacant as well. That left only the closet. She stared at the door as she might an objective on a jig. The weird doorknob stared back, a young face locked eternally in a moan of either pain or ecstasy. Aliara took two long strides, turned the knob, and ducked into the closet, careful to avoid the painting that hung opposite her pitiful collection of clothing. She wanted to be near the watercolor now no more than she had back then.

Cut in simple, happy colors, a ring of smiling puka danced in the Abinoth sunshine, ribbons eddying between them, wildflowers beneath their feet. The image shouldn't have bothered her, but it was wrong, horrible in a way she could never articulate. The revulsion—almost fear, actually—was irrational. She'd tried once to touch it, rip it from the wall, but as soon as her fingers had brushed it, she'd blacked out. Syl found her later, still unconscious on the closet floor.

She blamed the connection between her closet and the visits to Orono's lab for her distress. The instant the old man came into her space, heaving his bulk toward her closet, she knew the rest of the day—if not the whole quartern would be spent in the cool sterility of the basement, at the mercy of his needles and knives. Her adult mind assured her that was the cause, but the child within insisted the painting itself was vile.

She hissed softly at the painting, cutting off the sound as the whisper returned, a low lull inside her head. The words were so close, almost real. She dashed out of the closet, out the room and into the hall. Syl was leisurely ascending the stairs.

"Stop," she said.

He halted mid-step, looked at her quizzically.

She bridled. "It's not cute anymore."

"What?"

"Your game. It's annoying."

His brow knit. "Really, Pet, I do not know what you mean. I have been outside, enjoying an orange."

She closed the distance between them. He smelled of orange rind.

"Who else is here?" she asked.

"I saw Schmalch in the dining room, providing the other two with his own brand of management. It did appear that they have made some progress."

She studied his face in search of a lie.

"Maybe it's just this place, Darling Girl," he said. "Being here is doing unpleasant things to me as well."

She snorted.

"The sooner we finish, the sooner we can leave." He ran a thumb over her lips and bent to kiss her.

She returned the kiss, willing herself to relax. It was just old ghosts, dark memories, nothing more. She'd been toying with herself.

"Were you looking for me?" he asked.

"I need the keys."

He drew the silver chain from his vest pocket and coiled it into her outstretched palm. "Any particular reason?"

"Keyholes."

"Yes, I assumed. Why not simply pick them?"

"*Fancy* keyholes." She jangled the blocky keys. "Easier this way."

"Very well. Let me know when you have broken through."

She grunted at him and jogged back down to the steel-paneled room. When she inserted the key, it stopped halfway up the teeth. She tried it in the other keyhole then repeated the procedure with the second key, each time receiving the same result.

She unfurled her tool roll, drew her short hook, and tapped it in each lock. Something obstructed the keyway. Though she might be able to breach it, she risked damaging the whole system.

She moved to the combo lock. Ear pressed to the door, she gave the dial a quick spin. Only a bright ratcheting *zizz* replied. She sat back, scowled at the thing, and rubbed the tickle from her jaw. Slowing herself, she tried again, but heard only a more leisurely version of the same crisp chatter, unable to discern the click of pin against fly beneath the din.

Working by touch was tedious, and far from her favorite approach, but it wasn't impossible. She closed her eyes and took the dial gingerly, feeling the internal movements in her fingertips, searching for the slightest hesitation, the subtlest hitch in the dial's motion.

When she found the final notch and the fence collapsed, a metal *snick* rewarded her. She tried the keys again. Barrier retracted, they slid in easily. She turned one in each lock. From inside came the delightful *whir* of something mechanical. Aliara sat back, ready for the door to rise, revealing the concrete stairs beyond.

Instead, it did nothing.

SCHMALCH

Being boss suited Schmalch. The two workers he was in charge of, Glech and Munk, didn't question his authority. They worked pretty fast, too. They'd tried to run off at first when they saw the dried-up blood and guts. With a bit of pleading, however, Schmalch snagged them each an extra Calla a night if they stayed and worked. It was twice what they'd been promised. They stayed.

The Duke and Rift had been shuffling around the place all morning, talking in low tones and generally acting weird. Schmalch heard their footsteps on the stairs, pacing the floors of different levels, wandering to one side of the building, then the other. It seemed strange.

When Rift last came downstairs, she stuck her head in the dining room, eyebrows pressed low, nostrils flared.

"Leave me alone," she'd snapped.

Schmalch enthusiastically swore he and his crew would stay away.

The Duke hadn't seemed much like himself either. In contrast, he was quiet and distant. Quite the change from the smart guy Schmalch was used to. He wasn't sure what was going on with either of the chivori, but leaving them both alone seemed like the best idea. Schmalch would keep his head down and stay out of their way until they left for the night. Pretty soon they'd both be back to normal and they'd appreciate everything he was doing for them. His crew had accomplished plenty in just a few hours today, and this was the worst room. The Duke would be pleased with his decision to put Schmalch in charge.

An insistent rumble from his stomach interrupted the puka's enjoyment of his own success. A peek through the missing window showed the sun had started its descent. They'd long since missed lunchtime.

"Men," he said from his perch atop the dining room table, "it looks good in here. Good enough for Sviroosa to see, even. Let's break for some food. We'll finish clearing and board up this window when we get back. Then we'll call it a day."

"Good," Munk said. He dropped a shovelful of rotting leaves and started toward the door.

Glech stood and wiped his forehead. "How long?"

"Ummm…would an hour be good?" Schmalch asked.

His crew nodded.

"We're not from 'round here," Glech said sheepishly. "Where can we, uh, afford anything?"

"Right. Hmmm…it's kinda' a walk, but we're close…there's a guy with a tri-wheel grill that rides up and down the North Pipe. Stops near the desal plant around this time before he heads back south. You should still be able to catch him."

Glech nodded. "Comin' with?"

"Maybe tomorrow." It was nice to be included, but he had other ideas of what to do with the time. "I need to check out this place a bit more, see where we can bunk. Can you bring me back something?"

"Sure."

Schmalch fished out ten coppers. "This should cover it. Put the leftover on yours." He was a good boss.

When they'd gone, Schmalch hopped down from the table and stuck his head in the room where he'd last seen Rift. A big piece of the wall was open, and he could hear her muttering inside. He decided it would be wise to leave her alone as requested and explore on his own.

He wandered through the level, flicking open the shutters on the lumia lamps, recently resupplied and fed by Munk, as he passed each room. Most rooms featured crank-powered cap-lights too, but the Duke had announced that he preferred the subdued glow of the lumia algae, as the glare of the mechanical stuff strained his eyes. Schmalch didn't understand why chivori were so fussy. Light was light.

The kitchen, which looked like a waterspout had hit it, would be tomorrow's project. He and his crew would need someplace to cook. Munk said he made a pretty good version of his grandma's neha root stew, and Schmalch loved home-cooked food. He picked up a couple pans, checked the plumbing, and opened a few cupboards before noticing a door at rear of the kitchen. He jiggled the knob. Locked.

Drawing a bent metal rod and an old hairpin from his vest pocket, Schmalch tickled the pins and the door swung open. Inside was a narrow room with an open sliding door at the rear. Past that, he could see another doorway and another, all ending with a one-seater lav. The place looked in good shape, things still in place, no spatters. Only the dust needed cleaning. Sviroosa could come in here without them doing anything. He should take a good look around first, though. Just in case.

Schmalch pawed the geegaws in the first room, pocketing a pair of old Callas wasting away in a candy dish. Nothing else seemed worth his effort. Through the first door he found a tidy bedroom. On the bed lay what looked like something he'd seen when the Vintonae Circus had visited Dockhaven. The temple elders had taken them all to see the marvel, doling out three wondrous coppers per child to spend as they wished. Some kids saved theirs, but Schmalch spent his on food and a visit to the cabinet of curiosities. Everything inside was weird and fascinating—bugs with chivori eyes, fish with legs, birds with two heads—but the main attraction really caught Schmalch's attention. It was a woman-ish creature laid out in a glass box. She had funny lumps all over her throat and green hair. Schmalch couldn't tell what species she was. She was slight like a chivori, but her skin was pinkish-brown like a karju and her eyes, or rather the empty sockets, were large and set wide, toward the sides of her head like a puka. He edged toward the display cautiously, jumping when the cabinet's owner spoke.

"She was a lady in waiting from the courts of lost Vosharilim," he told Schmalch. His eyes twinkled beneath a tall, ratty velvet hat. "Under the sands of Tehtaemah she slumbered for untold centuries before the tomb was found by an unlucky herdsman. He took her back to his family's homestead, and that night she rose and consumed their flesh." He opened his dark cape and waved an arm toward a worn brown curtain. "Through this veil waits her sisters and their king. Only twelve more coppers and you can gaze upon a monarch, my lad."

Schmalch neither had the coin nor did he care to spend any more time around creatures who might eat him. He hurried away, but the monstrous thing stuck with him, haunting his dreams for days. He forced himself awake, convinced she would come for him if he dared close his eyes. Only when Elder Eliigia caught Schmalch sleeping during lessons did he confess the truth of these nightmares. She rolled her eyes and told him it was just a wax dummy, made up to attract and frighten chumps. He'd slept easy that night.

Nothing to be scared of here either. He stole forward and touched the thing's foot. When nothing happened, he moved up to the head. The face was puka-like and still, features sunk in on themselves, nothing like the cabinet woman at all. The skin clung to the bones and teeth, the eyelids were pulled slightly apart to reveal blackness behind them, the once-proud nose had collapsed into a sharp fin proceeding from the crown to the deflated lips.

Schmalch poked the thing's cheek. The surface turned to dust. His finger went through, touching dry, smooth teeth. This was *not* wax. He yelped and hopped back, waiting for the fiend to rise and try to eat him. After a long moment, Schmalch scampered out the door, re-locked it. Munk and Glech would need to help him deal with this before any of them could sleep tonight. Definitely before Sviroosa could be allowed inside.

Still unconsciously rubbing corpse dust from his finger, Schmalch climbed to the second floor, past a depressing-looking little bedroom that hadn't been touched by the blood spatters found in the rest of the house. Further down the hall he found the Duke in a room filled with row after row of book-lined shelves and stacks of books and papers. He was in the room reading and tossing things about. Also good to avoid. Schmalch wasn't much for books anyway.

He skulked along the corridor, stopping at each of the fancy bedrooms. All four were gory like the first floor, but they weren't as ruined. It wouldn't take much effort to make them good enough to use tonight. He *could* get a head-start on prepping the rooms while Munk and Glech were gone, but a third, unexplored floor loomed overhead, waiting for his inspection.

The third level was quiet and hot and featured only three doors, two of them locked. The unlocked room had a balcony and a big lav, along with some unpleasant drag marks and obliterated furniture. The whole place smelled like dock night at the Barnacle.

Schmalch covered his nose with his sleeve as he poked though the assorted dross. One of the walls was dusty-black and covered in white writing, another was hung full of paintings of some doughy baldish man alongside shiny pieces of paper in frames. All the walls and glass were blood-spattered like everything else around here. Even the ceiling was stained, though judging from the color, it probably wasn't blood. He was considering what the blotch might be when his eyes drifted down to where a safe half-again Schmalch's height lurked. He ran his tongue over dry lips. He might be able to crack it. Amazing things could be inside. He took two steps toward the safe and stopped, shaking his head. This was the Duke's stuff, and messing with what was the Duke's was a bad idea. Plus, he had to get away from that smell. He'd put Munk on this room tomorrow.

His crew should make a first pass before Sviroosa and her crew had to deal with that stink. He slipped out, locking the door behind him.

The door furthest from the stairs was as easily picked as the one in the kitchen. Expecting another dried-up corpse, Schmalch entered cautiously.

He found only an empty bedroom, big and in such perfect condition, it looked as though someone might still live there. He pattered across the sun-bleached rug and sat on the bed, bouncing a little. This room was nicer than the ones downstairs and wouldn't require much cleaning. This room should be his. After all, he was the boss, so he should have the best room. He poked around in drawers, moved some bottles on the vanity and wandered into the spacious closet. It was packed with beautiful clothes, the kind Rift had stolen from the Yenderot cave. The kind he saw the Duke wear.

He backed out of the closet, suddenly aware of whose room this used to be. He couldn't sleep here. The Duke would…would… well, Schmalch didn't know what the Duke would do, but it probably wouldn't be good. He needed to leave.

He made it all the way to the exit before he noticed a second door right by the one he'd come in through. It stood open, dark room beyond tempting him. He hesitated a moment then reached in and cranked the light. It was the biggest lav Schmalch ever seen—even bigger than the common one at the orphanage, or the public pots at the Barnacle. Twenty puka could have fit in the tub and more than twice that in the shower. A little room within the room sat alongside the big shower. Courage screwed up, he pushed the door open.

A lone toilet sat inside a cubby bigger than the bunk room he had shared with three others at the orphanage. He couldn't imagine why anyone would need this much space to use a pot, but he certainly wanted to find out. Staying at the Duke's was the first time Schmalch had used a private lav, and he'd grown to enjoy the time alone. This could be quite the experience. He'd just have to wait until the new dibucs were installed.

He left the luxury stall and opened the room's remaining closed door, opposite the one he'd entered. He was unprepared for what waited inside.

Enormous animals looked back at him. They were poised to attack, with teeth and claws bared. Schmalch yipped, slammed the door, and hid in the big stall beside the pot. He waited to be attacked, but there was nothing—no clawing, no growling, no gnashing of teeth.

He crept back through the washroom and peeped in again. The animals were still there, ready to pounce, but they didn't so much as glance in Schmalch's direction. He paused, barely breathing, waiting for them to move. They didn't. He crept into the room and poked the ceiling-high bear in the thigh. A bit of dust blew back at him. Its body was soft and furry, but cold and still. He'd heard about this sort of thing from a trader who visited the Barnacle a lot, but until visiting this weird house, he'd never believed in such things. He'd seen that big cat thing downstairs and the heads on the walls, but this was way more. Kind of silly. Why would anyone want to stuff a bunch of dead animals and keep them in their bedroom?

A big black bird missing a wing posed on one foot between the bear and a selachai with raised paw. A bit away from the others, a beaver taller than Schmalch crouched on its haunches and gnawed a piece of wood, smiling at him with big teeth, so stained they looked like hearth bricks A shiny little plaque was stuck to the front the platforms on which each animal stood.

He squatted in front of the bear. He knew it was a bear because it looked like the drawings of bears from the picture books of his youth, with a brew-barrel chest, flat head, and pointed muzzle, long forelegs, and thick claws. Schmalch gingerly poked one of the claws and stroked the coarse, rust-brown fur on top of its foot. Even if he were daring enough to rub the white belly fur, he doubted he could reach it. With a sigh, he squinted at the bear's plaque, but couldn't make out the weird words. He didn't want to come close enough to check the plaque of the grey-furred selachai, whose big fangs looked perfect for tearing pukas to bits. He recognized "*swamp*" on the bird's plaque, but nothing else. When he came to the beaver, however, he knew all the words: "*Giant Tolknor Beaver.*"

These big creatures flanked a wall of shelves littered with smaller, age-worn stuffed animals—squirrels, hares, chiviot, lotsa different birds, even a regular old cat with one of its fluffy bent ears missing—mixed with a bunch of multi-colored, multi-shaped clocks. Schmalch had never had his own clock before and, given his record with mechanical things, neither the temple elders nor the Duke allowed him to touch their clocks. He reached out and spun the longer arm on a particularly shiny clock covered in twisted blue barbs. He giggled softly and picked it up. Jutting from its back was a metal wing-shaped thing that turned. Lover of knobs and levers, Schmalch rotated the wing-thing until it would move no more. The clock ticked delightfully for a few clicks before a *bwoing* abruptly ended his fun. Unsettled, Schmalch set it back in place and edged away.

He looked around the rest of the room and gasped. This was a magical place—like its own little house inside the big house. The main attraction was a canopy bed, covered in pink and black fabric and so big stairs were required to climb into it. In front of some fancy glass doors that opened onto a balcony sat a dinky round table and two chairs covered in shiny pink velvet. Set inside the big round bump-out—part of the colorful, twisting tower outside, he guessed—were a bunch of dirt-filled pots. Dried feck that might once have been plants littered the area around them. A single oversized chair sat in front of a hulking fireplace, an empty glass on the tiny table beside it.

He briefly wondered if this had been Rift's room but dismissed it. He couldn't picture her here no matter how hard he tried.

He was delighted to find there was more bedroom around a corner, two fluffy chairs on one wall, two tall cabinets opposite them. They both looked really old. He dragged a chair over, climbed up and, inspected the two weird cabinets. The first was more of a stand really. On top was a metal toy the style of which he'd never before seen. A shiny silver ball the size of Schmalch's head jutted from a steel spoke poking from a stand. Just below the ball, three metal arms of varying lengths stuck out of the spoke. At the end of two of the arms were other, smaller balls, one painted green, one white. Attached to the third arm was a flat disc that ran a ring around the main ball. Underneath the whole thing was a plate painted with the marks he recognized as the calendar. He batted the green ball. It spun in a circle on its post while the arm rotated around the silver ball in the middle. He shrugged. A weird toy, but he could see the entertainment value.

The other cabinet, a box roughly the height of the Duke and twice as wide, was covered with pretty, painted carvings of flowering vines and long-tailed birds. On its front were two pairs of doors, one on top of the other. A row of vertical slits ran along the top of one side, a fancy brass crank sticking out below them. Schmalch went straight for the crank. With each turn, a pleasant ratcheting vibration echoed from inside the chest, tickling his hands. He cranked until it wouldn't move. Brimming with anticipation of something amazing, he released his grip. Nothing happened.

He frowned at the crank, hopped off the chair, and opened the lower set of doors. Inside was a stack of metal discs covered with little holes. They reminded him of cake plates attacked with a hammer and awl. He closed those doors and shifted the chair and opened the uppers. A lone disc stood there like a platter on its edge, held it in place by a swing arm, toggle switch nestled where arm joined cabinet.

Not wanting the disc to fall on him, but desperately needing to meddle with something inside the box, Schmalch flicked the switch. The disc began rotating. A slow, sickly music tinkled from the slits on the box's sides, gradually picking up speed as the disc spun faster and faster until it found its pace. He stood in awe, listening as a happy tune poured out. He'd never seen a melody engine quite like this.

"Mister Schmalch?" Glech called from out in the hall. "Vrasaj?"

Schmalch scampered back through the luxurious bath and out the Duke's bedroom door, locking it as he left. He knew which room he'd claim while staying here.

HAUS

After handing off the property to his employer in the morning, Haus enjoyed a well-deserved nap through the shank of the day. Emptying the estate had become ugly toward the end. Booting people out of places they called home was never pretty. Since this place had never belonged to the squatters to begin with, Haus had little compunction about his work. Plus, they had been given more than two days; they knew what was coming.

He sauntered down the stairs of the Belvedor Inn toward its lounge, the Zephyr Room, essentially another windless Dockhaven alehouse with a fancy name. Rej sat at a high-top, empty stools flanking her, a glass held lightly in her fingertips. She'd dolled herself up tonight. Delicate metal feathers hung from the pointed tips of her ears, her shapely legs visible beneath a shiny red skirt. With an amused smile, she watched Uuron parked at the bar, petting and cajoling some big-bubbed trawler sitting on his lap. No one enjoyed the looser things in life like Haus' cousin.

"—then I grabbed that big hairy wolf and pulled until its leg came off," Uuron said, his voice thundering yet jolly.

Haus recognized the story as a wildly inflated version of work they'd done last winter on Cammoranth. A starving pack had grown a bit too friendly with some local farmers' livestock. His crew was hired to run them off or exterminate them. Few creatures were as relentless as a hungry wolf, but they'd done the job quickly and with no further herd losses. No wolves, however, had been dismembered in the manner Uuron described. The entire experience consisted of nothing more than several late nights waiting for the prowling beasts, and a few well-placed shots.

Made a great story, though, when Uuron told it.

"Even with one leg missing, it came after me. It was snarling and slobbering and bleeding all over the place. So I whacked it with its own leg. Bam! Snapped its neck," Uuron continued. He slid a hand into the woman's blouse, she giggled and ran a hand over his lightly stubbled tawny head. "I swear to you, the thing was as big as me—bigger maybe."

At that, Rej barked out a laugh. Uuron turned his mischievous smile to her and winked. She raised her glass to her mouth but continued shaking with amusement.

"Victuur was there that night," Uuron said, fingers enthusiastically working beneath the woman's shirt. "He can back me up. Worst wolf we ever saw, right?"

Haus nodded obligingly. "Terrible thing."

"What'd I tell you, lovely? And I'm still here to tell the tale." He paused and winked at Haus, who knew what was coming. Uuron tipped his head toward his cousin's multitude of scars. "Plus, I don't look nearly as bad as this dirty old razee, now do I?"

The woman again giggled and smoothed a finger over the tracery covering Uuron's scars. Haus wondered if she was even capable of speech, or merely communicated in giggles. Uuron peered past her bosom to where another woman sat.

"Have you met my cousin?" he asked the woman, gesturing to Haus.

She shook her head playfully and twirled a shiny gold curl around her finger. Haus suspected she giggled a lot, too.

"Maybe later," he said, then aimed a finger toward Rej and gave Uuron a nod.

The big man coaxed the trawler off his lap. "Back in a bit,

sweetheart. Don't you go jogglin' with someone else while I'm busy."

She and her friend swung their hips to a table where a crowd of sailors' wives burbled. Haus recognized the type: Beached and bored by their husbands' absence.

Uuron held up three fingers and whistled to the barman before he joined Haus and Rej at the undersized bar table. "Where's Nyyata?"

"Haven't seen her since she went up the tower," Haus said.

Rej nodded, a whimsical look on her face. Haus eyed her. "What?"

"She mentioned something about a fat jig near Guunaat," Rej said. "Though last I talked to her, she was leaning against it. Too risky."

Haus' eyes narrowed. He didn't like his crew taking jobs without his knowledge. They were welcome to other work, but he wanted to know about it.

"That gal she's been seeing from somewhere up in the Nors— went by Despoilt or something equally self-important, her name's actually Rhuran—anyway, Rhuran was taking the jig. Maybe Nyyata had her arm twisted." Rej gave them a lascivious grin. "Or somethin else twisted."

Uuron chuckled, his big form shaking the aging wooden table.

"Owes me a Bildvald," Haus said. "Employer didn't much like adding that rifle. Don't want to lose it."

"She took off with the weapon?" Rej asked. "That doesn't seem like her."

"Maybe she's gonna bring it back after that gloss jig, Rej." Uuron said.

"Maybe." She shrugged. "But she hasn't been with us that long. I might have misjudged her."

"Don't care," Haus said. He scratched the scar on his arm. "Just want it back."

The barman sloshed their drinks on the table. Uuron sucked the foam off the top of his before downing it in a single gulp. Rej nursed hers. At almost half the body mass of Haus' big cousin, she couldn't keep up with his intake, something they'd proven more than once. Haus leaned back in his chair and listened to their mindless banter, barely tracking the topics they covered.

He liked his crew. Uuron had been with him as long as he'd been doing this work. After their service in the Estoan force—and Haus' stint in a Guunaat prison—Haus had been talented enough to turn Toh, but Uuron couldn't hack the subtler skills. His thick fingers could never quite get the hang of picking a lock, and he wasn't one to plan before doing. He'd signed on with the Abog Union. When Haus had formed his crew, Uuron was his first pick.

Rej joined a few years after. She'd been working for a tariff-runner who moved goods between the Haven and Locnor Bay. Haus held the contract to eliminate the man. Rej had made the job difficult. Haus finally resolved the situation by offering her a place on his crew. She'd sealed the deal by putting a bolt through her employer's throat.

He was disappointed—and more than a little angry—that Nyyata hadn't joined them here. She'd been with them just over a year. He wondered if he'd mislaid his trust.

Rej gave Haus a quick smack on the arm, "So what's with this duke and Rift?"

Haus shrugged and leaned forward, arms crossed on the table. "Best I can tell, seems to be her mate."

Rift had worked with them on more than one occasion. The only way they'd known her was as Toh, appropriately scary and effective. It was jarring to peek into her personal world.

"No 'fuge?" Uuron said. "He doesn't really seem like…well, you know… He's kinda fancy."

"But pretty." Rej sighed with affected wistfulness. "If I were into the lanky grey ones, I bet he's got a story or two to tell."

Uuron punched her playfully in the shoulder. "You were into that one when we did the jig down in Imt Hold."

"Exception to every rule."

"Pays well and on time," Haus said.

"Got a nasty glint in his eye when that nut was yelling in the courtyard," Uuron said.

Haus and Rej nodded.

"Aimed the bow for me," she said. "I kinda liked it."

"I'm sure you did," Uuron said.

She kicked him under the table.

"So now we just sit here and wait?" Uuron asked.

"Seems that way." Haus said.

"Not a bad way to spend a quartern." Uuron looked over his shoulder to the table of poovies and flashed a grin that showed all his teeth. "Ten days of a little drink, a little time with the ladies, and a bit of silver for our trouble."

"'Bout as far as we could get from a warehouse job up in the Rabble," Rej said.

"The one where—" Uuron started.

Rej broke in. "—where you bet that puka—"

"Lolf! That little twitch."

"Yeah, you bet Lolf you could go longer without a bath than he could."

Uuron shook with amusement.

"Sax! That place smelled like a used diaper warehouse by the time you two were done," Rej said.

"True, but it wasn't nothing like when we were stuck out in the swamps on Gal."

Rej shook her head. "I never wanna work in Chiva'vastezz again."

Uuron rumbled a laugh, and the pair rambled on about their marginally-fabricated reminiscences.

Haus leaned back again and let their yammering roll over him, trying not to think about Nyyata, and why she had up and vanished.

SYLANDAIR

Syl slouched into the steel-paneled anteroom and dropped crossed-legged beside Aliara. "I had to get out of that library," he said. "You would not believe the things the old douse kept in there."

She ignored him. She crouched so close to the still-sealed door that her nose almost touched it.

"I've found drawings that would turn the stomachs of most lechers alongside sequences for genomes that could have furthered his fortune...if they worked." He chuckled without amusement. "He was a man of varied interests."

Aliara did nothing to acknowledge his presence.

"Are you listening to me?"

She whirled on him, anger in her eyes. "Stop haunting me."

He recoiled with a frown. "What are you talking about? I've not seen you since mid-morning."

For a long moment, her only reply was a glare. Finally she answered in a growling whisper. "I've seen you, hovering at the edge of my vision, watching me."

"Not me, Pet, I have been occupied, poring over dusty documents full of unpleasant details of doings that not even we knew about." Syl ran his thumb and forefinger over his mustaches pensively, examining her, considering. He indicated the door. "Any luck yet?"

Her chin sagged to her chest and she let out a sigh of exasperation, whether for him or the locks, Syl wasn't sure.

"The keys worked. Something inside moves when I turn them. Then nothing. I've pawed the windless door all over. I've listened to it, touched every rivet, pressed every panel on the twitching thing," she said, punctuating the words with a smack to her nemesis.

The door clonged quietly.

"You have inspected the other panels in the room as well?" Syl stretched his legs and stood.

In one slick move, she rose and turned on him, one eye narrowed, the other wide.

Syl saw that the idea hadn't occurred to her. It was unlike Aliara to miss such an obvious possibility. "Let me help you look."

"No," she said, then added in a mocking tone, "I'm the best for the job, remember?"

He causally eased away from her, but kept a wary eye as she rounded the room, fingers crawling over the panels, rivets, and bands. Not yet halfway down the first wall, she whirled on him.

"Quiet!"

"I said nothing."

"I *heard* you. I can't think with all your noise. No wonder it's been hours and I still haven't cracked this thing."

Syl moved a few steps closer. "Darling Girl, perhaps we should call it a day. This place seems to be getting to y—both of us."

"You think I can't do it?" Her eyes were on fire. One lid twitched subtly.

She shifted toward him, one hand hovering near the stiletto strapped to her thigh. Syl took a step back, bracing himself should she actually come at him.

"Hey Duke?" Schmalch's voice preceded him into the room. "Rift?"

Aliara's eyes shifted from Syl to the doorway. Her fingers curled around the pommel of her weapon.

"In here," Syl called.

"Yeah, um, my men and I just finished the rest of the first floor." He hopped over the threshold as though it might burn him and jerked a finger back into the music room. "Should we start cleaning in there?"

"Does it look like I'm ready for you?" Aliara turned her frustration on Schmalch. "I have enough distractions without your manks in here nattering away."

Schmalch seemed to shrink into himself. He raised both hands and crept back toward the exit. "Right, right, Rift. Apologies. Stupid of me to ask. You're real busy. I'll just gam off and get busy upstairs."

"Yes, you do that, Schmalch." Syl positioned himself between the two. "One of us shall notify you when you may clean in here."

"Yeah. Right," Schmalch said, still backing away. "I didn't mean to bother you, Rift. I...I... Sink it." With that, he turned and ran.

"Seems you put the fear into him, Pet."

Aliara didn't seem to hear. Syl turned to find her once again focused on the door. She punched it, kicked it, dug her fingers at its base, accompanying the fit with a blend of screams and Vazztain invectives. Finally, she wilted, forehead against the cool metal. With a moan, she slumped to the floor.

"What else is there?" she asked, voice small.

Syl squatted and held her against his chest. He needed to return to combing the library for any cipher that would give their purpose direction, but he couldn't leave her like this.

"We've missed our mids, Pet. You need the rest. We both do," he said. "Let's leave Schmalch to supervise, take Sviroosa, and return home for a quiet evening. Forget about this place until morning." The part of him that wanted all trace of the old man gone hoped she would disagree.

She shook her head. "I won't be able to stop thinking about it."

He smiled weakly and kissed the crescent-moon scar masked by her spiky cap of hair. "Very well. Why don't you lie down and take a nap here instead? It's not ideal, but your old room is adjacent to the library. I can continue my work and be nearby should you need me."

"I hate that place."

"I know, but I would be close at hand."

"Lay down with me," she said. "In your room."

It was his turn to object. "I want to be there even less than I suspect you want to be in your room." He paused. "I could drag some cushions into the library, pile them up over by the fireplace. He kept enough of them. Does that satisfy?"

Her shoulders hitched, but she didn't resist as he led her upstairs.

ALIARA

Orono shuffled into her room with his usual disregard for her privacy, entered her closet, and pulled the door to behind him. It had been months since his last experiment. She'd hoped it might be his last, that she was too old, too battered to continue.

He emerged from the closet and tossed a loose lime-green dress at her—the same hateful sack dress as always.

"Put it on, girl." He shuffled out.

Aliara knew the routine: dress as told, meet at the basement stairs, be quiet. Deviation meant punishment. And punishment was usually worse than what waited below.

She needed shoes. The floor down there was so cold. Horrible gown tugged on, she dashed into the closet and burrowed through the mess for a matching pair. She glanced over her shoulder, long black braid flipping as she turned. It was back there, watching her. She watched it in return. He made her keep that horrible painting—even nailed it up so she couldn't move it. She hated that painting. There was something wicked about it, despite all appearances to the contrary.

Both shoes found, she rolled out of the closet, dodging the menace of those ogling baubles the puka called eyes. She spent hours each day with Flibuul. He was puka with eyes set so far apart they were almost on the sides of his head, just like the ones in the painting. He didn't bother her. So why did this? She slammed the door and raced downstairs.

As usual, Orono was waiting for her, hidden panels already open onto the concrete stairs. No matter how quickly she dressed, she could never beat him down here, never see the trick to opening the door. He was so decrepit. That shouldn't be possible. Yet here he was.

Aliara crossed the room's mosaic floor, hopping over the tiles that fashioned the pretty green and white moons, lest Aessatal punish her for treading on them, and ducked into the stairwell. Orono slid the door shut behind her.

"Get down there, you stupid girl," he said and swatted in her direction, barely catching the tip of her plait as she dodged his hand and scrambled down the stairs.

The heavy sound of his heaving bulk followed her down the steps, door locked fast behind him. "Room one," he called.

She dawdled while she waited, playing with specimens he'd left out on a lab table. She made a frog corpse dance, rearranged a pile of loose teeth by size, shook a vial of pink liquid until it foamed. When the huffing and puffing grew close enough, she slipped into room one and stretched out on the cold, shiny table obediently, face carefully neutral.

Restraints were nothing unusual. He'd done things before that required her to be still. Who could expect a ten-year-old to stay motionless for hours while being prodded with knives and needles? The bindings were necessary, she'd come to accept them.

The buzzing sound—that was new. It grew louder before something cold and alive grazed her head, running gentle arcs across her scalp. She smelled singed hair. She cried.

Then came the brace, turning tears into pleas. It clamped onto both sides of her head, pin-point pain in each temple, an indescribable pressure crushing her skull. She begged him to stop. He slapped her mouth, reopening the split in her lips.

"Quiet, or I'll immobilize that, too."

It went on like that—more whirring, a new and foreign burning odor, different pains, then the endless questions. She compared every whirl and dent in the pressed-tin ceiling to the inventory in her memory as he worked. The questions were a surprise, abrupt and puzzling. She tried her best to answer correctly, but as usual, she could never satisfy her owner.

He rummaged around behind her, pressed his fingers to her scalp. "What do you see?"

"I smell flowers."

"That's completely wrong, you stupid girl. What do you *see*?"

"The ceiling."

A pained sigh. "We'll try again."

The process was as old and well-known as that ugly green dress. Over the months, she never did give the right answer, see whatever it was he wanted her to see, but to the girl in the dream, it was all new and frightening. Though she'd never known exactly what he was doing to her during any of his experiments, she'd always been able to move her head to watch him work. The immobilization was the worst torture of them all.

In her sleep, Aliara shook her head—there *was* something new here. She couldn't see or hear anyone, but someone was there. Had they been there all along? All her senses showed her was the dirty metal ceiling, the smell of antiseptic and the squeezing pain of the brace, but she felt someone here who wasn't familiar.

The whisper she'd heard so often today was back, but at last she could make out a word. "*See…*"

Her eyes jostled her sleeping lids in search of the source of the voice. All the while, Orono continued his work—drilling holes, inserting needles, asking inane questions.

"*What do you see?*" The strange voice spat out each word like a rotten berry.

Aliara strained against the straps, tried to turn her head, but the brace held her firmly.

"Stop your wiggling," the old man said. He turned away from her, muttering as he fiddled with tools on the nearby tray.

"*Show you.*"

The voice was silky like Syl's and demanding like Orono's, but it belonged to neither. It was soft, fluid, and...and angry.

"Who are you?" Aliara yelled.

Orono smacked her mouth again. "Quiet."

She tasted blood, felt his hands against her scalp.

"Now tell me what you hear, stupid girl."

"*See.*" The voice ignored her question.

In the dream, Orono shook her, called her name. Aliara's eyes snapped open. Syl was there. He patted her face, worry etched in his expression. He shifted so her head lay in his lap and stroked the dark bristles of her hair much as he'd stroked the stubbly, sutured scalp so many years ago.

SYLANDAIR

Concerned about her mania and nightmares, Syl persuaded Aliara to stay home the following day. Their return to the old mansion was having a more profound effect on her than he'd expected. He kissed her scowling face and left her hovering on the patio, robe draped loosely over her shoulders. She watched him descend the stairs, keeping vigil until he was out of sight.

When he returned that evening, she was waiting on the top step and petting one of the area's many stray cats. She was still frowning, still wearing the black robe. Syl wondered if she'd passed the entire day like that.

By the following morning, Aliara seemed to have returned to her usual self; no nightmares, no outbursts. Before he finished breakfast, she was dressed and pacing the foyer, aubergine catsuit flashing beneath her dark cloak with each marching step. He needed only one glance at her face to know nothing could keep her from the puzzle of the lab door any longer.

He was glad to have her again at his side, though her unusually anxious demeanor stirred his unease. She said nothing on their pedicab ride up the Pipe, merely sat there, hands clamped to her knees. Even when they arrived, she remained silent, heading straight into the steel-plated room to resume her battle with the door.

Syl left her and returned to the study, reviewing basket after basket of antiquated data and smut before sending the vast majority to the trash pile outside. One of Schmalch's men fed the discarded material to a newly dug fire pit, incinerating brilliant thoughts and perverse visions alike. Syl's head throbbed from reading Orono's tight spidery scrawl, his mouth felt like paste from the sediment he'd stirred up, but a monumental accumulation of documents still loomed.

The cleaning crew had made more progress than either he or Aliara, so much so that Schmalch even agreed to admit Sviroosa and her cleaning crew to the main house. No great evil had leapt out and swallowed anyone whole. The source of this foulness had quite obviously been the squatter cult themselves.

Syl dumped the last of one pile into Schmalch's wheelbarrow and glared at the next mound of papers and books. He yawned. It was getting on toward time for their midday rest, yet as tired as he was, he was more tentative about Aliara's mood. He'd expected her to blow into the library hours ago with news of her success, yet here he was, still alone. He hoped she was herself, that this malady was a passing thing brought on by nothing more than the stress of their return.

He left his work and strode to the library's rear wall, home to his childhood textbooks. The shelves here were truncated by the bank of windows that topped them. He'd once required a rolling ladder to access the uppermost shelf. Today he easily looked outside, onto the blue-roofed desal plant.

Vases, framed drawings, and other disparate knickknacks were sprinkled between groupings of books. Syl remembered many of the titles and curios, but a handful had escaped his recall. He crouched and picked up a bronze cast of a starfish. This he remembered well. It had been part of his lessons on local marine life. After they'd finished with the model and accompanying texts, Orono had insisted he dissect a real one. The specimen had been rough on the outside, greenish-grey and disgusting inside. Syl could still smell the bitter fumes of the preservation liquid. He knew then that he had no future in zoetics or biology of any kind. Orono had not been pleased.

Returning the model to its perch, he examined what appeared to be a well-worn lady's shoe on the top shelf. Why his old master would possess, let alone display, such a souvenir was beyond him. Gently pinching the black leather tongue between thumb and forefinger, he lifted the shoe and peered in. Stains and the door of mildew greeted him. He shook it once, heard nothing, and moved to return the bootie to its shelf. He noticed a small switch, previously hidden by the shoe. It was set into the wood, almost flush with the shelf. Syl flicked it from left to right. One end of the bookcase groaned forward. Shoe forgotten, he pulled the shelf open, inanely hoping the information he sought would be waiting inside on a pedestal, bathed in divine light. Instead he was met by a low-ceilinged cupboard lined with stacked boxes. He opened a few. All were packed with papers, drawings, and notebooks.

Syl sagged.

He left the daunting mess behind and headed downstairs, strolling into the steel-lined room casually, hands in pockets. "You would not believe what I just found…" he began. The words froze in his throat.

Squatting atop her cloak in front of one of the truculent keyholes was Aliara, all the music room's bells arranged in a zigzagging line between her and the door. Her tools were organized by size, laid out in a precise row to her right, boots arranged at her left, their laces like groping tentacles. The sleeves of her catsuit were rolled up so tightly they had pressed pale rings into her upper arms. Dark half-moon marks of fingernails were dug into her forearms. Index fingers and thumbs blocking both the upper and lower lugs of her ears, she rocked back and forth and muttered. Clearly a single day at home had not been enough.

Syl watched her quietly, almost afraid to disturb whatever was going on. Periodically, the rocking stopped, and a shoulder or arm would twitch. Then she'd shake her head violently and resume swaying.

Syl laid a hand on her shoulder. Aliara twisted to look at him, startled black eyes bloodshot and unblinking. She warily unplugged her ears, her expression swinging to anger.

"What?" she snapped.

"It's midday," he said. "I thought we could have a snack, perhaps our nap."

"No."

"I could use the company," he smiled as warmly as his anxiety would allow.

She didn't deign to reply, turning back to the door.

"Maybe I should hire a second set of eyes for this project," Syl suggested.

"He can't win."

"Hm?" Syl asked. "Win what?"

"Win what, win what?" she asked, tone derisive. "Idiot."

He squatted on the edge of the cloak.

"Get off!" Her arm lashed out.

Syl hopped back, remaining at eye level. "Why don't we head home? Have a nice shower together? Enjoy the rest of the day?"

He reached to touch her, but she slapped his hand away.

"Sax!" she swore. "You just want it your way. Like always."

"What?"

"You were his favorite."

He stared. "What?"

"You had all the luxury you wanted."

"Luxury? Here? I was a prisoner like you."

"You had the good bed. You ate at the table. You had anything you ever asked for."

"Pet, you know that's—"

"I'm *not* your pet. Throw her some scraps and she'll stick around. He told you to, didn't he?"

Syl gaped.

"*I* had to live in the hole. *I* was his lab rat, his stupid girl. You got a pat on the head and a shiny new toy whenever you wanted it."

"Shiny new toy?" Anger flooded in. Syl stood, glaring down at her. "You didn't have to suck his disgusting old fid while his fat belly rested on the top of your head, did you? That's luxury? You could have had the scruddy bed and the table and whatever else it is you think you were denied."

She rose and unzipped her suit, revealing the scars that traversed her torso. "Do *you* have both lungs?" On tiptoes, she forced herself into his face. "Did he stick pins in *your* brain? Test what a kidney could take before collapse? Take off a toe and sew it back on again just to see if it would stay?"

Her words drained the ire out of him. They had never before spoken so openly about the ordeals of their childhoods, simply accepting that Orono had maimed them both in their own distinct ways.

"Will *your* hair ever grow back properly?" Aliara grabbed a wisp of his hair that had come loose as he'd worked and yanked it out by the roots. "Let's see if it will."

Syl winced, hand going protectively to the sore spot on his scalp.

Aliara stomped to the far side of the room, muttering to herself, voice now mimicking Orono. "'Farspeech, farspeech…we are superior to the puka. I will make it happen. Now pay attention, girls!'" She whirled on Syl, finger pointing accusingly, voice again raised. "It was all he could say for months while he drilled and poked and slapped."

"Stop," Syl said.

"Why? Does it bother you to know what was happening to me while you were out taking lessons and playing with your manky ponies?"

Before he realized he'd moved, Syl swung, catching her cheek with his palm. Aliara's head snapped to the side, connecting with the steel door. She crumpled like a loose sail.

Syl couldn't breathe. He'd never struck her in anger before. He squatted and laid an ear against her chest. Her heart still beat, though it was racing. He threw her over his shoulder and carried her out of this blighted house. He was having no more of this nonsense.

SCHMALCH

Over the past four nights, Schmalch had become quite comfortable in his new digs. He'd discovered an old, dusty cellarette situated in the back corner of the cush bedroom. The liquor inside still had kick. He hoped the job went on longer than planned. He could live like this forever.

Rift had been gone since some ruckus a couple days ago. The Duke had drifted in and out at odd hours but limited his time to the library. That left Schmalch in charge. He was very, very good at being a boss. He'd even shared his hooch with Munk and Glech. Maybe not the best stuff, but they still were pleased.

Halfway through a gloss bottle of caba and dressed in one of the Duke's old smoking jackets, Schmalch tipsily swirled his way around the room to the tinny music of the antique melody engine. Wrapped in his arms was the giant Tolknor beaver, tail dragging the floor like the train of some important lady's gown. He and the taxidermied animal ignored the storm outside, inelegantly drifting through the moonlight that dappled the room.

When the tune ended, Schmalch adjusted his partner to gaze into its eyes. "Sviroosa, I knew you couldn't resist me forever," he told the Tolknor beaver, trying his best to replicate words he'd heard the Duke's use. "You'll like your time with me a lot."

The beaver stared at him blankly, unmoved.

As the moonlight disappeared behind a storm cloud, Schmalch stroked the stiff fur away from the creature's eyes. "Your skin's so smooth…such a pretty shade of green. And your nose…so hooked and pointy." He sighed dramatically and touched his nose to the beaver's. "Wait here."

He arranged the animal in one of the chairs overlooking the courtyard, then cranked the music box again and returned to his dance partner. "Where were we?"

The beaver remained aloof.

"Ah, yes…your eyes, such a sweet shade of brown. Almost like Garl's coffee."

Cheek-to-cheek, he danced the moth-eaten taxidermy around the room, so caught up he didn't notice when the moonlight disappeared behind a cloud. When the music wound to a close, he shifted the rodent to gaze once more into its glass eyes, inadvertently poking himself with the branch clamped in the beaver's hand.

"Balls!" he said, rubbing the new scratch across his nose. "Stupid critter."

The fantasy broken, Schmalch rested the beaver against a blanket chest, took another drink, and studied the mounted animal. The illusion wasn't quite right yet. The black and tan fur and long, flat tail did little to boost his imagination. No, this Sviroosa-substitute needed something else to create the perfect fantasy. He gulped the last of his caba as the answer hit him: a dress. There were loads of dresses in this room's closet. With proper clothing and maybe a hat—or better yet, a veil—the beaver would be far more convincing. Maybe some perfume, too.

Schmalch gave the walk-in closet light's crank a quick turn before wandering unsteadily inside. The big dresses up front sported all kinds of wild prints and garish colors. Schmalch liked them, but they didn't look like Sviroosa. He closed his eyes and tried to picture her clothes. She liked things simple and plain. High necks, long skirts, solid colors.

"What do you think, Sviroosa?" he called to the stuffed beaver, who waited patiently beside the chest. "Pink with green or orange with yellow?"

The beaver voiced no opinion.

"I know you don't care so much for patterns, but whoever lived here liked them." He belched and soured caba gushed onto his tongue. "Maybe there's more further back. You wait there."

The beaver complied.

Schmalch pushed deeper into the rack, where the fancier dresses hung. These were mostly solid colors, decorated with embroidery, fringe, and beads—the kinds of things the real Sviroosa might like. A pale-yellow dress with green swirls embroidered along its hem and cuffs caught his eye. He tugged, trying to remove it from the hanger, but it clung fast. Schmalch dragged the chair from the closet's dressing table to where the dress waited, clambered up and worked the catch at the neck.

Schmalch was respectable at picking pockets and locks, but he had no experience working fancy hooks and buttons. This clasp gave him fits. He twisted, tugged, and even bit it, but it gave no quarter. Finally, he settled on shaking until it came free. He had forgotten, however, that he was both fully in his cups and perched atop a narrow, high-backed chair. Two shakes of the hanging dress and over he went, slamming hard against the back wall. A few items fell from the rack, fluttering around him. He snickered at his own antics.

Head reeling, he crawled between the dangling dresses. Thunder rattled the windows and he gasped. The gasp turned to hiccups. He needed another drink. He pushed the fallen chair out of his path, scraping it against the floor with a harsh scree that faded into a persistent, grinding rasp.

His fuzzy brain latched onto the sound. He looked back at the chair. It lay still, but the rear wall of the closet moved. It was a door! Maybe the Duke stayed late and was coming for a visit. Or maybe Munk and Glech found something they wanted to share.

Schmalch flopped onto his ass and watched the door's slow progress, excitement building in his chest.

Four pale, twisted fingers emerged from the crack. Their nails were split and chipped, the knuckles knobby. The third twisted hard toward the first and second, as though trying to change its place in line.

That didn't seem right. Schmalch swallowed hard and rubbed his eyes. His excitement washed away, replaced by anxiety.

The closet cap-light's charge waned; he hadn't given it much of a crank. In the light of the flickering bulb, a head emerged from the behind the door. Maybe he'd had more to drink than he realized because the head didn't make any sense. The right eye was larger than the left and bulged from its socket. The nose and jaw slid heavily toward the smaller eye. Mounds of knobs and bumps covered the left side of the head, the rest was covered with matted hunks of dark auburn hair. The thick, rosy lips, cracked and peeling, stood out against jellyfish-pale skin. The thing opened its mouth to show rotted, crooked teeth and a pasty pink tongue.

"Faaahh-uuurr?" it said, mismatched eyes sweeping across the closet.

Terror cut through the cloud of alcohol inside Schmalch's skull. A voice inside commanded him to run, but his body was rooted to the floor, unable to so much as twitch.

The horrible, green eyes swung down. The thing spotted him. It smiled, teeth green and gritty.

The light overhead winked out.

"Fooooood," the thing said.

Schmalch felt warm wetness as his bladder released.

GLECH

It had been four nights since Glech had left his family and their cozy cuddy above Phyyll's Bread Basket. In his dream, they were celebrating the Sower's Festival. Fohmsquah wore her rusty orange linen dress, ring of forsythia blossoms circling her lovely bark-brown head as she rolled out crust for his favorite blackberry pie. Glech slid up behind and wrapped his arms around her delicate waist. She started, but giggled, admonishing him against ruining her baking. As she turned to kiss him, he heard something strange.

"What was that?" the dream-Glech asked.

Fohmsquah only smiled.

The sound came again. Glech's eyes batted open, wisps of the dream drifting away. Thunder clapped outside. The storm must have woken him. A sort of bump followed by shuffling and more bumps echoed from somewhere outside his room. No, this was what he heard. Glech lay in the warm, comfortable bed for a moment, trying to figure the noise's origin. It was a big house, almost as big as the building where he lived, but this one wasn't jammed up against other buildings and filled with tenants. Its vacancy created echoes, made it difficult to tell where sounds started and where they ended.

He rolled over. It was probably just Munk sneaking down to the kitchen for a late-night snack. That boy could eat more than anyone Glech had ever seen. Of course, when his Chisev hit that age, he might be the same way. Ten was a hungry age for a puka. How he and Fohmsquah would manage to keep enough food around was beyond Glech, but he couldn't worry about that right now. He closed his eyes and encouraged sleep to return.

This had been a good job—two Callas a day, plus food and the softest bed he'd ever slept in. The other rooms had good beds too, but this one was magnificent. His only regret was that his sweet Fohmsquah couldn't join him. She would have loved this bed. But then, who would have taken care of their little ones? If this went on much longer, maybe he could talk to Mister Schmalch, see if his family could move in, maybe take up another one of the bedrooms if they all helped out.

Glech yawned and pulled the blanket close, drifting back into his dream.

On the edge of sleep, he heard another noise, similar but closer. Glech rolled onto his back and held his breath. The sound was more consistent, and definitely coming from upstairs. If it had been Munk on a food run, there was no reason he'd go upstairs. Glech sat up and eased himself out of bed. He pulled on a fresh shirt and drew yesterday's workpants over his threadbare white shorts. The ruckus continued. He frowned and peeped out the door.

At first he saw nothing, only empty hallway. Abruptly Mister Schmalch ran down the stairs yelling unintelligibly. Lightning flashed and Glech saw a shape, large and brown, maybe a little fuzzy, tucked under his boss's arm. An unfamiliar figure appeared on the landing behind the still-screaming Mister Schmalch and pulled him back upstairs. Someone or something else joined the screaming.

Glech had to help! He picked up an old hairbrush from the room's vanity and hurried into the hallway, almost bowled over when Mister Schmalch tumbled down the stairs. He picked himself up, screamed "monster!" and ran down the next flight. Glech's brain whirred through possibilities until it clicked on the work they'd been doing. Whatever had left the awful mess had come back.

"Munk!" he shouted. "Get ou—"

SYLANDAIR

Syl shrugged into his robe as he trotted down the stairs. Some dimwit was outside pounding and screaming, assaulting the bell. Pistol in hand, he was prepared to end the noise one way or another.

He yanked the door open. "What?"

Schmalch stood on the patio, storm-drenched and shaking. Beneath his arms was a large, soggy taxidermied animal staring apathetically skyward. On his back was a sodden, but familiar smoking jacket.

"It came for me I don't know what it was terrible chased me through the rooms don't know what happened to Munk and Glech I can't go back there Duke it's gonna kill me I ran and ran." His words spilled out in a frantic jumble.

"Enter," Syl said. "And leave that...whatever that is in the foyer."

Schmalch gingerly placed the dripping creature on the hall tree's seat and followed Syl to the parlor, still muttering random nonsense.

"Sit," Syl pointed to a sofa.

Schmalch pressed himself into the crook between back and arm, drawing his knees close.

Syl rang a bell, and a groggy Sviroosa appeared.

"Khuit, two glasses. And a towel." When she left, Syl dropped the pistol into the large pocket of his dressing gown and settled in opposite Schmalch. "Now, what's all this twaddle about? You're supposed to be watching my property, not wearing it."

The little douse resumed his babbling.

Syl held up a hand. "Stop. No one can understand that."

The khuit and towel arrived, along with a sparsely clothed Aliara, who curled up beside Syl.

"Dry off and drink this." Syl filled a shot glass for Schmalch. "Now, start again. And think about what you're saying before you say it."

Schmalch made a cursory attempt at drying, then sat on the towel. He gulped the thick, yellow liquor and made a face.

"I was in my bedroom," he began, voice still high and strained.

"Good."

"I was in the closet, looking at the dresses, and fell down."

Syl pursed his lips but nodded.

"Then the back of the closet opened and...and...this thing came out and it was horrible and it looked at me and called me a name and said I was 'food' and I don't want to be food and I've been sleeping there for days while it was there all..."

"Stop." Syl again raised a hand. He poured another glass, draining this one himself.

Aliara slipped away into another room.

"Which bedroom?" Syl asked.

"The big pink and black one on the third floor."

Syl looked at his lap, head wagging from side to side. He'd been distracted by Aliara's malady. "You should not have been in there. I should have been more specific in my directions to you."

Schmalch stared blankly.

"Continue. You were in the closet."

The puka nodded.

"The back of the closet opened and then what? Slowly this time," Syl said

"This thing poked its head out. It wasn't right." Schmalch shook his head violently. "It was all lumpy and white. The eyes were funny. It said 'food'—or I think that's what it said—and I ran."

"Was it glowing?"

Schmalch screwed up his face. "No, I don't remember anything like that."

"No dead-eyed children lurking about?"

Schmalch's brow furrowed and he frowned. "What, Duke?"

Syl raised his eyebrows and batted at the air.

"Oh," Schmalch drew out the word. He shook his head. "Un-uh."

"So you simply ran away?"

Schmalch's head bobbed. "Uh-huh."

"Did you warn the others?" Syl asked.

Schmalch's cheeks flushed dark olive. "I screamed a lot, so maybe they got out. That thing was chasing me. I think there were more, too."

"Oh? And why is that?"

"I...I heard something else and...and I got that feeling, you catch?" One side of his mouth pulled back and he shook his head. "I just wanted to run."

Syl motioned for him to continue.

"I threw some stuff at it while I was running, but it grabbed me on the stairs, but I had my knife..."

"Did you kill it?"

"I don't think so. I closed my eyes and stabbed at it until it dropped me. It screamed, too." He picked up the empty glass. Syl refilled it, and Schmalch gulped. "When I ran out the front door, I heard this awful roar. I thought it was chasing me. I ran all the way here."

"Ran? From the Big Island down to the Rabble?"

Schmalch nodded.

"With that stuffed monstrosity."

"Uh-huh."

"In the storm?"

"Er, yeah. I was, uh...I didn't realize..." He trailed off with a shrug.

"Impressive," Syl said. Schmalch was nothing if not enduring.

Aliara returned, dressed head-to-toe in black. Her stilettos were strapped at each hip, the hook of her copper-plated sickle knife poked from its forearm holster beneath her cloak. She stood close, eyes shifting between he and Schmalch as she fidgeted and plucked at the sleeves of her catsuit. Though their minds were in concert as usual, she still wasn't quite right. If it was Orono, he needed to be driven back to his hole until a true solution could be devised. If, however, this was something else, it was only a distraction. The sooner it was removed, the sooner they could finish examining the artifacts of the old man's once-great intellect.

Schmalch ran a finger around the inside of his khuit glass to collect the rest of the syrupy drink and stuck the finger into his mouth, waiting for direction. Despite yet another attack on his life, the puka was fine. He could be relied on.

"Go to the Belvedor, Schmalch, and wake Haus. Bring him and his crew to the mansion. We will meet all of you there."

"But I…" Schmalch protested.

Syl rose and cut him off. "No, none of that. I'll send their pay with you as well."

Schmalch nodded, shoulders drooping.

"Wait here while I retrieve their silver. And remember, if you are exaggerating or hallucinating, the mercenaries' every Calla will come from your pocket. You will be working for me for a long, long time."

"I'm not, Duke, I promise."

When they were alone in their bedroom, Syl took Aliara's face in his hands, ran a finger over the lovely bow mouth that always seemed to hold a frown. Syl didn't particularly want her going back to the old house, but *he* intended to return. Voicing his opinion would do little good, perhaps even be counterproductive. She'd go there without him anyway.

"Are you certain about this, Pet? You want to go?"

She nodded.

At least he could keep an eye on her this way.

"Very well." He kissed her forehead and considered appropriate attire for the evening.

SYLANDAIR

Hands clasped, Syl and Aliara walked along the rise of Temple Row, its cobbles slick with rain and smoothed by years. The ticking of his boot heels was muted by the autumn downpour, her boots silent no matter the weather.

The estate's basalt brick wall ran alongside the street, time-worn hunks of coral and shells jutting from the mortar. As they reached the gatehouse, lightning struck a distant roof high on the Nest. Thunder rolled over the city. Aliara tackled Syl around his middle, driving them both to the ground, barely dodging a falling pier cap. They rolled out of harm's way while the coquina sphere that once topped the neglected masonry bowled down the quiet street.

Motionless for a moment, Syl propped himself above Aliara, rain pelting them both. Their eyes met. The corners of his mouth turned up. He'd missed her these last few days. An impulse to take her right there in the street struck him, quickly replaced by a greater inclination to spark his flinter to the remaining papers in Orono's library and watch the whole thing burn. A satisfying idea, but not beneficial for their end goal. He rose and retrieved his hat, wiping away the clinging leaves. Mud spattered his charcoal topcoat. The legs of his navy trousers were soaked.

"If the little douse merely scared himself with an old housedress or caught sight of a trapped moon owl flying around or…" he trailed away, kicking at a hunk of ruined wall.

Aliara grinned beneath her hood. She got to her feet and gave her cloak a snap, shaking detritus to the street.

Syl adjusted his hat. "Shall we go in now or wait for the others?"

Without answering, Aliara slipped through the gap in the front gate and made for the house. Syl followed. The door was wide open, dim light from somewhere within illuminated the bunched-up foyer rug, but everything else looked as it had when they'd left—better in some cases, thanks to Sviroosa and her assistants. The domestic was so scrupulous in her work it seemed as though she'd even brushed the stuffed caracata's ratty old hide.

"Shhh," Aliara admonished Syl.

He'd said nothing but kept his own council and watched her closely. Draping his filthy outerwear over hers on the hall tree, he followed her upstairs. Somehow, she ascended the ancient staircase without a single creak. He tried to do the same, but failed, flinching at every faint squeak beneath his feet.

Halfway between the landing and second floor proper, Aliara stopped. She shook her head and rubbed her eyes before letting out a little huff and turning to him. With two fingers, she pointed to her eyes, to his eyes, to the hallway before them. Syl nodded. Aliara leaned against the wall, allowing him to climb high enough for a good look.

Blood was everywhere. Not the old dried spatter Schmalch and his men had been rubbing away, but fresh, dripping blood, almost brown against the white floor tiles. Too dark for karju blood, the wrong color for chivori. At minimum, one of the pukas had not been as lucky as their supervisor. Noting the chunks of khaki flesh mixed in, Syl held out little hope for either's survival.

Turning back to Aliara, he jerked his chin toward the ground floor, encouraging their retreat. She shook her head once, pointed to the string of open doorways and raised her eyebrows inquiringly. Which rooms had the cleaning crew slept in? Syl wasn't certain, but were he one of the pukas, he would have chosen an opulent guest room over the austerity of Aliara's old space. As she seemed bent on moving on without assistance, these rooms seemed the best starting point. Someone might still be alive.

Before he could agree, Aliara's head flinched back. Her eyes, still focused on him, registered surprise and confusion. Her brows scrunched together and she touched his lips. For a heartbeat, he was afraid she would break the silence, alerting whatever lurked within to their presence. Instead, blinking rapidly, she jammed her fingers in her ears and crouched into a ball. Syl gave her time, arm around her slowly rocking figure.

When she stood and nodded, he kissed her forehead, drew his pistol, and set off to investigate.

HAUS

Haus was none too thrilled to find a quivering puka at his door in the middle of the night. There'd been no trouble on this jig for four days. He'd relaxed, allowed himself to assume things were settled at the estate. This visit doubtless meant otherwise.

"What?" He looked down at the familiar puka, who fiddled nervously with the belt of an oversized smoking jacket.

"The Duke told me to come get you," the puka said. "He wants you to meet him at the mansion."

"Why?"

The dinner-plate brown eyes rolled. His words came out in a rattled staccato, "Something attacked me. Came out of the closet. Wanted to eat me. The Duke and Rift are there now. I hope it didn't get Munk and Glech."

"Get in here." Haus dragged his visitor inside. "Your name?"

"Schmalch. The Duke's top assistant." He attempted a smile, but his eyes kept zipping back to the puckered scars that tore their way across Haus' chest. Each time he surveyed them, the corners of his mouth pulled back in an involuntary grimace.

"Schmalch." Haus idly scratched the inky patterns that bubbled their way out of his old wounds.

"He said to give you this." Schmalch pulled a resin box from his rucksack, silver glittering inside.

Haus took the box and grunted. "How big was this thing?"

"Big," Schmalch said, pulling his eyes away, face scrunching up in thought. "Not as big as you, but big. And lumpy—really lumpy."

"Lumpy?" Haus wandered over to the iron-framed bed, where last-night's woman lolled half-asleep. He picked up his pants and began to dress.

Schmalch nodded, hands convulsively fluttering around his head to indicate where these lumps had been. "I never saw anything like it before."

Haus studied him for a moment, rubbed the missing tip of his ear. "You been drinking?"

Schmalch's eyes drooped toward his feet. "A little."

"Uh-huh." Haus pulled a rigid leather breastplate over his shirt and buckled it shut on each side.

Schmalch looked back up. "But I know what I saw, and it wasn't right whatever it was. It woulda' eaten me if I'd stayed."

Haus rolled the woman out of his way and sat on the dingy bed. He eyed the puka for an uncomfortable beat then pulled on boots. "Any weapons?"

"Me or it?"

Haus paused, boot halfway on. "Start with you."

"I had my knife." He lifted the cuff of his pant leg and proudly patted a little blade hidden there. "I think I hurt it when it grabbed me. My eyes were closed, though."

"Uh-huh. How about it?"

"I didn't see any. Or…or feel any." He patted himself as if checking for previously unnoticed wounds. "But I ran when it dropped me."

"Just the one?"

"That's all I saw, but I guess I think there were more."

"Oh?"

"Yeah." Schmalch looked at his feet.

"Why?"

He shrugged.

"Your gut?"

Schmalch nodded.

"Good man."

A smile cracked across the worried puka's face.

Haus stared into the wall and scowled. Unknown hostiles, likely no weapons. The way it looked, they knew this place better than his client did. His mind drifted back to the Rector's nonsensical rant, but he found no information there of use.

Haus strapped his hunting knife to his thigh and grabbed the cudgel off the dresser.

"Wake up Uuron and Rej," he said. "Rooms thirty-eight and forty down the hall. They won't be happy to see you."

ALIARA

The cleaning crew had not been as fortunate as Schmalch. One of them appeared to have exploded in the entrance to a guest room. The door was off its hinge, its frame chipped, and the stench of oozing vital fluids was so coppery and raw that Aliara could almost taste it. She poked at a severed finger with the toe of her boot, its stub ragged and bloody. It had been torn, not sliced from the body. Syl made a soft retching noise and moved on, doing his best to avoid the blood.

Though obviously slept in, the damaged room was empty, as were two others. The fourth was locked, but hardly a challenge to spring. The room inside was serene, bypassed by the horror outside. Passing clouds danced moonlight over the walls. A tendril of smoke drifted up the chimney from the dim fireplace embers. The bed was turned down and rumpled. Puka-sized work clothes were laid tidily across the divan, shoes tucked beneath its edge. The soft pulse of rapid breath came from somewhere within.

Aliara squatted and peered into the gloom beneath the bed. A shadow shivered there, small and pressed into the far corner between wall and bedpost. Aliara laid a finger to her lips and motioned the frightened man to come out, but he only shook his head and pressed himself harder against the wall. She looked up at Syl and shrugged. He crouched beside her.

"You can come out now," he whispered.

The shadow didn't move.

"This may be your only chance."

Thunder clapped. A jump, a moan from the puka.

"We don't have time for this." Syl sat back on his heels. "Shall we visit your quarters, Pet?"

They left the cringing puka, locking him in, and wended their way down the hall.

The only thing in her room not as Aliara had left it was a bloody streak that ran from the doorway into the closet. It ended abruptly at the wall opposite the hated dancing-puka painting. Yet another trick door. This one had been a secret even to her. Who knew how many nights Orono had stolen into her room as she slept?

"It seems we had no inkling of how many clandestine routes he had here," Syl said.

Aliara pushed the hanging clothes to one side and tapped at the paneled wall. Hollow. She patted its edges and ran her foot along the floor in search of the trigger. Only a few steps in, pain shot through her skull and she crumpled to the floor, mouth open in a silent scream. Syl called to her, his voice far away. His hands on her felt like he touched someone else.

The shadowy closet faded, resolving into a small, dim room. Before her was a dull white wall with a metal handle jutting from the top, convenient to only the tallest members of the household. Though she could not remember seeing the place before, it felt familiar and comfortable.

She turned. A coiled wrought-iron staircase with cobwebs threaded through its balusters broke through both floor and ceiling. She reached for the handrail. Instead of her grey fingers, the hand she saw was pale and skeletal, malformed, and strikingly white, yet the change seemed perfectly natural. She climbed up, out of the room, body lurching lightly with each step.

She heard Syl calling to her, his voice a hollow echo of reality.

She passed through a second, similar room and climbed into a large, murky space full of shuffling sounds. Indistinguishable shapes shifted here, their outlines uncanny, almost comical. She moved through the place easily, unrushed, fully aware of her surroundings, calm and sure of the nearness of loved ones. The further she went, the dimmer the scene. Before she could reach the strange shapes, a burst of brightness exploded against the dark, and the vision vanished.

A clap of thunder rattled the house's windows and Aliara rolled onto her back, familiar closet around her. She reached up and touched Syl's face. He was real.

"What in the depths happened?" he asked.

"Don't know," she murmured.

"Sink it. I am taking you out of here." Syl lurched to his feet, inadvertently ramming his head into the clothing rod. "Bugger!" He clutched his head and roared. "Enough of this of this house and its ridiculous secrets!"

Turning his rage on the false wall, Syl kicked the paneling repeatedly with his steel-toed boot until he had shattered the cedar, revealing the dingy white cubby beyond. Anger spent, he crouched by the opening, panting

Aliara crawled over to the aperture and peered in. The bloody trail continued on the other side, ending at a wrought-iron spiral staircase that wound through ceiling and floor.

Syl crouched beside her. "Where do you suppose *that* leads?"

"The attic," Aliara said. She studied her hand, expecting the pale bony thing again. "I was just there."

SYLANDAIR

"You were here? What does—?" Syl began, cut off by the thudding vibration of footsteps from below.

Pistol drawn, he reached the hallway as Haus and his crew topped the stairs, Schmalch close behind.

Uuron whistled as he took in the bloody mess. "Sweet mother Jajal, what is all this? Or what was it?" His laugh rumbled through the enormous chest.

"Evenin', Duke." Haus said. "Little guy said you had a problem."

"Mister Haus, I appreciate you coming on such short notice." Syl gestured the group into Aliara's old room and waited as they took in the situation.

Haus broke the silence. "Schmalch gave me a quick rundown. You find anything new?"

"Indeed we did."

"Didya find Glech and Munk?" Schmalch asked from behind the larger bodies.

"That, I assume, is one of your comrades dispersed all over the hallway," Syl said.

Schmalch blanched a lighter shade of green.

"The other one is cowering beneath the bed in the far guest room. He refused to come out. Perhaps you can do something about him."

Schmalch looked nervously into the hallway, took a deep breath, and dashed from the room. There was a squeak and soft thump as he slipped in the blood and collided with the wall.

"Fill us in," Haus said.

"We found a hidden room," Syl said.

Haus followed him through the closet into the room beyond, where Aliara crouched by the stairs. "These go all the way through the house?"

"We are unsure. You arrived just as we managed to open the door." Syl touched the growing lump beneath his hair.

Haus squatted by Aliara, and the pair began a conversation consisting largely of grunts and hand gestures. An artifact of their previous work together.

Syl turned to leave, but found Rej and Uuron wedged into the closet behind him, leaving no escape.

"So, you think one of the little guy's haints did all of that?" Rej asked, indicating the mess.

"I can only assume so, yes," Syl said.

"Pretty brutal."

"Sure is." Uuron waved his hands as he spoke, oblivious to the spiked knuckle dusters that brushed increasingly close to Syl's face. The man was a head taller than Haus, and thoroughly unaware of how fully he dominated any space he visited. "Haven't seen anything like this since that job over in Guunaat. Remember that, Rej? Us Estoans do know how to make a mess. Course, that's why we work with Fist." He chuckled.

"I remember that one…head was up in that tree." Rej rubbed her fair, freckled chin. "Where *did* we find that hand?"

"If you'll excuse me…" Feeling like a kisselball bouncing amongst bumpers, Syl left Rej and Uuron to their discussion of forceful vivisections of the past and returned to Aliara and Haus. "Find anything?" he asked.

"Not yet. Looking, listening." Haus stood, rubbed his palm over the back of his head. "You have a plan, Duke?"

"I have you for that."

"Fair enough," he said. "Uuron, Rej, get in here. Bring the puka."

Uuron batted away the last dangling vestiges of the battered wall and poked his head through the doorway. "Where'd he go?"

Syl pointed in the general direction of the hall. The big man nodded and disappeared.

Rej squeezed her way into the little room and laughed. "What *is* this place? I mean, who does this kind of thing?"

"I assure you," Syl said. "You are just as well not knowing."

"After this is all done, Duke, you gotta tell me. Crazies, hidden doors, spooks in the closets—I thought this was gonna be a simple eviction jig." She scratched the back of her neck where her slung crossbow's stock tickled.

"Certainly," Syl said. "When this is done, we'll sit down for drinks and I will tell you the delightful story of the eccentric genius who not only brought fresh water to all of Dockhaven, but also kept the two of us prisoner for decades, victimizing us on a daily basis. Is that the sort of evening you envisioned?"

The smile melted from Rej's face.

"Got him, Victuur—er, Fist." Uuron stood at the threshold between closet and hidden room, Schmalch tucked under his arm. He dropped the puka, who threaded his way between legs to stand by Syl and Haus.

"The other one ran off downstairs," Uuron said.

"Fine." Haus pulled a long, well-honed blade from the sheath on his thigh, thumbing its saw-toothed spine absently as he spoke. "We break into three groups. Uuron, Rej, go up these stairs. Duke, Rift, you go down. It's a blind climb, so be prepared for ambush. Either direction."

Syl welcomed the opportunity to descend. Since claiming the mansion, one of their goals had been the basement lab. Peering into the darkness below, he couldn't be sure how far down the staircase continued.

"Follow the stairs as far as they go. If you find nothing, come back here and wait. If you find something, kill it." Haus met their eyes in turn, holding his gaze until each one nodded. "Schmalch'll show me where he saw this thing. If there's nothing there, we come back here. If you're in trouble, yell. You hear someone else yelling, head toward them and help."

HAUS

"Which room?" Haus asked Schmalch as they crested the stairs onto the third floor.

Schmalch pointed to the door directly ahead. "It's s'posta' be open. I left it open."

Haus drew a long breath, held it, and released. The hope that Schmalch's creature was the result of a naturally fearful puka's imagination vaporized. Whatever the thing was, it was clever enough to hide its tracks. He scented the air, snoot twitching with the effort. Beneath the expected smells of a long-deserted house lay the odor of a predator's den, musky and foreboding. He had turned from hunted to hunter before, but this was not the mountains of home in winter, and this quarry was unknown.

"Anything else I should know?" Haus asked.

"Like what?"

"The area adjoining the closet, any blind spots?"

Schmalch bit his lip. "There's a *lot* of area aj-adjoining it."

Haus wasn't sure if the puka even knew what "adjoining" meant. "How so?"

"The room I was in is big. 'Bout as big as the library."

Haus nodded

"There's a big lav—washroom, I mean—between it and another bedroom. Plus, there's a funny sliding door that connects both bedrooms."

Haus added the detail to his mental map of the place. "Any spots someone might hide?"

"Uh…" The big, brown eyes rolled toward the ceiling. "Under the bed, I guess. Oh! Or around the corner. I might be able to hide in the fireplace, but I don't think that thing was short enough."

Haus nodded and waited to see if Schmalch would add anything else. When he didn't, Haus stalked up to the door, tried the knob, and found it locked. Choosing speed over silence, he thrust his shoulder into the stile. The jamb gave with an unobtrusive *crack*.

Schmalch tugged at Haus' pant leg and motioned him to bend down.

"There's a bunch of dead animals in there, all stuffed up, you catch?" he said. "They scared me sideways."

When he swung the door open, Haus was glad for the warning. The taxidermy littering the bedroom would have been shocking at any time, but given the circumstances, he might have unstuffed the bear with his blade before realizing the truth.

Lumia lamps inside glowed dully, their shutters left open after the puka's escape. Two other doors near the entry were closed, yet scattered around the unmade bed were empty liquor bottles, a half-eaten duck carcass, and an array of crumbs. The scene felt wrong— all the care taken to close the doors, yet Schmalch's mess remained.

"Which one's the closet?" Haus asked.

"That one, the other's the big lav." Schmalch leaned in, feet still in the hall, and pointed to the far end of the room. "The sliding doors are over there, 'round the corner."

"You still have your weapon?"

Schmalch reached to his boot and pulled out his wavy blade. He displayed it proudly.

"Good. Watch the closet door. If you hear or see something before I do, holler and cut anything that comes at you. I'm going to check the rest of the room."

Schmalch nodded uneasily.

The "big lav" was quite possibly the largest and least tastefully decorated washroom Haus had seen this side of a bathhouse. He squatted, checking that nothing was hiding in the stall and waited a few breaths to be sure the room was empty. Behind him, lightning blazed through the bedroom windows, illuminating the washroom and casting Haus' crouching shadow on the closed door opposite him. Thunder chased it with a resounding crash.

Schmalch yelped.

"Just weather," Haus said. He stepped back into the bedroom, closing the washroom behind him.

The puka gulped air and nodded.

Under the table, under the bed, inside the fireplace—all were unoccupied. Haus rounded the corner, into the nook, where more taxidermy joined an antique melody engine and dusty old orrery. The pocket doors separating this room from the next were closed. He sheathed his knife and gently tugged at the cupped handles, attempting to separate the doors. For an optimistic second, he thought they'd slide smoothly and silently, but before they'd parted far enough for him to peer through, the wood stuttered in its tracks. Its squeaking rattle kicked a final few notes out of the antique melody engine. Haus gritted his teeth and jerked the doors a chest-width apart. Nothing made a move inside; the adjoining room was as hushed as he hoped it would be.

Lightning flickered again, giving the bedchamber beyond a moment of muted color. Haus slid the panels closed, their chatter paired with the low growl of thunder in the distance. He shifted the delicate orrery and its stand front of the opening, painted balls spinning giddily around the central orb with a metallic *zing*. Anyone who entered from this direction would bumble into the contraption.

Haus strode to the closet, edged Schmalch to one side, and drew his knife again. He cracked the door and peered into darkness. When nothing leapt at him, he swung it open and cranked the light. The space was big, more dressing room than closet.

Haus poked through the hanging and heaped clothes and swept the area below the vanity, but found nothing. He crouched by the fallen chair at the closet's rear and raised a brow at Schmalch.

"I did that," the puka whispered.

"Which wall opened?" Haus asked.

Schmalch pointed with his kris to the wall behind Haus and the upset chair.

Haus shoved the chair and fallen dresses to one side. He tried lifting the clothing rod to no effect. It had been too much to hope that the lunatic who designed this place would make it obvious. While he worked his way through the search for a trigger, Schmalch pawed through the vanity drawers, opening bottles and toying with jewelry.

A distant *thud* interrupted Haus' search.

"Quiet," he told Schmalch, who dropped his handful of silver chains into an open drawer with a clatter.

The storm outside strobed and rattled the windows, reminding Haus of its presence. The noise he heard could have been nothing more than a bit of the rundown mansion's exterior coming loose in the wind and rain. A louder *thud* echoed from upstairs, followed by shuffling footsteps and Uuron's unmistakable roar.

Haus started for the exit. He made it only two strides before a tell-tale click and scrape halted him. He turned back, fist tight around the grip of his blade. From the corner of his eye, he saw Schmalch curl into the shadows beneath the vanity.

When the head emerged from the trick door, Haus could only reflect that the puka hadn't seemed nearly frightened enough.

GIRL

Girl and her children were hungry. The little grey woman and little green man hadn't filled their bellies. Since Boy had gone out to hunt so long ago and never come back, the Outside People brought food when the white moon was whole, half, and gone. Girl hadn't seen the Outside People for days, and without Boy, she and her children were hungry. Food had been here tonight. Just not enough.

They had huddled in their home for days, waiting for the sounds of food to arrive. Food always yelled, "Help me," "Let me out," "Why are you doing this?" Food liked to yell.

She knew Stupid Girl and Beautiful Boy had been here. Girl had heard them, smelled them, even seen them prancing around the outside place Father never let her go; the place he'd taught her to keep locked and safe. Stupid Girl was pretty and free. She would make good food. Girl would eat her and keep Beautiful Boy for herself. She'd watched Beautiful Boy for years—until Stupid Girl took him away. Girl loved him. But he loved Stupid Girl and Father loved him.

Girl wanted Father to love her. Father wanted her to make Stupid Girl see, but Stupid Girl wouldn't see. Father made Mean Man beat Girl when she couldn't make Stupid Girl see. Stupid Girl wanted her to have beatings, *that* was why she wouldn't see. She didn't want Father to love Girl. But these past few days, Girl had *made* Stupid Girl see. It hurt Stupid Girl to see, and Girl liked doing that. She would hurt Stupid Girl again before eating her.

Girl heard sounds on the stairs and crouched. Maybe *this* was Stupid Girl. So easy.

"What do you see?" asked a woman's voice from the stairs.

Girl giggled. That was what Father always asked Stupid Girl.

A brown head moved slowly into sight.

Girl could hear her children shifting behind her. They complained of their hunger. They were angry, eager. She told them food was on its way.

A bright light appeared beside the brown head. Girl and her children scattered on silent feet, hiding from the light. A body followed the head. This brown man was big. He would fill their bellies.

"Nothing, just a lot of trash and broken stuff," said the man. He put a large hand over his nose. "Smells like a thousand sick gutter babies shit in a slaughterhouse up here."

"Nice," said the other voice. "Still have to check it."

The man came all the way into Girl's territory. His light moved back and forth across the room, but not fast enough to catch Girl's family. A big pink woman appeared behind him. The family would eat until their bellies were big!

Both the man and the woman held shiny things. Girl recognized them. They cut and they hurt. Knife, Father had called them. Sister had been cut with one earlier when she'd chased a little green man. Her hand still oozed bright red from the wound. The grey woman had cut Daughter, too, but her red ooze had turned hard and brown by now.

"Damn, you weren't lying," said the woman, pinching the bridge of her nose. "I haven't smelled anything this foul since we stayed at that one-shitter camp up in the Tiavis Range."

The man laughed, his light still sweeping back and forth, back and forth.

"Hey, look—we found the dormers." The woman wandered to

one of the windows, separating herself from the man. She pointed at the sky. "You can count the rings from here."

The big brown man's grunt turned to a yelp as Brother dropped from the rafters onto his back. "What in the depths?" he said. He dropped his light and twisted around, grabbing at Brother with one hand, slashing the knife behind him with the other. The light spun on the floor between their feet. It made them look funny.

From her hiding spot behind Father's old trunk, Sister laughed and clapped before racing forward to help Brother, nipping at the brown man's legs. He made more noises each time she bit him.

The woman turned from the window, shiny knife raised. She stared, blinked as the brown man's moving light slapped over and over across her face.

"What is it?" she barked. She held a hand in front of her face, blocking the light.

Son hit the pink woman from the side, knocking her to the floor. The shiny thing flew from her hand. Son put his knees on the woman's chest and pounded at her face. Her arms flailed at him, scratching, hitting, but Son kept beating until her arms slowed and dropped.

Girl was proud of Son. He was her first born. He was strong. He twisted off the woman's head and brought it to Girl. Such a lovely gift.

Brother whined when the brown man's knife hurt him. His arm oozed red and he let go, falling to the floor. The man kicked at Sister, pointed his shiny thing at her.

"You windless freaks!" the man said. "I'll kill every last one of you!" He jabbed his knife at Brother and Sister.

Daughter grabbed the woman's dropped knife and scooted up behind the brown man. She poked the shiny thing into him. He yelled and turned, his knife swiping at her. Daughter ducked and giggled. Sister jumped onto the man's back. Daughter poked and slashed again, and the man's guts came tumbling out.

"Son of a dibuc!" he yelled. He pawed at his shiny, slick insides. "What'd you do, you ugly quim?"

Now he sounded like food.

He slashed at Daughter, ignoring Sister as she nipped at his neck. Daughter grabbed the trailing guts and began to gnaw, circling the man, ducking his shiny thing, grinning at him.

When he tired of their play, the man fell to his knees and dropped the knife. Brother, holding his wounded arm, ran up and kicked the brown man, who fell over and made a burbling noise. Daughter poked him a couple more times until he stopped twitching and groaning. Then Brother joined Sister and Daughter in their meal.

Girl squatted beside Son, who smiled his bright-red smile. The brown man's still-spinning light flashed on and off of Son, on and off. Girl stroked his face, told him what a good Son he was.

But there was still work to be done. She heard more sounds downstairs. The big pink woman's meat would wait. No more food should be allowed to enter their den, she told her family. Son nodded. Girl sent he and Daughter down the twisty steps to find the source of the noises. If more food waited down there, Son would deal with it. Or if, as she hoped, Father had come back, Son would bring him to Girl. Son understood.

Girl stood in the shifting moonlight beside the windows, cradling the big pink woman's head in her arms. She felt a familiar presence below tickling at her. Her lips curled in a smile. *She* would deal with Stupid Girl herself.

SCHMALCH

Just as Haus had been about to leave him, Schmalch heard the trick door scrape open. He wound into the tiniest, most compact ball he could manage and hid beneath the closet desk. He didn't even breathe, just watched, unblinking, from his hiding spot.

He liked the big karju. He really hoped these things wouldn't call him food, too.

"What in the Worn Book?" Haus murmured.

First, the big man's thick legs backpedaled past. Next came two more pairs of legs, naked and brilliantly white. One set worked normally, the other bent backward at the knee like some animal.

Tears blurred Schmalch's vision. He wanted to close his eyes, pretend it was all over, but he couldn't. He had to watch.

"C'mon," Haus growled.

The wrong-legged one scrooched down. Schmalch saw jutting hipbones, ribs like a thumb piano, sagging balls. It sprung. He heard a struggle, the grunting of effort, the *thwap* of flesh striking flesh, but no calls for help. When Haus yelped, Schmalch bit his tongue to keep from screaming.

When the last set of legs ran toward the fight, Schmalch knew it was time to get gone. He leaned out of his cubby. In the bedroom, Haus and the white man-thing with the wrong legs were rolling around on the floor. A similarly pale lady-thing was kicking and throwing clocks and stuffed animals at them. The hullabaloo blocked Schmalch's exit through the bedroom. That left only one choice, and not one he liked.

Schmalch slipped from his hiding spot and crept through the monster's door, into the dingy white room, and wound down the spiral stairs.

SYLANDAIR

The promise of the spiral staircase was quickly extinguished for Syl. After descending one flight, Aliara and he found themselves in a room smaller and gloomier than the one they'd left. He calculated their location relative to the rest of the house and grimaced. This path would get them nowhere. He considered ignoring this riddle, simply turning around and climbing upstairs to assist the others.

Aliara had different plans. She hopped over the stair rail and pointed. "There."

Syl regarded the unlit room until he spied her objective—a small metal handle situated where the wall met the ceiling. An average karju could have pulled the lever with ease—even a flabby, decrepit karju. Aliara strained on her tiptoes, finally hopping to catch the lever.

The wall creaked open and dim light shone in. Aliara gave a small, unhappy squeak. As Syl suspected, they once again were in the dreaded steel-paneled room. Syl studied Aliara in his peripheral vision. Her shoulders were pulled high, eyes narrowed, but she showed no sign of panic or mania. He stood with her, undecided on how to proceed, until she broke the silence.

"No," she said, her voice tight, controlled. "It's not here."

"What's not here?"

"The last catch."

This was the most rationally he'd seen her behave in here since she'd first opened the Duin-forsaken room. If the last piece of the puzzle was in here, his darling girl would have long ago found it, quite mad or not. She'd been looking in the wrong place.

"That would make sense," he said.

"Mmph." Her long eyes drawn in a thin line, she stared into nothingness, her thoughts almost visible.

The low rumble of calm but unintelligible voices drifted down the staircase.

Aliara's shoulders relaxed at last. "He was fat and old. The trigger couldn't be far. Music room—" she paused to look at him. "—or my room."

"Logical. He *was* fat and old…and profoundly lazy," Syl smirked, hoping to keep her from giving into another fit of frustration. "Shall we start with the music room, since we're here?"

With a curt nod, she began the search.

HAUS

Haus had done some research on the jig, knew the previous owner of this house had been a zoeticist, but the monstrosities before him were beyond anything he might have expected. If this was the price to be paid so the masses could enjoy indoor plumbing, crankless lighting, and replacement limbs, Haus would gladly go back to shitting in a hole in the dark and wiping with his one remaining hand.

He drew his blade and took in the naked, bony aberrations lurching toward him. The male stood on hock-jointed legs. Blood still dripped from scratches on his face and shoulders. Haus hoped the wounds had come from Rej or Uuron. Its jaw thrust so high into his face that the mottled lower teeth cut through callused flesh and back out again, grazing the occipital bone. Distantly, Haus wondered if the thing licked its own eyeballs like a lizard.

The female sported three arms. One was stumpy and vestigial, sprouting from below her breast. The other two, though of normal length, were horribly malformed. The forearm bones curved and bowed so brutally that Haus could see light between them. She ran a pink tongue over her cracked lips and leered at him with her one good eye, the other obscured by a fleshy lump sprouting from her forehead.

From jaw to crown, the left sides of both their heads were covered in clumps of tumors. To the hunter in Haus, those masses looked tender and vulnerable.

The too-familiar ruthless joy of the predator glowed in their malformed faces. His best hope was to direct the fight, hold the closet so they could only attack one at a time.

"C'mon," he said to the male, who crouched and pounced.

Haus raised his arm to block the snapping, drooling maw. He barked an oath as teeth sunk into his flesh while knobby, blood-soaked fingers scratched at the hard leather plate covering his chest. The impact threw him off balance, sent him stumbling backward.

The female rushed them, slamming into her companion and driving them all through the doorway into the room proper. He drove a knee into the male's exposed testicles and tried to push the monstrosity away. The male hitched and curled and groaned but held tight. Haus thrust with his knife. The thing skewed aside, the blade slicing into its shoulder instead of its chest. It growled and yipped.

The female pelted Haus with anything handy. He took a stuffed rodent to the head, something metal to his thigh. Ignoring the barrage, he pulled the knife from the male's shoulder as the creature came at him again.

With a bellow, Haus grabbed the gaunt body, lifted him into the air, and slammed him onto the floor. Volley of projectiles still battering him, he straddled the pathetic creature and raised his blade. The male swung a blood-slicked arm, deflecting Haus' strike. The knife slipped to one side, slicing into the spongy growths on the creature's head. Its tip snapped off against the floor with a sharp *tink*.

The male opened his mouth as if to scream but produced only a rusty gurgle. His arms punched and clawed. Haus dragged the blade through the hunk of irregular masses, severing a large chunk. Clear liquid gushed from the grey slickness inside. The thing's yellow eyes rolled in its head, the flailing arms slowed. Haus raised the blade again, this time finding his target in the creature's hollow chest. The male went still almost instantly.

Haus rose and rounded on the female. She was gone. So was Schmalch. If there was a chance Uuron or Rej had survived, they needed him. Haus wished the puka luck and ran to the iron stairs, scaling them in great leaps.

SCHMALCH

The howl of a badly played instrument barely registered as Schmalch barreled down the stairs toward the second floor. He hadn't been as sneaky as he'd hoped. He'd nearly made it into Rift's closet when a bony hand snatched his collar and tugged.

Schmalch slipped free of his jacket, but lost his balance and pitched forward onto hands and knees. Before he could move, the monster lifted Schmalch like he was nothing and slammed him face-first into a picture of happy, frolicking puka. Alongside the familiar sound of his nose breaking, he heard a distant *clank* and the grate of metal on metal from inside the wall. The whole painting sunk into its frame like a giant fancy button.

He wailed and let himself go limp, faking a blackout, and the creature let him drop to the ground. He rolled over with a groan, barely aware of the kris in his hand. Against his instincts he opened his eyes. Like the first head he'd seen, this one was half-covered in those lumpy things, but this was worse. Far, far worse. The figure was pale white and skeletal, female. Though a disturbing stubby arm twitched beneath one sagging bub, his eyes fixed on the larger one reaching for him, its bones so bowed he could see the sneering, feral face through the gap between them.

She grabbed him by the throat and lifted, squishy pink tongue dancing over her lips. She snapped teeth at him. Schmalch squeezed his eyes shut against the terror and slashed. When she dropped him with a yowl, he rolled to his feet and sprinted for the exit.

Schmalch slid across the bloody bedroom floor into the hallway and careened off the wall. Behind him, he heard the lady-thing thrashing across the slippery floorboards. He got his feet back under him and lurched toward the nearest door.

The room behind it was the library, where the Duke had hid out for days. Schmalch had only visited briefly, just long enough to talk to the Duke and leave. He didn't know it as well as he knew the rest of the house, but escape was escape. He darted inside. Rows of books and stacks of papers loomed around him. He started off to one side, hopped back, and groaned, see-sawing from one foot to the other, bewildered by his options.

He'd only paused a heartbeat, but the lady-thing moved fast. A low growl and slapping footfalls announced her arrival. Schmalch made a choice. It didn't matter which way he went; all paths led away from her. He darted down one row with her so close at his back, he was sure she would snag him at any moment. He turned and dashed up the next row. Up and down the stacks they circled. Until she got wise. Schmalch veered into the last row and slammed into her sweat-slicked stomach.

He bounced and fell back. She lunged. He rolled under a big table, hopping to his feet on the other side. She hissed, all three arms grabbing at him across the desktop. He feinted and faked, but she was fast, guessing his every move. He'd trapped himself in the rear of the room by the bookcase under the windows. He backed up to the shelves, blindly grabbing things, hurling them at her, one eye always on his pursuer, the other seeking any escape.

Off to his right, a section of bookshelf was misplaced, hanging open like a door. Schmalch couldn't see beyond it, only that it was open, which meant it led somewhere else. Still grabbing and hurling, he edged toward the door. He didn't know what might be waiting for him inside, but it had to be an improvement. He would *not* be food.

The horrible monster crouched for attack, ready to spring

over the table and devour him. Schmalch sprinted toward the open section of bookshelf, leapt inside, and tugged the heavy door after him. The lady-thing tried to stop him, her fingers scrabbling against the polished wood, but they slipped off. She screeched as the latch snicked into place. He was safe.

Schmalch dropped to his knees and crawled far, far behind the piles of books and papers packed into the shallow room, listening to her scream and beat and claw at the concealed entrance. He curled into the corner, knife ready, wincing at each rattle and crash.

SYLANDAIR

More than halfway through the room's inventory, Syl and Aliara had pulled horns from their mounts, tapped drums, even spun the glass armonica, but the door had remained stubbornly closed.

One foot on the wheelharp's drive pedal, Syl tapped the keys of the long out-of-tune instrument in search of a trigger. With each note, he relived the tedium of his lessons. This wheelharp, the clavichord, the spinet—if the instrument had a keyboard, Orono had demanded he learn to play it, his calves lashed black for each wrong note. Syl had spent far too many evenings dressed like a festooned confection, churning through song after song while Orono's guests ogled and petted him.

Syl slammed both fists against the keys, and the wheelharp caterwauled in protest. Aliara turned to stare. He brushed an obstreperous wisp of hair back into place, shook his head, and moved on to a shelf of ocarinas.

He'd only picked up the first when a garbled shout echoed down the stairs. The vibration of running feet on metal steps clanged, followed by the familiar keening of Schmalch. Aliara dropped a small drum and drew her stilettos. Syl readied his pistol. Something mechanical growled in the ceiling and with a metallic scrape, the door that had bedeviled them for days flew upward, exposing the basement entry.

Aliara pushed Syl back down the stairs. "Get the wheelharp."

Weapons holstered, they rolled the ungainly thing into the doorway, strings vibrating a discordant cacophony as it rumbled across the floor. Should the door close on it, the wheelharp would no longer be playable, but it was bulky and durable. The door would not slide shut again while they were away.

A bone-chilling howl spiraled through the house. As they bolted for the spiral staircase, Aliara collapsed, momentum driving her across the metal floor. Her body was rigid, head once again clutched in her hands. Tiny blue-black rivulets of blood trickled from her ears and nose. Her mouth yawned open but made no sound. Syl knelt by her, hand hovering above her face, afraid to touch.

From the small white room behind him, he heard a low *clunk, clunk, clunk, clunk*.

Stooped beside Aliara, he slowly turned, breath still, mouth dry, watching as the shaggy ball bobbed its way down the stairs. It hit the floor, rolled to a stop.

Rej's dead eyes stared dully back at him.

GIRL

Girl listened as Son fought another of the intruders. He screamed and was gone. She couldn't feel him, hear him anymore. The others clamored, calling his name, begging him to answer, but he was silent.

Girl wailed, anger hot inside her. Stupid Girl brought these monsters here to kill Girl's family. This was Stupid Girl's fault. She had to pay.

Girl closed her eyes. She could sense Stupid Girl below. Smell her, feel her.

Girl ran down the stairs to Stupid Girl's room. Daughter was nearby, in one of Father's favorite rooms. She had the little green man trapped. She wanted to taste him, ruin him for hurting her just as he'd hurt Sister before, but Girl had other plans. She called Daughter to leave the food and join her.

Footsteps clanged above Girl. She frowned. She wanted to protect her territory, but she had to stop Stupid Girl. Girl would hurt her. Make her see. Take her Beautiful Boy. Crush her pretty grey head. Girl called a warning to Sister and Brother. They were crafty. They would take care of this new threat. Father would be so proud when he came back.

Daughter arrived. Girl stroked Daughter's pretty brown hair, told her the plan, told her of the things they would do, the prizes they would take. Daughter giggled and twirled with glee.

Girl crouched. She thought hard. She made Stupid Girl see. She showed Stupid Girl the little white room, showed her the stairs, showed her the beauty of Daughter.

Below, she heard the thump of a body, the rhythm of feet. She felt Stupid Girl inside her, felt her see. Beautiful Boy was with her. Girl's mouth turned up. He would do for Girl what Boy had done before. Beautiful Boy would help Girl make a new Son.

It was everything Girl wanted.

She rose, bent over the railing and tossed the big pink woman's head, showing Stupid Girl every graceful bounce of the gift she offered to Beautiful Boy.

HAUS

A reek like a diseased animal left to die in the sun hung in the air like wet cotton. Haus made it two strides into the attic before wisdom replaced rage and he checked himself. In the dwindling beam of Uuron's crank torch lying on the floor, Haus saw a creature hunched over his cousin's carcass, gnawing on something unsavory. This one made the two from downstairs seem normal enough to take out to dinner.

The woman—her nudity made that determination simple—regarded him with hateful cold green eyes. *Three* cold green eyes. One was situated in her forehead, the others arranged equidistant on either side of a long, broad nose. Two jaws flanked the head, a mouth centered above each chin. She gazed unblinkingly at Haus as she crammed hunks of Uuron into her gory maws with both hands.

"Hey!" Haus barked.

The two-faced nightmare rose and smiled her double smile, revealing bits of bloody flesh caught between her jagged, decomposing teeth. Involuntarily, Haus stepped back. She eased closer, squatted again, and stroked her dark red hair like a trull flirting with a trick.

As they stared at one another, something splashed on Haus' shoulder, its spatter tickling his cheek. Haus touched his shoulder and drew back a blood-tipped finger. In the dimness, he thought he saw the woman nod. Weight and flailing limbs fell on him. Teeth sunk into the unprotected soft spot between his neck and collarbone. He dropped and rolled onto his back, pinning the assailant, who twitched and scratched, teeth still lodged in Haus' muscle. Haus drove his fist into its face until the mouth tore away, a hunk of his flesh going with it. Haus rolled to his knees, reached back, and grabbed the thing by its matted scalp and heaved it over his shoulder toward a dormer window. The attacker landed on the plank floor with a whump, coming to rest against Rej's decapitated body. Both combatants scrambled to their feet.

"Sweet mother Jajal," Haus echoed Uuron's earlier sentiment.

Silhouetted in the dormer against the stormy moonlight, the creature—this one was male—rose on legs nearly as long as Haus was tall. His limbs were elongated, spindly, and, as with all the horrors here, fish-belly white. He regarded Haus with lopsided eyes so far apart they seemed almost puka-like.

Suddenly, he crouched, folding his legs like a cricket, and cocked a head that grew directly from the shoulders without benefit of a neck. He raised his hips, palms on the floor like a sprinter waiting for the starting horn. The female, once again at Uuron's remains, giggled and clapped. At the sound, the male shot toward Haus, who pivoted away in the moment before impact. The thing caught only his side before bounding away into the darkness. The impact knocked the knife from Haus' hand, sent it spinning away, but he kept his feet. Haus gulped a breath and groped for the cudgel hooked to his belt. He spied the neckless spider-thing half-crouched by an upended trunk.

Haus bent low and charged, his wounded, bloody shoulder slamming high into the thing's chest. Teeth clamped down on the raw meat of Haus' neck. He roared. The creature flailed gangly limbs in search of a handhold as Haus drove it forward toward the dormer window.

Instead of resisting, the creature wrapped powerful spider limbs around Haus, pinning his arms and hugging him tighter than a mother's embrace.

Teeth gnawed at his head. Face buried in the horrible thing's chest, the reek of sweat and rot and blood-filled Haus' nose and snoot. Something salty and bitter oozed into his mouth. Haus thrashed around, trying to dislodge his attacker. His foot caught Rej's carcass and he tripped, sending he and the thing enveloping him crashing through the dormer window.

ALIARA

The pain in her head was enormous. Aliara no longer saw Syl or the music room or the at-long-last open basement door. She saw only the white room with the metal stairs.

"*See,*" the voice in her head commanded. "*See Daughter.*"

Her eyes settled on something vaguely female; nasty and unlike anything given form by the cruel minds of the Duar. Muddy brown hair framed a malformed grinning face, mouth filled with piano-key teeth. Clusters of tumors pushed their way out of one side of the head. One mashed against an eyeball that could not possibly see. Red gore ringed the mouth, dappled the gaunt cheeks, speckled the teeth.

"*See, Stupid Girl.*"

Aliara watched her hand, once again bony and white, toss a shaggy and blood-splotched orb onto the stairs. As it bounced down the treads, she recognized the face of Haus' archer.

"*Gift for Beautiful Boy,*" said the voice. "*My Beautiful Boy.*"

The head rolled to a stop at the foot of the stairs, empty eyes staring into the room. A giddy glee blossomed inside Aliara. Her pale hand patted the malformed woman's shoulder.

"*Go, Daughter, go.*"

The lumpy woman with the matted hair began to descend, and Aliara saw a body more horrifying than the face. It bent and twisted in ways that should have hampered movement, yet the woman descended the steps without struggle.

"*Stupid Girl die.*"

Aliara followed down the spiral, watching her filthy feet settle on each step. An explosion rang out. Louder than thunder. It hurt her ears. The aberration below her jerked, blood sprayed from its chest. The undersized arm below one breast wriggled as though trying to free itself from the maimed body. The woman's head looked up, meeting Aliara's gaze. Blood poured from its mouth and it folded, slid to the floor.

"*Daughter!*" the voice cried.

Aliara almost felt sympathy.

She hurried down the stairs. Syl stood there, lips pressed in a thin line, eyes narrowed. He patted his pockets with one hand, pistol in the other. Her own familiar body lay behind him, arched in seizure.

She squatted next to the wounded form crumpled at the base of the stairs and stroked the bloody brown hair. The woman was dead—face, neck, and chest spangled with oozing holes.

She turned to Syl, a dark effigy against the steel walls.

"*Beautiful Boy?*" the voice asked.

HAUS

As he plummeted from the fourth-story dormer window, freakish man-thing wrapped around him, Haus was ready to die broken and bloody in this horrible place on this rainy night. He was almost disappointed when their descent ended far sooner than expected.

His overloaded mind had forgotten the balcony stretched across the back of the mansion's third floor. Together, he and the creature bounced against the railing and rolled across the terrace toward the house. They crashed into the glass doors, shattered a few panes, then rebounded toward the railing. Haus heard the opponent's ribs crack, felt its gasps of pain with each impact, yet its bony arms and legs held tight.

Blood trickled into his eyes as the creature continued nipping at his scalp. Haus reared back and rammed the bleached body against the balcony's cap rail. The thing groaned and its legs relaxed enough for Haus to free one arm. He groped at his attacker's body, found an open wound in his arm, and jammed his fingers inside. The creature vibrated, his arms released as he pawed at Haus' invading digits.

Rain-soaked and off-balance from blood loss, Haus struggled to his feet. He grabbed the thing's shoulder with his own gnarled arm and lifted it off the ground, pinning it against the railing. The rain- and blood-slick monster snarled and snapped and writhed. Haus drew back with his free arm and struck. The head snapped back, but the face was so broad Haus' strike hit only the nose; both eyes remained unscathed.

He drew back for another punch, but hesitated as lightning zipped across the sky, teasing the tips of the waterworks' blue domes. The thing chomped down on Haus' restraining arm, struck the steel skeleton beneath, and drew back shattered teeth with a yelp.

"Didn't expect that, did you?" Haus landed the second blow. The creature's eyes rolled back, his limbs slackened. Haus picked up the pale body and hurled it into the night. Its skull exploded against the flagstone patio below. Haus stood in the shifting moonlight with the smile of a lunatic as he watched the beast's blood dissolve into pools of slanting rain.

That was two. At least two more needed his attention. One had gone after Schmalch, another still lounged upstairs, feasting on Uuron and Rej with her dual mouths. That had to end.

Haus rammed an elbow into the glass doors to the study, reached in, twisted the lock. The blustery night sucked the door open. Standing in a puddle that grew around him, Haus scanned the room. He tore a strip from one of the curtains and wrapped his gaping wound. He dried his hands and dripping hair with the remainder.

Most of the furniture in here had been removed by the cleaners. Atrocious portraits of a fat man in hunting garb and various finery still hung from one wall alongside scattered awards. Mostly empty shelves occupied another wall, a chalkboard on the third. A giant safe hunkered in one corner. Haus grinned. The lunatic owner of this house seemed to have been a hunter of some sort. That meant he had weapons and if weapons were anywhere, this was it.

He strode across the room and crouched by the dial. It was set five forward of aught, an old shopkeeper's trick to speed access. He suspected the same applied to lazy scientists. He laid his ear to the door and turned the dial back to zero. The final tumbler clicked as it found its mark, and he swung the heavy door open.

Inside was a handful of age-worn weapons—a bent harpoon,

a pneumatic pistol missing its barrel, two mag-rifles with rust-locked slides, bags of ammunition, and a rounded, metal helmet painted with some variety of roaring wildcat and the words *"Nireer's Naturalists Club."*

Haus zeroed in on the biggest, meanest, least corroded thing in sight: a blunderbuss as long as his arm and thick as his thigh that would vaporize whatever it hit. He snatched a heavy sack of grapeshot, dropped some into the barrel and clicked the weapon on. The hum of its magnet seemed to run through his body, raising the hairs on his arms. He swung the weapon over his shoulder and left the room.

This time, he didn't care about stealth. He wanted this twitching quim's attention. He stomped through the house back to the spiral staircase and up into the dark of the attic.

The distant, slurpy chewing still going on there turned his stomach. Uuron's crank light had fully wound down, leaving only the broken light from the dormers. Haus could make out only the outline of his target's white shoulder and the side of one face. She seemed unfazed by his angry presence, by the weather blowing in against her naked skin, by anything at all.

He took two steps toward her. Her head swiveled up to look at him, gobbets of flesh dangling from the dual jaws.

Another flash of lightning revealed the full scene. Thunder shook the building.

Haus pulled the trigger.

SYLANDAIR

His gaze pinned to the staircase, Syl groped in his pockets for ammunition. He knew he had more, but its location had departed his mind. A second pair of white legs appeared on the stairs, and Syl knew Schmalch's assessment had been correct, more than one bogy haunted this house.

This body was not as deformed as the first, but its head was no less horrifying. As tall as Syl, she wore a child's smock the color of an overripe lime. Its high, ragged hem revealed her gender, though she seemed indifferent to the exposure.

She crouched beside the fresh remains and looked up at Syl. One eye bulged wide, the other seemed to recede into the head; sorrow swam in them both. The crooked jaw shifted.

"Wyyy?" she asked. "Wyyy Booful Booy?"

The rheumy green eyes slid down to the pistol in Syl's hand and hardened. They drifted to Aliara's body, then back to Syl's face. The lips, red as the blood pooling around her, pulled back in a scornful smile.

"Toopi Gurl," she said and lunged on all fours toward Aliara.

Syl dropped the spent pistol and grabbed a handful of dark reddish hair before the monstrosity reached his mate. She spun and clawed at him, wrenching his fingers painfully in her tangled mane. Her serrated nails tore through his bespoke shirt and scored his chest and neck. He pressed a foot against her thigh and shoved. Knotted bits of her hair tore away, stuck between his fingers. She rolled and sprung up, anger focused now on him.

He grabbed for the dagger nestled at his back, but she was too fast. She leapt onto him. He groped for balance, but finding none, pitched backward and slammed into the music room, lunatic monster riding him through the fall.

Something in his left wrist snapped when they hit the floor. He cried out and raised his right arm against her attack. She clawed and tore at him, shrieking and spitting with each swipe. Syl pressed knees into her gut and threw her off. He scrambled to his feet as she again bounced up. This time, she came at him low, crashing into his chest, driving him against the glass armonica, which tipped and shattered. Syl stumbled back but kept his feet.

The woman-thing grabbed a handful of his hair and tugged, hissing something unintelligible. Feeling roots pull free, Syl twisted and struck her square in the face with the heel of his good hand. She staggered back, shook her head, then sprang forward, wrapping him in a fierce embrace that pinned his arms to his sides. He could not reach his dagger, could not strike at her, or do much more than pinch her thigh.

Her teeth clamped down on the meat of his left bicep and pulled. A hunk ripped free. Then another. Pain clotted the scream in his throat. The monstrous woman leaned her head back, his inky blood coursing down her chin and smiled, showing him the chunk of his own body held between her teeth. She gulped it down and snapped foul teeth at his face as Syl reared back and rammed his forehead into her nose as hard as he could.

Stunned, she released her suffocating grip and tumbled to her knees. Syl drew the Voshar dagger. As though on springs, she popped up again and ran at him, mouth wide in a rusty battle cry. He raised the weapon and swung, meeting her charge. The honed edge sliced through her cheeks like a well-cooked roast before catching in the hinge of her jaw. She gurgled, her body twitched, and her hands flapped limply against his chest.

Syl leaned his weight into the attack, pushing her back, back until her flailing form slammed against the wall. Flutes, ocarinas, and fifes tumbled unnoticed from their wall mounts. Syl pressed the weapon until he felt it pop through muscle and bone. Her body crumpled at his feet. The top half of her head rested on his blade, watching him until the light within her muddy eyes vanished forever.

HAUS

With shaking hands, Haus poured shot into the blunderbuss' mouth, tendrils of spittle sailing from his lips with each ragged pant. Elimination of the two-faced horror brought his total to three. At least one more lurked around here somewhere.

As he stood there, waiting for it to leap from the shadows, the fury clouding his mind ebbed, his logic returned. If one was here, it would have jumped him by now.

Haus turned and pounded down the spiral staircase; he wanted them to know he was coming.

On the first floor, he found a misshapen white body crumpled at the foot of the stairs, a ragged hole where her breastbone once was. A few feet away, the Duke crouched protectively in front of a partially conscious Rift. Haus had supposed the man helpless, yet here he squatted, body protectively shielding his mate's prone form, ugly arm wound bleeding freely, pistol pointed at the stairs.

"Everything fine here?" Haus asked.

His narrow face spattered with his own blackish blood alongside his victims' karju red, the Duke relaxed, lowered his pistol. "I suppose we are. What of upstairs?"

"Took out three of...of whatever those were. Rej and Uuron are dead."

The Duke nodded toward the stairs. "I had reached that conclusion regarding your archer."

Haus followed the Duke's gesture to where the severed head lay. He growled. He wanted to pick up Rej's head, return it to her body, but that was just sentimentality. He'd see to them later. He returned to his clients.

"The little guy?"

"Schmalch? We've not seen him since we parted with you," the Duke said.

"Left him in the closet when those…things came out. Gonna go find him." Haus made it up two steps and stopped. "If you don't need me."

Rift eased herself into a seated position. "Go."

"We will meet you outside," the Duke said. He looked down at his maimed arm. "Neither of us could best them if there are more prowling about."

With a nod, Haus took the stairs two at a time toward the third floor, where he'd last seen Schmalch.

HERGIS

Hergis Savesti had endured this story before. At least twice before. It was insipid the first time, irksome the second, and barely tolerable now, but Most Illustrious Master Pryor Skeln Emat was well-known and well-liked by both the politicos and literati of Dockhaven. His title was as impressive as a Mucha could hope for, and his works more widely known than any other in the city. So Hergis dared not complain or walk away—both things he desperately wanted to do. He would have much preferred to join the conversation of an adjacent group, enmeshed in gossip surrounding the recent hubbub at the neighboring Orono mansion.

Instead, he stood, glass of caba in hand, gazing up at the yellow bird flying around inside the cage woven into Skeln's towering coiffure and wondering why the man had ever thought this story was amusing, let alone worth repeating. Even when he had not been forced to endure it personally, Hergis had overheard Skeln retell the dreaded thing at every cocktail reception since he'd joined this Mucha Hall.

"—and, as you know Savesti, I told Mayor Raan—pernicious little pip that she was—that Tehtaemanian steel simply wouldn't work. Too brittle." Skeln flicked a bit of something from the cuff of his crimson bespoke jacket, an eight-button piece with besom pockets. "I insisted on Ukurian because it is far and above the finest quality and most durable, and I'll have nothing less for a Skeln Emat project. But then, you already know that."

The round ruddy man nodded and leaned down to slap Hergis on the shoulder as though they were great chums. The gesture left a dent in the puffy shoulder of Hergis' lavishly expensive lavender frockcoat. "But they crowed about expenses. Naturally. And you simply will not believe what they wanted me to—"

Each time Skeln nodded or shook his head, the bird was jostled from its roost. It attempted to fly, but merely bumped off the clumps of bluish-green hair swelling between the cage bars before settling back on its perch. Hergis himself had spent five hours in the stylist's chair today preparing for this month's meeting at the Mucha house. The conch-like coils wrapping his scalp were lovely, works of art actually. The stylist had woven Hergis' long buttery mustaches into the hair-sculpt before dappling it all with a coral dye, effecting a sunset-like appearance. Hergis hadn't considered adding wildlife— but he certainly would next time.

"—wouldn't allow me to move the statue, but how would one possibly achieve the effect they hired me to achieve if I was not allowed to adjust that bloody thing?" Skeln spread his arms like a lecturer soliciting classroom response.

Hergis shrugged, knowing full well that the statue did eventually get moved. "How indeed?"

"Yes, yes, well, it was merely a matter of using my acute negotiating skills," Skeln continued in his artificially cultured voice. "An architect must be one part artist, one part engineer, and one part diplomat. Not so simple, like you medical types. *We* must have an entire battalion of skills at our command." He sucked in air, ready for the next burst of his interminable tale. Hergis was certain he heard a strained squeak from the contrast stitching of Skeln's pink pinstriped trousers. "Utilizing those particular skills, I spoke to them each in turn and informed—"

An incongruous noise from below drew Hergis' attention. He peered through the ornate gallery railing into the crowded hall below.

A kerfuffle appeared to be brewing near the entrance. Gathering all these great minds and burgeoning egos in one room often led to petty squabbles and even minor physical altercations. Hergis enjoyed watching them, considered the spectacles the finest entertainment Mucha gatherings had to offer. Sometimes he would even be treated to a de-wigging—a horrifying embarrassment to the victim, but delightful fuel for gossip for months to come.

This scene, however, seemed different. Instead of colorful bodies bickering and slapping at one another, Hergis saw only a dark-cloaked figure wending through the room so nimbly it seemed to follow a ready path invisible to all others. The small troop of Abog Union goons, hired as security for the event, bumbled along behind, working their way upstream through the crowd. In a room full of overindulgent hairstyles and garish garments, this person's simplicity stood out like a tumor among healthy cells.

The figure stopped every so often and spoke with someone. Shock-faced Mucha shook heads and pointed to others, then whispered among themselves as the stranger moved on to the next person.

Now openly ignoring Skeln's monotonous story, Hergis strained to follow the stranger's path through the room, always a few steps ahead of security. His eyes widened with curiosity as the cloaked figure ghosted up the marble staircase, snaking closer and closer to his location.

Gradually, a hard-looking chivori woman took shape beneath the dark hood. She paused by Well Sovereign Master Enan Ranaran and muttered something. Enan's sharp, tapered face flushed, then pinched, lips drawing away from her perfect teeth.

"I think *not*," Enan said in a raised voice. She placed a bony grey hand over the breast of her ruffled burgundy frock in shock at the audacity of being spoken to by someone so prosaic. "I do important work, not that birdlime you people do out there. You won't drag me into this."

The woman scowled and murmured something else. Enan huffed and pointed to Hergis. The woman drifted over, stood with her dusky grey face turned down to him. She closed her long eyes for a silent moment. Hergis' curiosity could hardly bear the pause.

"That one," the woman opened her eyes and pointed to Enan, who quirked overpainted blue lips in a mercurial smile, "sent me to you."

Skeln gave an outraged huff and marched away to relay his tedious story to a new audience.

"Oh? Why would she think we should speak?" Hergis asked.

"Are you a surgeon?"

"I am. A Supreme Sovereign Master, holder of a tertiary degree from the Mucha Colleges of Ukur-Tilen, to be precise." He gave an almost imperceptible bow.

She stared blankly with dark, angled eyes that looked either sleepy or bored, he couldn't decide.

"My specialty is the brain—healing, altering, enhancing, and such."

She frowned. "That's it?"

He chuckled. "That is not enough?"

She shrugged.

"If you inquire as to my abilities with other facets of the body, then yes, I can do more. Much more. As with all my medical counterparts, I too was fully trained as a mere physician before conquering my specialty. The Colleges enforce very stringent standards before one can reach the pinnacle of mastery."

She stared for a moment as if waiting for more. "So you can sew up wounds?"

"Of course. Easy as a sigh."

"Will you follow me?"

"Oh now, why would I do that?" He swirled the caba in his glass and raised an eyebrow decorated with seed pearls.

"At least two people need a surgeon to—"

Hergis held up a hand and shook his head, dangling arcs of his mustaches shimmying. "No, no. For that, you'll simply have to visit a general surgeon. We are all here tonight to enjoy the company of our intellectual equals, not to be dragged away to sew up some heathens after their street skirmish."

Again, she closed her eyes and paused. "Is there anyone else?" Her voice sounded deflated.

"To assist you?"

She gave a single nod.

He shrugged. "You might try Rour Onati," he gestured to a man with flaming red hair and a bright blue unitard a few groups over. "But you will likely find the same answer throughout the room."

Her eyes narrowed. She made no move, but Hergis most definitely felt menaced. "Useless," she said. "The whole twitching lot of you. Can't be bothered to walk next door."

"Next door?" Hergis asked, interest piqued.

She spun on her heels and started down the curving staircase.

"Would that be the Estoans' Lodge next door?" he called.

She didn't answer, didn't even look back.

The woman didn't look like an Estoan, but the alternative would be surprising—and tantalizing. Hergis opened his mouth to call after her again, but decided it would be best not to yell this question. Others might find the answer as provocative as he.

Short legs pumping, he hurried after the woman and tugged at her cloak. She whirled and glared down at him.

"Do you mean the Orono mansion?" He noticed several well-coifed heads turn at the mention of the location. It had been the subject of much conversation this evening. The rapscallions who'd been living there for years had disappeared after an evening where—according to rumor—flares were thrown from the tower, followed by shouting and a gruesome death.

"Yes."

"*In* the Orono mansion?"

"Yes."

"Wait here."

Hergis scurried away to claim his cape and umbrella from the coatroom. He couldn't believe the luck. His love had always been zoetics, but at the colleges in Ukur-Tilen he'd been informed in no uncertain terms that he had no skill for the craft. His enjoyment of the subject, however, had never dwindled.

As a hobbyist, he'd studied the works of the magnificent zoeticist Kluuta Orono for decades, arriving in Dockhaven mere months too late to meet the talented scientist. Gathering at this Mucha Hall every month, so close to the sealed-up mansion, was maddening. Many times Hergis had considered hiring an Abog crew to help him pay a surreptitious visit to the abandoned place. Tonight, he might seize an opportunity to do so legitimately. Even if these patients were in residence illicitly, a surgeon of any stripe could not be blamed for lending medical assistance to those in need—regardless of their location.

Plus, a visit inside the mansion, so intriguingly active lately, would make him the darling of the next Mucha meeting. He giggled, giddy at the prospect.

Glittering blue wrap and matching umbrella in hand, he scurried back to the stairs. The woman was gone.

Panicked, Hergis scanned the bustling room in search of that lone black column. He spotted her long-limbed figure at the exit, only a few steps in front of the enthusiastic security staff. He threaded his way through the tall bodies and out the front door after her.

"Wait, wait, miss," he called as she drifted away from the hall's entrance. "I am here."

She stopped and examined his empty hands. "Tools?"

He opened his umbrella and stepped into the pattering rain to meet her. "Sadly I did not bring my medical valise this eventide. For that, we would need to pay a visit to my office, but it is many blocks from here, in the North Point district."

He rolled a bit of mustache between two fingers and met the woman's stern gaze. "It does not sound like you have that sort of time. It is quite possible the type of equipment we need would be available in Master Orono's laboratory. I could make a quick survey. You would not have happened to see that facility while inside, would you?"

Her eyes narrowed again, though Hergis felt less menace in this glare.

"I'm familiar with it."

"Excellent, excellent." He quivered with excitement. "Shall we go then?"

"You don't want to go in there."

"Oh?"

She started off toward the mansion's gate, gliding over the damp cobbles like a wraith. Hergis struggled to keep up, quietly speculating about what sort of delightful mystery he'd become enmeshed in.

As they closed on the massive iron gate of the Orono estate, the figure of another chivori resolved against the darkness, a tall column of a male, blood dripping from the hemline of his coat. The rain pattered against the wide black brim of his hat and the expensive, if dirty, trench coat thrown over his shoulders. Through its opening, Hergis could see the man's once-elegant clothing was in tatters, his wrist and left hand swollen grotesquely.

"Oh my," he said.

"*This* happened inside," the woman told him.

Her eyes glowed like a tabby's in the reflected light of the streetlamps. The scientist in Hergis knew the effect was merely the layer behind the retinas of chivori that both helped them to see in dim light and hindered their vision in brightness. The nervous man who had stumbled into this capricious adventure found the sight discomforting. He glanced around, realizing for the first time that he was alone with these demonstrably violent strangers. He swallowed hard and stroked the arc of his left mustache. "Who or what...

ahem...I mean to say, how did this happen?"

The man rolled his pale grey face slowly toward Hergis. Lightning flashed, brightening his eyes like lumia bulbs and highlighting the deep hollows of cheeks on a beautiful, haggard face. Hergis guessed the wrist was not the worst injury this man had sustained.

"I cannot say who or what. A thing? Another victim? I've no idea. Words fail me, sir." The man lifted the corner of his coat and removed a wadded hunk of dark, wet fabric from high on his arm. Beneath, he was missing a chunk the size of an adult fist. "Can you stop this bleeding?"

"Goodness, no, not here in the street." Hergis couldn't help glancing at the mansion. "Is there any safe place we can get inside?"

"The servant's cottage is behind the main house. It has been cleaned." The man looked at the woman and shrugged.

She slipped beneath his good arm and helped him shamble along the cart path.

"I will meet you in a moment," Hergis called. "I will attempt to locate gauze and antiseptic at the Mucha Hall. Perhaps Enan brought her kit..." He trailed off as he hastened back to his society's meeting house, shaking his head and muttering, "Oh my, oh my."

HAUS

Now that he was observing, not hunting, Haus found himself almost offended by the gaudy oversized bedroom. Pink and black-and-white were woven into a flurry of patterns across almost every item in sight. Hand-stenciled floral patterns covered the walls. The satin-draped bed reminded him of a pleasure den he'd visited in a less-reputable region of the Nors. And the rugs, while plush, looked as if they'd been designed by a colorblind spastic. What few spaces weren't tarted up were filled with taxidermy and assorted useless geegaws. Haus decided he'd rather sleep on a dirt floor than have to wake up to this each morning.

"Schmalch?" he called.

No answer.

He went to the closet and stood, straining to recall details. His unconscious mind had picked up the little guy ducking under the dressing table, but he wasn't there now. During the fight, the route out of the closet had been blocked by Haus and his opponents. That left the hidden stairwell. He'd seen no evidence of the puka or his remains in the attic, so he descended to the second floor.

In Rift's old bedroom, he found footprints and slide marks in the gore leading to the hallway where a body—no, two bodies—had slammed into the wall. Small, dragging bootprints and larger barefoot tracks led from there into the library entry, where a matted mess of prints led up one row before fading into nothingness.

Haus looked back out the door. If Schmalch had run out of here, he would have made more marks. If he'd been caught and eaten, there'd at least be some remainder of a carcass. He started into the room.

"Schmalch!" he bellowed.

Faintly, he heard a sound between a whimper and a cry.

"It's Haus."

A distant shuffling and weeping.

Haus held still. "Where?"

He heard a tapping like a fist against wood.

"I hear you. Keep it up."

He followed the sound to the bookshelves at the back of the room, squatted, and banged on them.

"You there?"

"Mister Haus?" came the muffled reply.

"How'd you get in?"

"It was open."

With most everything knocked off the shelves, it was no work to find the switch. The panel sprung open.

Schmalch darted out and hugged Haus' thick, scarred arm, barely avoiding the bite wound. Haus patted his bald head.

"That thing chased me, and I thought it was gonna get me!" Schmalch said, eyes rolling up to Haus' face from either side of his head. "So I hid in there and held really, really still. Where are they? Are they still around here?"

"Dunno. Five're down so far. Could be more."

Schmalch's eyes widened. He backed toward the hidden room.

Haus put a hand on Schmalch's shoulder. "No. C'mon."

The puka just about hopped on and rode Haus downstairs and into the courtyard. Once there, Haus stopped in the rain for a moment, enjoy the sting against his wounds.

"Where's Rift and the Duke?" Schmalch asked.

The front gate was open, but the Duke had been in no condition to walk anywhere. He'd indicated Rift was in bad shape as well, though outside of some blood on her face she hadn't looked it. Haus had seen her strangle a man with his own belt while two daggers were sticking out of her back. She was durable. Whatever had flattened her must have been bad. Either way, standing in the rain probably hadn't been on their agenda.

"You know the buildings out back?" Haus asked.

"Yup," the puka answered.

"We'll try them."

Schmalch nodded and trailed Haus as he led the way around the main house toward a squat building near the rear garden wall, smiling at the smashed corpse as they passed the flagstone patio. When the pair ducked under a tall fruit tree, Rift emerged from the smaller building's doorway, hood drawn over her head.

"Surgeon's inside," she said when she reached them.

They stood in silence, Schmalch shifting nervously from foot to foot.

"Are there more?" she asked.

"Didn't check it all," Haus said. "No sign of any more so far."

Her eyes were shadowed, but her mouth sharpened its perpetual frown. "We'll hire Abog. Let them sweep."

Haus grunted. "Right. What were those things?"

"Experiments."

"Here the whole time?"

She shrugged. "My best guess? Yes."

Haus gave a low whistle. "Gotta do something about Uuron and Rej. Family'll want to return him to the sea from home shores. Don't know about her."

"Have them sweep first."

Haus nodded.

Schmalch tugged at the rough edge of Haus' chest plate.

"Go on in," he told the puka.

Schmalch scampered into the warm, dry building.

"What's this about?" Haus asked.

Rift's face turned into the moonlight that peeked from behind storm clouds. Rain stippled her cheeks. She sighed.

"Zoetics?" he asked.

"Among other things. Sylandair should tell you." She nodded to toward the small house. "You could use a surgeon, too."

"More scars for the pile."

SYLANDAIR

"I see this was quite a tussle," said the burlap-colored minikin examining Syl's oozing shoulder. He stood on a short stool beside the bed, his gut brushing Syl's forearm. "My my, that looks just terrible. Is it a bite?"

"Yes."

"From what?" His rapid lilting voice rang in the ear he hovered by. "I am unfamiliar with this particular form of predation."

"As I told you, I am unable to say what exactly."

The surgeon clicked his tongue and stood back, rummaging through a bright-yellow valise ornamented with the initials *ERR* in burnished silver. "I can unquestionably provide some basic care here, but this will scar terribly if we don't get you to my office for further treatment soon. I am certain your lovely companion has informed you that I am a well-respected surgeon with offices here on Dockhaven's Big Island."

"She said you were a titled Mucha surgeon, yes."

He beamed. "Yes indeed—Supreme Sovereign Master Hergis Savesti. To keep it simple, you may call me Supreme Sovereign Master Savesti."

Syl had no intention of calling the little man any such thing. He'd strongly encouraged Aliara to take the extra time to find a proper physician who didn't look like a lunatic with unforgivable fashion sense, but she'd insisted on the more expeditious route of acquiring one of the Mucha from next door. Syl had been too weak to dispute with any enthusiasm, so he'd accepted the situation. However, his tolerance for the Mucha's codified eccentricity ended when he was called upon to participate.

"Savesti. Is that Norian?" Syl asked.

"It is Orasian."

Syl was silent.

"Ah yes, never fear," Hergis looked up from his excavation of the borrowed bag. "I was not raised there. I bear none of the foolish cultural prejudices that likely concern you."

"I see."

Syl thought he might bleed to death before the man actually did anything. But after a few more minutes of muttering and digging, he turned around and took hold of Syl's shoulder.

"And you, sir?"

Syl forced himself not to wince at the grip. "Hm?"

"Your name?"

"Ah, yes. Sylandair Imythedralin, Duke of Isay." He ground his teeth as the man palpated raw flesh. "You, Master Savesti, may call me whatever you like."

Hergis' eyes darted to Syl's pale face, then back to his work. He shoved the loopy mustaches over his shoulders, careful not to catch them in his enormous jade lobe rings, uncorked a bottle of clear liquid and poured it over Syl's shoulder.

"Sax's tit!" Syl shouted and drew away, angry glint in his eye.

"Yes, yes, that antiseptic certainly does sting a bit, doesn't it? But it will kill anything unpleasant that may be lurking in the flesh. And here's the anesthetic." He took out a syringe, tapped it twice, and injected it into the wound.

Syl's arm burned hot for a few seconds before the pain tapered off a bit.

Hergis donned a multi-lensed monocular, braced between one ear and the broad, bridge of his nose. He wiggled the blunt tip of the nose like a bunny as he ogled the wound, tilting his head this way and that. Again, he clicked his tongue. "Looks as though you've nicked a vein. Lost a good deal of the old ink, I should guess." He leaned back and took in Syl's face. "That would explain the pallor."

"Will it take much to sew up?"

"Not at all." Hergis went back to the bag and withdrew a device that looked to Syl like a very long, very narrow needle at the end of a hand drill. "Here we are. A lovely little device for just such a purpose."

He bent over the injury again. Syl felt a pinpoint burning in his arm, smelled his meat cooking. Beads of sweat popped out on his forehead and upper lip. The spit in his mouth vanished.

"Better, better. That will stop the leak. You were quite lucky it was a vein in lieu of an artery. No matter how expert my ministrations, you would have bled to death before I had the opportunity to repair you." Hergis patted the wound with gauze and soaked a surgical thread in the dreaded antiseptic as he chatted. "Owing to my abilities, you will live to reign another day. A duke you said, correct? How lovely. From the Dominion of Chiva'vastezz, I assume?"

Syl nodded, eyes watering despite the anesthetic, as the surgeon stitched up the wound. Somehow knowing the torture was coming, being required to sit still during it was worse than the initial injury.

"And your companion?"

"Aliara Rift," she said from the open doorway.

"My mate," Syl said. He winced. "Could you stop tugging there?"

"Apologies." Hergis kept tugging. "Your duchess, I presume?"

Aliara snorted.

Syl chuckled. "She is my darling girl most certainly, but I doubt Duchess of Isay is a title she would claim."

From the corner of his eye, Syl saw the surgeon's eyebrows shoot up.

"You are not married then?"

Syl raised a brow. "Do I look karju?"

Hergis chuckled. "It is not unknown amongst your people."

Syl huffed a derisive laugh. "Yes, under the most political of circumstances."

Hergis nodded. "Very well. And what brings you to our modest atoll?"

"Who would not want to visit the Haven?" Syl replied, wry quirk to his mouth. "It is such an idyllic vacation spot."

Hergis chuckled. "It is unusual to meet a member of the Vazztain court here, you must admit."

"I suppose."

"Especially unusual to meet one lurking about an abandoned house with such a tremendous hunk of flesh missing from his arm."

"Unusual, I concur."

Undeterred by Syl's vague answers, Hergis continued to probe. "You do know whose house this was, do you not?"

"I do," Syl said as he watched the physician bandage the long line of stitches. "I also know whose house it *is*."

"Oh?" Hergis began spreading ointment on the dozens of scratches crisscrossing Syl's torso, face, and arms.

Syl let the question hang.

"Might I ask who the owner is?"

Syl gave him a surprised face, as though the answer were obvious. "Why I am, of course."

He saw a pleased smile niggle the physician's mouth.

Hergis stepped back and examined his work. "There now. You have lost a great deal of your blood. Yes. No matter the color, it works the same as the rest. You will need to make more. Rest for three to four quarters so your body can replenish itself. Rest, rest, rest. Eat properly and leave that wound alone. Do not move the arm." He waggled a shaming finger at Syl. "No nonsense, understood?"

"Of course."

"A colleague at my office specializes in replacement flesh and framing. She could fill it in for you if you like."

"A decision for another day."

"Very well. I will instruct Madame Rift in the manner of continuing treatment for all of this," he waved his hand over the assortment of bandaged wounds. "But the wrist…" He shook his head and gently raised the broken limb. "I have an ossein catalyst that will help you heal more quickly, but I have no stronger medications with me, Duke Imythedralin, nothing to fully dull the pain. You will not enjoy the treatment."

"I'm certain I will not."

They stared at each other for a moment.

"I have had bones set before, Master Savesti."

"Yes… In that case, shall I proceed?"

Syl nodded.

The pain was exquisite. Because the bones were not in proper alignment, setting and splinting the wrist required Hergis to perform a series of intensely unpleasant adjustments. When it was complete and the ossein injected, Syl could do little more than flop back onto the bed and sweat. At least Nushgha wasn't here to mock him for his weakness.

As he drifted in a state that wasn't quite consciousness, Syl listened to the pattering of the rain outside and snatches of conversation between Aliara and Hergis. She squatted beside the surgeon just outside the room, pot of ointment in her hand, eyes flashing to Syl each time she nodded.

When they returned to the room, Syl sat up with a groan and a wince. "What do I owe you, Master Savesti?"

Hergis brushed imaginary lint from his garish lavender jacket, a tragic waste of fine Vazztain flannel, in Syl's opinion. "I've never before made a house call, so I cannot say that I have any sort of fee structure in place, let alone one that would take into account the interruption of my social gathering," Hergis said. "Perhaps…we could strike some sort of agreement in lieu of payment?"

Syl raised one brow. He didn't trust causal arrangements. "Such as?"

Hergis made a great show of considering. He tapped his foot and doodled with his bizarre hair, the style of which gave Syl the impression the man had attached flaming seashells to his scalp. The longer the performance ran on, the more closely Syl scrutinized him.

"I am an enthusiast," Hergis announced at last. "I once had dreams of becoming a zoeticist, but it was simply not to be. My love for the art did not diminish, however. Though I was unable to obtain a degree in the subject, I have studied it extensively through my many decades."

Syl's lips pressed into a tight line. He saw where this was headed.

"It has long been my dream," Hergis continued. "To view the contents of Master Orono's laboratory. For a peek—an extended peek—inside, I should gladly call your debt settled."

"You are a devotee of *Master* Orono's?" Syl gave a derisive intonation to the title. Although trained by a Mucha, Orono was hardly one himself.

"Indeed I am. He was a magnificent creator." Hergis' face brightened. "Few among us have devised and developed such a diverse and advantageous catalogue of genomes. And without attending a single session in Ukur-Tilen."

"He had a teacher, I assure you."

The façade of his professional society falling away with the rise of enthusiasm for the subject, Hergis climbed up and relaxed at the foot of the bed. "Yes. I have heard rumors," he said with a knowing nod.

"Not the best ones, I'm sure."

"You knew the great man?"

Aliara, bored or disgusted, left the room.

"After a fashion." Syl could not stop the sneer that crept onto his face. "He would enjoy that you called him a great man."

"Oh, but he was. If I was one sliver as brilliant as him…" Hergis sighed. "May I ask how you knew him?"

"He owned me." Syl had no energy remaining for pretense. He enjoyed the shock on the Mucha minikin's face. "Aliara as well. Bestowed the beastly house to me upon his death."

Hergis did nothing but blink.

"One of his brilliant genomes did this to me." Syl tapped his fingers lightly against the bandaged bite. "Are these the sorts of things you were hoping to learn through a visit to Master Orono's laboratory?"

Hergis swallowed hard. "I suppose there is a private side to us all that would change the world's opinion of our public face."

"Some more private than others."

The surgeon nodded, then tilted his head to one side. Syl could almost see him weighing his options.

"Do you still wish to strike that agreement with me?" Syl asked. "Much of what you see will quickly disabuse you of the notion that he was a great man."

Hergis stared into nothingness. Syl held his tongue, certain it was a difficult thing for the man to meet the potential truth of his hero.

"Yes," Hergis said at last. "I may learn things that will turn my stomach, but they will not change the brilliance of his work. A chance to learn from a genius in any field is rare. Such an opportunity will likely never be mine again."

Syl nodded. "Very well. However, I have terms."

"Proceed."

"I have need of consultation on the contents of documents we have found and will find. We are in search of specific information that will necessitate a more scientific mind than my own. Your presence would be required for several hours daily."

Hergis nodded. "Acceptable. For this opportunity, I will happily leave my practice in the capable hands of my partners."

"I would also request your services as a surgeon for anyone who chooses to join us in our efforts."

"Naturally."

"For these services, I will pay you two-hundred Callas a week as a retainer." Money made an agreement formal, more difficult to break. "While I am certain you earn far more from your practice, you will—as you have indicated—receive supplementary benefits from this situation."

"Remuneration is unnecessary but appreciated." Hergis bowed his head politely.

"Excellent. The final condition you may not so willingly accept, but it is immutable." Syl paused, waiting for Hergis' nod. "I alone decide the fate of anything found inside the house, on the grounds or in any way bequeathed to me." He held up a finger. "Correction: In my absence, Aliara will make such decisions."

The front door creaked open. Syl heard a squishy scuttle; Schmalch had arrived.

Hergis' brow wrinkled. "I see no reason to dispute that condition."

Syl watched for signs of duplicity in the physician's face and assessed him guileless. "Ah, but you will. There are plans and sequences and experimental notations inside that will rouse you. You will see considerable possibilities in what you find, and you will make arguments concerning their benefits to society. I will have none of it."

The puka appeared in the doorway. He rushed forward and hugged one of Syl's legs that dangled over the edge of the bed. Both surgeon and patient ignored the assault.

Hergis nodded, visibly excited.

"I have already burned many such papers and books."

The surgeon's face fell. "But—but why?"

"I will be very clear. I do not want the name of Kluuta Orono any further glorified or paid tribute to. He was an awful man, a blight on the karju, and on any species capable of reason and compassion. He will not be further lauded. Perhaps when you examine the bodies of those things inside, you will consider the cost of his brilliance and find a way to agree with me."

Boots thumped down the hallway in a familiar gait. Aliara entered, followed by Haus, who appeared chewed but not swallowed. Schmalch released Syl's leg and scurried over to the mercenary.

"If you can agree to my terms, Master Savesti—" Syl swept his uninjured arm toward the newcomers, "—Victuur Haus and my assistant, Schmalch. I would ask that you see to their wounds as well."

Hergis, head shaking softly, looked up from his lap. He almost flinched as his gaze fell on Haus and held for a long beat. "Goodness…" He seemed momentarily befuddled. "Yes…er… sit—Victuur, was it?"

Unconcerned by the negotiation in progress, Haus grunted and anchored himself in the room's lone chair. Schmalch squatted beside his legs like an obedient pet frightened by a storm.

"You look almost as bad as this one," Hergis told Haus before hesitantly returning to Syl. "I believe I can agree to your terms, Duke Imythedralin. Though I cannot say I fancy them."

"Feel free to steal the old quim's ideas and call them your own." Syl smirked. "Do not pilfer his paperwork or attribute anything to his name."

"I would never!" At the idea of passing off someone else's work as his own, Hergis adopted a shocked expression. He fidgeted and looked away, avoiding all other eyes.

The artifice was clear. Syl studied the tells, fully versed should the surgeon attempt further deceit in the future.

"I have one condition of my own—though it is negotiable," Hergis said.

"Yes?"

"I have a pair of assistants. My sister and another…a rather unconventional one. May they join us? I assure you they will have no interest in anything we find."

"I should like to meet them before agreeing, but tentatively I see no reason to object."

Hergis hopped off the bed and withdrew the antiseptic and gauze from the medical bag. Haus, well aware of what came next, removed his leather breastplate. Syl was pleased to see even the indomitable Victuur Haus wince at the antiseptic's sting.

As he worked his way across the mercenary's many injuries, Hergis added. "Since we are to be so close, Duke Imythedralin, do call me Hergis. Master Savesti is so formal."

"Sylandair."

Hergis turned his head, but he couldn't hide the smile.

HAUS

2085 DANURAK 21

"Victuur." With a smile, Curate Isako took one of Haus' big hands in his own. "Morning greetings. It's been a while since you last joined us."

"Come when I need to," Haus said.

"As do we all." He winked. "You arrive empty-handed."

Haus cracked a brief smile. "No time to stop at the market."

Isako nodded. "Then you shall present the meat after forms."

Haus scented the air. His stomach, empty and forgotten for hours, rumbled at the smoky aroma of fish cooking in the pit oven.

"Tuna. Fahroo caught it in the wee hours this morning." Isako smiled. "He cleaned it before he arrived, so you can avoid that unpleasant duty."

Haus dipped his head and left the Curate to welcome the others waiting for entry. He forewent mingling and headed upstairs to the form ring to wait for the rite to begin. He stood at one of the open windows, staring at the walled estates lining Temple Row. They were crammed so tight, so unlike the ragged, transitory settlements he and Uuron grew up in on Ukur.

His gaze brushed past the Mucha Hall to the candy-colored spire of the Orono mansion. Beneath the building's ratty shingles, his cousin had died. Horribly.

Haus closed his eyes and pictured Uuron, smiling, laughing,

fighting—all the ways he wanted to remember the man. He was determined to remember the laughing warrior, not the half-eaten carcass on a stranger's attic floor.

The echoing *tick* of Isako's cane and rattle of his tiger-tooth bracelet stirred Haus from his thoughts. He left the window and crossed into the ring, studying the rest of the assembly who wandered in behind the Curate. Most of the faces were familiar. Some had come to lodge alone, as Haus had, because that was the way of their lives. Some were lone sailors in search of a touchstone while in port for the day and some were families, displaced from Ukur for whatever reason. Haus had been a member of this small lodge, the only option for an Estoan in Dockhaven, since his arrival in this crowded island-city, and through the years, the scarcity had made this scattered group his clan as much as the one he'd been born into back home.

Isako moved among them as the group arranged for forms. His attitude was one of ease, his movements haunted by the occasional wince or twitch. The Curate's old body was still hard and strong, but injuries earned in ceremonies performed and participated in had taken their toll. He moved with the discomfort, lived with it. The man was proud of his pain.

Haus flexed his own aching body and assumed the waiting-hunter pose.

As they went through the forms, their collective bodies moving as one, Haus felt the strains and twinges from the previous night loosen and ease. He let his mind blank, focused only on the movements and sensations of his body, the perfection of the forms. His banged-up knees creaked as he bent them to the proper angle, bruised knuckles protested as his fingers aligned with palms, and his spine crackled with the memory of last night's altercation as he bent and strained. When a stitch in his shoulder snapped with a nearly audible *pop*, he disregarded the pain. The Duke's new pet Mucha could sew him up again and again, as many times as it took.

Sweaty and animated with the energy of exercise, the assemblage left the ring and moved en masse back to the nave below. Some split off to prepare dinner, others settled on canvas cushions surrounding the massive circular table at the building's heart. There were no corners here for Haus to lurk in, so he leaned against the casement separating two windows, waiting for the meat to be ready, waiting to perform his role in the day's ceremony.

"Today," Isako announced in a resounding voice that rose above the casual chatter of those gathered, "I will read from 'The Ascent.'"

Murmurs of approval rippled beneath the kitchen talk.

Isako retrieved the Worn Book of Andak from its case and feathered through the pages until he found the one he sought. The book was not the original—that rested safely under guard in Fort Andak on Ukur—but this was a rare copy, to Haus' knowledge the only complete one in the Middle Sea. It was a privilege to be part of this lodge, to be so close to the hand-copied words. Haus had sat on these scratchy cushions, listening to recitations from the book many times. It was a reminder of the strength and resolve of his people. And of the careless way the Duin watched over their children.

He found himself curious and a little excited to hear which passage Isako had chosen today, and he smiled reflexively as the man cleared his throat and began to read:

'It was in the darkest twilight of the War of Whispers that Estoas heard the warning call of his father, the Duin Kaniral. A battle was building on the moon of Opoli, Imt opposing Wetac, brother against brother.

"'Be wary,' was the warning. 'Be prepared.'"

The Curate's deep, rolling voice seemed lifted by the clink of plates and flatware being laid out on the table, the crisp thud of wooden spoons against ceramic bowls.

'Kaniral's words had barely passed through Estoas' mind when the ground beneath him shook and then from its silent heights, Mount Cordrach growled and spat. Estoas was on his feet in a heartbeat. Without time for armor or even shoes, he burst from his yurt into camp.

"He needed no words, only a great bellow. His clansmen dropped their daily drudgery, drew up weapons, and fell into step behind him. Together, they scaled the mountain, which spat fire and living rock, threw bits of its own burning heart at them.

"The seas chased them up, up, licking their boot heels, promising watery death to those loath to face the mountain's heat. In the sky above, the pink moon tore herself asunder. A hail of her carcass, unwilling to remain in the sky, drove deep into Ismae's skin."

Isako paused to sip from the mug placed beside him by a woman with skin almost as brown as the tea she served. "Gratitude," he murmured as she hurried off. He returned the mug to the table and continued.

"Only when all before them was a burning river, all behind was water, and all above was chaos did Estoas pause, eyes scanning for the refuge he sought. In his youth, the clan had settled in the cliffs. He and his kin had played in the hollows formed by Jajal's sand, Aessatal's winds, and Leloloom's waters. He remembered them and sought their shelter."

A man, arms laden with buns and loaves, elbowed Haus, jerked his chin toward the pit-oven. Ears still on the Curate's reading, Haus crossed to where the meat waited, digging it from beneath the hot rocks, unsealing it from the sea-tangle that wrapped it. As he sliced portions from the bones, the heat scorched his fingers with a welcome, pleasant pain.

"Together they sat in their stony nave, watching the living rock pour over the cave mouth, listening to the sizzle of flame against sea and scenting the long, slow burn of the world outside. Each uncertain if they would be sealed in alive, Estoas gave them solace; the Duin would ensure their favored children survived."

As the tale progressed, and Isako's voice rose, the chatter of the clan dimmed until the only sound in the rotunda was the story, the disparate group united by thoughts of their ancestors' survival. Haus found a peace in the ritual he'd been unable to find on his pillow last night. By the time he'd served and sat with the others at the table, Uuron's death howl no longer rang in his mind, replaced now by that bawdy laugh that had been Haus' companion for so many decades.

Isako closed the book and let his gaze scan over the assembly. "We seek that wisdom each day, Estoans. In each situation, we must find the understanding of when to oppose a seemingly insurmountable foe and when to retreat. There is no shame in survival. This is The Way." His mouth slid from grimace to smile as he cast his gaze around the table. "The meal smells wonderful."

All was silent for a moment before the din of eating and conversation rose to fill the room. Haus let the sound lull him like stiff liquor, even listening with unfeigned enthusiasm to stories of daily life from the red-faced man at his left and the round-bellied woman at his right. Only occasionally did the absence of Uuron still stab at his chest.

When the dishes were cleared and the crowd had tapered away, Isako eased himself onto a cushion beside Haus. "Something troubles you, Victuur."

"I need your help, Curate."

He laid a thick hand on Haus' shoulder. "Anything."

Haus drew a long breath. He hated to utter the words. "Assistance shipping Uuron's body home."

"Body?" The man paled. "He's dead?"

Haus nodded.

"I had not heard," Isako said.

"No one has."

Isako shook his head, let his fingers tie and untie on the table. "How?"

"Brutally. Working for me." Haus let his eyes slide up to the long bank of windows and the fighting pit in the yard beyond. "Going to gather his remains today."

"I'll visit the farspeaker office immediately to make arrangements with your clan." Isako paused, rubbed the flap of his snoot. "Will you return with him?"

Haus shook his head. "I have business here."

SCHMALCH

Schmalch stood across the street from the Temple of Spriggan, the only home he'd ever known. A girl costumed as their patron darted around the recreation yard. Schmalch knew the spots where she stopped and looked around—he'd done the same himself. She and her friends were playing scour the shadows, and these were the best hiding places the orphanage had to offer. He knew them like he knew the bumps on his skull, having stashed himself there sometimes for fun as these kids did, but sometimes by necessity.

The girl ducked into an angled drain pipe jutting from beneath the main building, her black cape flapping behind her. After a moment in the dark, she reappeared. Her head bumped the lip of the pipe and she hurriedly righted the costume horns stuck to her grey forehead. A puka boy scampered out behind her. She'd captured one of her targets.

Wandering this far up the Prick had been way out of his way, but Schmalch had wanted to watch the kids play. The elders may not want him at the temple anymore, but he still needed them every now and then.

When the elders appeared, calling the children to breakfast, Schmalch went on his way. He didn't want a confrontation, didn't need to be reminded he wasn't welcome.

He scurried back down the Prick and wound his way up Central Row, past shouting shop-callers and jangling bells of pedicabs, and across Bay Bridge, which connected the Lower Rabble to the Upper.

A little bell jingled as he opened the door to Domestic Consignment. An elderly puka woman, back humped and eyes cloudy, shuffled out. A few of her teeth were missing, and her wrinkled skin seemed to flap around the ridge of her nose like gills.

Schmalch hated coming here. She gave him the dithers.

As she headed to the counter, the old woman croaked, "Welcome to Domestic Consignment. What service can we provide for you today?"

"I need a couple more people for cleaning," Schmalch said. "For Duke Imythedralin."

The woman perked up. She pushed her scratched glasses up her nose and gave Schmalch a good looking over. "You again? I heard what happened." She clicked her tongue, shook her head. "No, you get no more of my people. Can't return 'em properly."

"The Duke says we'll pay more. And…and he hired some Abog for guards."

She stopped wagging her head and considered him. "How much more?"

"Double."

"They gotta sleep there?"

"Not this time."

"What're they cleanin'?"

Schmalch looked at his feet, unsure of how to phrase it.

"Oh, I see. They'll be cleanin up Glech, will they?" she asked.

He nodded. "And some other stuff like that." He raised his eyes. "It should only be for this quartern at the most."

She squinted, her lips faintly moving, then said, "Triple. That's six Callas a day each. And you only get two of 'em. They work dawn-to-dusk. One of those guards watches 'em the whole time. They don't sleep there."

"Sure, sure." He grinned at her. "When can they start?"

"Hold on there." She wagged a finger at him. "I'm not done yet.

Poor Munk can't work cause'a what he saw, and Glech left a wife and little ones. What's your Duke gonna do about that?"

Schmalch considered possibilities and found his mind empty. "What'd you think he should do?"

"Both'd make about twenty or thirty Callas in a good month—less my commission, of course."

Schmalch suspected the old woman was exaggerating, but having never held a paying job outside of doing this and that for the Duke or Garl, he couldn't be sure.

"Munk'll get back on his feet in a couple months, but poor Glech's family'll never replace him. I say your Duke owes Munk fifty Callas and ten times that to Glech's family." She waggled a finger at him. "Less my commission, of course."

Schmalch sucked in air. The Duke had given him free rein to haggle, a surprise he'd chalked up to extreme blood loss. He was comfortable negotiating for amounts like six Callas a day, but this woman was talking about hundreds! Injured or not, the Duke might skin him if he came back with that price.

Schmalch shook his head. "I…I can't make that deal. I gotta talk to the Duke first."

"Then get goin'." She turned and shuffled toward her office but stopped after a few steps. "And don't go runnin' off to any other cleaning companies in the city. I know 'em all. I don't like you, I'll make sure they don't either."

SYLANDAIR

"Meet Tatumi," Hergis said with the tone of a sideshow barker presenting the main attraction.

The flamboyant minikin waved his hands proudly at the most absurd creature Syl had ever seen. Taller than Haus and nearly as broad, the thing was covered with coarse black fur. His watery eyes stared out at nothing, greasy bits of something collected in their corners. Hergis had dressed him in bright blue knickers and a black, round-topped hat with a narrow brim, fluffy peaked ears poking out below. The cut and color of the trousers matched the frilled blouse Hergis wore. Only a Mucha would dress a wild man in such an inane manner.

"A hiisi?" Syl tried to rise from the parlor sofa where Aliara had parked him, but thought better of it when his wound screamed in protest.

"Yes, yes, I know we civilized people consider them brutal killers and all-around savages, but...bend down, Tatumi...but you see this?" Hergis lifted the hat and pointed to a large, diamond-shaped scar just above the creature's broad, flat forehead.

"I do," Syl replied.

"Good. You may stand, Tatumi."

The beast straightened, hat cockeyed on his head. One ear fluttered as though annoyed by the adjustment. An unfortunate-looking woman with a neck like corduroy stepped forward and offered Tatumi a large beetle. The hiisi snatched the treat and shoved it into his mouth while she scratched behind a stubby ear and straightened the hat. A soft smile spread over Tatumi's blunt, rounded snout, revealing the tips of fangs that poked over his lower lip.

Syl kept an eye on the brute as Hergis continued his lecture. "Tatumi was my final project before I left the Colleges. His transformation is the prized work that earned my tertiary degree for neurobiology. He has been with Nihal and me for nearly a quarter of a century. Since my alterations were completed, he has not once stuck out at anyone. He is a loyal and wonderful servant."

Having once been touted as a loyal and wonderful servant himself, Syl remained dubious. "How did you find him?" he asked. "Hunting?"

Hergis covered his mouth to stifle a laugh, though his gut still jiggled with amusement. "Oh my, no. Nothing so madcap as that. I obtained Tatumi from a circus as it passed through Guunaat. The owner had deemed him too violent for performance and was set to destroy him." Hergis' smile broadened. He stroked his blond mustaches, tightly coiled against his face today. The oceanic theme had been brushed out of his hair, which was instead wound in a matching coil at the base of his neck. "I saved his life. A little adjustment, and Tatumi no longer desires the blood of every man, woman, and child he meets."

Tatumi scratched the stubbly fur on his chest and snorted.

Syl wondered how many other hiisi had been saved in this manner before the process was perfected. "Does he speak?"

"He does not, but I believe that is a choice rather than a result of my work. Not that hiisi speech is very elegant to begin with. When he initially came into my care, his communication consisted largely of his people's guttural tongue mixed with Plainspeak curses and threats. Perhaps once he was no longer angry, he had nothing left to say." Hergis chuckled at his joke. "Tatumi is fully capable of understanding Plainspeak and following orders. He has proven to be an able assistant and protector through the years."

"I see." Syl adjusted his sling, pain sizzling down his arm. "And you want him to join you in the lab?"

"My sister as well." Hergis gestured to the tall, colorless woman who hovered behind him. She sniffed and stepped forward. "Nihal Savesti, my beloved sister, may I introduce you to Duke Sylandair Imythedralin, the benevolent courtier of Chiva'vastezz, who has given us leave to work in the home of the late Master Kluuta Orono."

Hergis was being a bit obsequious, but Syl detected no cunning. Likely the result of decades enmeshed in the Mucha culture.

"A pleasure, Madame Savesti. I would stand, but…" Syl gestured to his damaged arm and abraded face.

The woman wore a long grey dress and a group-appropriate bright-blue apron. She was old, easily in the last quarter of her life. Her once-blond hair had gone white, her eyes puffed with a softness that would never dissipate, and lines gathered around her pinched mouth. A narrow, pale scar ran from cheek to cheek just beneath her eyes. Even a wedge of her nose bridge was missing near the snoot. It was a curious injury, as though at some point someone had wished to horizontally bisect her head with an axe.

"And you, Duke Imythedralin." She managed something resembling a curtsy. Her spiritless, almost colorless eyes flicked from Syl to her brother, something like disdain in the gaze. "As my little— pardon—my *younger* brother says, we appreciate this opportunity. It has long been a dream of his."

"You assist him in all aspects of his work?"

She nodded, sniffed.

"You, too, must be quite brilliant."

Her sallow face flushed, broad, flat nose going red with embarrassment.

Before she could speak, Hergis interrupted. "She *is* quite intelligent for one unschooled."

The woman flushed darker. Her thin upper lip threatened to curl, quickly twitching back into place.

The hiisi reached out and picked at Nihal's braided hair. She seemed not to notice.

Syl's eyes slid over to Hergis. "These two only?"

"Indeed, Duke Imyth—" Hergis smiled and corrected himself. "Indeed, Sylandair. I require very little assistance in my work."

Nihal stepped back into place behind Hergis. She rubbed her nose and sniffed.

"Then we shall see how things go today, Hergis," Syl said. "If all is well by day's end, they may stay."

"Very good." Hergis gave a polite half-bow. "Where should we begin?"

"I had been combing the library. Until last night's unpleasantness, we were unable to obtain access to the basement lab facilities. To begin, I would like to consolidate everything from both locations."

"An excellent plan. Tatumi will carry things from the library to the basement. I would find it most efficient to centralize my work in the laboratory. If you are amenable, of course."

Syl nodded. Tatumi seemed not to hear.

"Nihal will assist me in sorting through the documents, separating the potentially useful from the useless. Once that stage is complete, we will look more closely at what remains."

"A fair plan," Syl said. "I will join you from time to time. Though I fear my injury will make me less helpful than I once was." He had no intention of doing any more of the initial sorting, only examination of unearthed items related to The Book and their goals. "I would like you to focus on two things as your work commences. First, I want to know more about those things living in the attic. The bodies will be made available to you for study."

"A matter that piques my curiosity as well."

"Yes. Aliara is at this moment hiring some Abog, who are to ensure no more of those things are lurking about." He frowned.

"Though it appears safe at this moment, this place has done nothing but surprise us. They will be kept on as guards afterward."

"An excellent idea."

"Secondly, I am interested in any research pertaining to The Book."

Hergis paused, his jaw working before he spoke. "Of Omatha?"

"Yes."

Hergis' eyes widened. Syl noted Nihal's did as well.

"Master Orono was pursuing that old myth?" Hergis asked.

Syl nodded. "Review anything you find on that subject and bring it to me."

"What exactly was he st—"

Syl cut off any further questions. "All other documentation should be destroyed in the house's incinerator, found in the basement."

Hergis winced, but, knowing he'd already agreed to the terms, held his tongue.

"There are many things I would hesitate to call 'documentation,'" Syl continued. "You will likely want to burn those items as readily as I do. However, should you find anything containing my image or my name—or those of Aliara—do notify us."

"Very well. Shall we beg—"

The front door banged open.

"Duke, Duke!" Schmalch ran into the parlor and skidded to a stop when he saw the looming tower of furry muscle standing there. He backed up, eyes swiveling from Syl to the hiisi and back again. "What in the depths is that?"

"That, my dear Mister Schmalch, is Tatumi, my hiisi manservant." Hergis repeated the theatrical wave of his hands as he introduced the beast. "And this is my sister, Nihal," he added with far less pomp.

Tatumi turned his heavy head and stared at Schmalch with flat brown eyes. The woman nodded at Schmalch, then returned her gaze to Syl. Tatumi's dark purple tongue fell out of his mouth.

Schmalch didn't seem to notice Nihal. He had eyes only for the beast. "A hee-see?"

"No, no. Hih-ee-see." Hergis pronounced the word carefully.

"That's what I said." Schmalch never took his eyes off Tatumi.

"No, you're missing a syllable."

"A what?"

"A syllable. There are three in—"

"Enough," Syl said. A diction lesson with Schmalch could take days. "Tatumi and Nihal are Hergis' assistants. They shall be with us during the organization process."

Schmalch and Tatumi remained locked in a stare. "You said it was fine, Duke?"

"Yes. What do you need?"

"I…it can wait until you're done. I'll be in the hall."

"Oh my, do not delay on our behalf," Hergis said. "Unless you think otherwise, Sylandair, I believe we will investigate the library and basement, then begin the transfer of materials."

"Proceed," Syl said.

"Very good." He looked sternly at Syl. "You, my dear Duke, are to rest today. No shenanigans."

"I shall be on my very best behavior."

"I should hope so. Come, Tatumi, Nihal." Hergis picked up his purple medical bag and strode into the music room, delivering directions to his aides as they went.

Tatumi turned away from Schmalch only when Nihal touched his arm. When he and his keepers were fully gone, the puka edged slowly to where Syl sat, grave expression suggesting he suspected the beast might leap back into the room at any moment.

"Unsettling, isn't he?" Syl asked. He found the creature repellant, but then he also found its master relatively unappealing. Hergis' knowledge and assistance were needed, and Syl could tolerate anything for a couple quarterns.

"Yeah," Schmalch said. "Why would you want…want that thing

as an assistant?"

Syl shrugged, wincing with the movement. "What do you need?"

"I went to hire more cleaners. She wanted triple the daily rate."

"Fine."

"That's what I said. But then she wants more Callas—*lots* more Callas—for Munk and Glech. Or she won't assign anybody to us."

"How many more?"

"She said fifty for Munk and…" he paused, rubbed the back of his neck, "…five-hundred for Glech's family."

Syl's eyebrows shot up. "There are other cleaning services in the Haven. Go hire from one of them."

"Yeah…she said she knew all of 'em…"

"—And would prevent them from working with us."

"Yeah."

"She, naturally, would take a cut of whatever we paid?"

"She kept saying something about her com-comish—"

"Commission. Yes, her cut." Syl relaxed into the orange overstuffed sofa. "Extortion. How very unexpected from such a source."

Schmalch shrugged. "She's not wrong, though, Duke. At least for Glech. Munk'll get by, but Glech had kids."

"Agreed, though I do not appreciate being coerced. Especially not by a charwoman."

Syl tapped his lips with a long index finger. Schmalch stood by, awaiting a decision.

Money wasn't an issue. Syl was happy to waste every copper of the ludicrous amount Orono had left him, but he would not capitulate to some dried-up old puka's demands. If he allowed her to pressure him, who would be next?

"Your coworkers will receive recompense. The withered quim, however, gets nothing."

Schmalch looked at him, brows knit in confusion.

"When Aliara arrives, she and I will tend to an errand. Tomorrow,

I will send you with Callas—and perhaps something more—to both injured parties."

Schmalch smiled.

"In the interim, you should begin cleaning until assistance arrives."

The smile vanished.

ALIARA

By the time Aliara arrived, Syl had sunk deep into the one of the tacky orange couches, a rolled-up paper and silver pen on the low table in front of him. His head was tilted back, eyes closed. Not sleeping. Exhausted.

She stood at the parlor entry and studied him. His face was drawn and gaunt, closer to white than its familiar oyster-grey. The dark rings circling his eyes reminded her of their time in the duchy, of his self-imposed misery. The angry scratches covering his face and neck pained her. The attack on him, as witnessed though that creature's eyes, replayed in her head.

He stirred, sensing he was observed. His eyes popped open and he sat up.

"Pet," he patted the cushion beside him and smiled. Even his gums looked pale. "Join me. How was your errand?"

She settled in beside him, laid her head on his uninjured shoulder. "Two Abog will arrive by midday. Well-armed."

He put his arm around her, ran his fingers beneath the neckline of her saffron waistcoat, a gift from him months back. "Satisfactory." He kissed her bristly head. "Hergis has begun his work."

She curled into him. "You met the assistants?"

A shiver ran through Syl. "I was shocked—and admittedly repulsed—to find the first is a hiisi. It seemed more an inappropriate pet than an assistant. His sister is the other. Older woman, wicked-looking scar."

"A hiisi?" Outside of a zoo Orono dragged them to as children, Aliara had never seen a hiisi. One in polite society was unheard of.

Syl patted the top of his head. "Seems our Master Savesti tinkered a bit with the thing. Docile, he says."

"You believe him?"

Syl shrugged and winced. "I intend to keep my pistol loaded when working near the hirsute terror. He seems to do a fine job with heavy lifting, something I doubt Master Savesti is too fond of. He's been carrying boxes from library to laboratory. Oh yes, and Schmalch doesn't care much for the thing either."

"Wise."

"Indeed. It looks at him with a certain relish. Speaking of, we have a little errand related to our assistant."

"Oh?"

"The proprietor of the cleaning service is attempting to extort money from House Imythedralin."

Aliara chuckled. Syl didn't. She sat up and looked at him. He wasn't teasing.

"Is this person a douse?" she asked.

"It seems she is. I have an idea, though it requires your particular skills."

Her brows rose.

"Not that skill. If I am unable to rid myself of an aging puka without resorting to assassination, I've lost more than the use of one arm."

She nodded. Outside of Nushgha and another in Chiva'vastezz, Syl preferred to resolve his entanglements with less radical measures, relying on more vindictive tactics with sustained penalties he could witness and enjoy.

"We shall see to her tomorrow. But today…" The fingers on his free hand awkwardly worked the buttons on her vest. "Balls. This is more difficult than anticipated with only one hand. It seems, Pet, you will have to do most of the work."

She watched his exertions with amusement. "Haus will be here any moment."

Syl abandoned the buttons, leaned in, and ran his hand up her skirt. "He is welcome to watch."

Aliara closed her eyes. With Syl out of commission, she would be required, as he said, to do most of the work. There were things to attend to before they stilled that wicked glint in his eye. She hadn't even made it downstairs to sweep the basement for herself.

With great reluctance, she stood. "Later."

Syl put on an exaggerated frown. "I shall sit here and—what?— make more blood while everyone else works?"

"Yes."

He sighed and slumped back into the cushions. He needed a distraction, regardless of what the minikin surgeon said.

"Have you been downstairs yet?" she asked.

"No."

"Join me."

"You actually *want* to go down there?"

Her shoulders hitched noncommittally. "Does no good to avoid it."

She watched him struggle to rise until she could stand the entertainment no longer and extended a hand, hoisting him up.

"These atrocious sofas go," he said, jabbing a finger at the furniture. He straightened his shirt in an attempt to regain his dignity. "I'll sit on the floor before I drop into one of them again."

She took his hand and led him into the music room, where the door, her one-time nemesis, had been spiked open, the wheelharp rolled back into place. Aliara hadn't yet discovered what finally triggered it to open, but she hadn't spent time in search of an answer either.

At the bottom of the familiar stairs, she paused, surprised. Only dust and the transferred materials from the library stood out as different from the lab of her memory. The shelves of specimen jars still stood behind the long table covered in papers, baffling apparatuses, and desiccated remnants of unfinished projects. The tall, cylindrical gestation tank, now empty except for an indistinct heap on its floor, loomed between the cooler and the massive steel chemical cabinet. Opposite them was the sooty mouth of the incinerator, flanked by a pair of swinging doors. The first of them she knew well.

Hergis and his peculiar assistants milled around the lab proper. The stunted surgeon picked up specimens and glanced at notes as he wandered around, muttering to himself. The woman sat on a stool at the far end of the bench, hunched over reams of documents and diagrams, her legs surrounded by the sorting bins Syl had used in the library. The hiisi roamed in and out of the room, transferring things from the library or loading them into the incinerator, a look of banal stupefaction on his face.

When Hergis spotted them, he scurried over, the black-and-blue spatter print on his white pants blurring with the motion. She didn't care for the man. Though her objections had little to do with his flamboyant style that so maddened Syl, she had to agree the group's fashion coordination was curiously off-putting.

"Duke Imythedralin," he said, then stopped and smiled. "Sylandair, I mean, of course. You are not resting."

"Merely a visit. I assure you there will be no escapades."

Aliara drifted away from the pair, an ear on the conversation, and peeked into operating theater one. Much like the main room, it was a neglected likeness of her memory. A metal table, which had once seemed huge, sat in the center, darkened capacitance light above it. A fireplace dominated the far wall, old ashes piled inside around a cauldron-like sphere Orono had called his autoclave. She let the door swing shut and leaned against the wall.

"I hope you do not mind, Sylandair, but I sent Tatumi out to retrieve a new heat eater." Hergis gestured to the cooler, where the hiisi lingered. "The old one...well, you can imagine. If I am to preserve these specimens, a proper cooler is absolutely necessary."

"Fine," Syl said. "Should I reimburse...Tatumi?"

Hergis chuckled and clicked his tongue. "No, no. If you were to reimburse anyone, it would most certainly be me, but do allow this to be my part of the effort. It was nothing."

"Very well. Notify Schmalch if there is anything else you require."

"Very good. We have retrieved some of the..." He stroked the ruffles of his blindingly blue blouse as he searched for a word. "... individuals who attacked you last night. Tatumi fetched both bodies from the room upstairs. I wished to stem their deterioration as quickly as possible. I hope you do not mind."

"Not at all. You may want to wait until the Abog have swept the house before you go retrieving others."

"I am certain Tatumi could defend himself."

Aliara considered a clash between the attic people and this dapper hiisi. If Garl were allowed to hold such a contest at the Barnacle, she was certain the winner's purse would be impressive.

"But," Hergis continued, "I would hate for him to be unnecessarily injured."

"Of course," Syl said. "The Union representative said two would arrive by midday."

"Excellent. And where would we find the bodies of the other individuals?"

"Speak with Victuur Haus when he arrives."

Hergis colored a bit as his head bobbed agreeably. "I will do just that."

"My darling girl and I are going to look around a bit, then we will leave you to your work."

Hergis shook his finger at Syl. "I told you no nonsense. You are to rest."

"Yes, and I have been doing so all morning. A quick pass though this dungeon, and we will repair upstairs for mids."

"Good. See that you do." Hergis' attention drifted to a multi-legged thing floating in a small jar on the bench beside him. "Oh my, it has been ages since I saw one of these." He picked up the jar and wandered away.

Shaking his head and smirking, Syl followed her into operating theater one.

"I was in here," Aliara said.

"As appealing as you had indicated."

She ran a finger along the groove in the steel table where her blood once ran, eyes on the set of swinging doors that led to the second operating theater.

"I wasn't allowed in there," she said. "Once or twice, I peeked while waiting for him."

She pushed open the doors. Like its companion, this room featured a metal table and overhead fixture. Neither of them noticed these details, focusing instead on the gaping hole that loomed broad and low in the far wall, a scatter of fallen bricks piled at its base.

"The technique looks rather familiar," Syl said, reaching for his pistol.

Aliara squatted, peered in. "Nothing in there now."

"A potential ingress to where he lurks?" Syl knelt beside her. "For now, however, we should have it blocked."

"Or explore it."

"I would prefer to hold off on that until Hergis has found at least something of value to our cause. I shall direct the Abog to push that chemical cabinet in front of it when they are done with the sweep."

Aliara nodded. The enormous steel thing would at least delay any intrusion, if not prevent it fully.

"Duke?" A familiar nasal voice came from the room beyond.

Aliara stood and ushered Syl through the swinging door back to the main lab room.

"You in here, Duke? Rift?" Schmalch's head poked out from the stairwell.

"Yes?" Syl asked.

"There's a couple guys here. And…and if it's fine with you, I'm gonna help Haus with something."

"Of course. Haus is welcome to all of your assistance he can bear."

"Gloss!" Schmalch almost smiled before noticing Tatumi lurking in the background. He wheeled and hustled up the stairs.

HAUS

Haus stood in the courtyard of the Orono estate, studying the pile of lumber he'd gathered overnight. Some he'd collected from the remnants of ruined furniture and floors removed from the gaudy house, others he'd salvaged from the shed.

He'd learned to build at his father's side. Before the service, before prison, he'd believed carpentry would be his life. When things overturned, they'd done so spectacularly. The shaping of wood, however, never left him. He still enjoyed the task; he only wished the motivation were different.

The front door banged, and Haus looked up to see Schmalch scamper out. He took a wide berth around the two Abog men lolling on the front porch while waiting for the Duke. The little guy had good instincts. He, too, had disliked this pair on sight, found them sketchy, even for Union types. He didn't like having them around, but he couldn't fault Rift for hiring them; Abog were far more disposable than their Toh cohorts.

"So, what're we doing?" Schmalch asked as he skidded to a stop in front of Haus.

Whether motivated by coin or the need to belong, the little puka had stuck around despite last night's scare. Whatever the reason, Haus needed a lackey, and Schmalch seemed glad to be included.

"Seeing to Rej and Uuron," Haus said.

Schmalch blinked a few times. "They're still, uh...still inside, right?"

Haus nodded.

The big eyes flicked to the attic dormers and back. "Are you sure there's no more of those things inside?"

"Nope." Haus nodded at the Abog men. "That's why they're here."

"Oh." Schmalch waited, absorbing the idea. "So we wait to, um…to get them till they're done?"

Haus nodded. "S'pose so."

"Wha'do we do in the meantime?"

"Build a boat." He gestured toward the pile of rough planks.

Schmalch goggled. "Build a boat? In a day?"

"Not a fancy boat."

"Why?"

"For Rej," Haus said. "Sending her back to the water from here. Uuron, I'll ship home."

Haus wanted Uuron sent to rest by the clan from their home shores. Rej, however, seemed to have no tether. He'd asked around but found no trace of her family. She had no patron to speak of, and in ten years, he'd never once heard her mention any of the Duin in anything but a barroom curse. That made the disposition of her body his responsibility. He had no idea what she would have wanted, so he settled on treating her as he would any of his kinsmen.

"When someone died at the orphanage," Schmalch said, "the Spriggans all cried a little, said nice things about them, and burned the body. Dumped the ashes in the sea."

Haus glanced up at the scree of the front door hinges. The Duke and Rift emerged looking as grey and graceful as ever, despite the new wounds. All placid on the surface, churned up below.

Both Abog popped up and barked about their own importance until the Duke cut them off with a wave of his hand. He spoke softly for a moment, then gestured at Haus, who stared back at the group through narrowed eyes. They were leaving him in charge of these two douses. While he appreciated the confidence, Haus didn't much relish a day as warden.

He nodded, accepting the temporary role, put a hand on Schmalch's head, and guided him to a set of makeshift sawhorses. Work progressed smoothly, despite Schmalch's many splinters and banged thumbs. The little guy made a fair assistant, but on the one occasion Haus handed him a saw, Schmalch sliced into his finger before he could touch tool to wood. Hergis was dispatched to bandage the wound. The accompanying lectures about safety were the surgeon's own addition.

Afterward, Haus tried Schmalch on other tasks, but though he drew no more blood, the little guy also showed no talent for carpentry. Haus relegated him to carrying and cleaning. Schmalch's relief at the change in duty was almost palpable.

By the time the boat's keel and ribs were laid, the sun had burned away the morning fog. The Abog duo stopped by to announce the mansion was clear. Haus nodded at them, kept working. They stood there for a moment as though awaiting praise or coin before the taller of the two asked about the carcasses inside. What were they? Why were they there? Haus grunted, and Schmalch followed suit. After a bit more loitering, the pair muttered something derogatory and returned to the house.

As if conjured by the job's completion, Hergis reappeared, slobbering, dandied-up hiisi in tow. Neither were as easy to ignore as the mercenaries. With far too many words, the surgeon asked where he could find the remaining bodies of the "pale individuals who had resided in the attic."

"Two in the music room," Haus said when Hergis finally shut up.

"Yes, yes. We retrieved those two earlier. I was informed there were others and you, Mister Haus, were to person to speak with regarding their location."

Haus scowled down at him, focus on his work broken by the

intrusion. If Hergis hadn't sewn him up so well, he might have batted the minikin away like a squawking bird.

"One's on the flagstones out back," Haus said. "Another in the master bedroom. Last's in the attic."

"Good, good. I shall send Tatumi to retrieve them." The surgeon fondled his spiraled mustaches and turned to leave, jerking to a stop when Haus grabbed his shoulder.

"Leave the attic one," Haus said. "Schmalch'll tell you when it's ready."

"Do be sure you hurry, Mister Haus. The longer they lay there, the more they decompose." Hergis clicked his tongue. "Rot, I suppose I should say."

Little douse thought Haus was stupid.

"Don't care. I get Uuron and Rej, you get the other." He released Hergis' shoulder. "Good luck finding its face...both of them."

Hergis' expression blossomed with curiosity before he forced it into a look of polite disgust. All proper on the surface, cracked below. He trotted back into the building, lobotomized beast loping along behind. Haus was no fan of this new presence. Nor was Schmalch, if his cringing stance behind the skeletal boat was any indication. The Savesti trio was simply disquieting.

Shaking off the visit, Schmalch asked, "What's next?"

"The boat can wait; time to get the bodies."

Schmalch released a grating whine akin to the pleas of a starved cat.

Haus pointed a thick finger at him. "No."

The noise cut off and Schmalch slumped, arms dangling limply from his shoulders, and followed Haus to the attic.

The carcasses had intensified the lingering shit and sweat smell. Despite pulling his shirt over his snoot, Haus gagged repeatedly as he collected the scattered parts of Uuron and Rej in crates.

In the far corner, near the area apparently demarcated as the residents' toilet, Haus found the missing mag rifle, a pile of still-gory chivori bones beside it. He slung the rifle over his shoulder and called back to Schmalch. "Found Nyyata. Need another crate."

The little guy shot downstairs and returned in minutes with a picnic basket. "I couldn't find a crate, but I found this in the kitchen. Will it work?"

Though the basket was half the size of the crates, what little remained of Nyyata fit inside, even with the lid closed. Haus didn't know much about his sniper, but she'd been Toh, so Luugrar would have some information. Haus would drop her carcass off at the contract house when he had time. Maybe after he delivered Uuron to Isako at the lodge.

He dropped the last of the bones into the basket and held it out. "Take her to the basement cooler, then find Rej's head. Meet me out front."

Schmalch's lips peeled back from his teeth, but he accepted the task with only a small groan and shudder. Basket bumping against his knees, the little guy hurried downstairs while Haus carried the two crates out to the courtyard. Schmalch emerged from the building with Rej's severed head held arm's-length before him. If it hadn't been such a somber occasion, Haus would have laughed at Schmalch's pained expression. He couldn't have looked more appalled had he been carrying his own head.

Gruesome task complete, Schmalch again asked, "What's next?"

"Cleaning. This part's mine," Haus said. "Sit."

Schmalch settled onto the ground and drew pictures with his finger in the loose dirt as Haus washed and reassembled both bodies on wide planks that had once served as roof decking. So much of Uuron was missing. He seemed half the size he'd been in life. At least they'd left his face intact.

When both were as whole as they'd ever be, Haus laid Uuron's knife on his chest and folded his hands protectively over the weapon. He repeated the maneuver with Rej, then opened a bag filled with long strips of white cloth and held one out to Schmalch.

"Wrap them," he said. "Tight."

This, the little guy was good at. Haus held the disjoined bodies still while Schmalch bound them to the boards until both figures were nothing but loose silhouettes of the people they'd once been. Haus stood beside the bigger of the two, the face beneath visible only as shadow. He touched Uuron's forehead and sighed. The weight of his grief at the loss surprised Haus. His young cousin had visited him in prison nearly every quartern during his five-year sentence. The rest of their family—their clan in general—had accepted Haus' guilt as truth, shunned him.

"Poison," Uuron had ranted and spat on the ground at the first of their visits. "Those windless twats think *you* would resort to poison. Coward's weapon."

Haus had no reply, still too mired in the loss of his wife to care about incarceration.

"It was that scug of a mother of yours, wasn't it, Victuur?"

Haus didn't answer. He knew it was, but he'd never say. Muunoa Haus had warned him—she'd tolerate Yoni as her "son's trull," but she'd not have him wed to Clan Rutuunae jetsam. But he was willful. They'd married anyway. Yoni was dead in days.

"They think she's a sweet, harmless old woman, not the hate-filled bigot you and I know," Uuron continued, slamming his hand on the battered prison table. "Kaniral knows how hard it was on you. I only had to live with her two years while Mooma and Buuwa were overseas." He slapped Haus on the shoulder and shook his head. "Poison. It's just insulting."

When Haus emerged from his fog of grief, Uuron's visits kept him going through the endless fights, horrible food, and general squalor of prison life. What his cousin had done for Haus during those bleak years was a debt he could never repay. No matter the price, Haus always made a place for his cousin in his life.

Haus let the memory go as he looked up into the clear midday sky. Part of him wished he could return to Guunaat to take part in the ritual, but the business here had to be cleared first, or Uuron would never rest. Haus owed him that. Those twisted things from the attic might be dead, but overheard snatches of conversation between the two chivori told Haus the man responsible was still out there.

As he and Schmalch finished planking the rough, ugly boat's hull, Haus kept one eye on the front gate, watching for the Duke and Rift to return. He planned to ask them to attend the rites for Rej this evening. Rift, he knew, would join him—she had before—but Haus wasn't sure about her mate. He'd proven to be a dichotomy, not at all the man Haus had expected, given the package. Neither reaction from the Duke would surprise Haus. Afterward, he had questions.

Schmalch squeaked when Haus added the final touch to the boat—boring holes in the hull with the brace and bit. "Why're you doing that?"

"At dusk," Haus said, "we sink it."

SCHMALCH

Schmalch had waited patiently on the stoop for Haus to return for what seemed like hours. He'd enjoyed the day with the big mercenary, though his hands were hazeled with bruises, and several of the splinters under his skin itched like ants. He was disappointed Haus hadn't allowed him to come along on the trip to the Estoan lodge to drop off Uuron. It was just a couple plots down the road; he wouldn't have been any trouble.

Instead, he was stuck here watching the day dwindle away with no one to talk to. Sviroosa was back at the apartment. The Duke and Rift were inside enjoying their nap. The only other people around were the Abog Union guys or the two weird scientists and their scary pet. Schmalch wasn't interested in any of them, so here he sat.

The sun was threatening to disappear behind the big domed building next door and the shift-change hubbub had begun by the time the Duke finally pushed open the front door. Schmalch turned and studied his swish dark pants, grey shirt and matching vest, silver-rimmed sunshades, and clean, dark hair pulled back in its usual smooth tail. Even with a face covered in scratches and his arm in a sling, the Duke still looked fancy.

"Is it hard to put those on with only one hand?" Schmalch asked, pointing to the shiny line of buckles running down the Duke's boots.

"Yes." He scratched the soft hair on his chin. "Aliara tells me we are set for a genuine Estoan funeral this evening. I assume you shall attend."

"'Course I will." Schmalch sat up straighter. "*I* helped make the boat."

The Duke's face tipped down, one brow raised above his dark lenses. "We are to meet Haus at the Pipe's outer docks after sundown," he said after a moment. "Are you ready?"

"Yeah." Schmalch popped up. "Yeah."

Rift drifted out the door, and without a word led them off the grounds and down the hill from Big Island to North Pipe, where the docks jutted into the sea.

Haus stood at the far end, ceramic jug dangling from one hand, smaller jug by his foot. He'd tethered their new boat to a pylon, Rej's white-wrapped body laid out across the thwarts. Around him, the evening fishermen continued their pursuits, unworried by the sight. Burials of all sorts were common here.

Schmalch fought his instinct to rush down the pier. The somber occasion made him feel somehow that his excitement was wrong. He was proud of his work on the boat, but, he reminded himself, that wasn't why everyone here. He could crow about the accomplishment later.

When they reached Haus, everyone nodded politely to one another, but said nothing. Schmalch leaned on a piling and studied his work, curious how the boat floated with all those holes. They were all filled with something that looked like waxy sawdust.

Haus uncorked the jug in his hand and squatted, carefully pouring clear liquid over the corpse. When the liquid hit, thin white wisps of smoke rose from the wrappings. The weird plugs did the same when the liquid ran over them. It was unnerving.

"May your flesh feed the sea, may your spirit not wander the depths," Haus said as he poured.

He picked up the second jug and stood. Rift held out her hands. The Duke held out his one good hand. Unsure why they were doing this, but not wanting to be left out, Schmalch copied the gesture.

Haus poured the contents of the jug over their hands, then over his own. Schmalch's nose wrinkled and he sneezed. Whatever it was smelled like pickles, or those onions Garl stuck in fancy drinks.

Haus turned back to the boat. "From the waters you came, to the waters you shall return."

Rift cut the tether, and together they watched Rej and her little craft drift away, water seeping into the bottom through the holes. Schmalch leaned against the Duke's leg and, for once, wasn't pushed away.

When the irregular little craft disappeared into the darkening sea, Haus turned to the Duke. "We need to talk."

HERGIS

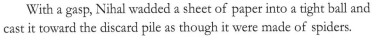

With a gasp, Nihal wadded a sheet of paper into a tight ball and cast it toward the discard pile as though it were made of spiders.

"Is there a problem, Sister?" Hergis asked.

She shook her head, lips tight, face flushed.

"We were warned there would be shocking content."

She sniffed and picked up a thick tome, cautiously opening it.

"Yes, it has been worse than I had anticipated," Hergis said and resumed digging through the detritus of Master Kluuta Orono's life.

Initially, he'd attempted to shield his sister from the startling images, but they were mixed so thoroughly with the scientific documents that he'd abandoned the effort. Though neither he nor Nihal could be considered prudes, the things Master Orono had deemed entertainment left both uncomfortable. Only the allure of the scholarly texts and schemas found amongst the mess kept them both working.

Hergis hoisted a complex spark model, its interwoven chains spiraling this direction and that. "And far more magnificent as well. It pains me to see so much brilliance go to the fire." He ran a finger down the model's smooth curve.

"What is it?" Nihal asked, her voice soft.

"Unless I'm mistaken, a genome for a modified lusca that would allow the creature to detoxify as well as desalinate liquids."

"Bacteria or poisons?"

"Both, I suspect. A pity." He sighed and gently laid the model on the to-burn pile. After a moment, he turned to his sister. "With an upbringing like this, how in the moons did Sylandair become a Vazztain duke?"

Nihal sniffed derisively. She had a sniff for every attitude and occasion.

"What?"

"You have only his word that he is a duke."

Hergis' lips twitched as he considered. "I find I believe him."

She shrugged. "Then I would say trickery and violence."

"Oh?"

She raised her head from the book and sighed in that ever-suffering way he so reviled. "He is Vazztain, Hergis. They do not toss around duchies like candies. I find no other acceptable explanation—beyond the obvious one that he is lying."

Hergis grumbled noncommittally. "You are so bleak sometimes, Sister."

She returned to her book.

"He told me I could co-opt what I like," Hergis said, "so long as I did not credit Master Orono. I would have to claim them as my own."

Nihal snorted her disapproval. "You? He thinks you can pass yourself off as a zoeticist?"

"I know, I find it difficult to accept the idea as well." He opened a large folio of loose sheets.

"It's not that," she said, looking up from the book. She glanced around, as though guilty of some misdeed, and lowered her voice. "You can't trust these chivori."

"Speak up, Sister. You know my hearing is not what it once was."

She frowned, undoubtedly paranoid that one of their employers lurked above, their nonpareil hearing soaking up her every word. "Very well. This Duke may say that now, but if you became rich off his gift, he'd arrive with his hand out."

"Perhaps. However, I find myself asking whether it is a greater immorality to take credit for another's work, or to allow the world to live without such important advances."

Hergis flipped a sheet and stared a long moment at a photograph that lay next in the pile. It must have been quite costly. Such prints were relatively rare and special in any but the most wealthy of homes—or as implemented for industrial purposes. This image depicted a chivori boy, in an unsavory pose. Sadly, it was one of the least offensive images Hergis had seen today.

He let the photo flutter into the reject bin at his feet, soon to join its too numerous cousins in the incinerator. "I must admit that I also find myself understanding why Duke Imythedralin insisted on his terms."

"You always were the sentimentalist, Hergis," Nihal said. "Father was right. Not enough of a pragmatist to flourish."

He shrugged off her insults and worked on, quietly considering the idea of adopting one of the sequences as his own. Perhaps that would be pragmatic enough for Nihal.

As he cast away a handful of useless and pornographic feck, he stopped. One side of a folded sheet lay at his feet. The visible portion showed a sketch of a head covered in abnormal lumps. Hergis picked it up with the tips of his fingers and carefully unfolded the sheet, smoothed it on the floor. "Sister, come look at this."

She bent over him and gave an approving sniff. "A diagram of an altered brain and what appears to be an implanted zoet." She pointed to words scrawled in the upper right corner. "'Farspeech.' Was he trying to recreate this in other species?"

"It certainly could be. That has potential to explain the deformities." Hergis rifled through the pile. "Let me see...what associated materials are here?"

He yanked out an illustration showing part of a skull, its twin aural openings, homes to the superior and inferior tympanums, identifying it as chivori. An arc indicating an incision began above and behind the ear and extended back roughly the length of Nihal's index finger. Notes around the illustration indicated a recognizable, though uncommon, brand of intracranial surgery. Hergis studied it for a moment before handing it to Nihal. She held the page between fingertips as a curator would an artifact and sniffed again.

Hergis returned to his excavation, thrilled to find an oversized book with a similar sketch doodled on its cover. He plopped to the ground, hefted it on his lap and flipped pages.

Nihal hung over his shoulder like a snuffling bird of prey. She seemed to hold her breath as she read along with him.

"Tatumi," Hergis called to the hiisi, who squatted in a corner. "Put this load into the incinerator and set up the headless corpse in operating theater one. Be sure to bring the head as well."

Tatumi rose and lumbered away, the acrid scent of burnt papers floating along behind him. Hergis suspected it would take months to rid his assistant of the odor.

After slightly more than an hour of dissecting the pale corpse, Hergis and Nihal agreed they had found the answer to one of Sylandair's questions. The alterations they found in the brain of the least-deformed creature, the female who had been born a natural karju, mirrored the sketches and the notes. Master Orono had made an attempt to replicate the puka's gift of farspeech in the higher species. Most dramatically, if the notes were to be believed, one of the subjects still lived. Had it worked? Hergis was virtually bursting to share his information by the time Sylandair and Aliara arrived.

"You simply will not believe how quickly we have managed to elucidate one of your mysteries, Sylandair." Hergis hurried to the two chivori as they entered the basement lab, words spilling from his mouth like brew from a tap. It was superb work, and he was delighted to share it. Only someone with an acute knowledge of both zoetics and neurobiology could have so quickly comprehended such complex work.

"What is that?" Sylandair asked.

"Your attic people. They were experimental subjects."

"Yes, we had come to that conclusion on our own."

"We now know to what end." He raised a finger and turned to Aliara. "Madame Rift, would you allow me to examine you?"

Aliara looked at Sylandair, who raised his eyebrows in return. "Your decision, Pet."

"Why?" she asked, gaze rolling back down to Hergis.

"I believe you are connected to the research. One of the subjects, it would seem. There are sketches…" he tapped the overlarge book, "…that appear to be your face, your head, your brain. Younger, but most certainly yours."

"What do you intend to do to her?" Sylandair asked.

Hergis shook his head. "No, no, nothing invasive, to be sure. I merely wish to get a closer look at her scar, her eyes, ask her a few questions."

Aliara lowered herself cross-legged onto the floor beside Hergis. The crescent moon scar on her scalp indeed mirrored Master Orono's drawings. A few other dots of scar tissue surrounded the old wound, camouflaged, but not hidden in her short hair.

"He opened your skull," Hergis muttered, unaware he was speaking aloud.

Aliara drew back.

"Terribly sorry. I am certain it was an appalling experience." He looked into her eyes, so black he could nigh see the pupils. They reacted normally. "Did Master Orono work on your head?"

"Yes."

"And tests?"

She shrugged.

"What did he do? Intracranial procedures? I should say, what specific operations did he perform on your head."

She glared at him, glanced up at Sylandair, who gave her a one-shouldered shrug. Her eyes returned to Hergis. "He did something with needles, asked me what I saw. Sometimes what I heard."

"Did you see and hear anything…out of the normal during these tests?"

"No." She paused. Her eyes slid away from him and grew distant. "Not then."

Hergis took a startled step back and bumped into Nihal, who straightened and hurriedly returned to her work area. "Oh?" he asked. "You experienced something at another time?"

"Last night."

He clapped his hands. "Brilliant, utterly brilliant."

Sylandair reached down and held Hergis' clapping hands together. He'd forgotten himself again.

"Explain," the Duke said.

"You know of farspeech?" Hergis asked.

Sylandair released the clapping hands. "We are not rubes, Master Savesti. It would be difficult to operate in this world without awareness of the puka's wordless communication."

"Yes, yes, but it only manifests in one of about one-hundred puka. They consider it very elite. It is a standard rite of passage to test them all for the ability as children. Those with the ability earn a fine living. For their species, at least."

Farspeakers were employed as intermediaries, delivering and receiving messages across the islands for those with the coin to afford their services. Hergis had made prodigious use of their skills during the homesick days of his tenure at the Colleges of Ukur-Tilen.

"So I am told," Sylandair said.

Aliara watched Hergis, eyes narrowed, frown deep.

Hergis continued. "Yet this skill remains elusive to us higher species. Certainly, we karju and you chivori know the occasional mystic walks among us. Even they, however, do not possess the skill of farspeech. Master Orono sought to rectify this situation."

Hergis put a hand on Aliara's shoulder. She looked at the hand, then back to his face. A chill seemed to run from her into his arm. He withdrew it.

"I fear that you, my dear, were part of his experiment. It must have been a loathsome experience for you. Though not as horrible as that of your counterpart."

Aliara stood. Sylandair wrapped his arm around her waist.

"Why would you say that?" Sylandair asked.

"Her counterpart was the one you beheaded last night."

Sylandair blinked.

"Stupid girl," Aliara whispered.

Hergis let the curious comment pass. "The girl, referred to in the notes only as Subject Sender—you, my dear, were Subject Receiver—was taken as an infant and…" His face puckered. It was hard to describe what was done to the child as simply "being altered," but he knew no other way to say it.

"Well, horrific things were done to alter her genetic makeup, specifically the communication centers of her brain. A heretofore unexplored segment of the thalamus in the puka brain was integrated with her own. In the hands of a lesser zoeticist, you both would have been dead within days, but Master Orono…" Hergis trailed off with an admiring smile that faded into a sad sigh.

Nihal handed him the book, open to a diagram of Subject Sender's head. Labels and notes dotted the page. Though Hergis was certain neither would understand their content, it was important his employers see the evidence.

Sylandair took the book and flipped through pages. "The dates," he said, passing the book back to Hergis. "This girl, Subject Sender, lived here while we grew up?"

"I can only assume so. The notes are not specific regarding her accommodations. Perhaps we will find more as we continue to sift through these papers."

"The others?"

Hergis puckered his lips and glanced back at Nihal, who nodded. "Our best guess is offspring. There was another before Subject Sender." He held the book tight against his chest and leaned toward Sylandair as though revealing a secret. "Master Orono *grew* him. He was to be Subject Sender. The idea was that it would be simpler and less painful to create a body with the genetic alterations already in place, rather than manipulate an existing body."

Aliara turned and vanished up the stairs.

"Oh my, will she be all right?"

"I have no doubt she will be," Sylandair said without a glance at his mate. "This first creature—why wasn't he used?"

"Too many flaws, apparently. As you may know, the growing of an entire sentient creature has never been perfected. Most bits and pieces of our bodies are simple to recreate, as is the growing of lower lifeforms such as lusca, but as a whole, something seems to be missing when attempting to replicate sentience."

Hergis realized he was still wearing his blood-stained autopsy apron and quickly removed it. "Apologies, apologies. Master Orono was unclear on exactly what the issues were with this first attempt. The notes only indicate the lab-grown creature, a male, was flawed and ineffectual. He was kept around, however, for other scientific purposes. Nihal and I believe the male who was grown and the female who was altered were left alone here when Master Orono failed to return. Nature…took its course."

Sylandair drew a deep breath and leaned against the lab table. "You shall have to pardon me, Hergis. This is a bit much to take in." He paused, slowly letting out the breath. "That we lived here for so long with people we never knew existed is incredible."

"Of course, of course. I wish they had left notes as well, so we could discover how they survived. They must have resorted to cannib—" Hergis' speech faltered as Haus strode in, large body dominating the spacious lab.

Hergis rarely considered his own size, but in the presence of this man, he acutely felt the inequality of his proportion. His parents had never given him a moment's grief about it. Nihal had occasionally mocked him as a child, but that was the way of siblings. Even these chivori, who he knew reviled his kind, failed to make him feel his genetic shortcomings. But this hard, tattooed man, whose eyes barely acknowledged Hergis' existence, made him feel small and inadequate. This Victuur Haus left Hergis wanting more from himself and more from a world that had, in truth, already given him so much.

"Pardon me." Hergis cleared his throat. "We can continue this conversation another time, Sylandair. Did you require something, Mister Haus?"

The tower of scarred sallow skin and hazel eyes glanced down at Hergis. "Just the Duke."

"By all means."

"Rift doing all right? She flew outta here like the building was on fire."

"A bit of a shock is all," Sylandair said.

Haus grunted. "You 'bout done here?"

"Yes." Sylandair turned back to Hergis. "If we are needed, you may find us at our apartments. Lock up when you have finished. We shall discuss this further tomorrow."

SYLANDAIR

Syl slipped onto the sofa beside Aliara, her legs curled beneath her. Haus sat across from them, pensive frown on his face. He had refused to have this discussion with Hergis and his group nearby. His distrust of them seemed to far exceed Syl's own. So they'd retired to the penthouse. Syl was just as happy with the arrangement. If it was not essential for him to be at the old estate, he would leave it be.

When they were all comfortable, he asked. "What is it you would like to discuss, Haus?"

The big man's eyes focused as though seeing Syl for the first time. He rubbed his palms together and leaned in, elbows on his knees. "Uuron was my cousin," he said. "Rej was a friend."

Syl nodded. He regretted the man's losses, but pity would offer little beyond insult.

"Those things ate them. They knew the job," Haus said, "but those things *ate* them."

"A bit of you and me as well."

"We lost our piece of flesh, I know, but we're still walking." Haus swiped a palm over his face. "I hear things. You talk, little guy lets things slip when he doesn't know what they mean. Guy who made them…he's still around, isn't he?"

Syl puffed out a sigh and leaned forward, careful of his arm. "We believe so," he said quietly. "After a fashion."

Schmalch arrived, carefully balancing a tray loaded with a bottle

of caba and three pony glasses. "Sviroosa said she'll bring ap-appi-…
snacks."

"Excellent." Syl poured, handed glasses to Schmalch and Haus,
took the last for himself. "Sit," he told Schmalch. "I only care to
review this once."

Face brightened by surprise, Schmalch climbed into the
remaining sliver of space beside Haus and nervously gulped his
drink like he feared it would be stolen.

"You want some?" Haus offered his glass to Rift, who shook
her head.

"My darling girl does not imbibe. Not so much for professional
or nutritional reasons, but because the monster who owned us
removed most of her liver." Syl ran two fingers across his wispy
mustache. "In addition to several other bits and pieces you and I
take for granted."

Haus' face darkened. His eyes flicked from Syl to Aliara and
back.

This was more than either shared with most people, yet Aliara
did not object. For whatever reason, she trusted Haus, so he would
do the same. Though he had no intention of thoroughly detailing
their past, he saw value in drawing Haus into their situation.

"All of these mutilations were performed in the name of science,
naturally." Syl sipped his drink, ran his hand across Aliara's cheek,
and studied her impassive face before returning to Haus. "You have
heard of The Book of Omatha?"

Schmalch sniggered.

Haus' brow furrowed. "The Duin's recipe for immortality? That
old myth?"

Syl nodded. "Not so much of a myth, it seems."

Schmalch guffawed.

Syl turned his flat gaze to the puka. "Remember that glowing
heap of glass beneath the city? The children around it? Their defiled
skulls?"

The laugh dribbled away. Schmalch nodded, eyes wide.

"I thought you might." He returned his attention to Haus. "After Schmalch departed, we encountered a rather unpleasant tail that remade itself when severed. Aliara and I believe this appendage belonged to what remains of Kluuta Orono. Judging from the tumorous weapon she cut from this tail—twice—he may no longer be the man we knew."

Schmalch shook his head.

"Well over a century and a half on this planet, wreaking his particular brand of havoc. It is my belief—" He glanced at Aliara, who nodded. "Apologies, *our* belief that we can credit The Book for his continued presence."

Haus sat his glass on the low stone table with a clink. "You're saying the guy who created those things," he waved toward Aliara, "and did whatever to Rift—and I don't want to know what to you— is still alive? The guy whose statue's in front of the water works?"

"The same."

"And this legendary book has something to do with it?"

"Well, not so much of a book as a miscellany scattered across the isles, but yes." Syl leaned forward and poured himself another glass. He offered the bottle to Haus, who accepted more.

Haus looked at Aliara. "You agree?"

She nodded.

"Why?"

She sighed. This explanation required more conversation than she was normally comfortable with. Syl considered speaking for her but held his tongue. Aliara's words would carry more weight with Haus precisely because they were so spare.

"We grew up with it as fact," she said. "I retrieved things for him from all over the islands. He called them 'ingredients' and 'keys.' He gathered ancient writings and rubbings. Didn't need me for that part. We traveled with him, listened to his conversations with archivists, curators, temple leaders." She waved a hand to indicate the length of the list. "He even fed us Portent in attempts to reach Omatha."

"All of that could be an old man's fear of Ruru when his time came," Haus said.

"True." She shifted, straightened her legs and wiggled her violet-tipped toes. "At the end, he performed a…a ritual? Maybe an experiment. Something between. He worked it out in the lab, took his ingredients and keys to an underground room." She crossed her legs and arms against the memory. "He killed a lot of children. We were entering our second decade, so we were spared. We ran."

"So you never saw what happened?" Haus asked.

Aliara shook her head. Syl ran his good hand over her hair.

"How do you know it worked?" Haus poured another drink for himself and filled the glass clenched in Schmalch's hand.

In the brief silence, Sviroosa slipped in, dropped off a plate of food, and slipped away.

"We needed to know he really did die in that explosion," Syl said. "At least I did."

Aliara nodded.

"After years away, after I had made my own place," Syl continued, "I needed to see him dead, to really know the explosion had done away with him. We visited the Haven here and there over the years, but for this we formalized our residence. "

"You came back. And?"

"The original path from within the plant was no longer accessible to us. It required some time and effort, but we found a way back to the chamber." Syl swept his hand toward Schmalch. "With a bit of help."

Schmalch blinked and took a drink, caba sloshing as he did.

"I did not see his face, but I am certain he was down there," Syl said, "dreadfully transformed."

"With all those bogy kids," Schmalch added in a soft voice.

Haus again looked to Aliara. "Was it him?"

"Yes."

"Why didn't you kill him?"

She shrugged. "We threw a grenade at him."

"Among other efforts," Syl said. "Yet children continue to disappear in abnormal quantities from the streets near the plant. It is his hallmark."

"So you think he's still down there. Right." Haus tossed back the rest of his drink. "You still want him dead?"

"Of course," Syl said. "There is, however, no point in returning to his...his lair until we know more about how to end him."

Schmalch nodded.

"Right." Haus leaned back, almost squashing Schmalch, who scooched toward the sofa's arm. "How do we do it?"

"We?" Syl smiled.

"Yeah. Owes me now, too."

"That is where our Master Savesti and his carnival of the bizarre come in," Syl said. "I have employed them to learn whatever they can about The Book in all the mess of that house. I tried, but my knowledge and my tolerance were tested by what I found. Someone with a more scientific disposition was required."

"You worry about trusting him?"

"A bit, but I was left with little choice."

Haus nodded, studying the striations in the stone tabletop as though the map to his life lay there. Finally, he looked up. "Don't trust him. Or any of them for that matter."

"I rarely do."

"Let me watch them. Put the Abog upstairs. Put me down there with the lot of them."

"Fine."

Haus gestured something to Aliara in their hand cant. When she nodded, he returned to Syl. "You trust me?"

"My darling girl does. I do by proxy."

"And him?" Haus nodded to Schmalch.

Syl chuckled, image of Schmalch in his mind, teeth latched to the back of the big draas' knee. Syl knew exactly with what and how far the puka could be trusted. "Yes, I would say he has proven himself."

Schmalch sat up a bit straighter and grinned.

"Good." Haus scratched at his wild mass of brown hair. "Anything else I should know?"

They sat silent for a moment.

"He has a tunnel into the estate basement," Aliara said.

Schmalch squeaked. The glass slipped from his hand, spilling caba all over the antique rug.

HERGIS

Hergis found himself obsessed by this work. Now that he'd finally made it inside the Orono Mansion, he could hardly bear to leave. Nihal had coerced him into a brief late-night dinner—only three courses versus the usual five. She'd been right. He returned to the work energized and ready to begin anew.

Payl, the Abog Union man hired to guard them, was none too happy about the overnight duty, but tolerated it with only a few mild curses, the leftovers from their meal placating him briefly. After eating, he fell asleep curled into a corner much as Tatumi might, mag-rifle hugged to his chest.

Once the proverbial shine wore off the discovery of the "Farspeech Addendum," as Hergis had begun to call it, he and Nihal returned to combing through the torrent of papers. His interest in the farspeech situation still itched at the back of his mind, but he had been hired for other purposes and intended to fulfill them first. Plus, he couldn't deny his interest in the requested subject: The Book of Omatha.

No, he would resume the autopsies later; the data he could extract from the attic creatures' genetic makeup alone would win him swaths of awards amongst the Mucha. And it would be his work, not stolen. He had even convinced himself that Sylandair would allow him to publicize that the creatures had been created by Master Orono. It wasn't as though anything about these travesties of science would glorify the man's name. It would be vindication for all those rejections, for the flat refusal even to allow him to attempt to earn his degree in zoetics. He only wished Father was alive to see this success. The acknowledgement by his peers might even heal those old paternal wounds.

"A common surgeon," Father had called him, voice raised unreasonably. "I didn't leave my home and pay the Mucha all those Callas for you to be mediocre, Hergis. It's vulgar, that's what it is."

Hergis had tried again and again to enter the zoetics college until his mentor forbade any further attempts. It was just as well. By that time, Hergis likely couldn't have tolerated any more parental rebukes.

Certainly, he'd become a brilliant neurosurgeon—and Mother had been proud of his every accomplishment—but he might have become a brilliant zoeticist as well. He hadn't even been allowed the opportunity to fail. The mind reeled at the possibilities where the two schools of knowledge intersected. He glanced at the cooler door and smiled. His future was secured inside.

With these dreams and memories swirling around his tired mind, Hergis stumbled on the first of the notations regarding The Book of Omatha. The information began so gradually, he almost missed it. Brief notes of archaic language, hints of places and hidden objects grew into fully realized plans filled with descriptions of sites, translations of lost languages, and formulas for compounds Hergis had never seen. He was rapt. He loosened the smooth collar of his acid-blue blouse, ruffles pooling on the polite lump of his belly, and dug into the research like a sand mole excavating a new home.

Like most, he hadn't believed The Book existed. He'd heard the legends of those who had purportedly found it and how it had changed them, but he'd always chalked it up to cautionary tales. To find out the thing was real was beyond anything he had ever considered.

When it became obvious he was engrossed in something, Nihal joined him, quickly losing herself in the texts as well, occasionally muttering "no, no." Even her sniffling tapered away. The knowledge was intoxicating to them both. When he had absorbed one document, Hergis found himself burrowing into the mess until he located another. He no longer cared what was burned and what kept to benefit the world. He cared only to learn more about this marvelous amalgam of science and the divine.

Collected here, the plans seemed quite simple, though Hergis had to admit some of Master Orono's conclusions confused him. He set the more perplexing documents aside for later review with his sister. The process necessary to implement the transformation would be challenging for even the finest zoeticist, but the items Master Orono called keys were ordinary objects, uncomplicated and often easy to procure. Hergis considered what it would take to gather them. He mentally mapped where several could be found and wondered if he should send agents to obtain what was so readily available.

The swishing sound of a door disturbed his concentration. He looked up to find a jaundiced girl in the room with them. Her jaw was slack, eyes glassy, chin lolling toward her chest. A bit of drool dangled from her mouth onto her floral frock. She looked rather young and ill for someone wandering the streets of Dockhaven at night.

Hergis clicked his tongue, shook his head, and grudgingly returned his work to the lab table. If their guard down here had fallen asleep on duty, it was likely the one upstairs had as well, allowing this poor, itinerant child to wander in. Perhaps she had been part of the squatters' collective and believed she still lived here.

"Vrasaj, little girl," Hergis said.

Nihal looked up from her work and kicked Tatumi, who napped in a ball at her feet.

Hergis slid off his stool and walked over to her, almost eye to eye. She stank of rot. The odor sent him back to his residency days, when he'd irrigated an infection from the cheek of a man who'd endured a slapdash dental procedure. Hergis lay a finger over his snoot and wished—not for the first time—he wasn't burdened by his species' superior sense of smell.

"Little girl?" he asked.

She didn't respond. Not even a blink of the lids. Something deep in his mind told Hergis things were wrong, off in some terrible way.

"This is not your home, young woman. You need to leave."

She swayed slightly like a reed in the wind.

Tatumi growled in a way Hergis had not heard in years.

"Hergis, get away from her," Nihal said, voice hushed.

"She is only a child, Nihal. What could she possibly do?" He reached out and touched her arm.

In that instant, the girl snapped to life. Her head jerked up and she hissed. The arm he'd touched swung toward him. Hergis lurched back and fell with a shriek onto the burn pile.

His cry woke the Abog man who sprung up, rifle to his shoulder.

"Shoot it!" Nihal yelled.

"Yes, yes, shoot it," Hergis echoed.

"She's just a little girl," Payl said. "I don't earn my coin shooting kids."

Growling and hissing, the girl fell onto Hergis. He struggled to hold her off as her thin, ragged fingers wrapped around his neck. This was no child. It was another monstrosity produced by this terrible house, and it was going to strangle him! Here on the moment of his greatest triumph, Supreme Sovereign Master Hergis Savesti would be killed by some abomination he was attempting to assist.

Payl traced the action with his rifle, unable to reconcile what he saw with the idea of murdering a child. Then he too shrieked. "By the dead hand of Leb, what happened to her head?"

"Just shoot it!" Hergis gasped.

Tatumi's growl, a low constant since he woke, became a bark, then a roar. He bounded over the lab table, shattering glass, scattering paper, and heaved the girl off his master. Hergis rolled away from the burn pile and scrambled to his feet.

The child turned her fury on Tatumi. He held her in both hands at arm's length and roared, his purple tongue and yellowed teeth bared, his spittle peppering her face. Unable to reach any vital points, she scratched at Tatumi's arms. His hair offered some protection, but her jagged nails raked the flesh beneath. The hiisi yelped at the pain. In a single movement, he ripped her tiny body in half. He threw both pieces aside, crouched on his haunches, and commenced grooming the blood from his massive hands.

The Abog man lowered his rifle and shot up the stairs. Hergis leaned over and vomited. Nihal cautiously went to Tatumi and offered him another of the large beetles he loved so much. He gobbled it up and grinned at her.

"What in the depths was that?" Hergis asked when he'd regained both his breath and his composure.

She wasn't like the pallid malformed things stored in the cooler. She was something else entirely. Something he'd not been warned about.

Hergis eased his way to the top half of her corpse. The back of her cranium was caved in, a narrow spike with the appearance of bone protruding from the damaged tissue. He gently reached to retrieve it but thought better.

He stood, brushed off his beautiful blouse, and scowled at the mess. "Tatumi!" he shouted.

The beast gave a curious grunt and stopped licking his paws.

"Put that body—all of it—in the cooler with the others. Then go to the Lower Rabble and retrieve Sylandair. Our Duke either needs to see this, or he owes me an idrit-sized explanation."

SYLANDAIR

Syl leaned out the window of the gondola and watched the contrasting patterns of light and dark beneath the water bend with each passing ripple. Even in the near blackness of the naught-moon night, they swelled like great ink stains on freshly pressed paper. Watching them as he crossed the bay always made Syl a little dizzy.

Tatumi had arrived at their penthouse toward the end of the conference with Haus. After nearly scaring the skirts off Sviroosa, the hiisi had tipped his hat and removed a pretty blue ribbon from his neck. Tied to the ribbon was a note from Hergis that summoned Syl to the mansion, saying only that there had been "a visitor" earlier that evening. The blood on Tatumi's hands and pants spoke of urgency, so they followed.

Schmalch clung to the gondola wall as close to Haus and as far away from Tatumi as possible. His eyes shifted from the animal's dull face to the drying blood on his hands and back again. The hiisi's gaze never left Schmalch.

"Why didn't Hergis send someone who could talk?" Schmalch asked.

"Would you send your sister out for a nighttime walk in the Rabble?" Syl replied.

Schmalch's lips puckered and danced from side to side as he considered this. "Probably not…if I had one."

Syl waved his hand.

"Still—" Schmalch started, but interrupted himself with a jaw-cracking yawn.

Haus and Tatumi joined in. The monotonous chirp of pulley on cable and the soft sway of the gondola as it climbed toward the cliffs of the Big Island seemed designed to induce sleep. It was well past midnight, creeping into the pre-dawn hours. Only the long midday rest he'd enjoyed with Aliara gave Syl the stamina to press on. Even that was waning.

The brilliant lights of the Caba Club welcomed them as they stepped onto the tram station's platform. People sauntered in and out the revolving door beneath the club's glowing red sign while shadows shifted suggestively inside the orbs lining the building like glasses round a punchbowl. Syl had visited the establishment with Aliara several times. It couldn't exactly be called a pleasure house or a cocktail lounge or a cabaret. Somehow it was all and none simultaneously. He did enjoy renting one of the opaque glass private rooms whenever he visited. There was something so wonderfully exhibitionistic about knowing other patrons could see his silhouette as he enjoyed whatever flavor of entertainment he'd selected for an evening.

They left the glittering lights behind, travelling from the hubbub of late-night business into the peace of Temple Row. Though the street was home to many chapels and shrines of the Duin, the name was something of a misnomer as it also housed several walled estates, trade societies, and the occasional private residence of those not quite wealthy or well-bred enough for the Nest.

Orono's estate sat at the east end of the road, near where the Pipe met the Big Island. It was a section of land Syl suspected no one else had wanted, fearing their worship would be interrupted by shift changes at the desal plant, or by the raucous chatter of groups traveling up the Pipe toward the diversions of the Big Island. He remembered hearing them as a child and wanting to join them.

As they pushed open the main gates, Syl spotted Hergis and Nihal settled in tall-backed dining chairs on the front porch. The surgeon hopped up the instant he spied them and scurried across the courtyard. His natty appearance was frayed, blouse unbuttoned and torn, and his mustaches were in disarray.

"So sorry to reach you this way. I would have sent a chit with further explanation, but I fear Tatumi…" Hergis' cheeks puffed out. "Well, he eats them."

"Of course he does," Syl said. "What is it you need at this hour, Hergis?"

"Come, come." Hergis hurried toward the house. "I do hope you do not mind. We dragged some chairs out here, not wanting to be inside without Tatumi. You will understand why momentarily."

The basement looked much as it had when Syl left earlier. The burn pile had changed in size and the floor looked as though it may have been washed, but nothing else seemed out of place.

"I apologize profusely for the accidental breakage of laboratory equipment," Hergis said.

"Breakage of what equipment?" Syl asked.

"Tatumi was forced to vault over the research table, and a few odds and ends were shattered." Hergis opened the cooler. "Tatumi!" he called.

"A loss for you more so than for me. I would not know what to do with most of this," Syl said.

"Get the body," Hergis directed the hiisi before returning to Syl. "True, true, but I do still apologize."

Tatumi reappeared, two halves of a girl in his arms. Syl tried not to look at the bits that dangled from the ragged ends of her body. The back of her head was a familiar travesty.

"One of the bogies," Schmalch whispered as he ducked behind Haus.

Syl marched to operating theater two, Aliara at his heels, and pushed open the door. "Those Abog fecks didn't so much as try to cover the breach," he said. "To the depths with them."

Haus leaned in behind Syl. "That the tunnel Rift mentioned?"

"Yes." Syl let the door swing shut. "I instructed those two buckets of offal to push that storage locker in front of it after they had finished their sweep." Syl pointed to a mammoth steel cabinet near the cooler.

Hergis made a "hrumpf" and frowned. "Mister Payl did nothing to protect my life when this child was trying to squeeze it from me. He ran out like his pants were aflame."

"We can move it," Haus said. "Might take all of us, but it can be done."

Syl squinted, his nostrils flared. He tapped his lower lip. "No… well, yes. Get it close, but do not actually block the hole."

"Right." Haus turned to Hergis. "Can I get your pet's help?"

"Of course." Hergis whistled. "Tatumi, assist Mister Haus."

"Schmalch," Syl said. The puka appeared from behind the research table. "Go to the Abog Union hall. Get the men who were here earlier. No one else. No substitutes. Understood?"

Schmalch nodded.

"Tell them the job was not completed. They'll ask for more Callas. Agree to anything they ask."

"Anything?" The puka blinked a few times. "You sure, Duke?"

"Yes. Whatever they request, agree to it. Just get them back here."

Schmalch hurried off into the night.

"Now, Master Savesti," Syl said. "I believe I owe you an explanation. Shall we proceed to the…" He paused, remembering his difficulties with the terrible tangerine sofas. "…parlor. I believe we will find a pair of still-serviceable chairs there."

He and Hergis settled into the hideous green-and-rust pattered armchairs, while Nihal chose one of the sofas. Before any of them could speak, the piercing scrape of steel against concrete rang from below. Syl cupped his aching jaw and lower lug to still the vibration.

He couldn't fathom how Aliara could stand to be in the same room with the noise.

The sound died away, and Syl drew a long breath, considering how much to share with this group he did not particularly trust. He settled on only the most basic of facts.

Hergis' excitement and intrigue faded with each disclosed detail until his frown drooped as severely as his frazzled mustaches. When Syl finished his account, the group sat quietly for a long moment while the Mucha muttered wordlessly and fiddled with his ruffled cuffs.

"The data I have found," Hergis said, breaking the silence, "mentions no physical transformation, though it does focus on the reinvigoration of the body's cells—in great depth actually. 'You will live as you truly are within the glow of the moons,' so said one of the pages, though I suspect it was far more lyrical in its original language."

Nihal released a scoffing sniff.

"My goal for your research is to determine a way to finally put an end to my old master," Syl said. "Have you found anything to that effect?"

"Nothing thus far, but I fear I have been focused on the process Master Orono utilized to facilitate this transformation. Fascinating reading."

"I am certain it is. However, I would prefer you channel your efforts in another direction."

"I am quite sure I can follow both lines in tandem."

Syl watched Hergis' face and considered if this was acceptable.

The front door slammed open. Schmalch hurried in, out of breath and sweaty. He rushed to the parlor, slid between chairs, and sat on the hearth. "They're on their way. Settled for five times pay."

The pair of Abog lumbered inside, clearly annoyed by the late hour. "What is it?" the shorter of the two asked. "Payl said the minikin wanted him to fire on a little girl. We won't shoot no kids."

"Of course not." Syl rose, economical smile on his lips. He found it curious that neither Abog mentioned that the little girl in question was subsequently ripped in half. "It seems there is an area of my estate that was not scrutinized in your inspection. I require you to finish the job."

The taller man, assumedly Payl, clung to his rifle, eyes wary as though he expected to be attacked at any moment. He shook his head. "Not going back down there, Starn."

"Shut it, Payl. You won't need'ta work for a month with the pay we're making." He nodded to Syl. "It's fine. We'll check it, but it better be quick."

"Certainly," Syl said.

"Right. Where do we go?" Starn asked.

"Follow me."

Syl led them downstairs into operating theater two, where Haus and Aliara lounged on the metal table. Tatumi stood by the door, tongue lolling out one side of his mouth.

Syl pointed to the ragged hole in the wall.

Starn raised his eyebrows. "Seriously?"

"Quite," Syl said. "You were contracted to clear all regions of the house and instructed to block this opening. Now, unless you intend to refund every Calla, you had best complete the job."

Payl and Starn conferred quietly between themselves.

"Fine, but we're gonna need an extra three ladies each," Starn said. "On the sly."

"Of course. Schmalch?"

Schmalch produced Syl's purse, withdrew six Callas, and placed them in Syl's palm.

"When you return," Syl said, "these shall be waiting for you, along with the rest of your fee."

Starn licked his lips. His hands fluttered at his sides, itching to hold the silver coins.

Syl closed his palm. "Proceed."

Payl crouched by the opening, peeked in. "You got a light?"

"I assumed you would carry your own tools," Syl said.

"Not much call for crank torches when we're guarding houses."

Syl shrugged.

Haus tossed a small crank torch to Payl, who caught it awkwardly, nearly dropping his pneumatic rifle in the process. He gave the light a quick turn and scanned inside the hole.

"Looks like it hooks right," he told his partner.

"Get movin'," Starn said, elbowing Payl in the ribs.

Payl crawled in, Starn close behind. Syl crouched and watched their bobbing light as they awkwardly moved through the low tunnel, guns swaying below them.

When the light from their torch disappeared around a bend, Syl rose. "Now," he told Haus, "you may block the hole."

SYLANDAIR

"Welcome to Domestic Consignment. What service can we provide for you today?"

Syl waited for the wizened old puka to trundle out from her back office in no particular hurry. Apparently customer assistance was not a pressing matter at this establishment.

When she saw Syl, she scowled. "You."

"Indeed."

"Unless you have a box full of Callas tucked into that sling, you best turn around and leave."

"I disagree," Syl said in a silky tone he reserved for moments such as this. With a flash of blue silk lining, he pulled a rolled-up document from the topcoat draped over his shoulders and extended it to the old woman. "You will assign four of your best cleaners to me this morning. For the previously agreed-upon price, the one we both know already was inflated."

She hooted, amusement trailing off into a coughing fit, then pulled a handkerchief from her sleeve and blew her sweeping nose. "I haven't laughed like that in years, chivori."

"I suggest you reconsider."

"Keep it up. I'll ruin any chance you got to get service." She leaned against the counter in an attempt at intimidation, but found it difficult to deliver a devastating stare from so far below her enemy's eye level. "Even your sweet little housemaid will abandon you when

I'm done."

Syl smoothed the sheet of paper on the counter in front of her.

"What's this?" She unrolled it and scanned the words. "A quit-claim deed? Of all the—"

She inhaled sharply as the fine point of a stiletto pressed into the soft flab beneath her chin. Aliara had entered alongside Syl, but slipped into the shadows as they'd waited for the old woman to reach the front counter.

"Had you not made your droll threats, madame, I likely would have agreed to your monetary requests without protest."

The woman opened her mouth to object. Aliara pressed harder. A trickle of blood ran down the wrinkled throat, soaking into the lacy collar.

Syl slid his silver pen across the counter. "It seems you have been called away quite suddenly to the fair village of Ebury. You are familiar with that quaint little hole on the isle of Kharanor? Yes, I see you are." He smiled. "Your stay will be...indefinite. Your ship sets sail at dusk. Sign."

She flat-eyed him, crossed her arms.

Aliara leaned in, hood brushing the hairless head, and sniffed like a hungry animal.

The woman's face went from resolute to disturbed. It never ceased to amaze Syl how effective that simple gesture could be. The old biddy reached for the pen.

"Take your eye, chivori," she cursed as she signed.

"I suggest you pack quickly. Meet the vessel *Rehaud's Anchor* at the Big Island docks." Syl retrieved the document and pen and slipped both into his coat. "Convenient that it should be located so near the bank. You should even have time to make a withdrawal."

He nodded to Aliara, who holstered her blade.

Syl leaned down, eye to eye with the puka, brim of his hat against the bridge of her nose. "You do *not* want to miss your departure, madame. Should you do so, my darling girl will pay you a much less pleasant visit." He stared until she looked away, then straightened. "I will expect the four cleaners by midday today. Do we understand one another?"

The old woman spat at him.

"I see we do."

With that, he left, Aliara on his arm.

SCHMALCH

Having resumed his place on the mansion's stoop, Schmalch spent the day watching the sun crest, waiting in vain for anyone to join him. He hopped up, waving and bouncing on the balls of his feet, ready to leap off the porch when the Duke and Rift strode up the walk. She hurried inside without a word, but the Duke, still paler than normal, sat down on the porch beside Schmalch and handed him a rucksack that tinkled pleasantly.

"The chiseler has been seen to," he said, hint of amusement in his voice. "Time for your errand. Open the bag, would you?"

"Sure." Schmalch peeked in. A canvas pouch and a resin box of Callas lay inside. "What's for who?"

The Duke pulled two coils of paper from his overcoat and handed them to Schmalch. "First, take the bag to your friend who survived."

"Munk?"

"If that is his name, yes. Then the box and papers go to the widow. Allow her to read them before you leave." He paused, pressed his eyebrows together. "Can she read?"

"Don't know, Duke. Glech was pretty smart."

"If she cannot, find someone who can before you go. Direct her to me should she have any questions."

"What's on 'em?"

"Directions for her family's compensation."

Schmalch didn't know why everything always had to be a mystery with the Duke. He put the coins and papers in the bag and slung it over his shoulder. "Right. What about cleaning up inside?"

"A crew will arrive soon. I shall instruct them in your absence. They are yours to manage thereafter. Aliara and I will be going home."

"Home?"

"Our penthouse."

Relief swept through Schmalch. He feared "home" meant the duchy in Chiva'vastezz, but no.

The Duke glanced at the sun through his dark lenses and frowned. "Only midday, and I am exhausted." He rose. "Until then, Schmalch."

The instant the Duke was inside, Schmalch scampered off the grounds and hurried down the Pipe. A few of the inmates on the Bag shouted insults and grabbed at him through the fence, and twice gutter babies tried to mooch off him, but he slipped past all of them unscathed.

He rushed up through the Lower Rabble and was nearing Bay Bridge, where Central Row crossed into the Upper Rabble, when he spied Sigrin Malpockey lurking in the shadows behind the Order of Omatha. The minikin had enjoyed taking out his own woes on Schmalch in the days when he lived on the streets. Spending most of his time in the Grey Boots' territory made it easy for Sigrin to target him, but it was the part of the city he knew—and street gangs turned over so often, he'd kept hoping some other group would get rid of Sigrin for him. No one ever did. Now Schmalch was important, a Duke's assistant, and he had important work to do today. No two-copper thief would stop him in his duty.

Schmalch straightened his spine, held his head high, and marched on past. Anxiety got the best of him, and his confident stride became a nervous scurry as he hurried across Bay Bridge. He angled north, along the Upper Rabble's western shore into Pukatown, where Munk and Glech's apartment building waited.

"What's in the bag, Schmalchy?" Sigrin asked in his usual whine as he sidled up, grey-booted feet matching Schmalch's brisk pace.

"A delivery for the Duke." Schmalch kept his eyes forward, kept moving toward his destination.

"Somethin' fancy?"

"Um…don't know. Just delivering."

"Don't know. Right, right." Sigrin produced a short blade and put a restraining hand on Schmalch's shoulder, bringing them to a stop. No one around them seemed to notice or care. "Hand it over."

"No."

"C'mon now. Not like you wouldn't do the same. Foia! I've seen you do the same." He patted Schmalch a bit too hard on the cheek with his grubby pink hand. "Don't make me hurt you again."

Schmalch clasped the bag to his body. "You're not gettin' it."

Sigrin angled his blade beneath the rucksack's strap. Without thinking, Schmalch balled his fist and punched the little man in the chest. Sigrin stumbled back, eyes wide for a heartbeat before narrowing. "Not smart, puka."

Schmalch withdrew his kris from its ankle holster and poked it at Sigrin. "It's not yours."

Sigrin hopped away. "Like that, is it, Schmalchy? You don't learn too fast, do you?" He lunged, shoulder low and set for a take-down.

Schmalch spun away. Sigrin tripped forward, landing on his hands and knees in the street. Seeing the opportunity, Schmalch wheeled and ran, not slowing until he reached the towering tenement Munk and Glech both called home. One side was a concrete column, probably eight or so stories high. It was linked to a glass and steel cylinder that looked like some giant had pinched it in the middle. The thing always gave Schmalch the impression it was going to topple at any moment. Though it hadn't done so thus far, he hoped that wouldn't change while he was inside. When his breathing calmed, he yanked open the door and steeled himself for this unpleasant task.

Munk's mother greeted Schmalch with a slap in the face when he introduced himself. She pointed to Munk, huddled in a pile of blankets on their ratty old sofa, and swore for a few minutes before taking the offered pouch. Her demeanor changed a touch when she saw the Callas inside. It changed more when she counted all one-hundred of them. She didn't apologize, but she didn't slap Schmalch again either. He was just as happy when she grunted and slammed the door in his face.

That episode left him anxious about his next visit. If Munk's mother was that angry because her baby had been scared, Glech's wife must be all-out furious. Schmalch really wanted to just leave the box and papers outside Glech's family's door, knock, and run away. But he was a good boss. He'd run out of the house without them. He needed to take care of this. He'd take whatever she doled out.

Her reaction was even more unexpected than the slap. Instead of anger, Glech's widow, Fohmsquah, welcomed him into their house, praised him for the Callas Glech had earned and for taking Glech's remains to their temple. Her smiling peat-brown face sent a tickle through his chest, and her kind words pushed a lump into his throat.

He thrust the box and papers at her and choked out, "From the Duke."

"Come in, Mister Schmalch," she said. "Would you like a drink?"

He shook his head.

"You just let me know if you change your mind." She turned around and walked into the apartment. "Come now, join us."

He crept inside, where two little girls who looked like twins talked animatedly as they played with rag dolls in a corner. One kept shoving the other and claiming things weren't fair. A boy about half Schmalch's age, sat at the kitchen table, drawing and making a show of ignoring his sisters.

"Chisev, Worch, Ilit," Fohmsquah said in what Schmalch assumed was a motherly voice, "come over here and greet Mister Schmalch."

The boy, Chisev, was downright despondent about being taken away from his work, but he obeyed. He shook Schmalch's hand and murmured a polite greeting. The girls hugged Schmalch around the waist and burbled. All of them were puffy around the eyes. He was pretty sure he knew why.

"Sit," Fohmsquah told them.

They sat.

"Have a seat, Mister Schmalch, while I see what it is you've brought us."

"Um, sure." Schmalch wriggled onto the couch between the boy and his sisters, uncomfortably aware of their closeness.

Fohmsquah opened the box and smiled. "Oh! This is so generous, Mister Schmalch. My babies and I can't praise you enough." She bent and pecked him on the cheek.

The little girl nearest to him—he wasn't sure if it was Worch or Ilit—hugged him again.

He colored. "The—the papers," he said. "The Duke said I gotta stay until you read 'em."

"Do you know what they are?"

"Huh-uh. Duke just said to stay here till you read 'em."

"You didn't read them?"

Schmalch looked at his hands folded in his lap and shook his head.

"Oh, I see."

He let her read. Chisev was brooding and not in the mood to talk. The girls chatted with each other in some language Schmalch didn't know, so he looked around the room during the pause. The place was tidy—the sort of home every kid at the orphanage hoped to go to, but never did. The furniture was aging, but in good shape, paintings of seascapes hung on the walls and everything was temple-clean. It even smelled like cooking.

"Oh!" Fohmsquah gasped. *"Oh!"*

Schmalch and the boy jumped up from the sofa. "What is it,

Moocha?" Chisev asked.

She hugged her son, dragging Schmalch into the embrace with them. The girls latched onto their mother's hip, not wanting to be forgotten.

"Oh, Mister Schmalch," she said. "I didn't know how I would raise my babies without my Glech. And you bring this?" Tears dripped down her cheeks. She released the hug and dried her eyes on her apron tail.

"What is it?" Schmalch asked.

"The deed to Domestic Consignment! Your Duke's note says Barlith had to leave unexpectedly and couldn't take care of her business anymore. He acquired it from her and deeded it to me."

"You'll be great at that, Fohmsquah." Schmalch turned away to hide welling tears. "I uh…I need to leave." He hurried out the door and down the long, echoing hall.

"You're welcome here anytime, Mister Schmalch," she called after him. "You'll come by for dinner soon?"

He grunted an agreement and rushed away.

Schmalch wandered through the Rabble for an hour or so after that, thoughts circling the events in the tenement. The Duke never failed to surprise him. The chivori had done some of the worst things Schmalch had ever seen, but he always came around to doing some of the best things, too. Schmalch couldn't understand it, but decided he didn't need to.

HAUS

Some five or ten years ago, during a happy bender, Haus had promised Uuron that should he die, Haus would find all of his "girls" and tell each one they were his favorite. Haus had laughed and said it would be a full day's work minimum. He hadn't been wrong.

After dropping off Nyyata's remains, he spent the rest of his day circulating through bars, peep shows, and pleasure houses, locating all the women who had enjoyed his cousin's company. Given that the big man's lady friends were scattered throughout Dockhaven and Guunaat, Haus quickly regretted his lighthearted commitment.

Fifteen stops, eighteen women, and fifteen beers in, he arrived at The Triangle, glittering darling of the Lower Rabble. The sun had just set, and though the entertainers and servers were ready for the evening rush, the customers had only begun to trickle in.

Haus dropped into an unforgiving iron chair at a small table and took in the room. A boxer whose face no longer resembled the one he'd been born with leaned over the bar to chat with the willowy woman pouring drinks. Two couples in varying states of friendliness occupied tables in the darker corners. Along the back wall, lone women and men penned in glass cages shook and teased and did all they could to draw the bar's few patrons into private booths while the melody engine thumped in the background.

A hollow-eyed chivori sauntered toward Haus' table and sat without invitation. He gave Haus a long, shameless once-over, crossed one ankle over his knee and reclined into the chair.

"Anything I can do for you today?" he asked, finger lazily drawing curlicues on the tabletop.

"Enali working tonight?" Haus asked.

The man's face soured. "Back rooms. Booth nine, ladies' side."

Haus flipped a few coppers on the table and snagged his sixteenth brew of the day. The private booths were quiet. He'd been back here before, knew that wasn't always the case. Male or female side, the narrow hall grew congested as the night went on. He'd seen Uuron stand for hours in line for his precious few moments with Enali. Haus was curious—he'd never seen the bym himself.

Inside booth nine, he swung onto the single tall stool and set his beer on the narrow bar. He dropped a Calla in the slot and a panel whooshed open, revealing a stage at bar height. A muscular blonde the color of sandstone sat there, straddling a chair. She wore a short skirt, limp garters hanging from it like overcooked noodles, and nothing else. Wisps of her wavy blonde hair glowed in the red lumia light, creating the effect of her head burning. Her chartreuse eyes, abnormally large in her narrow face, focused on Haus and she pulled an uurost pipe from between her thick, painted lips and smiled.

She still had all her teeth.

Haus drew a long pull of her through his snoot. Her smell reminded him of some of the better nights he had spent on the trail as a young man. He adjusted himself before his pants bound.

She dropped the pipe on the floor and took her time running hands up her strong thighs and round bubs, then stretching back in a deep arc. Satisfied she had her client's attention, she rose and walked to where he sat. Nothing between them. He could reach out and touch her, but uninvited, that brief touch would get him tossed out of The Triangle. She invited it, then no worries.

"Lookit you." She bent at the waist to get a better view of him, both hands overflowing with bubs. "Somethin' really took a bite outta' you, didn' it?"

"You Enali?"

She straightened, hands dropping to her sides. Haus understood Uuron's fascination.

"Why?"

"I'm supposed to talk to Enali."

She stared at him with suspicion, one eye narrowed.

"You know a big bald guy named Uuron?" Haus asked.

Her head turned slightly to one side. "Why?" She drew the word out this time.

"We're cousins."

Her face softened. "Why didn' you say so?" She dropped to her knees, legs splayed. The skirt climbed higher. Her scent grew richer.

Haus stared into her corpulent chest, now at eye level. "Uuron sent me."

"In that case…" Enali slid into the splits and began an act that was obviously well-rehearsed and oft-repeated, but enjoyable nonetheless. "He's thoughtful like that," she said as she went through her motions. "I don't see many customers outside'a work, but he made it worth my time. Always gave me a good joggle."

Haus nodded and appreciated her talents until the partition slid shut, puffing out the odor her warm body and stale uurost. He dropped in another Calla and enjoyed the show for a bit, hand drifting unconsciously to his own thigh, as he mentally debated when exactly he should break the news.

Turned away from him on all fours, Enali broke the silence, ending Haus' deliberation. "What'd Uuron send you for, uh…what's yer name?"

"Haus." He blew out air and scratched the neglected stubble of his chin. "Could you turn around?"

"Don't like this view?"

He spat out a laugh. "Hardly. Wanna look you in the eye when I tell you this."

She sat on the floor and spun around. The skin of her thighs squeaked against the polished wood. "Right. What'd'ya got?"

"Uuron's dead."

Both hands went to her mouth.

"Yeah."

"What happened?" The words came out between her fingers.

"You don't wanna know. He had a message. Wanted me to let you know you were his favorite."

Her eyes welled and her hands dropped to her lap, pulling her shoulders with them. The enormous breasts rested against her abdomen.

"Well, balls," she said.

The partition slid shut.

Haus gathered his beer and left. After that, he needed a break. There were at least six other places to hit before his promise could be considered fulfilled—the Dockhaven portion of it, at least.

Parked at the same table, he leaned back in the cruel chair and downed the rest of his beer as he watched the punters parade in from the dingy street. The timid and the two-copper losers among them wandered to the peep-show arcade machines, while the bolder ones headed straight for the private shows in back. Several merely plopped down in front of the glass booths and absorbed the less-raunchy free show. The bartender was too busy now to chat with the dejected-looking boxer. The couples who'd groped in the dark corners had moved on.

Haus studied them all. Most looked like ordinary working folks, but here and there fat-pursed gudgeons strutted around, all the companionship they might ever want clinging to their arms. Among them, Haus spotted a minikin with flashy blonde mustaches and a black-and-white gingham suit.

Hergis' yellow hair had been twisted into a series of bulging topknots that ran down the center of his scalp, his still-coiled mustaches were now stiffened at the tips and topped with what looked like tiny pink umbrellas. He chatted enthusiastically with the lithe, glitter-coated man whose hand rested on his back. When Hergis said something particularly funny, the man playfully tapped his index finger on the tip of the minikin's nose. Hergis chuckled as he casually turned his head toward where Haus reclined.

Hergis' eyes lost all amusement. His cheeks flushed as red as his neckerchief.

Haus smiled his most impolite smile. "Master Savesti."

"M-Mister Haus." Hergis darted a glance at his companion. He tried to smile, but his face was unwilling to oblige. "What brings you to...er...what brings you here?"

"Walking old roads."

Hergis patted his companion's arm. "Go along, Myyat."

"Will you visit me later?" Myyat leaned down and rubbed Hergis' belly, round beneath the gold blouse. "My supreme sovereign master." He glanced up with eyes as without conscience as those of the ratty cat Haus had seen pilfering the garbage out back.

Hergis' gaze flitted back to Haus, though he answered Myyat. "Yes. Perhaps... We shall see. Now off with you."

The man minced away. Hergis watched him disappear into the crowd. Finally, the minikin cleared his throat and looked back at Haus. "It seems you have caught me slumming."

"What do I care?" Haus shrugged and downed the last of his drink. "Got our own tastes, don't we? And the Duin know I spend more time in this hole than I care to admit. It's not like you're buying children to bugger." He paused to give the surgeon an exaggerated look of suspicion. "Are you?"

"My goodness, no!"

Haus barked out a laugh. "I know. Saw how revolted you were down in the basement."

Hergis shuddered. "How could such a brilliant man...?" He trailed off, head wagging sadly. The fine copper loops that hung from the pointed tops of his ears flashing in the bar's red glow.

"Makes you like the Duke a bit more, eh?"

"Or feel badly for him at the least."

"Doubt he wants your pity." Haus pushed out a chair with his foot. "Sit. Want a drink?"

"Perfection."

Haus stopped a passing server and placed their order. Hergis withdrew a monogrammed pipe from his suitcoat and tapped in some uurost. The pipe looked clean and new. Haus wondered if this was habit or if the pipe was a recent acquisition. After what the surgeon must've seen in the estate basement, he understood why the Mucha might want to numb his mind.

As Hergis worried a match, Haus studied his face. With makeup and medicine, he'd done much to camouflage the deepening creases around his eyes, and the mustaches went a long way toward hiding the drooping chin and burgeoning jowls. This close and in the punishing red light, however, Hergis looked far older than Haus had suspected.

Pipe lit, Hergis said, "After last night's escapade, I could not bear to stay in that house past dark again."

Haus nodded. "Can't say I blame you."

"Nihal was willing, but I required…shall we call it a 'diversion?'"

"Nicest thing I've heard it called."

Hergis' mouth twitched, turned up. He drew on the pipe, blew out the bitter smoke. "Would you care for some, Mister Haus?"

"Just Haus. I'll pass."

A brew and a caba thunked onto their table. Haus slipped coppers to the server.

"If you change your mind…" Hergis tipped the pipe to Haus.

"This'll be beer seventeen. Don't need to compound that."

"Oh my. Is it the loss of your mates? Salving yourself with drink?"

"Could call it that. Taking care of business I said I'd see to if Uuron went to the water before me."

"Ah." Hergis nursed away half the glass of caba. "It must have been horrifying."

"You find what the Duke's after, I'll even things out."

"Yes." Hergis' mouth twisted on one side.

"Having much luck?"

"More than I would have expected in such a short period of time. I owe a great deal to Nihal's efficiency in wading through the raft of documentation. It was little wonder Sylandair sought assistance."

"I saw some of the birdlime your hiisi was shoveling into the incinerator. I wouldn't wanna look at it either."

Hergis nodded solemnly. "The man's mind wasn't right. Most certainly in that manner, but at the end, even his brilliance seems to have faded."

"How so?"

Hergis finished his drink as he considered. "Sylandair mentioned that Master Orono had indulged in anti-agathics for some time. They can be quite effective but are rare and often quite polluted. Rumors of their long-term use tell terrible stories. It seems from the notes we found that Master Orono's brain had been failing exponentially—his brilliance no longer the light it once was." He shuddered. "I have considered anti-agathics for myself as I have gotten on in years, but the things I saw have caused me to reconsider."

As Hergis spoke, Haus signaled for another round. "What mistakes?"

"My sister is quite the linguist. She spent some time reviewing the translations Master Orono worked out over the years. The early ones seem quite accurate and thorough, but the later ones..." He pursed his lips in a frown, traced a finger around the coils of one side of his mustaches. "Well, they are full of gaffes. Many of the epistles he recovered are quite clear and direct in their message, their instruction, if you will. Others, however, are shrouded in metaphor and flowery language. I fear he woefully misunderstood some, unable to reason out the difference between literal and figurative. He mistranslated words, he mixed messages, he took colorfully worded missives quite literally."

"For example?"

Hergis let out a long breath through his nose. "There was a quatrain that directed the reader to obtain 'the finest grain from the desert's heart.' Given the remaining lines, I believe it refers to the genetic material—the spark, as the common folk say—of the voshari, first people of the Tehtaemanian deserts. It would make sense, given the context, correct?"

Haus nodded.

"In lieu of such a sample, Master Orono brought home a half-ton of sifted sand from Tehtaemah." Hergis shook his head, smiling ruefully.

Haus chuckled.

"We also found some notes about a direct message from Omatha regarding the need for children in this recipe." Hergis scratched at his forehead, eyes closed. "Undoubtedly—if this purported message even truly existed—it referred to genetic material un-degraded by age. I shudder to think how this information was actually employed."

Haus grunted.

"Yes...yes. Another mentioned 'a drop of the sorrowful passage that divides sisters.'" Hergis sipped.

"What'd your sister think that one meant?"

Hergis smiled. Both mustaches rose comically with the gesture. "It was a bit of a puzzle. Historical records tell us that after the Cataclysm, all terminuses connecting to the B'hintal Dadeyah egress were drowned along with the land and its people."

Haus nodded. He'd read the old records in his studies just like everyone else.

"Well, Dadeyah's round face hangs in the sky between Dormah and the rings of dust that once were Opoli." He leaned forward and raised his brows. "Nihal and I propose it is a reference to retrieving a sample of the spark from one of those terminuses. Given their locations, I am not certain that is even possible." He waved his hand to dismiss his ignorance. "However, Master Orono instead dispatched Madame Rift to retrieve one of the Cuundatay vials from the Seers of Dream and Waking. They are purported to contain tears of the Sisters of Augury—though I have doubts."

Haus gave a low whistle. "I knew Rift was a gifted thief, but swiping something from the Seers…"

"A little spooky, no?"

Haus grinned. "No. But we're in different businesses."

"I suppose we are."

"So, you and your sister, you think all these ingredients should have just been different sparks?"

Hergis tapped one of his showy rings against the bowl of his glass pipe. "There were artifacts he needed as well, but primarily—though not exclusively—for the information they conveyed. The sapia, for instance. They were a set of large copper ceremonial braziers scattered across the world long before the seas rose." He paused, toying with one half of his mustaches. "Purportedly they were placed in Omatha's temples by the Duin herself—something I never quite believed, though now I find I am forced to reconsider that position."

Haus grunted agreement.

"The story claims that she dispersed these vessels across the isles centuries before the Cataclysm. Master Orono had procured one both for the information engraved on it and as the receptacle for his experiments, though from Sylandair's description of events, I highly doubt that particular sapia remained intact after the conflagration."

The new round of drinks arrived. The pair sat in silence, drinking, smoking, and considering.

When the pipe died, Hergis tapped it out against the chair's arm. "It has been a bit of a revelation, I must admit, to learn that The Book of Omatha may not be merely a myth."

Haus nodded, wiped foam from the stubble over his lip.

"And that it actually does something," Hergis said, voice loose with intoxication. "Though in this case, it did not do what it was intended to do. I do wonder what it would do if the instructions were followed accurately."

"Not something I'd care to try."

"No, no. Of course not."

"So how's it work?"

Hergis looked around as though someone might be eavesdropping and spoke excitedly. "I am not entirely certain yet, but I believe the instructions allow the user to form some sort of—shall we call it a regeneration engine?—employing opoli as a power source. The genetic materials called for and the laboratory processes specified lead me to believe there is a bond created that transforms the body in some way on a cellular level. Assuming, of course, that our chivori employers are correct in their belief that he still survives, I suspect the extreme transformations Master Orono underwent were due in large part to his gross errors." He looked into the remains of his caba and shook his head sadly. "I fear he was a victim of magical thinking."

Haus scratched the sides of his crooked nose as he thought. "So we need to find this engine thing?"

"It is only a hypothesis. I intend further study before I fully concur." Hergis blinked slowly. "I believe we have located all of the relevant documentation. It is now merely a matter of plodding through it all."

"Right." Haus leaned back and stretched. "You up for another round?"

"Probably not the finest idea, though I do appreciate the offer. It gets on top of me a bit more quickly than it does on you."

Haus chuckled. "'Spose so."

"I think I shall see if I can dig up Myyat." Hergis slipped from his chair and stood with a drunk's affected grace.

"Have at it." Haus said. He leaned in close. "If you can't find him, a guy who used to be on my crew, he liked the gents. Swore by a fella here named Y'larn. Chivori, if you don't mind."

Hergis straightened his neckerchief and dipped his chin in appreciation. "Until tomorrow."

ALIARA

They returned to the mansion early that morning. Aliara had tried to coax Syl back into bed, but he simply smiled at her.

"We should arrive before the others," he said.

She'd tried some flirting, a brief pout, even a bit of groping, but still he resisted. Finally, she gave up with a sigh, threw on a black mesh shirt and bright blue pants and followed him north, prepared to spend another long day poking around the basement.

She was surprised when Syl started upstairs instead.

He took her hand and led her to his old bedroom, to the familiar green box chair.

She cocked her head, brows raised.

"Things change." He ran his good arm around her waist and pulled her in, mouth warm against hers.

After days of errands and constant interruptions, that single kiss was all either needed. Aliara eased Syl's suitcoat from his shoulders, let it slide to the floor beside the white triangle sling, and slowly worked her way down the buttons of his shirt while his mouth explored her throat. She slacked the laces of his pants and slid to her knees, peeling away the leather, enjoying the flavor of him. He flinched when she nipped his thigh, hissed as her tongue traced its way back up his body. He pressed against her, kissed her long and eager.

"Pet," he whispered.

She shoved him back into the well-worn cushions. He grinned, eyebrows waggling as she made a show of removing her own snug shirt and pants. Aliara paused, enjoying his strong, limber body before straddling him.

The aging chair creaked beneath them. Syl's hand skimmed her teacup breasts and belly, coaxed her, quickened her breathing. His mouth was all over her as he pulled her in.

Tucked in the old familiar chair, isolated between its high walls, they fell into rhythm. His stormy eyes on hers. His uninjured hand roamed her body, traced her constellations of scars. She mirrored him, fingertips grazing the healing wounds soon to match her own.

She clung to him, the one wonderful constant in her life.

His eyes rolled shut, breath held, and she hovered on the edge above him before the shudder ran through them both.

Loose and sated, Aliara collapsed onto Syl's chest, careful of his many injuries. His head lolled back against the velvet, and she licked the sweat from his neck. He always managed to taste a bit like vanilla.

"Almost like being young again," he said, smirk in his voice.

"Magic chair."

"It comes home with us." He kissed her forehead. "It would be lovely beside the fireplace in the bedroom."

She murmured agreement.

"We may need to reupholster it to match."

"No."

She felt his laugh.

"Cleaned then?"

"Fair eno—"

A distant scratch, like rasp on wood, cut off the pillow talk. Aliara straightened.

"Our army of employees are arriving," Syl said. "Or they've stopped in and realized their intrusion."

She relaxed. Though the third floor wasn't frequented, it had become difficult to find solitude in the old mansion filled with so many people. Soon enough, the whole melee would be over and forgotten. Privacy would once again be theirs.

"Did you close the door?" Syl asked.

She shook her head. "Wasn't on my mind."

He grinned and patted her ass. "Good point, but I'd hate for that furry catastrophe to walk in on us. Hergis hasn't kept much of a leash on him."

She gave him a pained look and rolled away.

He stood, awkwardly tugged at the dark leather pants around his ankles then looked at her, eyes amused and annoyed. "Help?"

"Come here," she said. Since the injury, she'd become the master of all buttons, ties, and buckles. Given Syl's vast and complex wardrobe, the role kept her busy. She yanked the laces of his pants tight.

Syl winced. "Watch it."

"More zippers in the future."

He left his shirt and sling in a puddle on the floor and started around the corner for the door. She made it no further than panties and shirt before the hairs on her neck bristled. Instinct turned her to Syl. He stood motionless, wounded arm curled against his stomach. His head was cocked awkwardly, jaw clenched, and eyes focused on the wall around the corner.

"What's wrong?" she whispered.

When he looked at her, fear flamed behind his eyes. Aliara knew only one reason for that look. His gaze turned back, and she joined him.

Just around the corner, clinging to the ceiling was a creature undreamt of in Aliara's darkest nightmare. Beneath layers of thick flesh like translucent adipocere, it glowed with the same frosted blue light as the glass heap they saw in the ritual chamber. Two tentacles dangled idly near its head, while an array of spindly limbs held it fast to the ceiling. Dagger tips of vertebrae protruded through the lucent skin. A long, reedy tail stretched out from the base of the spine, twitching randomly, like an animal on the hunt. At its end was the familiar tumorous growth, thick spike protruding from the top. Aliara gripped Syl's arm hard enough to bruise. He grunted reflexively.

The creature's tail ceased its calm twitching and traced the air in a rhythm of wide, searching arcs. Its head slowly rotated until it seemed to look down its own spine. Clouded eyes whirled in their sockets. The comically floppy ears leapt about in search of sound. A pinkish membrane low on the face quivered in a pantomime of sniffing.

Changed though he was, there was no mistaking the creature's face. This was Kluuta Orono. The man who had raped Syl almost daily, whose experiments had left Aliara forever scarred and broken, who had sought to make himself eternal, now clung to the wall above them like some malevolent, fleshy louse.

Beneath the translucent skin, she could make out the body that had once been karju: The arms hidden beneath the flaccid tentacles, the legs fused together to extend the knobby spine, the nose and mouth at work behind the lumpy membrane.

"He found us," Syl murmured.

Orono's tail curled toward his body like a snake poised to strike. His horrible face blindly swiveled around the room, slit of a nose opening and closing. The tail lashed out, swishing only a hand's breadth from Syl's cheek.

Aliara jerked him back, toward the doors separating his one-time bedroom from Orono's. If they could slip in and close them, they had a chance. Together they crept backward, unwilling to turn away from the sightless thing. Orono's reedy tail swept around him, jabbing at the space where they had stood.

When her heel bumped the door, Aliara realized she'd been holding her breath. She gulped air. Her fingers fumbled for the cup handles, finally finding their cold metal.

She placed Syl's hand in the companion cup and, each gripping a handle, they pulled the doors apart.

Had anyone asked him, Haus could have warned them about the aging door tracks, but household maintenance hadn't been a priority the past few days. The doors vibrated with a chattering squeal of wood on wood.

A deep, animal rumbling and scratch of skittering legs echoed through the old space. In a heartbeat, Orono was above them, long tail undulating with menace. Waxy flaps opened on what remained of his neck, their stiff flesh jutted to either side like miniature wings.

Aliara's heart thudded. She heaved at the door. It shuddered open enough to slip through.

Outside, carriage wheels crackled on the gravel of the drive. The burbling voice of Hergis drifted up. "—was very productive, but I do hope we are not visited again. Tatumi will monitor the burn pile before things get out of control. So much to go through."

Orono twitched, disturbed by the sound. The rumble building inside him piqued. The neck flaps pulsated like revolting bellows. Brown gas gushed out, a stench like old breath and rotting fruit.

Aliara managed to step one foot through the doors before everything went black.

PART THREE
THE FETE

ALIARA

Aliara was lost in darkness so empty and black it left her unsure if her eyes were open. It crushed her, soaked her brain, suffocated her with immobility.

A hand slapped her face. Her eyes flew open, and Syl's beauty floated before her, his palm against her cheek. The room behind him vibrated, everything bright edges and motion. Mischievous set to his mouth, he eased her toward sitting, propped her up on an orange sofa. He stroked her face, her neck, her breast, and she realized he was slipping away. The sofa sucked him down, drew his body into its crevices like filaments of paint down a drain.

Aliara grabbed for him with arms that seemed stuck in glue, watched his face disappear beneath the carroty cushions, and felt his fingers slip away. She dug into the sofa like a burrow dog hunting hares, half-buried, feet waving wildly in the air. A hand fell into hers. She pulled. The hand tightened and jerked, dragging her into the gloom below.

SCHMALCH

"Duke?" Schmalch kept close watch on all open doors as he climbed to the third floor. He would not be blindsided by more of those lumpy white people.

He hadn't dared come upstairs since the night of the attic people. He was none too happy about being here now. Hergis had offered to send Tatumi as his guardian on the search for the Duke and Rift, but Schmalch was even less comfortable with that than he was going alone.

"Duke? Rift? There's a lady here from the Abog Union." He unlocked the bedroom that had been his, however briefly, and peeked in. It was still a mess; the cleaners hadn't made it up here yet. "Duke? She wants to know where her people are."

Schmalch backed out and crossed the hallway to the room the Duke called the study. The midday breeze swept through the broken glass doors, carrying the still-lingering pong of the attic people's toilet above, but the room itself was quiet, empty.

"Rift? Duke? C'mon, where are you?" He crept on, constantly checking behind him.

The door to the Duke's old bedroom stood open. Schmalch relaxed. They were probably at it again. That was why they didn't answer. It was nothing he hadn't seen before. He stuck his head in.

"Du—" He choked on the word.

A motionless grey arm peeked out from the corner where the

room elbowed. He recognized it, long, muscled, fingernails un-lacquered. Rift.

Something had taken Rift down. Nothing that could do that could be good.

Schmalch turned tail and ran back to the basement.

HAUS

Over the shoulder of the woman Haus was scrutinizing, he saw Schmalch thump down the last few stairs on his ass. He hopped up, ran toward Haus, and grunted several syllables before actually forming words.

"Calm," Haus said and held up a hand. He stepped away from the mercenary rep.

Schmalch gulped air. "—Rift…Rift's arm. I saw it!"

"What?"

"I saw her arm on the ground. Nobody answered me."

"Where?"

"The Duke's old room."

Haus took two steps closer to the Abog, "It's time for you to go."

"You can't bully me. Where are my men? Where's our money?"

Haus grabbed her arm and pulled her to the front door, not pausing until he threw her out onto the porch.

The Union officer stumbled down the steps and righted herself. "Next time you see me, I won't be alone," she said with as much menace as she could muster and hobbled across the courtyard, leaving Haus to consider the threat, and just as quickly dismiss it.

He shut the door and snapped the lock behind their visitor, vaulted up the steps, and rushed into the far bedroom.

The smell here was different and horrible. This wasn't the

pungent bleach, vinegar, and lemon oil combination the cleaners had been using. It wasn't the old sweat and toilet odor of the freaks either. No, this was more like the funk of a sick hunting animal—damp, rotten, and oily.

Schmalch was right to get him. Rift lay on her back, half-naked, limbs splayed like a cast-aside rag doll. The Duke was nowhere to be seen. His boots and a crumpled shirt that looked like something he might wear were lying by the overstuffed chair.

Haus crouched and found her pulse. He slapped Rift's face, but she didn't so much as groan, her head pivoting with each strike as though her neck held no muscles. He scanned the room. Though most everything looked as it had when he'd last been here, the pocket doors had been opened wide enough for a chivori to pass. Knife in hand, Haus pulled the doors fully open and stalked into the master bedroom. It was just as he'd left it after the fight—disordered and unoccupied.

Schmalch was squatting beside Rift when Haus returned. "Is she alive?" the puka asked.

"Yeah. Can't find the Duke. When'd you see them last?"

"At home last night after we left here. They were gone when I got up for breakfast."

Haus let out a pained breath. He'd prefer backup, but he didn't want to wait. Whatever had knocked Rift out probably had the Duke.

"Get Hergis," he told Schmalch, then pointed to Rift. "See what he can do."

"Where're you going?"

"The attic."

The little guy made a sour face and ran off.

Pulling a small torch from his pocket, Haus cranked it and ducked through the closet and hidden room. He banged up the iron stairs into the attic and bit back a retch. The lingering stench of rot and drying shit mingled with the new stink to create a pong that made bile rise into the back of his throat.

He didn't dwell on Uuron and Rej's dried blood spattered the attic floor, didn't note the collected detritus crowding the space. He was alert only for movement and found none.

He took the hidden stair all the way down, stopping to quickly search each floor as he passed but finding them equally vacant. The basement, though, was a wellspring of activity, and one that housed an entirely new reek.

Dressed in a shiny black coat choked with embroidered pink and yellow roses and holding a matching pink hanky over his snoot, Hergis was barking orders at the hiisi as he dumped medical equipment into his bag. The sister, yellow kerchief covering the lower half of her face, sat serenely at the research table, undisturbed by the hubbub as she plodded through bales of paperwork.

Hergis glanced up, spotted Haus. "Pardon the odor, Mister Haus, it seems Tatumi spilled more chemicals yesterday than I initially believed. Can you tell me anything more than what Mister Schmalch relayed?"

"Only that Rift has a pulse and the Duke's missing." Haus could taste the chemicals. He tried not to breath through his snoot.

"My, my. Do you know how long she has lain there?"

"Not sure. When'd you last see her?"

Hergis fiddled with the silver pin at the collar of his yellow blouse. "Well, last night, of course. Before I saw you. I assumed they were here already when we arrived."

"Yeah. Probably were."

Haus left Hergis and pushed into the second operating room, the one with the hole in the wall. The caustic scent rolled over him. The room reeked so powerfully that Haus pulled off his shirt and covered his face with it.

The steel cabinet, as tall as Haus and twice as broad lay on its face, its contents having shattered and seeped out around the edges, turning the air bitter with fumes. The hole it had blocked, knee-high when Haus last saw it, was now broad enough for him to walk through with only a slight stoop. Something big, fast, and powerful had found its way inside.

ALIARA

She floated amongst whispers. Hands tumbled over her, lashed at her, forced open her eyes to a painful, breath-stealing brightness.

Lumia lights undulated and swayed above her. Aliara lifted her head, saw her small, pallid feet poking out below the old lime-colored dress. Her limbs were bound to the cold, steel table she knew too well.

Orono's moon face, bright and vibrant, hovered above her. His face was clear, but here again, the world beyond seemed to vibrate like the string of an over-plucked cittern.

Orono drew up her gown. His scalpel hovered in-hand for a moment above her sternum before slicing into her. As he cut, the hand dissolved into a waxy tendril, the change crawling across his body until only his monstrous, unseeing face tilted down toward her. His lips writhed beneath their fleshy shell.

She knew what they said. She *was* a stupid girl.

A scrabbling limb snapped forward, drumming at her mouth. He cut deeper into her, reached inside, and withdrew Calla after Calla. He passed them to young Syl, who dangled by his neck from the reedy tail, eating the silvery coins, tears floating in his eyes.

Hergis coalesced behind Orono like some obscene owl. His long mustaches danced in the air, looped around Syl, and groped inside her opened body. The little man opened his mouth and vomited a hideous blackness that enveloped her.

HERGIS

Hergis lifted Aliara's eyelids. It was difficult to separate pupil from iris in her eyes under the best circumstances, but now the dilation absorbed all but the sclera. Her pulse was strong, her breathing even, but she responded to no stimuli. He found no wounds or broken bones, no contusions on her head. He could only assume she'd been drugged or poisoned somehow. He administered chemical stimulants, first inhaled, then injected, but she remained inert. Despite the frustrating lack of results and the need to revive her, he ceased further experimenting, lest he kill her with his efforts.

Hergis' lips poked out as he considered his options. "Pick her up," he told Tatumi. "Bring her to the laboratory."

The hiisi complied. His floral-embroidered newsboy cap fell off when he bent to lift Aliara. A soft smile passed his lips.

"Mind the head," Hergis said, patting the staircase's twisted handrail. "We would not want to exacerbate her situation."

Tatumi trundled along obediently, descending with his master into the basement.

"On the table," Hergis said.

Tatumi stared.

"Room one."

The hiisi backed through the swinging door and laid Aliara on the steel table. Hergis rolled his stepstool to the table's edge, locked it, and climbed into place. Operating light bright in his patient's face, he examined her pupils through his monocular. Even in the bright glare, they remained dilated and fixed. Exceptional behavior for a species so fond of dilute lighting. He let her eye snap shut and rubbed his chin.

A metallic screeching sound from the adjacent operating room startled him.

"Savesti," Haus called. "Send your muscle in here."

Hergis flicked dismissive fingers at Tatumi. The hiisi swung the doors wide, and Hergis glimpsed the enormous metal cabinet, now knocked on its face, the back panel notched as though someone had gone at it with a sledge. The hole in the wall was more than twice the size it had been when last seen. It was far from a comforting sight. He put the image of the murderous little girl out of his mind and returned to his patient, considering alternative locations for his work.

From the next room, glass broke, someone cursed extensively, and something metal produced a reverberating clang. Haus stalked into operating theater one, followed so closely by Schmalch that he may as well have been carrying the puka. Tatumi sauntered in behind.

"Hole's blocked again. She all right?" Haus asked.

"I really cannot say." Hergis removed the magnifying instruments from his face and turned gingerly on the stepstool, at eye level with Haus for once. He smelled the sweat of effort and a distant whiff of last night's beer on the big man. "She appears uninjured. I have applied some medications that should have brought her round, but as you see, they were unsuccessful."

Haus grunted. He stared at Aliara as though he could locate the corruption. "Duke said she doesn't have much of a liver."

"Fascinating." Hergis stroked the coils of his mustaches. "That certainly could contribute to the situation."

Another grunt.

"Have you found Sylandair?" Hergis asked.

Haus shook his head, shaggy, unkempt hair waving this way and that. "Doesn't seem to be here."

"Given all that, may I ask for your assessment of our situation, Mister Haus?"

"Seems obvious."

Hergis nodded. "To me as well. What do we do about it?"

Haus looked up. "That's your bailiwick, isn't it?"

Schmalch's head swung pendulously between the two, frown fixed in place.

"In part, I suppose," Hergis replied.

"Any ideas?" Haus asked.

"One perhaps." Hergis scowled and rubbed his hands together as though cold. "I would like to research it further before I commit."

"Should we waste the time? The Duke could still be alive down there."

"Our Duke Imythedralin is either dead already," Hergis said. "Or he will not be killed—not intentionally, at least—so long as he cooperates with his captor. I would hypothesize the latter. From what I have learned of him, Sylandair seems to have a prodigious capacity for survival."

Both ignored the animal squeak from Schmalch.

"Why not kill him?" Haus asked.

Hergis cleared his throat, wiggled his nose. The subject was uncomfortable at best. "I am operating under the assumption that if Master Orono wanted our Duke, it was not simply for the purpose of killing him. Otherwise we would have found his body upstairs."

Haus tilted his head back to look at the ceiling. "Manky son of a trull wants his dolly back."

"Yes. That is my assumption."

"Why not smash his head, stick one of those needles in?"

"Ah, you mean as he does the children? Sylandair is what…well past his fortieth year? Perhaps even more."

"Never asked. Hard to tell with chivori."

"Hrm, yes. The girl I saw and the children described to me—the ones displaying the needle to which you refer, I mean—they all are children. I suspect there is a reason for this. Whatever biological mechanism Master Orono is utilizing to connect with these children, I believe it requires youth to function properly. We can hardly call Sylandair a youth."

Haus strode to the wall and back several times as he scratched the scars on his arm. When he returned to Hergis, he crossed his arms and frowned. "So we just leave him there with that thing?"

"By all means, go charging to the rescue and see how it unravels."

Haus' nostrils flared. "Yeah, yeah."

"Nihal and I will do our utmost to devise a stratagem by tomorrow. Will that suffice?"

"Have to, won't it?"

Hergis shrugged a tiny shoulder.

"What'd we do with her?" Haus asked.

Schmalch moved away from the conversation and took Aliara's limp hand. "We should take her home."

The room was silent for a moment.

"An excellent suggestion. I suggest we *all* vacate the premises and repair to Madame Rift's apartments." Hergis danced down the steps of his stool. "Nihal and I can gather the tools and materials we need and continue our study from there as well. I will be able to monitor her condition, administer medications as necessary."

"Agreed." Haus looked around the stark room. "Nothing good happens here."

SYLANDAIR

He drifted in a familiar darkness, a cousin of the one he'd known often during Orono's Portent quests to reach Omatha.

His nose woke first. Sviroosa was cooking breakfast. Badly. The reek of it turned his stomach. His eyes flicked open to a world that shifted and squirmed as though heat radiated from all surfaces.

Syl rose and wandered into the kitchen, where Sviroosa stood on her stool, stirring an enormous pot. He strained to tell her to do something about the smell, but his tongue flopped around in his mouth like a hooked fish. He put a hand on her shoulder and she turned. Where her face should be, there was nothing. Only smooth, sage blankness looked back at him.

He took the spoon from her, peered into the pot. Floating atop the dreadful soup, his own face looked back at him. The spoon clattered to the floor as arms shot out and pulled him in.

Syl sucked in air like a drowning man. His lungs chilled. His head throbbed. Shapes shifted outside; light wavered and bucked on the other side of his lids. The smell was strong. He could taste it. Like wet dog and curdled milk.

A smooth, cold touch stirred him, and he slowly opened his eyes. The horrific face of what was once Orono hovered above him, bigger than in Syl's youth. The old man had always dwarfed Syl, but now his bulk had expanded, his height elongated.

A slithery tentacle, alive with pale light, brushed Syl's cheek.

Revulsion overrode reason. He tried to sit, to backpedal, but raw lightning ripped through the bones of his left arm. He pulled the splinted arm close to his naked chest, rolled onto the uninjured side of his body and scooted away, eyes never leaving the monster who'd dared touch him.

Something cold tightened around his neck and tugged at him as he drew away. Syl choked and coughed, his fingers fumbling at his throat. A collar. A chain held it fast to an eyebolt driven into the floor beside the too-familiar glowing glass lump.

Syl's mind cleared, assembled facts. He knew where he was. That was good. He was deep underground, lying on a dais at the center of a ring of tiny bones, lifeless children standing watch beyond. That was not.

Orono whistled and clicked. Even without words, Syl knew the tone. He was being scolded.

Syl stood, chain pulled taught. "I am not yours to command anymore, you flaccid husk." He jabbed a finger at Orono. "I am no longer your plaything."

Orono's tail lashed out, clouting him across the side of the head. Syl slammed against the glass mound, instinctively recoiling from the warm pulse against his skin.

Orono produced more clicking, punctuated with a long, low whistle. He scuttled over and stroked Syl's hair as though fussing over a housecat. His expression seemed almost regretful. The little bellows at Orono's neck opened and pulsed, brown gas billowing forth again, and Syl slipped back into the black.

SVIROOSA

Though she was none too thrilled about the motley troupe she now played host to, Sviroosa tolerated the situation. She would tolerate an awful lot for her Duke Sylandair and Lady Aliara. Granted, they were often up to no good, and sometimes the things she had to clean up were revolting, but they took excellent care of her. They'd given her a good life away from her family in the Dominion. They paid her quite well, treated her with respect, and left her the run of the house during their holidays away from the Haven. Duke Sylandair had even funded her education. With the skills and experience they'd given her, Sviroosa was better off than anyone else in her family. She could earn a living in whatever way she desired should this job—or her employers—vanish for good.

So when Schmalch swung the door wide and invited inside the scarred and tattooed mercenary, the disquieting scientific contingent, and an unconscious Lady Aliara, Sviroosa set to work. Something had happened to her mistress, and—though the Duin knew why—she and Duke Sylandair seemed to trust the maddeningly irritating Schmalch. Sviroosa would do the same.

After settling them in the parlor, she dashed to the market for extra food. By the time she returned, the invading horde had set up camp, rearranging furniture and tromping all over her clean floors. The mercenary attempted to lay claim to Duke Sylandair's study as his temporary sleeping quarters, but Sviroosa's fit at the suggestion dissuaded him. She would have no shaggy lump of karju flopped on the room's sofa, booted feet propped on the imported leather as though he owned it. She reluctantly agreed he be allowed to sleep on one of the parlor sofas, but he was strongly admonished against putting shoes on furniture.

She was in the midst of frying soft-shell crabs and preparing a bean salad when Schmalch burst in, all eyeballs and nervous energy. He said nothing, simply looked around as though he'd never before seen the kitchen.

"What do you need?" she asked.

"What? Um…oh yeah…"

As she waited for him to settle, Sviroosa fished the last of the crabs from the oil. Their shells, once maroon-speckled white, were now a perfect crispy brown. She wasn't about to let this pest's distraction ruin her meal.

Schmalch swallowed a couple times and rubbed his upper arm, relaxing slightly. "I, um…I'm real sorry about all this, Sviroosa."

She snapped off the stove and stepped down from her cooking stool. "What exactly *is* all this?"

His brow wrinkled. "It's very complicated."

She put her hands on her hips.

"Right. Yeah. Well, you know the old mansion?"

"Yes, obviously." She wiped her hands on her apron.

"Right. Right… Yeah." His gaze dropped to his feet for a moment before he answered. "When did you last see the Duke and Rift?"

"This morning. They left about the time I pulled the biscuits from the oven. I sent them off with a few and some tea."

"So that was what? Pretty early?"

"Before dawn, yes. Now what's going on?"

"I didn't get to the mansion until midday, 'cause I had some other stuff to do. Anyway, this Abog woman shows up and wants to talk to the Duke, so I go to get them, but I can't find them, so I start hitting all the rooms—there's a lot of them to check—and finally I get to the Duke's old room. You know the one?" As he spoke, he picked up speed. "Yeah, well, Rift's laying there dead to the world, and the Duke's just not there at all, so I got Haus and he wanted us all to clear out of that nasty old building and come back here. Hergis is gonna do whatever it is he's doing with all that dross from the mansion, and his sister's gonna help, and I'm real sorry to bring that big, hairy critter of Hergis' into the apartment."

Sviroosa's eyes were wide. "What are they doing to find Duke Sylandair?"

"Well, that seems like it's got to do with—" His words cut off as the swinging door struck him in the backside.

Schmalch edged out of the way, rubbing his wounded rear as Haus stepped in.

"Going out for supplies," the big mercenary said.

Schmalch blanched. "You're leaving us here with that-that-that hiisi?"

He mispronounced the species' name. Sviroosa made a mental note to correct that when things were less chaotic.

"You'll be fine," Haus said. "I have a friend who knows a little something about chemistry. Planning to stop there while I'm out and see if he's heard of something like this."

"You're coming back?" Schmalch asked. "Soon?"

"Soon as I can. Few hours at worst." He noticed the heap of deep-fried crabs. "You mind?"

"They're for you and the others," Sviroosa said. "Help yourself."

Haus grabbed a handful and clomped out.

Schmalch positioned himself beyond the swinging door's reach. "So…what was I…?"

"What's happening to find Duke Sylandair?"

"Right. That's what Hergis and his sister are working on. He said either the Duke is dead already, or he won't be killed, and it's better to wait and figure stuff out before going after him 'cause he'll be fine.

Didn't make much sense to me, but Haus agreed. And, well, before all this Rift and the Duke really seemed to think Hergis knows what he's doing." Schmalch shrugged deeply.

"But they are going to do something?"

"That's what they said." He nodded hard enough to shake his brains loose. "Can I sit in here and eat? I don't want to be out there with that thing. I promise to be quiet and stay out of your way."

She pursed her lips. "Sit at the island and leave me be. If you get in my way, you're out."

"Great." He pulled out a stool.

"First, though, take some food out to the parlor."

The round trip took him less than a minute. He struggled onto the stool and commenced sloppy, open-mouthed chomping on the crabs and salad. Sviroosa worked on a lobster molga and did her best to ignore him. The soup was one of Lady Aliara's favorites. When she woke—and she would wake soon, Sviroosa was sure—she'd be hungry.

Molga was a complex soup that required gentle preparation of its many ingredients. Sviroosa took her time, dicing vegetables, measuring cream and seasonings, wrangling the massive and miserable live lobster. Schmalch watched her with a level of interest normally reserved for sporting events. She felt his presence behind her, aware of how desperately he wanted to hop off the stool and ask inane questions. He'd long since finished his meal, but he so disliked the hiisi that he sat quietly, waiting for the mercenary to return. Experience had shown her that any word to Schmalch gave him the impression she was interested in whatever he had to say, so she pretended he wasn't there.

She held the tip of her kitchen knife at the heart of the poor creature's cluster of eye stalks. The lobster made a last effort at escape, swiping vainly with its giant claw before Sviroosa punched the blade through its mottled dark-purple shell and into its brain. Ignoring the squeak of surprise from Schmalch, she dropped it on to boil as a ruckus started from somewhere beyond the kitchen door. Someone shouted unintelligibly, something was knocked over, and it was quiet again.

"What was that?" Sviroosa asked.

"Probably they're just moving furniture again," Schmalch said. He stared at the door and bit his lip.

They stood there, waiting for any other sounds. When Schmalch's shoulders relaxed, Sviroosa slowly turned back to her work. The lobster's shell wasn't the right brilliant violet yet but would be any moment now.

A horrible half-scream came from somewhere in the house. Sviroosa dropped the spoon. The scream tapered off to a gurgle, then quieted altogether. Schmalch hopped off his stool, drew the wavy little dagger from his ankle, and crept toward the door.

"Where are you going?" Sviroosa asked in a loud whisper.

He swallowed hard. "Out there. Somethin's not right."

"You're going to leave me here alone?" She climbed off the stepstool, boiling lobster forgotten.

"I uh... What if one of those kids followed us?"

"What kids?"

Schmalch shook his head.

"Isn't that shaggy thing out there a guard of some kind?"

"Yeah, but what if something happened to him? I gotta at least check it out." He grabbed a heavy, steel shellfish mallet from the counter.

"I'm not staying here alone." Sviroosa's fingers tightened around her knife and she edged as close to Schmalch as his odor would allow.

"Right. Anything happens, Sviroosa, you run," he said.

"You will, too?"

"After you're gone." He pushed open the door, and they crept into the distressingly quiet hallway.

ALIARA

Aliara hung in nothingness, immobile and bewildered. The dark seeped through her skin, crawled into her sinuses, swirled down the drain of her pupils. Her mind blurred, dizzied, all concept of time forgotten.

A thrill of hope ran through her as a smudged world took shape before her straining eyes. It was a lovely, sunny spring day. Green grass tickled her feet. A breeze fluttered her lashes. She felt a hand in each of hers, looked down. Grinning green puka surrounded her, spinning madly in a ring as they chittered and laughed. She tried to jerk her hands away, but they held her tight, dragging her around the circle with them.

The one to her left opened a mouth filled with jagged reptile teeth and clamped down on her hand, tearing at her flesh with shark-like determination. She tugged on her right hand, hoping to beat her attacker, but the puka on that side bit down as well. She kicked at them, but they danced out of reach, tugging on her like a Sower's Festival goose. She screamed. The happy circle spun on, faster and faster.

Her body ripped and her mind seeped away until she was once again lost in black obscurity.

NIHAL

The year Nihal Savesti turned twelve, her parents sparked a new life that extinguished any hope she had for her own.

They'd wanted two children so badly, a girl and a boy. At the end of each season's fertile cycle, the whole family waited to find out if Father had managed to make Mother pregnant. Each time they were despondent when she wasn't. Nihal tried to cheer them, tried to be enough to fill their lives, but she could never be that boy they wanted so badly.

When they finally became pregnant, the celebration had been near constant. Even Nihal was caught up in the excitement. Yet when they brought her baby brother home, their faces were not the jubilant ones she expected.

"Meet Hergis," Mother said as she lowered the infant for Nihal to see.

He was tiny in her arms. Ugly and all puckered looking, too. A big drip splashed onto his head, and Nihal looked up, surprised to find Mother crying.

"We need you to help us pack, Bubble," Mother said, voice catching in her throat. "We're moving."

"Why?" Nihal asked.

Mother straightened and looked at Father.

"She's old enough to know, Faida," he said.

Mother's chest hitched as she tried to speak, but all she managed was a warbling sob.

Father stomped forward and brushed her out of the way. He bent down on one knee and took Nihal by both shoulders. "Your baby brother was born minikin."

Nihal stared at him, shrugged.

"He's too small," Father said. "He'll look like us and talk like us and act like us, but he'll never be as big and strong as the rest of us."

"So? Why do we need to move?"

His eyes flicked to Mother. "The Emperor's law—we either leave Oras or turn little Hergis over to the priests so they can send him to be with the God-Emperors."

Nihal internally debated which choice she preferred. Before she could voice her opinion on the matter, Father released her and stood. "Now go pack everything you need," he said. "And hurry."

That night, the Savestis abandoned their lavish estate on the island of Oralin for a three-bedroom apartment teetering nine stories into the stinking sky of Dockhaven. All the privilege Nihal knew in her first years—the education, the friends, the servants—was gone. Instead, she was put to work in a laundry on the Upper Rabble, her fingers puckered by the constant dampness, her skin forever stinking of other people's filth. Eventually it stole her beauty.

When she came home each night, she cooked the meals, cleaned the house. She became the family's lone servant.

Little Hergis never lifted a finger. Too delicate, too anemic, too twitching precious; the excuses were endless. He burped too loudly, and Mother rushed him to the physician. Nihal could chop off a finger, and she'd be told to bandage it and quit complaining.

The precious child's tenth birthday arrived with a ray of hope. As he grew, Hergis displayed impressive intellectual aptitude. Nihal had as well at his age, not that her parents would recall that. Because Hergis would never be able to hold a laborious job—or so Father claimed—a month of the family's wages were spent to send him to the Mucha Colleges in the city of Ukur-Tilen for admission testing.

If deemed adequate, the Mucha would keep the child, train him until he either became Master or washed out as Onaman.

Nihal pushed Hergis to study, reading to him, quizzing him, taking him to libraries in her spare time. If he was accepted, if he left their household, the family could return to Oras. She was still young. She could marry well and lead the life of a proper Orasian. If he went off to the Colleges, she'd never have to see her baby brother again. He would be out of her life, no longer her burden.

When Hergis left for the island of Ukur, Nihal could think of nothing but that freedom almost within her grasp. Nearly a quartern later, a farspeech runner arrived with a chit. The family clapped and hugged when Father read the news that Hergis had been accepted as a Mucha entrant.

Nihal rushed to her bedroom and packed. When she strode into the parlor, her parents goggled.

"Why are you carrying luggage?" Mother asked.

"We can return home," Nihal said.

"What?"

"With Hergis gone to his new home, we can go back to Oras."

Father laughed. "Hardly. Once the die is cast…" He waved his hand.

"But…" Nihal began. At Father's glare, she wilted. The little trunk, filled with everything she owned in the world, dropped to the floor with a *thunk*.

"Anyway," Mother said, "Dockhaven is far closer to Ukur than Oralin. We'll visit Hergis as often as possible. Now, put your things and your silly notion away and run to the market. Your father is peckish for whitefish stew tonight. See what you can find."

These memories and more roiled in Nihal's mind as she glared at her brother from behind one of Master Orono's books.

They were settled in their chivori employer's parlor. The situation was far from ideal, but Nihal managed to ignore the discomfort and distractions and progress with accurate translations of the source material. She'd made impressive headway—until now.

The sheets of her research notes lay on the low table between Hergis and her, puddle of water blurring her fresh ink. Hergis muttered and clicked his tongue as he blotted at the pages, her words vanishing into obscurity with each wipe. The clumsy boor had spilled a glass of water all over *her* hard work while his remained fresh and crisp and untouched.

Her vision went dark, focused down to a pin-prick. She saw only Hergis, only the decades lost in service of the pusillanimous little twat while being denied her own wants and needs, hiding herself behind a well-honed mask of placid obedience. Behind the wrinkles of more than six decades and the pompous garb of his profession, Nihal still saw the little boy who had ruined her. She'd spent her entire life following him, caring for him, keeping him safe. All she was to him was an assistant, someone to command alongside poor, brain-addled Tatumi.

Everything she lost over the wasted lifetime flooded her mind. It had all been denied her simply because this runt was allowed to live.

"Stop it! Just stop it, you douse!" She rose from the sofa and swatted at his hand.

"Sister?" Hergis massaged away the sting of the slap and looked up at her reproachfully.

"It's as though you don't really want to know these things. These pages hold insights you could never hope to glean on your own, and you dump water on them. Fool!"

"That was an accident. You know that." Hergis stood, put his hands on his hips. "Perhaps you should take a few hours, take your mind off this, spend some time at the market? We have obviously been working too hard."

"We?"

"Well, I suppose I did take an evening off. I certainly needed a break. That can't be helped," Hergis replied.

Nihal grunted. "Yes, you enjoyed your break while I dragged our work to your apartments to continue into the night, while *I* finished your part of the Varsak temple translation."

"You should have enjoyed a respite as well." He smiled placatingly. "I do appreciate your labors, Sister. I may be a Supreme Sovereign Master of the Mucha, but I still value my fine assistant's efforts."

Her lips pulled back in something that was less of a smile than a baring of teeth. "My *efforts*? My efforts have been far more productive than yours, Brother. You and all your opportunities, your Mucha, your bank account."

"I have always seen to it that you have money."

"Oh yes, my precious allowance isn't at all degrading." She leaned over, palms flat on the low table. "*I* never had the chance to attend the Colleges. *I* had to stay home and serve Mother and Father, helpless feck that they were."

Hergis edged away from her toward the end of the sofa. His voice took on a patronizing tone intended to be calming. "Now, Sister, I am certain you do not mean that. Mother and Father loved you so."

"They loved what I did for them. Serving them, spending *my* coin to keep them fed and housed." Nihal straightened, gesturing spasmodically as she spoke. She stepped around the table, her skirt, black with floral embroidery made to match Hergis' jacket, swishing softly. The mask of servile humility she'd worn all these years was gone.

He edged out of the sofa grouping toward Tatumi, who waited on the slate hearth by the fire, tongue out, eyes glassy, as though unaware of the tension in the room.

"I had no idea you felt this way," Hergis said. "What can I do to…to…to make it better?" His little body shook beneath the expensive clothes. He feared her. She liked the sensation.

Nihal closed, bent over, and shoved Hergis. He tumbled backward, flopping against one of the wood-framed chairs. It careened into the smoking stand, cushions popping out of place with the impact. The little stand tipped onto the hearth with a *crack* that made Hergis jump.

Nihal stood over him, finger poking at his chest. "I am done with you and your precious needs. I will clean out your bank accounts and take what I've learned and build myself the life *you* kept me from living. All of this…" She jabbed the finger toward the piles of books and papers behind her. "This will allow me to live the life I should have lived all along."

"Sister, surely you do not mean that—"

"Don't I?"

"You have been told of what happens when one dabbles with… with all that." Hergis waved his hands dismissively.

"I've been told what happens to a foolish old man who can't understand metaphor. *I* will discover what happens when the method is applied correctly."

Hergis' expression was horrified. He struggled to stand.

"Tatumi," Nihal said, "help your master to his feet." She pulled a snarl beetle from her apron, fed it to him.

Tatumi munched the treat, smile that never looked quite right wrapped around his muzzle. He pushed the undone chair out of his way. It clattered halfway across the room.

"Now give your master a big hug," Nihal said.

Tatumi lifted Hergis, wrapped his arms around the undersized chest and squeezed. Hergis released a grunt and a *whoof* of breath.

"Sister…what are you doing?" he grunted out.

"Tighter, Tatumi, hug him tighter." Nihal moved closer. Eye to eye with her brother, she smiled. "He needs a big hug."

Hergis tried to shout, but the sound came out as pained gurgle, like a squeeze box full of water.

Nihal watched his exertions with glee.

"What's going on?" asked a small, nasal voice from the hallway. She spun. Two pukas stood in the entry. The chivori's servants.

The male brandished a tiny blade and some sort of kitchen implement, a meat mallet, perhaps. The female clung to his shoulder. He tried to look menacing, but Nihal could see the fear in both their faces.

"Get out, pukas," she said.

"What're you doing to Hergis?" the male asked.

"That's none of your concern."

He scurried forward, close, but out of reach. The female caught up with him.

"Put Hergis down, you big ugly thing!" he shouted at Tatumi. He slashed the pathetic weapons through the air.

"Ignore that insect, Tatumi. Hug tighter," Nihal said. "Do not let Master Savesti go."

Tatumi's tongue lolled happily against his chin. He squeezed.

Hergis' face was red, his eyes rolled back, and his lips moved with silent pleas.

The male tossed the kitchen mallet at Tatumi, who unwound one of his arms and batted it away. The steel head clanged into one of the room's picture windows. Nihal heard the crack of glass.

Tatumi resumed his hug.

"Let him go!" the male shouted.

"Schmalch, no!" the female reached for her companion as he hurried away from her. With the shield of his body gone, she clenched her own weapon, a kitchen knife, to her chest.

Wavy blade raised, the male rushed at Tatumi, who kicked the little creature away. His huge foot slammed into the puka's chest, impact knocking the air from his body and the knife from his hand. The male slammed into the damaged window. A maze of spider-web fissures crawled across the glass wall, a few glittering bits breaking away and spilling into the darkness. The puka struggled for balance, waving his arms in an attempt to right himself, but inertia held him against the disintegrating pane.

With a sound like shells sliding across sand, the glass shattered, cascading toward the sea. The puka's little green body tottered on the edge for a moment before he pitched into the darkness with a feeble squeak.

"Schmalch!" the female yelped. She lurched forward as though she might run to him, but her eyes flicked to Tatumi and she stopped.

The group of them stood there, Hergis still tight in Tatumi's arms, listening to the few soft thuds and distant splash as the male puka tumbled through the night.

"Oh Schmalch," the female moaned. She took a step backward.

Nihal smiled, curled her fingers toward the remaining invader. "Come here, puka."

The female ran for the doorway. Nihal grabbed some vulgar wooden statuette from the mantle and rushed at the scampering creature. A quick strike to the revolting hairless head, and the female collapsed in the hallway, hook nose buried in the ostentatious rug.

Nihal returned to Hergis. "Now, where were we?"

Hergis made some vain attempt to speak, froth trickling from between his swollen lips.

"Oh, yes…" She bent and picked up the puka's stray knife. "Big hug, Tatumi."

The hiisi squeezed tighter. Hergis moaned. A trickle of snot ran from his nose.

"You won't be needing these anymore. Brother." With two quick cuts, Nihal removed her brother's precious mustaches and draped them over her shoulders like a burlesque dancer with a pair of shaggy snakes. "Tighter, Tatumi."

Hergis' eyes bulged, his tongue protruded, darkening until it was black with pooling blood. At the crack of his ribs, a spike of pain rushed across her brother's face. Blood from his punctured lungs burbled from his mouth. He blinked helplessly at her with red-stained eyes that could probably no longer see, tears streaming down his fat cheeks.

Nihal's cold, straw-colored gaze never left her brother's as the life was squeezed from his body.

CHISEV

After Mister Schmalch's visit, Moocha put Chisev to work as her assistant. Taking care of the house and the new business would be too much for her to handle alone, she told him.

Chisev was almost an adult, and his mother's trust had delighted him, but after a whole day at it, he was so harried with cooking and shopping and keeping Worch and Ilit out of trouble that he'd barely had time to paint or enjoy his books. The job wasn't the fun he'd imagined it would be. At least Moocha wasn't crying anymore, he reminded himself. The new business gave her—gave them all—something else to think about, and Chisev couldn't be angry about that. Plus, he'd already met a lot of interesting people at Domestic Consignment. It was a world he never would have known otherwise.

Lots of pukas worked for the agency, of course, but Chisev had been surprised by how many of the workers were chivori, many with nasty scars or missing limbs they couldn't afford to replace. They were mostly fugitives or liberated rou, Moocha told him, the lowest caste in Chiva'vastezz, the big country to the west where most chivori came from. One or two were even runaway slaves from Oras, that paranoid country so far to the east. Moocha said the Orasians he met were especially lucky; it was far less likely for a someone to get away from Oras than from anyplace else across all the islands. The whole idea of castes and slaves was so foreign that it fascinated him.

He wanted to ask them dozens of questions, but the first time he'd tried, Moocha cuffed him in the back of the head for being rude, so he kept his mouth shut and made up his own stories.

She hadn't needed Chisev in the office this morning, so she sent him to the Big Island's wharf market to pick up tonight's supper. Worch and Ilit tagged along, jabbering and running around the colorful vendor tents while Chisev tried to pick out the best food for the coin like a grown-up. He lost out on a perfectly good melon when he had to go chasing after them instead of paying the vendor. He gave the girls each a pinch on the noses and called them a pair of scruddy twitches. They only laughed, with Ilit promising to tell their mother he'd cursed. Chisev said he didn't care, but that wasn't true. The fear of Moocha's reprisal was swimming laps in his chest when they stopped at the family's favorite fish stand.

"Stay there," he said, pointing to a bare spot by the fishmonger's knockdown booth. He wasn't about to lose out on the freshest catch thanks to their shenanigans. "Do *not* get up until I come back. You understand?"

The girls' dark-olive heads bobbed, round eyes perfectly sincere. Chisev took a couple steps toward the iced fish display and spun around. They both sat in place, legs crossed, serene looks on their faces.

He pointed and gave them a stern glare. "I'm watching you."

He scanned the ice-filled bins in search of the perfect fish for tonight's dinner. Some, he was certain, had been lying around since yesterday—cheap, but no good. If he saw film over their eyes, Chisev moved on, no matter what kind of discount the fishmonger offered.

A display of scorillion looked promising. Eyes were clear, scales shiny, gills bright. He could fry those up and serve them with some of the herbs growing in Moocha's window box. After a bit of dickering over price, he paid three coppers, dropped the wrapped parcel into his bag and turned to where his sisters waited.

They were gone.

"Worch?" he called. "Ilit? It's not funny. I'll tell Moocha you made trouble."

He expected them to emerge from behind one of the stands. But they didn't.

"Worch?" he asked, voice catching in his throat. He looked behind the stand, ignoring the fishmonger's protests. Finding nothing, he hurried down the aisle, calling their names. His heart thrummed. He asked after them, ducked into booths, and generally annoyed the vendors in search of their hidey-hole. They couldn't be far. Mostly the pair was outgoing and curious. Though they loved playing scour the shadows, they quickly grew bored. If Chisev kept searching, he'd find them soon enough, no doubt playing with a street cat or bothering some fruit seller.

He started winding his way through the market, calling their names, telling himself they'd show up right quick.

SYLANDAIR

The world quivered; each crisp line a frenetic harp string. A row of Orono's puppet children sat at an ornate bar in front of him, empty glasses in their hands. Syl struggled to speak, his mouth working with a metallic ache, his voice like an unbending wire. His soldered fingers filled glass after glass after glass with iridescent powder that always blew away before it could be consumed. The dust filled the room, soaked into his pores, left him unable to breathe—

Syl woke with a gasp. He sat up, nauseous from hunger and stiff from the room's chill. In his sleep, he'd edged toward the glass pillar, the room's lone source of heat—negligible though it may be—and onto the copper skirt encircling the thing. Once an intricately engraved missive from the Duin in the centuries before Orono had melted it into a puddle, the metal was now faintly warm beneath him. He scooted as far away from it as the chain would allow, happier to freeze to death than to receive comfort from the foul thing.

His wounds complained, and Syl cursed them silently. Were it not for blood loss and the weakness from his maiming, he might already be free. Rubbing the puckered and scabbed flesh around his stitches, he scanned the room. Though it was much as it had been when he'd last been here, two new openings had been dug into the concrete walls. One undoubtedly led to the mansion's basement; Syl couldn't be sure where the other would lead. A pile of debris heaped in one corner may have been new. Syl didn't remember it from his last visit, but wasn't convinced he simply hadn't noticed it in the chaos.

Silent, motionless children stood in random groups around the room. Beyond them lurked the thing that Orono had become, his mutated body bent over a little girl he clasped in his supplemental legs. She stared at him impassively as the slit that was once his nose worked furiously. A long yellow proboscis unfurled from it, and the child opened her mouth, allowing it inside. An identical tube extended from Orono's abdomen, attaching somewhere around the child's navel. The tubes pulsed like living siphons, the girl's body convulsing in a matched rhythm.

Syl leaned forward and retched.

Orono flinched at the sound and retracted the feeding tubes, leaving the girl in a crumpled heap as he scurried over to Syl. The reek of feeding time at the wharf's hog pens on a hot day returned with him. Fear fought to punch through Syl's wits, equal parts horror at the aberration coming for him and dread at once again being in the presence of his childhood tormentor. He tried to scoot away, but the collar and chain held him fast.

Orono's twisted form bent over him, and Syl braced for attack from the repulsive yellow tubes. Instead, the creature clicked and purred, stroked Syl's shoulder and cheek with a slick tentacle. The little bellows at his neck spread and pulsed.

As the world swam away, Syl watched other children drag the girl's husk into one of the room's many tunnels and wondered if Club Perpetual's theater still housed its grotesque crowd, or if Orono had been forced to find new dumping grounds.

ALIARA

Aliara couldn't breathe, couldn't move, could only stare at the familiar pale-blue ceiling of their bedroom. She willed her lone lung to draw air, but it ignored her. The world around her swished and swayed as though she were at sea.

On the verge of blackout, the lung capitulated with a loud gasp. She coughed and rolled onto her side, eyes watering as she drank in air.

She smelled something smoldering. Coughing again, she tried to call for Syl, but her throat was filled with grating sand. She swung her legs from the bed, tried to stand, and collapsed in a heap. One leg driving her, the other dragging uselessly behind, she crawled to the open washroom door. She dragged herself into the shower, turned the knob, and lay there, water pouring over her and into her mouth.

Gradually, her body began to obey, and she managed to stand and awkwardly walk. Clinging to the wall, she lurched into the hallway, dripping trail behind her.

With a voice like gravel, she called, "Sylandair?" A pause. "Sviroosa?"

No response.

Aliara sat on the top stair and worked her way down step-by-step, the acrid smell intensifying the further she went. Twice, she was forced to pause as the world wavered.

Near the foot of the stairs, she spied something in the hall, possibly an abandoned laundry bag. She slid off the bottom stair and grabbed the newel post, hoisting herself to her feet. She eased her way along the wall toward the rumpled shape that gradually resolved into the unconscious body of Sviroosa, bloody contusion on her skull.

Aliara whoomped onto the floor and patted her domestic's shoulder with all the grace she could muster. "Wake up," she croaked.

The little woman groaned and rolled onto her back. Her lashless lids fluttered, and she surged upright, shouted "Schmalch!" and grabbed her head as though it might topple from her neck.

Aliara leaned against the wall, wet hair darkening the silk wall-covering. "You're hurt."

Sviroosa patted her scalp wound with tentative fingers. "I'll be fine. You shouldn't be out of bed, Mistress." She stood, sniffed the air, and yelped, "My lobster!"

She wobbled into the kitchen, and Aliara heard some polite cursing, a clank of metal, and a loud hiss before Sviroosa reappeared. "No, no, no, no," the puka said. "Let's get you back to bed."

"No." Aliara's hand went to her throat. Her abraded voice hurt with each word. "What happened?"

"I'll bring you a nice glass of water." Sviroosa straightened with a groan and started back toward the kitchen.

"Wait."

She stopped mid-step.

"Where's Sylandair?" Aliara asked.

Sviroosa sucked her lips into her mouth and blinked rapidly. Her hands fluttered at her sides. "Let me get that water first," she said and lurched into the kitchen, bumping roughly against the frame before disappearing behind the swinging door.

When the doorbell rang, the little domestic whooshed back into the hallway, shakily depositing a mug of water by Aliara before heading into the foyer. Sviroosa climbed the door's puka steps and looked through the peephole. With a gasp, she hopped down and swung the door wide.

"Mister Haus," Sviroosa said. "By the Duin's grace. I…I…"

Haus stepped into the foyer and absorbed the scene. He laid a finger over his snoot. "What's that pong? The place on fire?"

"No, no, just something left on the stove." Her cheeks flushed the color of a pine in winter. "It's a little burned, that's all. There's been…something terrible's…oh! Come with me." She took him by the hand and pulled him into the parlor.

Aliara considered joining them, but chose instead to slop the mug of water toward her mouth. She heard Haus shout "windless son of a trull!" followed by scraping furniture and Sviroosa's murmur in heated conversation with Haus' low rumble.

When he returned, Sviroosa at his heels, Haus crouched in front of Aliara and reached for her face before noticing the red blood on his hands. Sviroosa offered him her apron. Haus cleaned his hands and cupped Aliara's chin, turning her head, studying her eyes.

When he was satisfied, he said, "Welcome back."

"Where's Sylandair?" she asked, voice still raspy.

"Gone."

Her eyes widened, she leaned forward, attempting to rise.

"Whoa." Haus gently pressed her back into place. "We'll get him."

"Where?"

Haus shook his head. "Let's get you settled and I'll tell you all about it. We have other problems right now."

"No. Where?"

Haus sighed. "Underground. We don't know exactly where."

She rose to hands and knees. That deviant had him.

Haus put a hand on her shoulder and eased her back into a seated pose. "Slow. You're not ready for that."

"I won't leave him."

"No, we won't. Neither of us like waiting, but you go rushing in like this, you won't do him any good. You'll just get yourself killed.

Get you on your feet, gear up, then we'll go."

She slumped against the wall. "I won't leave him."

"Nope, not for long. Savesti said if that thing's gonna kill him, it already has. If not, he'll keep."

Her eyes narrowed, her nostrils flared, and her mouth puckered. There was something in his tone that made her hackles rise. "What aren't you telling me?"

"Not now; when I get you settled." He turned to Sviroosa. "Where can I put her downstairs that's not in the middle of all that dross? I'm not letting another one out of my sight."

Sviroosa stared at a spot just above Haus' head for a long moment before nodding. "The solarium," she called back, hurrying toward the foyer. "I'll open the windows against this stink and Lady Aliara can take the sofa. It's one of Duke Sylandair's fa—" She trailed off with a shrill choking sound.

Haus slid arms under Aliara and lifted her as though she weighed as much as a leaf. She tried to hold onto the mug, but found her hand unable to maintain a grip. It spilled on one of Syl's prized antique rugs.

"Blast," she muttered.

SCHMALCH

He woke floating under a pier. Face up, fortunately. Something nibbled at his ear. Schmalch slapped it away and gathered his wits. He'd fallen out a window. Why? Panic hit him as he recalled the bloated blackening face of Hergis.

He'd left Sviroosa alone with that thing, with that woman.

He swam awkwardly to the nearest ladder and hauled himself up. He'd been beaten before, knew the bruising and stiffness, but this was a whole new flavor of pain. No one had ever thrown him off a building before. Even so, he'd been lucky. The Duke and Rift's place hung out over Rimadour Bay like a buck tooth, so the fall was a pretty straight shot from window to water. He remembered banging into one or two things sticking out from the neighboring cuddies on his way down, but nothing hard enough to break bones. Still eight stories of building was a pretty long way to fall.

Schmalch shook, little chunks of glass spraying from his clothes with the seawater. He held one nostril and blew. More glass. He repeated the procedure with the other side, then loped north. He'd floated only a few blocks away from the Duke's place. He had to know if Sviroosa was safe.

After a miserable climb up the building's tower of basalt steps, he banged on the door like a madman. When no one answered right away, Schmalch groped in his jacket for his picking rig. The hairpin was halfway into the keyhole when the door swung open. Sviroosa shrieked something and threw her arms around him.

For a brief second, everything was perfect. Then she stepped away, cheeks darkening. "You're alive," she said, staring at her shoes. "When you went out the window, I…"

"I, uh, I guess I blacked out and, uh, woke up in the water down by the piers." Schmalch rubbed his nibbled-on ear.

Sviroosa stepped back from the doorway. "Come in, come in. Mister Haus will want to see you."

He shuffled inside, ready to be chewed out for dripping on Sviroosa's clean floors. She didn't say a word.

Haus was crouched by the sofa in the room everyone called the solarium for reasons that eluded Schmalch. Rift sat there, half-dressed, just like she was when he last saw her, holding her head with a scowl. Both of them looked up as he squished his way into the room.

"Who in the depths woulda' guessed?" Haus said with a half-smile. "I was sure we'd lost you, too."

Even Rift sorta grinned. It was good to see her awake, though she looked like a walking shade.

"Fell in the water." Schmalch smiled and lifted one side of his shirt to reveal a bruise running chest to belt. "I hit something on the way down though. "

Sviroosa gasped and hurried away. He watched her go, noting with a frown the bandaged spot on the back of her beautiful, smooth dome.

"Wait." He turned back to the others. "Too?"

"Savesti didn't make it," Haus said. "He's in there. Planning to take him up to the mansion, stick him in the cooler for now, figure it out later."

"That big hairy thing was squeezing him," Schmalch said, voice picking up speed with anger and excitement. "He looked really awful—all red and purple. His tongue was sticking out, and that woman was shouting at him. He looked at me and his eyes were weird and bulgy. I think he was trying to ask for help, but he couldn't talk. I tried to stop the squeezing, but…" He shrugged.

Haus put a big hand on Schmalch's shoulder. "You did what you could."

"Hubris," Rift said quietly. Her voice sounded like she'd been eating chalk.

Haus nodded.

"What's that?" Schmalch asked.

Her drawn face turned to him. Her eyes were sunken, but still filled with their usual angry blackness. "He was reckless to try to tame a wild man."

Schmalch shook his head. "That lady with the weird scar was telling that…that Tatumi thing to do it. I thought she was supposed to be Hergis' sister."

"Hrm." Rift closed her eyes and returned to cradling her head.

Schmalch looked up at Haus. "Aren't we going after them?"

"Not now."

"Why not?"

"Duke's still missing, and we don't know where to start. One thing at a time."

"Yeah," Schmalch said softly. Haus was right, but it was frustrating to let them go after what they did to Hergis.

"Ugly quim took everything," Rift said, voice muffled by her hands.

"All the dross Savesti was working on, papers, books, all of it," Haus said. "We're on our own."

Schmalch gave a low whistle that changed into a yelp as Sviroosa laid an icepack against his bruised chest.

"Hold that there. It'll help," she said before leaving again.

Schmalch crawled into one of the chairs flanking the sofa, obediently holding the pack in place, even though it made him shiver. "So what do we do now?"

"Improvise." Haus took the other chair, leaning forward with elbows on his knees.

Schmalch had no idea what that meant, but he trusted these two to know what they were doing. If they didn't, he couldn't imagine someone who would.

Sviroosa appeared with a fold-out tray, assembled it in the middle of their group and disappeared. Schmalch watched her lovely figure swish around. He thought about that hug.

"Rift and I are agreed—we finish this." Haus ticked off points on his fingers. "Recover the Duke, end this man-monster thing that has him, do it soon."

Schmalch cringed. The comforting whine of fear built inside him, and a little eked out, but he gulped the rest down.

"You don't hav'ta come along," Haus told him. "Strictly voluntary."

Schmalch shook his head. The water in his ears sloshed, making him a little dizzy. "I'll come," he said quietly.

"Good."

"He'll pay you both," Rift muttered, eyes still closed.

"Not me," Haus said. "I owe that mank for Uuron and Rej."

Schmalch cleared his throat and kept silent. He was happy to know reward would come at the end of this. "So…" he said, dragging out the word. "Is it just the three of us?"

Haus grimaced. "Seems that way. We could hire some more Toh, but I'm not getting anyone else killed."

"What about Abog?"

Rift coughed out a laugh.

Haus' lips drew back in a disagreeable smile. "Don't think that's happening. Their rep showed up at the mansion last night when everything was falling to feck. Guess I overreacted. Tossed her out on her ass."

Rift laughed a little more.

Sviroosa deposited a pot of tea, some sort of fancy biscuits, eggs, and dinnerware on the tray and positioned herself by Rift's sofa. Schmalch abandoned his icepack and piled a plate high before returning to his chair. Haus put a biscuit in Rift's hand and took a couple for himself. He stretched out his legs, crossed them at the ankles, and ate.

"Bumped into Savesti the other night at The Triangle," he said between bites. "Had a few things to say."

Rift opened her eyes and glanced at the biscuit before focusing on Haus. "Like what?"

"Seems he and his sister thought old Orono mucked-up some of the translations. Gave me a few examples you wouldn't care about, but what he described seemed legit."

"How does that help?" She started to return the uneaten biscuit to the tray, but Haus caught her eye, shook his head like a disapproving father. She frowned and nibbled at it.

"Don't know, but Savesti thought it explained the old douse's current state of beauty."

Schmalch snorted. Bits of egg sprayed onto his lap and the rug below.

"Also said…" Haus rubbed his temples. "Said the old man made some sort of opoli-powered 'regeneration engine.' His words. He wouldn't commit to specifics, but I got the idea he thought if we could find and destroy that, we'd have a chance to kill your old buddy."

Rift finished the biscuit and reached for her cup of tea. Her long eyes had gone narrow again. "We saw one thing down there that might qualify."

Haus raised his eyebrows.

Schmalch swallowed his food. "The big glowy glass thing?"

Rift nodded.

"Explain," Haus said.

"A melted glass pillar sits in the center of the room, glowing opoli-blue."

"Sounds like a good place to start."

Rift stood, wobbled a bit, righted herself, and stretched. She looked at Haus. "Twelve?"

"Yep," Haus said. "Let's get you dressed and head to the Tail."

Schmalch looked from one to the other. "What's twelve?"

"Fella' we know who sells weapons, quick and cheap. Picks up a little this, a little that from the freighters passin' through." He chuckled. "And from a young group'a light-fingered gutter babies. He goes by Twelve 'cause he's wrangler number twelve out in the baluut yards."

"So we're going to the Tail out on Nireer's?" Schmalch asked.

"Yup."

The doorbell bonged. Sviroosa scampered into the foyer and climbed to the peephole.

"And we're gonna buy stuff there?" Schmalch asked.

Haus nodded. "Don't know what we'll find when we hit that tunnel, or what we'll need underground."

The door banged open and a recognizable voice, alive with panic, exploded inside. "Is Mister Schmalch here? I need to talk to Mister Schmalch right away!"

Schmalch hopped up, put his empty plate in the seat behind him and headed toward the foyer, where Fohmsquah gripped Sviroosa by the shoulders. Both their faces looked terrified.

"I'm in here, Fohmsquah," he said. "Come on in."

She let Sviroosa go and hurried into the solarium, words pouring out in one breath. "My babies, Mister Schmalch. My babies have disappeared. Chisev had them with him at Big Island market. They were gone when he turned around, and he looked and looked, but he couldn't find them anywhere. He came home and he thinks it's his fault, but Worch and Ilit liked to play and they wander off all the time. I shouldn't have sent them with him. It was too much too soon. I know the news callers keep talking about children disappearing, but I never thought…" Her outburst trailed off into tears.

"We'll take care of it Fohmsquah." Schmalch put his arm around her. "I think I know where to start."

ALIARA

From the mooring towers of the Big Island's aerodrome, Aliara, Haus, and Schmalch caught a ride out to the Tail on a baluut-in-training. It was young and ornery, according to the wrangler, so they should expect a bumpy ride.

Aliara, still wobbly on her feet, consoled herself that it was at least a short one. Her stomach rolled with every dive, wheel, jolt, and bump, the biscuit she'd been coerced into eating still lodged in her gut as though it was trying to form a pearl.

In an effort to distract herself, she stared out the carriage window into the sea below, where baluuts played and swam and snacked on sea life. Emptied of their buoyant air, the deflated zoets looked like giant fish. The fine array of fins running down both sides of their bodies fluttered in the water, their movements more beautiful in many ways that the wings of any bird in flight. Her gaze flicked up to where their inflated counterparts glided nimbly though the bright sky, their tough silvery-brown skin glinting in the dawn.

The baluut yawed, and Aliara's stomach moaned. She pushed her sun shades closer to her still-sensitive eyes and turned away from the window.

"Apologies for the rough ride," the baluut's pilot called back with a cackle. "Don't know why them zoeticists can't mix 'em up and crank 'em out already trained, eh? This pocky whelp's getting better, but he's still hasn't taken to the carriage."

Schmalch seemed oblivious to their erratic flight. Aliara was surprised the puka had still come along after she'd described what had been hanging from the bedroom wall—what had taken Syl—but he stuck. This was his first baluut ride, and he was handling the experience far better than Aliara had expected. He scampered from window to window, peering into the sky and sea with unadulterated awe, loudly pointing out schools of fish and ads painted on rooftops of the city.

Haus had positioned himself a few seats away, possibly because he knew she didn't feel like talking, though more likely he wanted to be out of range in case she did hork up that biscuit. He reclined in the flip-down chair, feet propped on the seat in front of him, eyes closed. To the casual observer, he would appear asleep. She knew that was a faulty assumption. He worked that way—playing on people's assumptions.

Their first jig together had been an extraction of a purported virtuoso of zoetic design from his position at Mopuk Marine Livestock and delivering him to Jihmdahl Agriculture. A simple job on land. A more complex one when the mark was aboard a not-so-secret research barge anchored alone in the waters at the northwestern tip of Nireer's Island. Aliara's plan was to climb on board, kill anyone in their way, and snatch the zoeticist. Haus had proposed a different plan, a cleaner plan.

With the client's money, Haus bought an aging, shabby fishing boat and filthed himself up—even rolled around in some dead fish, judging from the odor. He cruised in close to the research barge and faked a broken rudder cable and a moronic disposition. The guards tried to chase Haus away, while he played dumb. With their attention focused entirely on the big idiot who couldn't fix his own boat, Aliara had slipped into the dark water, climbed onboard, and snatched the target. They'd made a leisurely escape, their victims unaware they'd even been conned.

Haus had kept that nasty old boat, lived on it for years. The

Duin knew why.

His work was clean and clever, though Aliara doubted either of those traits would have much play in their current endeavor. Rather, she suspected he would rely on brute force tactics and his natural tenacity to contend with Orono.

"Rift?" Haus touched her arm.

"What?"

"You doing all right?"

"Yes." She blinked a few times and flexed her fingers. "Why?"

"You were…not there. Didn't seem to hear me."

She grunted. Whatever Orono had puffed in her face still lingered. "What did you say?"

"We're here."

She rose and angled toward the gangway.

Schmalch continued his oohs and aahs as they rode the mooring tower's lift to ground level. When they asked after Twelve, a semi-alert guard, shirtsleeves rolled above his elbows and sweat staining his pits, directed them to a far hangar.

Inside the high, hemicylindrical building, they found Twelve in the middle of the training ring, shouting at a small baluut who kept bumping into the barrel-vaulted ceiling like a drunk in the dark searching for a door. He was a crude, scraggly man in stained, piss-yellow pants and a woven brown jacket, frayed at the elbows. Over one eye he wore a black patch. The other was a baluut wrangler's zoet, a solid yellow ball with three green, vertical stripes. She didn't know how it worked, only that it allowed him to commune with the creatures he trained.

Absently, she rubbed the bane gland in her palm. Despite her ace zoetic surgeon, the gland's implantation had been painful and risky. She didn't care to imagine going through the process with an eye.

"Get down here, ya brat!" Twelve yelled at the baluut.

The creature ignored its trainer, continuing its attack on the ceiling.

"Get down here and I'll let you back in the water!"

The baluut stopped and faced Twelve, pectoral fins fluttering in smooth succession down both sides of its body while its small mouth opened and closed silently. Twelve stared at it, something unheard passing between the two. Then the baluut expelled a puff of air from its ventral flue and dropped to the center of the hanger, hovering just above the dirt floor. Twelve rush-shuffled to the back wall, pulled a rust-pocked chain, and the wall slid open. The baluut floated out, flattening as it descended until it slid into the water like a blade.

Twelve flipped up his eye patch, turned back to the training ring and jumped. "By Sax's dry socket, you scared me sideways."

"Didn't want to interrupt," Haus said, his sonorous voice echoing through the great, open space.

"Fist? That you?" Twelve squinted and sauntered over to them. "What in the depths you doing here? Don't tell me that mag-rifle gave out already."

"Need a couple things," Haus said. "You in the mood to help?"

"'Course I'm in the mood. When aren't I? Just surprised is all." His gaze flicked to Aliara. "Ah, and I see you brought a ray of moonlight into the dark night'a my life." He took her unoffered hand and kissed it. "Always gloss to see you, Rift."

She nodded as she retrieved her hand.

"Always happy to help two'a my best customers, too, eh?" Twelve looked down at Schmalch, half-hidden behind Haus. "And a new one, it seems."

"Schmalch," Haus said.

"Schmalch, a pleasure." Twelve winked the yellow eye.

Schmalch mimicked Aliara's nod.

"So what'cha need today, Fist?"

"What do you have?" Haus asked.

"Big, stonking troop'a toys." Twelve beckoned them with his

fingers. "Follow."

He led them into an enclosure set in the side of the hangar, its walls lined with training equipment and baluut food and all the things anyone might expect from this type of facility. Opening a segment of the wall with a quick push, he waved them into a tight, stretched-out room, closing the door behind them. One long wall was lined with hanging weapons, the facing one with cabinets and drawers.

"Have a look see," he said. "Gimmie' a shout if you find anything of interest. Got a couple'a smaller models of those Bildvalds you like so much, Fist."

"Still have the 700."

"Finest mag-slide work I ever seen," Twelve said. "Old guy's stuff is swish. Good you got one before he kicks. You should consider one for your lovely lady friend."

Aliara sneered. Guns were bulky, awkward, and made too much noise.

"Now, now, Rift. You say you don't like the firearms, but what'cha got strapped there under your arm?"

She was carrying Syl's pistol. She wasn't sure why, but it had seemed right. "Not mine," she said.

"Just holdin' for a friend? Awful nice Querlin 280 to go unused. Mind if I take a look?"

She shrugged, passed it to him. He balanced it in his palm, held it up to his ear then aimed it at the back wall. "Beautiful. Your friend ever wants to sell, you let Twelve know, right? See this here? Querlin's mark," he said, tapping a circle radiating curved lines etched in silver at the apex of the gun's butt. He handed the pistol back to her. "Beautiful maker—the work and the lady herself."

Aliara holstered the gun and resumed browsing. Twelve stocked some nice blades, but nothing to compare with what she already owned.

"Tell me about this one." Haus picked up a shiny, rifle-like weapon with a pair of tubby tanks mounted on top, one smaller than the other.

"Brutal thing, that one," Twelve said. "Vyyl Bush Burner. Spits gel fuel. Nasty stuff—sticks and burns."

"Price?"

"For you?" The fence sucked in air. "Let's say four-hundred-fifty Callas. You know it's twice that back on the Big Island."

"Three conchs," Haus said, referring to the platinum coins stamped with the familiar shell, "and you throw in a second fuel tank."

It was a big drop in price, and Twelve made a performance of considering. "Sink it. It's a steal, but for a good customer…" He flapped a hand in the air. "What else you need?"

"What is it?" Schmalch asked in an uncharacteristically soft voice.

"Flamethrower," Haus said, his gaze never leaving the inventory. Schmalch's brow wrinkled in surprise.

"Any carapace?" Haus asked.

"I got some implants and some wearables. Which you want?"

"Wearables." Haus lifted his reconstructed arm. "I've had enough work done for this life."

Twelve chuckled and opened a cabinet full of hard, glimmering shells that once had grown on the backs of idrit beetles. Skilled craftsmen had cut and molded the durable material to fit chests, arms, legs, shoulders, and any other body part that might require protection. Most were the idrit's natural glossy mud-brown mottled with splotches of oatmeal, though several had been decorated with various dyes, paints, and foils. Of the varying styles, the chest plates looked the most like actual beetle shells, though each was only a small fraction of what could be harvested from one beetle. Idrits, native to nearby Nireer's Island, were big as pachyderms, and far nastier. Hunting them was almost as prized a skill as working their shells.

Haus selected a small chest plate, dyed black and painted with tendrils of rough-textured white that crept in from one edge. He passed it to Schmalch, who stuck his arms through the straps. He allowed Haus to buckle it in the back, then spun around, admiring himself as though modeling a fancy gown for the Sower's Festival.

While he preened, Haus took a larger shell from the wall and slipped it on. Coppery with a compact swirling texture pressed into the surface, the chest-plate covered Haus armpit to armpit and collarbone to navel.

"Five conchs for the pair," Twelve said.

"Six-hundred Callas?" Schmalch whispered. It was likely more than he'd seen in his whole life. He ran a palm reverently over the chitin covering his chest.

Haus eyed Twelve and addressed Aliara. "Rift, you want any?"

"Too rigid."

"Ah! I have just the thing." Twelve opened a drawer and dug through some fabric, pausing every so often to look Aliara over. Finally, he withdrew a long sheet of jet black. "Ebb Weave. Just right for a lady like you."

Aliara ran the fabric through her fingers. It was thick, but pliable, stiffer than ordinary fabric. She'd seen it before, but never owned any. If ever there was a time to spend the money on such frills, this was it.

"Yup, Ebb Weave," Twelve said. "Manky name, I know. Don't know why Integrated Zoetics thought it was a good one, but it seems'ta've worked for them. Popular stuff. It's good against cutting, scraping, and light poking." He paused the sales patter to mimic attacking her with a blade. "Great against slicing, little less so against stabbing. 'Bout useless against shot, though. You wanna try it on?"

Before the words left his mouth, Aliara was out of her tank and weapon holsters.

"Coulda' gave you some privacy," Twelve murmured, "but no complaints here."

She squeezed into the suit. Dulled-steel zippers ran from each ankle, up the leg and torso, and over the shoulder to the back of skull. The high neckline, long sleeves, and pant-legs left only the head, hands, and feet unprotected.

Twelve gave a low whistle. "Pretty swish. Made to fit you, I'd say." He ran a bony hand through his retreating hair. "Normally runs four-twenty-five by itself, but because of that show, I'll knock off... let's see—"

"No," Aliara cut in, pointing to a leather vest lined with a dozen throwing knives. "Give me that."

Twelve shrugged. "Fine by me. You gonna wear the Ebb out? Or do we get another show?"

Aliara scowled at him. Twitching karju and their prudery.

Haus whistled. "Over here, ya letch."

Twelve left Aliara to change in peace.

"These." Haus held a set of spiked metal knuckle-dusters reminiscent of those worn by Uuron. "And whatever else the little guy needs."

Schmalch perused his options. "What about this?" He picked up a steel chain whip and began waving it around.

Haus grabbed Schmalch's wrist, retrieved the whip, and returned it to the wall. Aliara almost regretted it. She would have enjoyed watching Schmalch learn to use such an awkward weapon.

"No. Try this." Haus handed Schmalch a squat bullpup boarding gun. Its collection of narrow cylindrical barrels made the weapon thick and mean-looking.

Schmalch made a soft "ooo" as he examined the stubby gun. Pleased with the new acquisition, he tucked it under one arm and pointed to a group of hatchets hanging below the bulkier axes. "Can I have one of those, too?"

"Sure. Won't maim yourself with that one." Haus selected one with a brushed steel head and polished bonewood handle and plucked it from the wall. He hesitated before handing it to Schmalch.

"Probably."

Twelve stuffed some shot canisters for the bullpup into a sling-sack and tossed them onto the pile. "How about some more ammo for that Bildvald?" he asked.

Haus shook his head. "Close quarters, won't need it."

"Right. What else?"

"Grenades," Aliara said.

"Got no grenades." Twelve leaned close and smiled his gap-toothed grin. "But I know who does."

"Who?"

"Fella' by the name of Herrenny. Has a chemist shop up on the Big Island he calls Intermix." Twelve pulled a face to show his disgust. "Pompous twitch, you ask me. Any of you know him?"

Aliara's eyes narrowed to slits, the neutral set of her mouth shifted to a frown. She knew the man. He'd visited the Orono mansion often.

Twelve smiled at her and raised a bushy greying brow. "Yeah, I see you do, Rift. Seems like a nice old man, but he's got Imt's balls when it comes to coin. That's why I don't deal with him. Not direct, at least." He shoved his hand in the pockets of his fusty pants and shrugged. "Buzz is he's been brewin' up a big batch. I been having some of my kids keeping an eye out for a wayward crate that might find its way outta his shop, but no soap yet. I can let you know if any happen to land here, though."

"Grat, but no," Haus said. "We need them now."

"Guess that's your next stop, then."

SYLANDAIR

Syl swam in the tedious, seemingly interminable darkness. He felt his feet moving, opened his eyes. He was running. People were chasing him. He was sprinting down the streets of Dockhaven, but not those he'd left only days earlier; no, these were the erstwhile byways of his young adulthood. These were the days before they'd killed Nushgha, after the coin-hungry sycophants had turned them out.

The borders of buildings, the streetlamps, the glowing signs—everything around him quivered. He was dreaming, hallucinating, but the need to escape was so fresh and real, he couldn't stop.

He skidded into an alley, raced up some stairs, down a hallway, and scrambled up an age-pocked wall toward a hidden hollow between buildings. He squeezed inside to where Aliara crouched. He remembered this place. They'd nested here for months.

His pursuers stopped outside, confused shouts booming, then fading away. Panting, Syl curled up, laid his head in her lap. The surrounding dark walls seemed to breathe with him, pushing in, out, in, out. Aliara stroked his sweaty face and tangled hair. He loved the warm feeling of her, the safety.

As he lay there, eyes closed, smelling her scent over the stink of his shabby, unwashed clothes, her fingers became cold and clammy. He sat up. One of Orono's glowing tentacles cupped Syl's chin. With a happy chitter, the twisted creature tried to drag him back into his distorted lap.

Syl wheezed his way awake. He wasn't sure how much more of this he could endure. He hadn't eaten in a while. Hours? Days? It was hard to tell since the old goby kept knocking him out. If the healing of the scratches on his chest were to be believed, the duration leaned more toward days. He looked around, but found only a bowl of water, which he lifted to his mouth and gulped, examining the room as he drank. He was alone. None of the insensate children stood about. No Orono lurked on the floors, walls, or ceiling.

Sucking in the last drops of water, Syl coughed, the sound echoing though the empty space like a pistol shot. He braced for Orono's appearance, but all was quiet.

Syl rose and walked a ring around the glass pillar as far as his tether permitted, paying no heed to the rumblings from his gut. Though things were largely as they'd been when he'd last enjoyed consciousness, a makeshift cage now stood in the corner by the mound of debris he'd noticed earlier. It appeared to have been cobbled together from a curious variety of garbage and flotsam. One side looked like it once was part of an actual barred enclosure, probably from an animal pen. The rest was comprised of boards salvaged from boxes, panels stolen from local gardens and coops, and aging grates from who knew where, all held together with odd lengths of wire and sailing cord. A child-sized gap at the top was the only visible break in the strange enclosure. Whatever was inside was not meant to come out. At least not with any ease.

Despite his species scotopic vision, he struggled to distinguish any details inside the cage. He squinted at the shadows. Something inside, something not-quite-definable was shifting in a slow rhythm. No, several somethings—and they were breathing.

Gradually faces and limbs took shape from the darkness. A collection of small people lay still on the cage floor, flopped over one another as though sleeping in a communal nest like the draas. Their skulls appeared whole. Nevertheless, Syl was just as happy that any children found down here remained in a cage for the moment.

Beside the cage was the random pile of debris Syl noticed earlier. It appeared to consist largely of sand, though he could differentiate a large bowl, a palm-sized bottle, and several nuggets that likely were stones of some sort. Other items were too far buried to accurately characterize.

For a moment, Syl puzzled over what it all meant, why Orono would be collecting such random objects. Then his starving mind made the connection: Orono was preparing a new ceremony, one in which he intended to create a companion.

Unaware he was doing so, Syl crept away from the collection, whispering, "No no no no no no."

He had to get out. He dug fingers beneath the collar, scoring his skin as he fumbled for a latch, a buckle, anything that would free him, but found only the stout padlock. He tugged at the collar until even the inside of his throat felt bruised. He circled the dais, examining the floor for anything that might help. A handful of desiccated rats and other small animals were mixed with the bones circling the dais, as were small pieces of concrete. He picked up those hunks he could reach, but none were large or hard enough to break a chain.

Poking through a particularly large heap a few feet away, Syl spied the glint of metal within. He couldn't make out much detail, only that the piece was made up of at least two bars. He walked as far as his restraint would allow, strained against the chain, but his prize remained just out of reach.

Syl lay down and stretched out flat on his good side, foot groping in the debris until his naked toes felt the chill of metal. The cold collar cut into the flesh beneath his chin, pulled the fine hairs of his beard. He tried to drag the buried item, but it was heavy and awkward. Again and again it slipped out from beneath his sweaty foot, refusing to come free. Undeterred and no longer able to breathe, Syl struggled on. As bright spots appeared in his vision, the concrete gave up its hold and his reward slipped loose. Syl grasped it between his toes and gently, cautiously worked it toward his hand, guzzling precious air as the pressure on his chain relaxed.

It was larger, heavier than expected. Bits of rubble dragged along with it, making the process even more difficult. When he'd navigated the piece within reach, he sat up and pulled it close. About the size of his chest, it was a small group of bars welded together in a crisscross fashion. To Syl's mind, it looked like a child's sleebach game board, though he recognized it as a rusted segment of window muntins from some run-down house. Undoubtedly it was originally intended as a component for Orono's new cage. A few of the bars were bent off their welds, clinging to the whole by tenuous bits of solder. He broke off one of the loose lengths, about as long as his hand, and tinked it against the floor, tried to bend it. He'd expected the soft lead of stained glass, but the bar was solid and unyielding.

He was no Aliara when it came to lock picking, but he was no slouch either. If he found the right bit, he might be able to spring the old-fashioned lock mechanism that held him fast. Syl checked all the exposed ends, hoping to find one with a fine enough point, but all the tips were blunt and thick. That was probably for the best. There was a good chance he would stab himself in the throat in the attempt before anyone had an opportunity to find him.

He threaded the bar he'd broken off through the padlock's shackle and twisted, hoping the pressure would break the metal, but only succeeded in further bruising and choking himself. The links of his chain were too tight, so he laced the bar through the loop of the eyebolt that held him to the floor. Using the muntin like a handle, he turned it to one side and pressed as hard as he dared. Nothing moved. He turned the bar the other direction and tried again. He repeated the process, back and forth, feeling only strain on his new tool.

He closed his eyes and sighed. He had no other options. If this hunk of muntin broke, he would try another and another. The work would require patience, but eventually, Syl told himself, this ridiculous bolt would break free of the floor.

As he twisted the bars in their loop, a hunk of rust slit his finger and he barked in protest, wincing as the sound bounced around his prison like thunder.

"H-hey mister?" A small, quiet voice drifted through the stagnant air.

Syl looked up. The glint of eyes, reflective like those of a cat, winked back at him from within the cage. Another chivori. He left his work and walked as close as the restraints would allow.

A boy not yet ten years old clung to the bars. His skin was the sallow grey of bilge water, dark circles haunted his eyes, and his clothes looked like they'd been retrieved from a swamp. Syl wasn't entirely sure of what to say or do.

"Will, uh…" The boy swallowed hard. "Will you let me out?"

"Sadly, I cannot." Syl shook his head, put a hand to his collar, and rattled the chain. "No more than you can free me."

"Oh." The boy sagged. "Why're we here?"

A complicated answer. "A deranged man thinks he needs us."

"De-what?"

"Crazy person." Syl squatted, the collar tightening with the strain, turning his voice husky. He ignored it. "Though I suppose he doesn't look much like a person anymore."

In the dim light of the glass pillar, Syl saw the boy's glowing eyes widen, then close.

"Is it that old man?" he asked.

"What old man?"

"The one I followed here. He was kinda' fat and smiled a lot. I…I was waiting for my da outside his warehouse, and this old man showed up and waved at me." He frowned and looked at his feet. "I don't remember much after that."

At least this child was still alive, unlike so many others.

"Where are we?" the boy asked, looking around the cavernous room.

"Under the city."

"Where's my Mimmy and Da?"

"I've no idea."

"Oh." His voice dropped to a whisper. "I hope they're safe."

Syl had no answer. His last moments with Aliara crept into his mind. He'd not allowed himself to consider what might have happened to her when Orono had taken him. If she had been wounded when Orono bull-rushed them, Syl was on his own. Now he had a pile of children as well.

"I'm Jeruu," the boy said

"Sylandair."

"Are you here to save us, Sylandair?"

Syl's head drooped. "I shall try, but you need to be quiet. There is no telling when our captor will return. If he sees you up and about, I've no doubt he will gas you again. So remain silent...and keep any others that wake quiet as well."

"Right," the boy said. He shrank back into the shadows of the cage and lay down.

Syl returned to his work on the eyebolt, convinced—whether by delusion or reality—that he felt the subtlest of movement. Every now and then he heard another little voice in the corner asking where they were and why. Each time Jeruu calmed them, kept them quiet, assured them that the big man by the big light was going to save them. Syl did his best to ignore the promises.

When distant skittering echoed in from one of the many tunnels, Syl glanced into the corner and lifted a finger to his lips. What little noise the children were making hushed. He motioned them all down before he also lay on the cold concrete of the dais and feigned unconsciousness.

HAUS

Rift had been quiet since they left Twelve. She was taciturn by nature, but this silence was ominous in a way that unsettled him. Haus tried to credit the lingering effects of whatever had knocked her out, but he'd worked with her often enough to not entirely believe that.

The black line around her eyes was smudged and thick today, intensifying her distant stare. She didn't seem to notice the crowds as they walked the short distance from the aerodrome to the chemist's shop in search of grenades. The people broke around her, she never wavered.

Herrenny's shop, Intermix, sat just south of the aerodrome inside the Oblong, a pair of bowed streets that formed a sort of stretched circle in the heart of the Big Island. A green glass sign, alive with lumia, dominated the storefront.

A little bell tinkled as they entered. The place smelled like a cleaning service had exploded in an herb garden. Haus pinched his snoot and sneezed. Schmalch tugged his shirt collar over his nose. Rift didn't seem to notice, but most chivori he knew couldn't smell a turd in an outhouse.

"Be with you in a moment," called a man's voice from behind a kelp-green curtain.

Haus picked up a few pieces of equipment, sniffed cautiously at sprayers and tins, ducked between the hanging plants and dried herbs, and casually browsed the assortment of bosh while they waited. Schmalch followed him around, occasionally pocketing something too shiny to resist. Rift stood at the counter like a mannequin, staring at the green curtain.

"Welcome, welcome." An older man emerged, wiping his hands on a smeared canvas apron. He was fit for his age and tan, though paler than Haus, with a thin blonde beard and friendly, crinkled eyes. His gaze swept the group. "What can I find for you today?"

Haus stepped up to the counter beside Aliara. "You Herrenny?"

"Bytor Herrenny, yes. Owner and proprietor of Intermix for nearly half a century. Are you looking for something specific?"

"Rumor is you have talent with grenades."

Herrenny beamed. "I've been told I produce quality wares along that line."

"Right. Looking to buy some."

Herrenny clapped his hands together. "Marvelous. Now how many wo—"

"I remember you." Rift spoke in a low, measured voice, drawing out each syllable as though tasting the anger behind the words. She slipped off her sunshades. Even to Haus, her dark eyes looked deranged.

Herrenny took a step away from the counter. "Nonsense. I've never seen you before, miss."

One of Rift's brows rose. "Really?"

"Quite." Herrenny's approachable demeanor had turned cold. "I suggest you make your purchase and leave before I call the Corps."

In a flash, Rift drew a stiletto from her hip, leapt over the counter, and drove the blade into the soft flesh beneath the man's chin.

Haus heard Schmalch squeak.

Herrenny struggled to say something.

Rift leaned in, cheek-to-cheek, and hissed in Herrenny's ear. "I *know* you."

She pulled back, drew her other stiletto, and plunged it into his chest. Herrenny groaned and tried to shake his head. Rift held the pose, watching until the life left his eyes. Her features relaxed, she withdrew the blades and the meat that was once Bytor Herrenny collapsed into a puddle of blood.

"Help me look," Haus said to Schmalch. He started around the corner of the counter.

"Not yet," Rift said. She nodded to Schmalch as she wiped the blades clean against the curtain. "Find some gutter babies. Tell them there's free stuff in here."

Haus quirked a smile. No wonder she was still operating, despite her sometimes-volatile behavior. "Free" was every gutter baby's favorite word. No one would remember their faces from amongst the dozens who would tramp in and out of the store over the next hours.

Rift drew back the curtain. Two chivori children, young enough their genders had yet to develop, cowered under a table littered with chemistry equipment. Their grey arms were wrapped around each other, the younger one's face was buried in the older's shaggy black hair.

"He's gone." Rift squatted by the table. "You know where to find Our Lady of Artfulness?"

They nodded.

She handed them a fistful of Callas. "Go there. Now. Don't come back."

The older child snatched the coins and led the younger out just as the first cluster of looters entered. Foregoing the front room, they started around the counter to where the good stuff was kept.

Haus blocked them "Nope. Pilfer out here till we're done."

There was some grumbling, protests about "the big twitch scaling the gloss swag," but the group, having seen the carcass behind the counter, had enough sense to obey.

Others had flooded in behind them. The little guy worked fast. People filled the showroom, shouting nonsense and shoving anything and everything into pockets and bags, down shirts, or filling skirt tails. They didn't pilfer only the inventory. One couple maneuvered a large steel table out the front door while newcomers crawled in beneath. Another group was busy unhooking the lumia sign from its post in the front window.

Haus left them to their looting and passed into the back room, where Rift stood, staring at the wall, both hands resting on an oblong crate. To one side was dirty tank filled with what looked like cooking oil and chunks of something shiny that wasn't quite metal. On the other was a stack of cakey-looking yellow bricks wrapped in translucent waxed paper, "Intermix" stamped on each one.

"The grenades," she said without looking back. She tapped the crate rhythmically with gentle fingertips and flipped open the lid, revealing several dozen shiny spheres with little knobs on both sides.

"Should be plenty," Haus said. If it wasn't, they were in real trouble.

He picked up one of the yellow bricks, lifted it to his snoot and sniffed. Though Rift or Schmalch wouldn't have smelled it, Haus detected a nip of freshly turned earth tinged with a chemical tang like floor polish or paint. Trinite. He knew the odor well; his squad had used the explosive often during his military years. It was stable enough to be tossed around in a ship's hold during transport, but add a fulminate ignition cap, and it went off like Wetac's fury. Grenades were great for clearing a room, but trinite could take down a building or sink a ship. Plus, with an igniter, it would provide a little distance between them and the explosion, and Haus wanted to be as far away from the concussion as possible when it hit.

Grabbing a canvas satchel from the late shopkeeper's coatrack, he dropped in a strip of ignition caps, a wire spool with integrated plunger, and all the bricks. Leaning against the crate of grenades, Rift watched impassively. When Haus shouldered the loaded satchel, she hefted the crate and headed out, stepping over Herrenny's body without a glance.

ALIARA

The well-armed trio arrived at the Orono estate with only a few alarmed glances from passersby. The morning air was thick with the smell of cooking and the sounds of merriment from the Mucha estate next door. Voices chirped happily over an ensemble's insufferably cheerful tune and the soft clicks and thuds of a game that sounded like it was played with a wooden ball. This was the third such social event Aliara had overheard since Syl took possession of the property. She wondered if the Mucha did anything besides hold parties.

"Sounds like they're having fun," Schmalch said. He smiled at the neighboring hall's high, domed peak and closed his eyes, big orbs rolling beneath the olive lids. "I bet Hergis would have loved it. I wonder what he would have done with his hair."

"Something strange." Aliara ushered Schmalch into the house before he either lapsed into melancholy or scampered off to join the festivities.

The steel cabinet in operating theater two stood where she'd last seen it, but in a far different condition. Its doors were open, revealing a mess of spilled chemicals and broken glass inside. More of the same puddled at its base. Haus strode into the room, pressed his shoulder against the side of the cabinet and shoved it aside until he was huffing and red-faced with the effort.

The hole he revealed was far larger than it had been, big enough for Aliara to walk through upright. Good. She was just as glad to avoid another long scramble in the dirt.

"I'll take point," Haus told her, "you take rear."

"What do I do?" Schmalch asked.

"Stay between us and keep quiet."

"Right." Schmalch chewed on his lower lip and stared at the shimmering wire spool attached to the back of Haus' belt. "Will those creepy kids be in there?"

"Hard to say." Haus patted the knife strapped to his thigh. "Just need you to back me up. You ready for this?"

Schmalch blinked a few times, slung the bullpup over his shoulder, and opened the sling-sack that hung from his chest like some comical belly, whispering as he counted the grenades and ammunition canisters within. "Yeah." He cleared his throat and repeated, louder this time, "Yeah. The Duke needs us."

Haus adjusted the Bush Burner so it hung across his back next to the pack of trinite bricks and ducked into the hole. Schmalch followed with a groan like a child instructed to wash the dinner dishes.

"Quiet," Aliara hissed, and the lament died away. She followed, grenades in her kit shifting against Syl's pistol and boots, uncomfortable vest and its cache of little knives throwing her off balance. Anxiety fluttered in her chest. She hoped not only that Hergis' assessment of Orono's plans for her mate was correct, but that they could reach Syl before those plans were enacted.

This tunnel took a sharp turn only a few steps past the entry and opened up to a height comfortable enough for Haus to stand—though he had to watch for low-hanging rocks and roots. Soon after, they found the remains of the two Abog Syl had sent in only days ago. Rats had long-since ravaged the softer bits of both bodies and were now working on the gristle. A finger over his snoot, Haus kicked at a shifting lump beneath the shorter Abog's shirt. A rat popped out and scurried away, cursing at the violation.

None of Orono's corrupted children waited for them. Having gone in prepared for a fight, Aliara found their absence unnerving. Unease crept up her spine, danced in her gut to the beat of her heart. She was almost relieved when they rounded another bend and found the path sloped sharply down toward an exit that glowed with a blue light. Haus slid down the incline and settled beside the opening. Aliara squatted next to him while Schmalch stood behind, shifting from foot to foot as though his bladder was full.

The room appeared devoid of both children and the monstrous incarnation of Orono. And Syl. Only the ring of bones and big glass candle remained. A faint, repetitive *tink* and scrape of metal against metal told her the vacant appearance was an illusion. Something was inside and alive enough to make noise.

"Is this it?" Haus asked in the Thung Toh's hand cant.

She nodded.

"Cold," he signed.

Aliara pointed to the wall to their right, where dirt and stone poured from what was once the only way inside. *"Original entrance,"* she signed, then indicated the wall opposite their position. Orono and his children had cleared the tunnel to the theatre since the grenade blast that had allowed her, Syl, and Schmalch to block pursuit on their last visit. *"Came in through there last time."*

Haus squinted, shrugged. *"Too dark for me to see."*

She motioned to an opening in the left wall. *"That's new."*

"Where are those kids?" Schmalch whispered. "It's creepy they're not here, right? Where else would they be? And that sound. What's that sound?" He stopped his anxious dance.

Haus glared, and Schmalch quieted. His nervous dance resumed with fresh urgency.

"See anything moving?" Haus asked in cant.

Aliara shook her head.

The *tink* and scrape continued, its slow rhythm almost

mechanically regular.

Haus tapped his ear. *"Recognize that?"* he signed.

"No. Didn't hear it last time," she replied.

"You want the lantern?" Schmalch asked.

"Quiet," Haus hissed. "And keep that thing shuttered."

Schmalch nodded.

"Something new over there. Can't make it out," Aliara signed. She gestured to a shape that ran floor-to-ceiling in the far corner. Its base was a dark, irregular blob that bled into an array of blotchy clumps and streaks of shadows as it rose toward the ceiling.

Haus began to ease out of the tunnel. Aliara put a hand on his shoulder. *"Check the walls and ceiling."*

Haus nodded and rolled into the room, raising the Bush Burner as he stood. The odd, monotonous noise continued, but nothing pounced.

"Nothing here," he signed. *"You check the perimeter. I'll set charges."* He turned and headed toward the center of the room and the ominous glowing pillar.

Aliara frowned. She'd almost hoped Orono was hiding somewhere above them. The absence of the expected, coupled with this new peculiar noise, left her feeling off kilter. Were this a contract, she would have cursed the client's faulty info and considered scrubbing the whole thing right now. But Orono and his brood had to be somewhere close.

Aliara slipped out, Schmalch almost clinging to her hip. She nodded toward the fresh tunnel entry and tapped her chest, then pointed to the tall shape in the far corner and tapped his. Schmalch frowned and ran a rot-green tongue over his lips before hurrying away, the urgent patter of his feet like hail in the empty space.

SCHMALCH

Crouched low in an effort to make himself invisible, Schmalch edged toward the big blob in the corner. Best he could tell, it looked like a half-assed duck coop built by some tippled trash collector.

He edged sideways toward a pile of sand and shiny stuff blocking his path to the coop-thing. His foot bumped a half-buried glass bottle about the size of his hand and it rolled away with a happy tinkle, all glittery in the dim blue light. Before it spun out of reach, Schmalch retrieved it, opened it, sniffed the liquid inside. It didn't smell like anything, especially not like the liquor he'd hoped for. Schmalch shrugged. The glass was pretty enough. He bet he could sell it to someone for a few coppers. He pocketed the vial and dug into the sand in search of more swag.

He'd located a couple pretty rocks and a fancy washtub when a small voice disturbed his work. "Hey, mister."

Schmalch pitched head-first into his excavation. The voice giggled quietly. He righted himself, brushed grains of sand from his nose and forehead, and hopped back. "Who's there?"

"Dinara. I'm Dinara." Something the size and shape of a kid shifted inside the tall coop. "Are you here to save us?"

Schmalch was silent for a beat. This Dinara sounded like a child, but the children he'd encountered down here hadn't exactly been friendly. They hadn't said anything either, let alone told him their names. This one might be safe. He took two cautious steps toward her—close enough for a better look, but still well out of reach.

Inside what appeared to be a shabby cage stood a karju girl, her dark skin an eerie purple in the room's blue light. Her face was pressed between the slats of an old crate wired to a metal grid that was once part of someone's window. Other children crowded around, whispering and begging.

They all looked normal. None of them reached out to claw him or snapped teeth. They definitely weren't like the ones from before. But he kept his distance, just to be sure.

"What're you doing here?" Schmalch asked.

"Dunno," she said. "I was with my dibby at the wharf market. I remember seeing this other girl who looked sick digging around in the trash down an alley. I tried to tell Dibby, but he shushed me. But I...I wanted to help her. She looked really sick, and when I tried to talk to her, she just walked away." Dinara sniffed. "I shouldn't have followed her."

A few of the others chimed in with "me too."

"She led me down the alley where this old man was standing. He smiled a lot. He looked nice. He waved at me and I waved back, then...then...then I don't remember"

"He was shiny!" said one little boy, who clung to the window frame beside Dinara. "He wanted me to follow him and when I tried to leave...I can't remember either. We're stuck here like Sylandair,"

"Sylandair?" Schmalch perked up. "You mean the Duke? You know him?"

"He's over there." The boy jabbed a grey finger through an opening in the junk.

Schmalch followed the gesture. There, with Haus and the glowy glass candle, stood the Duke, chained to the floor like some circus animal.

"The Duke'll know what to do," Schmalch told the kids. He cleared his throat and called, "Hey, um, there's a bunch of kids in some kind of cage over here."

"Then get them out," the Duke said.

Schmalch eyed the cage. He couldn't find a door. "Uh, how?"

"Figure it out," Haus said. "And take them back above ground."

Schmalch stepped back and studied the slapdash cage. One side looked like it'd been snatched right off a jail cell on the Bag—or maybe from one of the bigger cages at the Pukatown pet shop he liked to visit—but the other side was just a lot of dross. He peered into the dark above. He could make out bits that had once been old crates, hunks of metal, even something that looked like an abused old iron headboard. All of it was lashed together by lengths of thick sailing line and wire.

"Right," he said, returning to the kids. "I'm Schmalch."

"I'm Jeruu," said the chivori boy who'd pointed at the Duke.

"I'm gonna get all of you outta' here."

Trying his best to smile, Schmalch drew his kris and cut into a rope that attached one side of a crate to a sheet of corrugated roofing about the size of the Duke's footstool. His blade barely nicked the thick line, so he started sawing. He should have sharpened it before they came down here; he'd do it first thing if he made it back above ground.

"Careful," Dinara said. "We tried push our way through, but—"

"But it all creaked and made like it was going to crush us." Jeruu indicated the high, rickety wall.

Schmalch imagined the mountain of feck collapsing on top of him, breaking over him, crushing him. He could almost feel the splintered bits of dross stabbing him until the life wheezed right out. He stopped sawing and took a step away from the cage. He needed to leave. This was too much. He didn't want to die down here under some pile of flotsam. He took another step back and another. He had to run.

"You're Mister Schmalch," squeaked a new voice.

"Huh?"

"You came to our cuddy."

Schmalch scanned the little faces and found a puka girl smiling at him from beneath the panel of corrugated roofing. Her round face was dirty and tear-streaked, but he still recognized her as one of Glech and Fohmsquah's twins. Her mother's pretty, panicked face came back to him, and he slowly walked back over to the cage. "Are you...are you Worch or Ilit?"

"I'm Ilit. Worch's still asleep." She blinked up at him with big, bright eyes. "My Moocha says you're real swish."

He flushed and returned to sawing at the rope. "Fohmsquah—your Moocha, I mean—she's worried about you. Your brother, too."

A big tear rolled down Ilit's cheek. Something in his chest hurt.

He patted her little fist, curled around a hunk of old board, and turned back to Dinara. "I...I know it's chancy to take it apart, but I don't see another way to get you out, so we'll have to risk it. Right?"

The karju girl nodded.

"Good. You and Jeruu get everyone back from here. I'm gonna cut this and try to make a door. Right?"

She nodded. Jeruu started shooing the others away from the ramshackle wall.

"When I get it open, you send 'em through the hole one by one."

"If it doesn't collapse first," Dinara said.

Schmalch paused, bit his lip, and pushed the images of death beneath the scruddy wreck out of his mind. "When you get out, you go in there and run all the way till you're in a basement." He pointed to the tunnel leading back to the mansion. "Got it?"

"*Yes,*" all their little voices replied.

"Something bad's coming," he said, "but you'll be safe there." He hoped he wasn't lying.

The kids huddled against the back wall, as far away from the impending collapse as possible, though the space was so small, it hardly seemed worth the effort. If he did this wrong...his bladder tightened and his throat closed at the thought. He kept cutting.

"Schmalch," Haus shouted, "move it!"

The need to bolt nearly overwhelmed him. He pictured Fohmsquah again, how scared she'd been when she showed up at the Duke's cuddy. Schmalch cut faster, little blade warming in his hand. When the line split in two and the kris chinked against corrugated panel, he nearly whooped. He unwound the rope, hooked his fingers behind the piece of roofing, and eased it open like a trapdoor. The rest of the wall groaned and trembled but held.

He peered inside. All their hopeful, frightened little faces looked back at him.

"Right," he said. "Sleepy ones first."

HAUS

The chamber's smell hit Haus like a sock full of Callas, making his snoot sting and his eyes water. It was the same stink he'd encountered when he found Rift unconscious in the mansion's upstairs bedroom, but here it was almost overwhelming, as though the cold air made the pong somehow more powerful.

Flamethrower at the ready, he put his free hand over his nose and eased into the ring of bones toward the weird glass fetish. The closer he came, the louder the unexplained metallic rhythm grew, almost as though it was coming from the inside the object. Only a few steps away, he felt warmth coming off it like a fat, lazy cat. This was no ordinary hunk of glass. If Savesti's appraisal was right, this *had* to be the regeneration engine.

He unshouldered the satchel of trinite bricks and dropped it onto the copper floor with a soft *thump*.

The steady clinking stopped. A dark shape rose slowly behind the glowing glass. Haus shouldered the Bush Burner, steeling himself for his first look at the horror everyone had described. Instead, black hair and an unmistakable pale-grey face eased into view.

"...Haus?" The Duke's voice croaked. He stepped shakily around the pillar, shirtless, shoeless, and even lankier than usual. He patted Haus' arm. "You *are* here."

"Yep. Rift and the little guy, too."

The Duke looked around the room until he found his mate. As he watched her with a smile, Haus watched him. The man was uneven, not quite himself. His pupils were massive. He was smeared all over with splotches of dirt, and his long hair was unbound and ratted. His old wounds stood out in the blue light, ribs and collarbones casting shadows. Clamped around his neck was a metal collar chained to an eyebolt set in the floor. A metal rod was threaded through the loop of the bolt, slightly bent and pocked with small dents.

Haus clasped the Duke's shoulder. "Shame we took so long. You look like feck."

The Duke looked away from Rift and waved away the comment. "Would you happen to have any food?"

"No," Haus said. "Apologies. That's the one thing we forgot."

The Duke shrugged. "What did you bring?"

"Hey, um, there's a bunch of kids in some kind of cage over here," Schmalch called from the far corner.

Haus squinted into the darkness. Mostly, he made out only shadowy lumps, though one he recognized as the well-armed puka. The others were a blur of small, shifting figures—undoubtedly the kids in question. Haus had to assume they weren't like the one who'd attacked Savesti. Schmalch wouldn't still be standing there if they were.

"Then get them out," the Duke replied, voice raised.

"Uh, how?" Schmalch asked.

"Figure it out," Haus said. "And take them back above ground."

Schmalch looked back at the cage, his response blurry and unintelligible.

When Haus returned his attention to the Duke, he found Rift wrapped around the man in a way that made him think of his last night with Yoni. Haus squatted and began unloading bricks, giving them as much privacy as anyone chained the floor could expect. When the sounds of lips on lips shifted to those of pick in lock, Haus looked up. Rift was working the padlock at the Duke's neck while he dug through the gear she'd brought.

"In my absence, did Master Savesti discern how to rid ourselves of…him?" the Duke asked.

Haus winced at the mention of Hergis. He glanced at Rift, who shook her head. This wasn't the time to deliver that news.

"Maybe," Haus said. "We're gonna blo—"

"Quiet!" Rift hissed.

Both chivori stared hard at the tunnel mouth behind them.

"He is coming," the Duke said. "And the children with him. I hear…" He cocked his head to one side.

"A lot," Rift said. She returned to the padlock, redoubling her efforts.

A pair of tall boys lurched from the tunnel, others stumbling out behind them in no particular rush. Their staring eyes seemed to see nothing. They walked aimlessly into the room, bodies moving with a weird, spasmodic gait, as though they weren't fully in control. They looked like puppets from the children's theater on the Big Island— puppets whose operator had a lot to learn. Haus had never seen one in action before, but he had no doubt these were like the one Savesti's pet had ripped in half.

Something big skittered out of the tunnel above the puppet children and hurried up the wall. Haus thought of the nest of beetles he and Uuron had found in a cave deep underground when they were kids. They were shaped like regular beetles, but like lumia algae they made their own pale light. This thing glowed, too, but blue like the regeneration engine, and it had no shell, only a covering both like and unlike flesh. A blur of knobby, thin legs carried it over the wall and ceiling. Two loose tentacles flapped limply near the head like oversoaked noodles. Wicked-looking barbs jutted from the heavy spine, and waving behind the whole mess was a long, thin tail tipped with a melon-sized bulb and single, hateful-looking spike.

"Sweet Mother Jajal…" Haus muttered.

The thing froze halfway across the ceiling, cloudy eyes rolling aimlessly, exaggerated ears drooping and stretching like a spritsail in shifting wind. Its blunt, distorted head turned toward them. The face stretched like some warm ball of paraffin and it produced a mouthless wail that made Haus' balls crawl up. It ran straight for them, tail swinging like a sailor throwing line. The kids followed, the listlessness of their motion gone.

Haus looked across the room and bellowed, "Schmalch, move it!"

The collar at the Duke's neck swung free, and Rift hurled it into the mass of children, striking a girl, who staggered and dropped, skidding across the floor before being trampled by her compatriots.

Haus aimed the Bush Burner at the thing skittering across the ceiling.

"No!" Rift shouted. "Set the trinite!"

She drew both stilettos, ran straight toward the two tall boys in the lead, and drove the slender blades into their chests. She let the bodies drop, then charged the next wave.

"Savesti suggested we detonate him?" The Duke finished tugging on his boots and gestured almost casually at the creature skittering across the ceiling. He set to strapping on the pistol harness.

"Something like that," Haus replied.

"You can explain later." The Duke loaded his gun from a little bag dangling from the holster. "What do you need me to do?"

Haus flicked off the Bush Burner's safety and offered it to the Duke. "Distract that thing."

SCHMALCH

"Balls," Schmalch swore as he watched those horrible-looking bogy kids rush toward the Duke and Rift and Haus. When the monster scrambled out of the tunnel, up the wall, and onto the ceiling like an enormous muck bug, Schmalch lost all his words—even the swears.

It was big and twitchy, a pulpy lump of pale, greasy meat that reminded Schmalch of the dead guy he'd found once behind the Barnacle. It had so, so many legs and flappy, pointed ears and a tail like a mace on a whip. He'd never seen anything like it. He hoped he never did again.

"That's the bad thing you said was coming," said a small voice behind him.

Schmalch nodded, terrified shriek frozen in his throat. He couldn't let it out, couldn't scare the kids.

The horrible bug monster let loose some high wail as it skittered across the ceiling, its tail swinging behind it like the train of some fancy lady's gown.

"Mister Schmalch?" the wavering young voice said.

He shook his head and looked away from the horror in the center of the room. The Duke and Rift and Haus would take care of that thing. It was why they were here, why they'd brought so much gear. Jeruu stood behind him, eyes wide and expectant.

"Yeah, right," Schmalch muttered. "Who's next?"

He helped the last few kids—the normal ones—out of the cage while Dinara and Jeruu herded them toward the mansion tunnel. When the last kid was out, and the relief almost overwhelming, Schmalch raced after them. Bullpup gun at the ready, he kept one eye on that monster-thing and its group of sick kids. If any of them came after these kids—*his* kids—he'd stop them. He was a good boss.

Two bogies, a boy and a girl, broke away from the crowd, running like sick twitches toward the line of escapees. Schmalch aimed the gun like Haus had shown him and waited until both were so close he was sure one of them would reach out and rip off his face before he squeezed the trigger.

The gun rattled and spit. The boy's midsection disappeared in a red haze, what was left of him dropping in a gory heap. The girl, who caught only a few pellets, kept coming, so close now that Schmalch could smell her rot. He pulled the trigger again. Nothing happened.

Schmalch reached into his sling-sack, groping for another cartridge. He tried to backpedal as he searched, but his feet tangled. He stumbled and righted himself, but she was on him.

Her limp-skinned hands wrapped around his throat. She squeezed with surprising strength. Blood thrummed in his ears. His eyes pulsed as though ready to burst. She leaned in and hissed, and Schmalch saw her tongue was gone. His stomach rolled.

He raised a knee and jammed it into the girl's gut. She lurched back but clung to him. Little dots of light appeared in Schmalch's vision, bright and glittering like candle flames in a window. He felt her ragged nails cutting into his skin, though he no longer felt the pain.

His hand closed over a new ammunition cartridge. He yanked it from the bag and banged it against the girl's skull until she let go. Schmalch kicked her again, sending her tumbling away, but she sprang back like some child's toy punching bag. He tried to jam the new cartridge into the gun, only to find the old one still in place.

The girl leapt. Schmalch pressed the cartridge release, and the old cylinder popped away with a clang just as her hands clamped around his throat again. He hammered the new cartridge at the gun, desperate to lock it into position. He couldn't find the catch, couldn't hold the cylinder like Haus had shown him. He pounded cartridge against gun, no longer able to think of anything else. His vision began to blur. All he could see was the black stump of her tongue waggling at him. This was how he was going to die.

As fast as she'd attacked, the girl's grip relaxed. Her body jerked, her hands slid from his throat and she crumpled into a little heap, her expression still feral.

Schmalch blinked at her, confused. His hatchet stuck out of her back. Jeruu stood there, shaking, staring down at the girl.

"I...I...I borrowed it," he said.

Schmalch put a foot on the girl's ribs, tugged the weapon free, and returned it to Jeruu. "Take it and go!"

He snapped the cartridge into place and took a last look around. Rift was throwing little knives from her fancy vest at the bogy kids while backing toward the center of the room. The Duke was there, spraying the shrieking bug creature he called Orono with fire.

Haus was crouched by the glowing glass candle. He glanced at Schmalch and pointed to the tunnel. "Drop a grenade behind you!" he shouted.

SYLANDAIR

Orono scurried across the ceiling, ears, tentacles, and tail waving insistently. Whether he was concerned with Syl's escape or the safety of his luminous glass fetish was unclear. His indecision made him a delightful target.

Syl awkwardly balanced Haus' flamethrower on his filthy splint and flicked it to life. A bright purplish-blue flame licked the air around its tip. He'd never used this kind of weapon before, never even held one, but he could conceive of no finer introductory experience.

He strode to the edge of the dais, aimed, and squeezed the trigger. The gun vomited orange fire, coating Orono in burning gel. The dismal room, dark and frigid for so long, came to warm, brilliant life. Screeching in pain, Orono scuttled this way and that across the ceiling in search of escape. His puppet children screamed with him. Bits of flame clung to the ceiling around Orono, others spattered to the floor, burning amongst the litter of bones. One clump fell onto a dried-out alley cat and the late creature burst into flame.

Orono dropped to the floor, rolling in the littered remains of his victims. Beneath the clumps of burning gel, his flesh bubbled and blackened like overheated salve. As each little blaze burnt itself out, flakes of char peeled away and fluttered to the floor. Fresh skin, whole and undamaged, took its place.

Fire wouldn't kill him, but it was a more effective deterrent than anything else they'd tried. At least it gave Orono pain, if only for a second. Syl glanced back at Haus fiddling with a spool of wire and hoped whatever Hergis had devised was a more long-term solution.

Syl marched into the ring of chained skeletons, spraying Orono, herding him toward the tunnel he'd so recently emerged from. The monstrosity feinted to one side, then skittered to the other in an attempt to reach his precious pillar. Syl fired another burst, this one right into that wretched face.

Orono slapped at the flame with his limp tentacles. He drew back his tail, swirling it around him like the fan of some hideous burlesque dancer. Syl traced the path of the barbed bulb with the gun barrel. A quick flick and a grunt, and Orono whipped the spiked tail at Syl, who lurched sideways. The revolting squishy bulb brushed Syl's skin, but the spike missed its mark.

Orono reared back and roared, the sound muffled by the membrane covering his mouth. Syl launched more fire at his exposed belly. The muted roar became a throaty squeal. Orono turned and raced into the tunnel, several of the children stumbling after him.

Syl shifted his aim into the remaining milky-eyed children. Aliara held them at bay, hurling knives at those who made for Haus and the pillar. Syl strode over to her and fired a gout at the cluster. Aliara, speckled with all shades of blood, smiled at him. She looked about to speak, but any words she had ready were cut off when an explosion rumbled through the room. Chills of fear wound around Syl's gut. He glanced back at the pillar. Though seeming a bit startled himself, Haus was still at work. The yellow bricks were still intact. Dust billowed from the tunnel that led to the mansion. Schmalch had done his job.

"Follow that thing!" Haus shouted, waving them after Orono.

"You go." Aliara paused to halt the progress of a child who'd wandered too close. "I'll follow."

Syl ran into the tunnel, ducking around or pushing over any staggering children blocking his way. He heard Aliara's breath behind him, her grunts of effort as she dispatched those he'd passed.

He raced up a sharp incline into a small dirt-walled root cellar lined with largely empty shelves. A battered old ladder on one wall led up to a freshly expanded exit, the upper rungs lost to the violence of Orono's departure. Daylight eked down to him through dirty glass panels in the ceiling of the structure above.

Syl slung the flamethrower and scrambled as far up the ladder as its remaining rungs would allow. Orono was close, chittering and wrecking his surroundings. The muffled sounds of a party overhead underpinned his fit. Syl locked his splinted arm in the upper rung and fired a burst of flame into the room above. Orono howled in chorus with his remaining children.

Syl clutched the lip of the hole with his good hand and pulled. Injury, hunger, and exhaustion conspired toward failure. One arm was not enough. He grabbed the edge with his damaged hand, flouting the pain that demanded he stop, and wrenched himself upward. He managed only a brief peek at a long-abandoned greenhouse and a raging Orono before another explosion shook the world around him.

Syl's grip slipped and he dropped back into the root cellar. Stunned, he lay on the floor, waiting for his senses to return. His jaw ached from the blast's concussion, his eyes watered, and his ears rang as though his skull had been used to muffle cymbals.

From the room above, Syl heard an eruption of shattering glass, the brittle clatter subdued by the ringing in his head. The sounds of jubilant voices poured in, quickly shifting to screams.

A dust-covered Aliara burst into the cellar. Blue-black blood seeped from her lugs, disappearing into the high neck of her catsuit. She extended a hand, hoisted Syl to his feet, and jerked her chin toward the ladder.

SKELN

It was an especially beautiful, sunny autumn day, perfect for the fete honoring Right Venerable Master Cedef Mlar's retirement. At age eighty-nine, it was about time the old mathematics professor packed up and returned to Ukur-Tilen.

Tucked beneath a private canopy, Most Illustrious Master Pryor Skeln Emat leaned back in the rattan lawn chair, sipped his Dormah's Rise, and considered his own retirement. Cedef had informed Skeln with no small amount of pride that he was giving up his work in the Haven to accept the position of professorial doyen in the combinatronics department of the mathematics college. Though far from impressed, Skeln had provided the obligatory smile and congratulations. When *he* retired, Skeln assured himself, he would be the doyen of the entire architectural college, not just of one pathetic department.

The fizzy cocktail tickled his nose, and Skeln sneezed. His hair wiggled with menace at the sudden movement. He'd allowed his stylist to remove the caged bird from his coif—it had begun to smell—but Skeln insisted he maintain the rich turquoise hue. Today, it was fashioned into a ridge fanned out along the crown of his skull, a style set off by a three-piece suit in a perfectly coordinating shade of mauve, its jacket extra-long and heavy for the season's chill weather. His was a well-assembled appearance.

Skeln waved at two of his grandchildren, who rode in lazy rings astride a pair of fat ponies. The youngest showed mental promise, but the eldest was thick—a real douse. Skeln held out little hope for that one.

Across the lawn, the middle one stood with her father, studying the statue of Jodidar Grifmuel positioned a few feet from where Skeln sat. He caught snatches of his bound-son's lecture to her about the brilliant Mucha Jodidar, the very man who had both harnessed the power of opoli and donated the lands on which they now stood. Skeln had delivered that same speech to his bound-son on the day the boy joined the Emat family. He hoped the young man was reproducing it properly.

Skeln's wife Klarin—not Mucha herself, but a passably bright specimen nonetheless—lingered around one of the entertainers, a man on red stilts whose upper body was costumed as an overdressed baby in a high chair. His clothes were largely red, set to match the stilts and skirting, but the puppet arms and legs were a brilliant blue, his bib and cap glittering silver. Even amongst this crowd, the man stood out.

Skeln found his performance irritating and absurd, if not a little creepy, but the fool seemed to entertain Klarin endlessly. Her plump midsection, swathed in black and white checks, jiggled and jostled with each of the baby-man's antics.

Klarin nearly doubled over with amusement when the performer hobbled over to Supreme Sovereign Master Enan Ranaran and asked, "Are you my daddy?" before shooting a stream of white foam at her from a device hidden in the crotch of his fake baby body.

Enan brushed the foam from her lovely shoulder and scowled. "I am a woman, you fool," she said and stomped over to the cluster of chairs arranged in the miniature orchard. She flopped into one, crossed her arms and legs, and glared at the clown, her silver curls and bright pink sheath dimmed by the shade. Too bad—Skeln had been enjoying watching her move around the fete.

"Apologies," the faux baby called after Enan in his falsetto, "I had a little accident."

Klarin wiped her eyes. She looked at Skeln and pointed to the baby-man, her belly still shaking with giggles. When her laughter tapered off into coughing, she hustled on over to her husband, hand extended. "Join me in the buffet tent," she said. "They're serving fried cod and potatoes with myylantyl pie."

"No." Skeln shook his head, the twist of his turquoise beard swaying along with it. "No. Bring me a plate. I don't want to lose this seat. It's the best one here, and Meela's been eyeing it." He scowled at a white-haired woman reclining amongst the miniature fruit trees.

"You're no fun," Klarin said and gave him a playful smack.

He leaned out and gave her round rump a pat as she trundled away. "And bring me another Dormah's Rise while you're at it," Skeln called after her.

He was certain Meela had started to rise when he leaned out to pat Klarin. That woman wanted his cush seat with its private shade. Well, she couldn't have it. He'd die before he surrendered his chair to anyone as low as a linguistics master. He leaned back and wagged his fingers at Meela in a patronizing wave.

"Would you toss that back?" A call came from his left. Something heavy hit his foot.

Skeln bent forward and found a red ball nestled against his expensive Ossquere-leather loafer. He palmed the ball and rolled it back to the troco players.

"Be more careful next time," he called with a practiced smile.

The little girl with the red spoon-ended cue nodded, then smacked the newly returned ball with unnecessary enthusiasm, wildly missing its hoop. The other girls with her scampered away, whacking their own green and orange troco balls with no respect for the way the game was supposed to be played.

Skeln grumbled and settled back, pressing a creak from the rattan as he adjusted his bulk. He sipped the dregs of his drink and watched the children run around the lawn, Mucha members circulate politely amongst themselves, and various spouses wag their chins about thoroughly unimportant matters.

His eyelids drooped, and he began to doze in the autumn breeze, startled by a sudden shudder in the ground. Perhaps he'd been dreaming. Some partygoers standing at the food tent looked equally perplexed, but most of the rest seemed not to have noticed. Skeln leaned back, ready to continue his disrupted nap when the clink of shuddering glass attracted his attention. He sat up.

The noise seemed to have come from the filthy old greenhouse in the far corner of the property. Skeln had petitioned the Mucha Hall's council for months to allow him to rid them of the eyesore. The structure was rarely used, and even then, only by the nigh-useless horticultural zoeticists. He had begged them too allow him to raze the thing and erect something more functional—a drafting studio, perhaps—but to-date, he'd been denied.

He twisted in his chair to glare at the windless glass structure behind him. Something was moving inside. The dirty panes blurred his view, but he could tell that someone most certainly was where they shouldn't be, tossing things around. Children, undoubtedly. Unsupervised and naughty children had broken in, intending to wreak havoc. Skeln didn't care for the greenhouse or its purpose, but he'd sooner shave his head than allow anyone to sully Mucha property.

He waved to a security man standing by the fruit trees, who jogged over.

"Find out what's going on in there," Skeln said.

The man nodded and trotted away.

Skeln returned to his relaxed musings, secure in his knowledge that the mischief would come to a swift halt. He'd only just closed his eyes again when he heard a commotion from the greenhouse, things inside being knocked around.

The guard shouted "What in—" and glass exploded, spraying Skeln and his precious chair from the rear. He turned in his seat and glared at the useless building.

Something indescribably hideous, some nightmare molded from scorched canning paraffin, had burst from the worthless old building. It was larger than a normal person, but not so massive as a rhochrot, though more horrifying by far. Little bits of glass stuck in its skin, which was blackened and blistered in patches. Wrapped in its long, prehensile tail was roughly two-thirds of the guard Skeln had dispatched to the greenhouse. The creature's near-featureless face jerked from side to side as though examining the expanse of lawn, though it seemed bewildered by the experience.

Skeln wasn't quite sure how to react, either.

Someone screamed, and others joined in. The thing lurched forward, skittering on crustacean legs into the crowd of partygoers.

It stumbled into Skeln's private tent, uprooting the runner pins, bending the poles. It thrashed against the canvas, whining like a stuck piglet, and succeeding only in tangling itself further. It uncoiled the long straw of its tail and dropped the guard's devastated corpse on the ground beside Skeln.

The creature lurched forward again, pulling all the supports from the ground, dragging the entire structure in its wake. It rolled almost comically across the lawn while people ran and screamed around it.

With a great rip of fabric, the dagger on its tail slit through the canvas. It leapt from the ruin so haphazardly that it caromed off the statue of Jodidar before racing toward the buffet tent.

The mounting bolts snapped with nauseating *pops*. The statue tottered on its base for a breathless moment, and the figure tipped.

Skeln had enough time to raise an arm before Jodidar's polished effigy smashed into him.

He never left his rattan chair.

HAUS

Haus stared hard at the plunger in his hand. He was deep in the tunnel, as far away from the trinite stack as the spool of wire would allow. He tried not to think about the scorched little bodies back in the chamber. If he detonated this, they'd never be sent back to the sea like they should.

He closed his eyes, pulled his shirt over nose and mouth, and pushed the plunger.

The world went white and bright. Thunder was everywhere.

Haus opened his eyes. He was flat on his back with no memory of falling. He tried to breathe. Someone had dropped an anchor on his chest. He coughed and rolled over onto hands and knees, gasping.

The air was bitter with chemicals and ripe with burning rot. His cough turned into a retch, and he spat out dirt and blood. A splotch of fire burned on his shirt cuff. He patted out the little flame and wiped his face with his sleeve.

Haus rose to his feet, hand on the wall to steady himself. He heard no activity from down the tunnel, no sounds that might be Rift or the Duke. In fact, he heard nothing at all. He stuck a finger in one ear and wiggled it. It came away bloody. By Inglahar, he'd deafened himself. He shook both fingers in his ears and made noises until the nothing became a ringing. The ringing grew louder and louder, until he thought his head would split and he wished for the silence again.

He stumbled up the tunnel, the whistling in his head tapering off into a manageable hiss. He emerged into someone's root cellar. A cacophony of hollers and shrieks poured down to him from a hole in the ceiling. Ignoring the dross that passed for a ladder, he jumped up, grabbed the edge of the opening and pulled himself into the ruin of an abandoned greenhouse.

Some of the pots with their dead plants still sat on shelves alongside rusty gardening tools and chemical containers, but mostly everything had been hurled about in some unpleasant battle. The Bush Burner lay on the floor, its tank showing empty. Everything was misted with a spray of fresh, red blood—no black. One broad section of the grimy glass-paneled walls was shattered. Dozens of voices outside were screaming. Haus realized where he was. *This,* he thought abstractedly, *is a celebration Dockhaven's Mucha would never forget.*

He stepped through the shattered wall into a combat zone.

The scene was as bad as any battlefield he'd known. Panicked people screamed and hid while the twisted monster that had called itself Orono ran amok in the middle of what was once a lawn party. Casualties were scattered across the yard. Those still on their feet fled in terror or stood and wept. Orono's spiked tail slammed into the head of a child fleeing hand in hand with its mother, bulbous tumor pulsing before it withdrew. The unlucky child turned and attacked its parent.

Haus scanned the crowd. He spotted Rift and the Duke running toward the rampaging monster. She'd taken one side, he the other. They planned to flank the thing. They needed someone to drive up the middle.

Haus drew his hunting knife and charged after them.

SYLANDAIR

Syl threaded his way across the lawn, pistol raised as he dodged both Orono's burning minions and the Mucha's frightened partygoers, who ran around the lawn like headless poultry. He couldn't get off a shot. Each time he aimed, some dunderpate crossed his path or slammed into him. He needed to be closer, close enough that no one else would be foolish enough to be near.

Orono rampaged through the crowd like some feral hog, trampling, slashing, and goring. He ripped the head off one fleeing woman, flung another across the lawn, impaling her on the stump of a tent pole. With his spindly legs, he snatched a man on stilts, who was inexplicably dressed like a baby, and shot his yellow proboscis into the man's screaming mouth, the other into his gut. The man twitched and heaved and groaned as his skin went pale. When he stopped moving, Orono tossed the body, stilts and all, into a banquet tent filled with people, yellow feeding tubes curling back into his nose and belly. When the cowering crowd inside screamed, Orono spread his segmented vestigial limbs and leaned in with a hiss. While they trembled and wailed, he opened those hateful little neck bellows and gassed them.

Syl saw his opening. He fired the pistol, steel shot ripping through the horror's dead-pale flesh. Orono howled and wheeled, brainless children miming in unison. The wounds did not heal. Instead of closing, these lesions wept pale ichor and blood. Hergis had been correct; the melted, glowing leavings of Orono's ritual *had* been the source of his remaking.

Orono hissed and advanced on Syl, one tentacle waving like an admonishing finger. Syl fumbled with the ammo bag that dangled from his pistol harness but couldn't free it. His heart hammered, anxiety and satisfaction circling his chest frantically. Orono scuttled closer, lecture cut off as Aliara swung onto his back in a slick blur of black. The monstrous bug—the man he'd once called papa submerged inside—bucked across the lawn like an unbroken steed, slashing ineffectively at Aliara with his spiked tail.

With a shout, Syl yanked the shot bag from his harness and dumped pellets into the pistol. He tracked Orono's thrashing with the barrel, ready to fire the instant Aliara was clear of his aim.

She reared back and raised her hand, the black nut of bane tucked in its center, and slapped the monstrous face, pumping toxin into Orono's waxy skin. His minions screamed and writhed. Orono flailed and groaned, the yellow threads of poison spreading through him like mold on a pudding. He threw himself around the area, tentacles groping his back in an attempt rid himself of Aliara. He succeeded only in trampling more partygoers.

Syl followed, still tracking with his pistol, as Orono rammed headlong into a full-grown tree, Aliara drew one of her stilettos and stabbed myriad holes in his neck and shoulders.

Orono staggered, shook his head, and roared. He swung the barbed tail, batting her from his back like a cow deterring a fly. She sailed toward the nearby cluster of sapling fruit trees, landing face-up on the tidy lawn. Those hiding there screamed, some scattered, none came to her aid.

Aliara began to rise, thrown back when the spiked ball at the tip of Orono's tail slammed into her chest like a maul. A mist of black blood filled the air for an instant, then her body jerked and went still.

Syl fired.

ALIARA

Aliara felt pressure, no pain. She lifted her head and saw Orono's tail withdraw from her body, dark blood dripping from its talon. She flopped back onto the ground. She couldn't breathe. She needed air.

Syl's face floated into focus above her. She tried to sit up but fell back. She needed to finish this, needed to kill Orono. Her lips moved. She needed to ask Syl to help her up, but all she heard were the shouts and crashes of the bedlam around her muted by the incessant ringing.

Where was the air? Her diaphragm pulled hard. She felt the tiniest stream leak in.

Syl's eyes darted from her face to her chest. His head shook. He pronounced her name. She reached up and touched his lips.

His gaze swept the area, lit on something. He slid both arms beneath her, face twisting with the pain of his injury, and lifted her. She tried to raise her head, but it would only dangle and bounce. She watched stitches pop in the wound on Syl's arm, their sudden snap like bangers blossoming in the night sky. Blood trickled from the scar, dripped off his elbow.

"Surgeon!" he shouted into a crowd of people cowering in a copse of little trees.

One of their heads turned, a pale grey woman with a mass of spiral curls and a pink dress. Syl loped over to her and laid Aliara down.

"Help her," he commanded.

The woman shook her head, frowning like someone who practiced the expression often. "I will not."

Syl rose, drew his spent pistol, and placed its muzzle against the woman's temple. "Do you have an operating theater here?"

Aliara's eyelids lowered, lifted. She tugged at the air. Threads seeped in; just enough to keep her conscious.

The woman nodded, cloud of silver hair bouncing, catching the light. "Under the dome."

"You!" Syl shouted at a big karju crouching behind a nearby tree, his green-spangled jumpsuit and matching hat lending him the appearance of a giant stalk of asparagus. Syl pointed to where Aliara lay. "Pick her up and follow. Carefully." His voice left no room for argument.

The man scrambled to his feet and hoisted her impossibly high into the air. He looked down at her, his face pulled into an expression she recognized: pity for the dying. Her head bobbled, loose on her neck, as the man carried her across the trampled lawn. She couldn't remember why she was here, what they were doing, why Haus was dancing with a huge white insect.

Her head lolled to one side. There was Syl. He was wrong-side-up. Everything was—the sky, the soil, the buildings, the screaming people.

She reached for him, but her arm was too heavy. It dropped, dangled. She called his name, couldn't hear her own voice. She blinked, pulled hard, and found no more air. Her vision greyed, and her eyes slipped shut of their own accord.

HAUS

Haus drove his shoulder into the creature's midsection, the Duke's pistol shot still ringing in his already abused ears. He and this thing called Orono bowled over one another and sprang to their feet, the mutant staggering like a tippler well into his cups; Rift's bane had done its work. Little holes mottled one side of its face and upper body. A big hunk had been hacked out of what might be called a shoulder. Something translucent and blood-streaked swelled at each wound like oozing scabs. The smell was appalling. Haus swallowed his gorge.

Orono drew back the spiked tail and swung. Haus sidestepped the blow but didn't anticipate the return swing. It caught him hard in the ribs, cracking his carapace plate and knocking him off his feet. Haus toppled, sliding across the blood-slicked grass, breathless and reeling. The horned lump of flesh slammed into the ground near his head with a solid *duumph*!

Haus rolled, bracing for another blow—one like Rift had received. Orono closed, skittering over him like some hideous lover. A pulsing yellow tube slithering out of the slit where his nose should have been.

Haus' stomach turned and, on instinct, he slashed up, across Orono's sagging abdomen. Hot guts flopped out, oozing across Haus' chest. Orono rolled away, clicking and screeing, his many thin legs scrabbling at the viscera in an attempt to pull it back inside.

Haus pivoted onto his side and drove his hunting blade through the thing's blind eye. Orono keened and flailed. His cold, slick tentacles fumbled with the invading object like a panicked animal. With a grunt, Haus twisted the blade. Something inside crunched, and Orono fell still with a thump and a faltering wheeze.

Collapsing back onto the grass, panting, Haus let the fading panic around him drift away as he laughed into the blue autumn sky.

SCHMALCH

The news callers in Pukatown were shouting about the Mucha's petition to remove the statue of Kluuta Orono from its position in front of the desal plant. A lesser story mentioned Mayor Carsuure's attempts to attract new Mucha talent to Dockhaven since the incident.

Schmalch stopped to toss a couple coppers to the closest caller and request a text chit. Sviroosa was teaching him to read, and he particularly enjoyed buying things that employed that skill. He'd even splurged and bought a couple of real books. He couldn't read every word in them yet, but he liked seeing them on the shelf in his room at home.

He wasn't quite used to that yet—calling anywhere home. When everything settled down, the Duke had made Schmalch his paid assistant. He earned five Callas a quartern—as much as Sviroosa—plus meals and his own room. The Duke even let him keep the stuffed Tolknor beaver as decoration. He'd been afraid Sviroosa would balk, but she'd not said a word. He was shocked when she washed his clothes for him and cleaned his room without him even asking. And she hadn't kicked him out of the kitchen or scowled at him once since that pocky Tatumi tossed him out the window. When she volunteered to teach him to read, he nearly went keel up.

Schmalch's first jig had been to find someone to replace the

Duke's shattered window. It took a full day and part of the night to find someone who was not only willing to pour the right-sized pane, but also had the crane and equipment necessary to install it. When the window was in place, the Duke offered Schmalch the assistant job, contingent on him not wasting *all* his Callas at the Barnacle or any other bar or pleasure house. Schmalch hadn't needed to consider; he'd accepted on the spot.

He finished scanning the news chit and smiled at the mid-morning activity in the Upper Rabble. The sun was over the tops of the buildings, there was barely any fog creeping around, and he had coins in his pocket. And he was headed someplace special. Again. He'd passed on Sviroosa's breakfast in favor of accepting an invitation from Fohmsquah, something he'd done nearly every morning since he brought Worch and Ilit home. She'd insisted. It was nice. Pretty close to the Duke's place, too. Close to *home*, he reminded himself.

He looked up at the tall, puckered building where Fohmsquah and the kids lived. He still couldn't quite pick out their window from so many.

"Spare a Calla?" a voice asked. Sigrin Malpockey grinned at him from the closest alley.

"Not for you, Malpockey," Schmalch said.

Sigrin spat at him. Schmalch chuckled and ducked inside, waving pleasantly at the nasty twitch. Sigrin slung a few curses his way before wandering off to panhandle someone else.

Schmalch's favorite part of every visit was the greeting. He liked to stand outside their cuddy a little longer than necessary to build the anticipation. No one had ever been so excited to see him before. It was really gloss.

When he'd fully savored the moment, Schmalch knocked. The door swung open, and he was mobbed.

"Mister Schmalch!" Worch and Ilit called in unison, clinging to him like sweet little leeches.

Chisev gave him a manly squeeze, and Schmalch rubbed the boy's head playfully. Then Fohmsquah hugged him, gave him the usual peck on the cheek. His face went green as a pine every time.

"Chisev's making poached eggs and sausage, Mister Schmalch," Fohmsquah said. "I'm making some lemon bread as well."

"Sounds real swish," he said as one of the girls dragged him through the cuddy by his shirtsleeve. He'd learned to tell the twins apart. Worch was the smiley one. Ilit was a bit more shy.

"Moocha bought us a puzzle," Worch said. "It's a wild rugaelk in the winter. Lots'n lots'a white."

"Bet Mister Schmalch can do it in minutes," Ilit whispered.

"I'll sure try," he smiled and sat down at the table with them.

He watched Fohmsquah in the kitchen with her son while the girls chattered and tried to force puzzle pieces into the wrong spots. The Duke had given Schmalch a pair of tickets to some fancy—but not too fancy—theater where they served food while people performed. As he watched Fohmsquah, her beautiful head smooth as the lump of bread dough she worked, Schmalch decided he would ask her if she'd like to join him.

HAUS

"They are yours." The Duke held up both hands in refusal when Haus offered to return the gear he'd purchased with the man's money. "Take them with you. You shall find them far more useful than I."

"Much appreciated," Haus said. "Hope I'm not leaving you in a bad spot."

The Duke shook his head and smiled.

Haus couldn't get used to seeing him without facial hair. The soft black mustache and hair at his chin had given him a masculine countenance that had vanished when he shaved. Without it, the Duke was a damn pretty man.

"You do me a favor by taking them," he said. "And by delivering Hergis. I will stop by the farspeech office on my way home and send word to the Mucha to expect his remains and the paperwork."

Haus patted his pack. "Have the papers right here."

"Excellent. If anything more than a delivery is required, I will send word."

Haus gave a single nod. The late autumn wind fluttered his unkempt brown hair. He sniffed the air, taking in the sea, the market foodstuffs, the fires from local stoves, and the ever-present scent of an overcrowded populace going about their labors. It had been overpowering when he'd first arrived years ago, but now he found he would miss the smell. He looked over his shoulder at the ship he'd booked for passage to Ukur. Even in dawn's dimness, it was none too lovely. He'd heard good things about its captain and its cook from Luugrar, so he gave it a chance.

Discussing the Duke's jig with Luugrar had been awkward. He'd been a fixture at the Haven's contract house for so long, Haus wasn't sure what he'd do without that hole to haunt. Luugrar was reluctant to see him go and agreed to wish him well only if Haus promised to complete the jig and return soon—in one piece. He'd promised to fulfill the contract. The rest was uncertain.

As rough as that'd been, the worst was the visit to his lodge. Isako understood, accepted his decision without explanation. Somehow that made leaving harder. The place had been his solace for years. He couldn't imagine belonging anywhere else or receiving guidance from anyone else.

"What will you be doing until the expedition sets out?" the Duke asked. "If I may ask."

Haus turned away from the ships. "Yeah. I still have some women to notify for Uuron. He wasn't as busy in Guunaat as he was here, but the man never met a bym he didn't like."

The Duke smiled.

"I'll see the family."

"Naturally."

"After that, the Nors."

"Mm yes," the Duke mumbled. "In search of the lady and her beast."

Haus nodded. From what Savesti had told him that night at the Triangle, Nihal would need a few things, mostly spark—antique in one case, drowned in the other. He and the Duke had debated for quarterns trying to decide which she'd go for first. When one of the Duke's agents had reported an impending archeological dive, the deliberation was rendered moot.

The Duke drew a long breath and straightened. "I will ensure you have a place when the expedition departs."

"Until then I'll wander, ask around. She's there, she'll be remembered."

The Duke chuckled. "Indeed." He looked out to sea, brow furrowed. "Keep me apprised of your location so I may send word should I hear anything relevant about either site."

"Will do. You'll find me?"

"If we selected the wrong objective? Yes."

"Right." Haus shifted his duffle from one shoulder to the other. "You'll be fine here?"

"Of course. Some of the Mucha have chosen to blame me— us—for what happened, but most see reason. A few well-placed words about the fact that Orono had been living under their property for decades assuaged much of the upset. Add to that my generous donation from the ancient parasite's bequest, which allowed them to make repairs and accommodate any injured parties, and I am quite confident they are satisfied for the moment." He half-smiled. "And I have Schmalch."

Haus chuckled.

"You are certain you do not wish to take him with you?"

"Comin' 'er stayin'?" the captain of the *Lespoto* shouted at Haus.

"Coming," he replied.

They gripped wrists and the Duke gave a slight bow. "I am in your debt."

SYLANDAIR

Melancholy wrapped itself around Syl's chest as he watched Haus board the little launch and set out. He'd grown rather fond of their evenings together, sitting around the parlor, drinking and rambling, and sharing stories of past exploits. He would miss the big man's company. Syl wished him well on his half of their endeavor.

He left the docks, comfortable dark grey topcoat flapping around his ankles in the autumn breeze. His wrist, though healed, ached each time a storm blew in. Wonderful, now he was one of those aging loons who could predict weather with a body part. With the chill of winter creeping closer, he shuddered to think what his wrist would have to say in that season.

He wandered through the market toward the tram, taking his time to enjoy the lingering whiff of seafood and dirt-caked vegetables. Large portions of the place soon would shut down for the night. Flower and vegetable stands didn't do well after dark in such temperatures. Fish and meat vendors, however, loved the colder seasons.

A little girl with black plaits bumped into Syl. She rebounded and danced away before he could speak. He watched her skinny form wind between larger bodies and vendor stands before resuming his stroll toward home.

He wished Aliara could have joined him to bid Haus farewell. The two had worked together so often and so well, it seemed unfair that she was unable to attend.

Syl left the market, headed up the slow arch of the Oblong South and into the Big Island's farspeech office.

"Where're you sending today, Duke?" asked the puka behind the counter.

"Ukur-Tilen," Syl said.

"Again? You sure do have a lot to say to those Mucha."

It was the fifth message he'd sent to the Mucha Colleges in the past quartern. Some of the Haven's more pleasant Mucha, whom he'd been so forcibly introduced to, had suggested Syl direct his messages about Hergis to Immaculate Sovereign Master Leehal Dentath. She was dean overseeing all the colleges of the Tangible school of study, which encompassed both surgery and zoetics. That had suited his needs perfectly. She had been oh so contrite to hear of Hergis' demise and promised to do all she could to honor the little man's memory, but she became far less enthusiastic when Syl asked her to see to Hergis' remains. Her attitude changed when Syl mentioned the extra item he intended to ship along with the corpse.

He'd found an intriguing genome sequence tucked into the documentation of Orono's farspeech experiment, the only useful bit of Hergis' work his sister hadn't absconded with. Clipped to the paperwork were notes from Hergis explaining the zoet's function in a way even Syl could understand. Though Orono's experiments on Aliara and the other poor creature had failed, he had managed to apply his work successfully to the common swamp leech, transforming it into a wearable short-distance communication device.

To Syl's knowledge, it was the last surviving invention from Orono's lab. In his communications with Master Dentath, Syl described the work as something found when gathering Hergis' belongings. If she would provide the talent, Syl told Dentath, he would fund the zoet's development. He suggested it be called "the Savesti," and offered to divide its profits between himself and a surgery and zoetics scholarship to the Colleges. He'd needed provide only a few intimations about what might happen were his suggestions not implemented.

Hergis might have been none too thrilled to learn someone else's work was being passed off as his own, but he was gone. It was, to Syl's mind, a grand way for the minikin surgeon to be remembered as more than just the man murdered by his own pet experiment.

After leaving the farspeech office, Syl stopped at the property now known as the Imythedralin Estate. Things were progressing well. Nearly all vestiges of Orono had been erased. The house was no more than rubble, the outbuildings gone, and the gardens transplanted to other, more appropriate estates. All that remained of his childhood home were a handful of trees, and he hadn't the heart to raze them.

The foreman spotted him standing at the gate and trotted out. "We're down to the basement," she said. "The salvage guy said he'd be back in five days to get the rest. Don't know why it's taking him so long to pick it up."

"He is transporting them away from Dockhaven," Syl said. "I am unaware of their final destination, but they will no longer be here."

"Oh." She looked at him curiously, but let it pass, accustomed by now to the peculiarity of her employer. "You got the chair?"

"Yes. It was delivered as you promised."

"Good." She removed her hat and ran fingers through her bushy, ginger hair before putting it back on. "Are you sure you don't want us to start work building something else here? A new house? Business? Seems like a lot of land to sit empty."

"I am certain," Syl said. He slid his hands in the pockets of his coat. "I have not yet decided what to do with the property, though I've no intention of letting it go."

"So you said. Just seems like a waste."

"Mm-hmm, so *you* said."

She waved a hand toward the Mucha Hall. "Your neighbors

keep stopping by to ask if you're interested in selling."

"Yes. They are quite keen to expand their property."

"I tell them I don't have any answers."

"The answer is no."

"Right." She looked at him from the side of her eyes and shrugged.

Together they watched the workers clear rubble for a few moments. Syl couldn't stop the smile that crept onto his lips.

When he'd seen enough, he patted the foreman's shoulder. "Continue the good work. You know where to reach me should you need anything."

"Sure do, Duke."

He strolled out the gate and down Temple Row toward the tram. He was ready to be home. Sviroosa should have breakfast ready by the time he arrived.

ALIARA

Aliara stood in front of the full-length mirror, examining the puckered scar where her left breast should have been. She ran her finger along its bumpy surface; it had devoured the one caused by Orono's removal of her left lung decades ago. If she'd still had it, the surgeon had explained, Aliara would have drowned in her own blood before she even reached the operating theater.

Now she had a new lung, enhanced ribs, and several organs that functioned better than the originals. Work on the new breast would begin as soon as the ribs beneath were fully developed. Most had required only ossein injections to heal, but three had been too far gone for repair, requiring full replacement with steel cores. Her body needed more time to finish their development. Maybe another quartern, Master Ranaran said during her last house call. Syl's Callas had calmed the surgeon enough to not only forgive him for holding her at gunpoint at the fete, but also to continue on as their personal surgeon.

Aliara still found the strangeness of the new parts unsettling. It had been so long since she'd had a whole body, the idea made her anxious. She'd reached peace with the mutilations, assumed that was the body she'd have for life. Initially, when Syl explained the plan, she had balked at the work, tried to argue against it, but he was persuasive. When he asked if she wanted to think of Orono each time she saw her naked self, Aliara was forced to relent. He was right;

that situation would be unacceptable.

Having seen enough of the wound, she pulled her robe closed and eased herself into the big green chair, relocated from the mansion to its new home beside their bedroom fireplace. She poked at the shirred eggs and toast Sviroosa had left on the side table. Aliara wasn't hungry this morning, but she ate a toast wedge anyway. She didn't care to endure Sviroosa's admonishments if she ate nothing. The little woman had become obsessively fussy since the incident. She'd prepare any dish Aliara had ever mentioned enjoying, and if Aliara didn't finish what she was served, the poor little puka lapsed into despondency. Though Aliara explained that she simply had no appetite, Sviroosa took it personally each time.

The bedroom door creaked open and she sat forward without thinking. Pain jabbed at her. Aliara dropped back into the cushion. It was most likely Syl or Sviroosa. If it was anyone else, she simply didn't care enough to stand.

"Pet, you are out of bed," Syl said. "On your own? Or did Sviroosa assist?"

"I managed," she said.

"Wonderful. I hope you used care." He tossed his hat and suitcoat on the bed and strode over to study her. "I would hate for you to overexert yourself."

The grey pinstriped shirt and snug black pants fit him beautifully. If she'd been able to move more freely, he wouldn't have been wearing them for long.

He bent and tousled her messy hair, something he'd not been able to do since she was a child. Her hair had gone untrimmed during her convalescence, leaving it shaggy on top and uneven with bald patches on the sides. She hated it, but Syl had taken to running his fingers through it as they lay in bed at night. *That* she enjoyed.

He kneeled in front of her, lifted her hand, and kissed the moonstone ring on her index finger. "Haus sends his regards."

She nodded. He was off to avenge everyone they'd lost. Haus

hadn't said as much, but he hadn't needed to. She would have been shocked if he'd stayed.

Syl took her hand, pressed his lips to her palm. "How are you feeling today, Pet?"

"Better."

He leaned in and kissed her. "How much better?"

"Strikingly."

He eased her forward in the chair until her legs wrapped around him. The wicked glint in his eyes had at last replaced the fear and pity she'd seen too often over the past quarterns.

"Well…" He ran his hand beneath her robe and leaned closer. "Master Ranaran did direct you to enjoy some exercise."

EPILOGUE: **NIHAL**

2085 ALSOLON 38

They'd been turned away at the dock outside Oranard's Glory, not even allowed to disembark the ship, let alone enter the city. She should not have been so proud of her name. Her branch of the Savesti family was forever exiled for choosing her runt brother over their emperor's command. Even dead, Hergis still kept her from her rightful place.

Nihal had considered visiting another port to obtain access to Oras under an assumed name, but she was angry enough with her homeland that she turned around and took Tatumi and her few possessions back across the Dawn Sea. She could begin her work just as easily in the Nors—perhaps with greater ease, if the legends were to be believed.

Over the past months, she'd collected many of the components specified in the fragments from The Book. She'd obtained the correct ones, not the useless tripe Master Orono had gathered. In her travels, she'd uncovered further details about others who had shared the same pursuit. Names like Erintajul and Sozaxai had been uttered in hushed tones at temples, libraries, and museums where she'd inquired. And of course, there was the situation on Rhalnor— not an acceptable subject for discussion in any academic circle.

As she looked out at the open ocean, Nihal smiled. *Fools.*

Tatumi sniffed at the sea air and whined. Nihal fed him a handful of snarl beetles from her pocket. With him at her side, she had no fear of traveling alone. Even dressed as Hergis had preferred, he was intimidating to most, but she'd allowed him to select his own garments, simple canvas pants and cotton shirt. No longer would he be required to dress like a dandy and perform like a circus animal, just as she no longer had to wear what was assigned to her. She brushed thin fingers down her white blouse and green linen trousers, proud of her new appearance.

They were to arrive in Lebnor tomorrow, barring any raids or storms. Many legends had collected around the islands, and she intended to investigate them all. She might settle on Dinor or Baetnor, maybe even a more populous island like Imtnor or Locnor. No matter which she chose, all were littered with pockets of native hiisi. They would be easy to find. She knew Hergis' methods better than he had. Soon, Tatumi would once again have a tribe.

She had plans that would make the dotard Orono's experiments seem facile.

Thank you for reading

If you enjoyed *Things They Buried*, **please leave us a review.** Your efforts do so much to help indie authors and keep us writing.

Visit ismae.com and sign up for our email list to receive bonus Ismae short fiction. You'll also be notified of new publications, concept art, and special promotions.

Follow Ismae Books on Facebook, Twitter, Reddit, Instagram, and Twitch, follow Amanda K. King and Michael R. Swanson on Goodreads, or reach us directly at contact@ismae.com.

Aliara, Sylandair, and Schmalch will return in *The Long Game*.

ACKNOWLEDGEMENTS

Our thanks to everyone who helped make this project a reality: Rob and Cassy Fenter, Christopher Bennem, Michael B. Fee, Jacob Walker, Emily Stansell Photography, John Helfers and Stonehenge Editorial, Cara Moczygemba, George Culbreth, Anne Bishop, Toiya Kristen Finley, Kelly McCullough, Gregory A. Wilson, DL, Hans and Tina Leck, Greg Lindholm, Corrie Jagger, Kevin Edwards, Tonya Perkins, John and Kelly Wikman, Elizabeth Oinen, Kamoria Art, and the town of Irvington, Indiana.

Our love and gratitude to our families, who have supported us through this and so much more: Will and Ellen King, Roland and Diane Swanson, Jeffrey and Sarah Swanson, and those who may not be blood, but are most definitely family.

A special thank you to TheGato, Marnoch, Wulfwin, Vreejack, Gonkbot, VladTheImprobable, IronMoose, and all the others who stopped by so long ago. You know who you are.

51449471R00302

Made in the USA
Columbia, SC
22 February 2019